Pemberley Manor

JANE AUSTEN'S
Pride & Prejudice
continued…

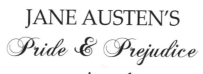
Kathryn L. Nelson

PEMBERLEY MANOR

Copyright © 2006 Kathryn L. Nelson
Cover and internal design © 2006 by Subtle Sisters--
Kaiine-Shapiro
Author photograph by Annie Hines
Cover image: Hewell Grange, 2005, taken by Leonig_Mig
for Wikipedia. With thanks to Marian Ebrey.

Sourcebooks and the colophon are registered trademarks
of Sourcebooks, Inc.

Published by Sourcebooks, Inc.
P.O. Box 4410, Naperville, Illinois 60567-4410
(630) 961-3900
FAX: (630) 961-2168
www.sourcebooks.com
www.austenfans.com
ISBN 13: 978-1-4022-1-2857
ISBN 10: 1-4022-1-2852

To my Mom,
who will read anything and
doesn't criticize... very much

Prologue

The morning that Jane and Elizabeth Bennet married Charles Bingley and Fitzwilliam Darcy might be seen by some as the end of a story of faltering and reviving passions, a tale of petty prides and prejudices solved and resolved into a loving state of eternal bliss for all. As for the eldest sister Jane and her Mr Bingley, this was almost certain to be the case, as it was evident that their kindly hearts and mutual affection rather assured them a calm and contented domestic life with a household ordered and cheerful by any standard. Mr Bingley's social standing and fortune exceeded even Mrs Bennet's hope for her eldest daughter, and his character was such that he considered himself honoured to be loved by such a beautiful and agreeable woman as Jane. To the opinions of some - that he had married beneath him - Mr Bingley appeared oblivious. Jane likewise felt herself the most fortunate of women, and she bore herself with a charming modesty that disarmed all but the most mean-spirited among those assembled. The only want that the Bingleys might be feared to suffer was the liveliness that occasional disagreement may supply in a marriage.

Of the second couple, a vast deal more must be said, and indeed, in Meryton that morning, a vast deal more *was* being said. That they were a beautiful couple could not be gainsaid, for their dark curls and comely good looks complemented an elegant bearing. Mr Fitzwilliam Darcy, however, had long since acquired the unfortunate reputation in that town of being an arrogant man with little inclination towards social delicacy; his kinder, gentler side, so recently uncovered by Miss Elizabeth Bennet, had heretofore been well disguised.

If Jane was generally considered the most beautiful of the five Bennet sisters, it was only that her sweet, complacent nature augmented a lovely but rather conventional beauty. Elizabeth was far the more interesting to lively minds. Alas for her, Meryton had more than its share of lively tongues, but a paucity of lively minds. That her early encounters with Fitzwilliam Darcy had stirred her to anger rather than admiration was not forgotten. It is widely recognized, however, that passionate anger and passionate love are often found to run hand in hand, and Elizabeth Bennet, aided by a most extraordinary improvement in Mr Darcy's manners, had soon awakened to an earnest adoration of him that rivalled his love for her.

For the guests who wearied of the topic of the Bennet sisters, a slightly more malicious diversion offered itself in the forms of Charles Bingley's sisters; Miss Caroline Bingley and Mrs Louisa Hurst. They were admired, to be sure, as their wedding finery reflected all of the benefits that superior birth and prodigious wealth may bring to a lady's wardrobe. And while some observers argued that their vanity befitted their rank, it is well known that in general, country ladies do not care to be found wanting in matters of dress or manners. It required only a passing glance to understand that these conceited women found nothing to their taste in Meryton.

Miss Bingley and Mrs Hurst were engaged in their own ruminations, which had very little reference to the opinions of those around them. As the sound of Mrs Bennet's prattling reached into the crowded church, Miss Bingley seethed, rolling her eyes.

"It is more than I can bear to be allied to that woman," she muttered. Louisa concurred, but being slightly more prudent than her sister, laid a warning hand on her arm.

Miss Bingley was not entirely unreasonable in her censure, for Mrs Bennet was indeed a rather silly woman and, with the exception of Jane and Elizabeth, her daughters bore testimony to a careless and frivolous upbringing, benefiting little from their father's kindly good sense. As she fluttered under the good wishes of her neighbours, she whispered much too loudly, "Oh, Mr Bennet! I knew that Jane's beauty could not be for nothing. Think of it! Who could have imagined a year ago that our daughters should marry so well?"

Mrs Bennet must be given credit for her diligence in the pursuit of

Mr Bingley for Jane, but she found Mr Darcy so formidable that she scarcely dared utter his name. Nonetheless, she found comfort in the fact that she was relieved of the difficult chore of finding a husband for Elizabeth, a daughter who often vexed and baffled her, and she was, in the end, prepared to celebrate both marriages.

Mr Bennet, as he paced about the narthex waiting for the brides to appear, was so engrossed in his own contemplation that he scarcely heard his wife's nervous chatter. He confided to his sister-in-law, an eminently more sensible and intelligent woman than his wife, "I am worried about our Lizzie, Mrs Gardiner, that she is not totally sensible of the difficulty of a temperament such as Mr Darcy's. Although she has assured me that he is a kind and good man, I confess I see only his pride. And she has not the easy nature of her sister Jane to allow her to overlook the faults of others."

Mrs Gardiner smiled complacently and patted his arm. "Lizzie has undoubtedly chosen the more difficult path of the two, but I daresay, knowing her energetic spirit, that she is equal to the task. My acquaintance with Mr Darcy leads me to hope that he only wants a bit of levity to make him an excellent husband, and who better than Lizzie to supply that deficit?"

Mr Bennet nodded thoughtfully and hoped that she was right.

Chapter One

Of all the guests at Meryton Church that morning, one pretty young woman glowed with unadulterated pride as she watched the proceedings. Georgiana Darcy, Fitzwilliam's only sister, turned to her cousin excitedly as Elizabeth Bennet started down the aisle. "Is she not the handsomest of brides, James?" Turning her attention forward to where her brother waited by Charles Bingley's side, she sighed happily. "I have never known my brother to be so animated. I believe he may even be a little nervous."

Her cousin smiled amiably. "Yes, he's a bit like a schoolboy, is he not? I'm delighted to see him finally settled." He did not add his reflection that the last time they were together, Darcy had been in such a melancholy state that James had feared for his sanity. Looking at his cousin now, he was content that the cause of Darcy's distress had now become his salvation.

Indeed, there could be no mistaking the look of rapture that Mr Darcy wore as his bride walked slowly toward him. When she was within a step of his side, she lifted her eyes to meet his, and the eloquence of their communion was enough to calm Mr Bennet's fears and fill Miss Darcy with a tenderness that brought tears to her eyes. Caroline Bingley, seated behind her, was so far from enjoying this uncharacteristic display of affection that she allowed a contemptuous snort to escape her throat. Her sister quickly touched her arm in a warning gesture, and as Georgiana turned inquiringly toward the source of the interruption, she found Miss Bingley apparently lost in blissful contemplation of the happy scene before them.

The 'I do's' were finally pronounced all around, with Mr Darcy's sounding rather like a prayerful whisper next to Mr Bingley's cheerful exclamation. The Bennet sisters were soon swept back down the aisle on the arms of their adoring husbands, and the onlookers were left to speculate, if they cared to, on the meaning of the tears in Mr Darcy's eyes. As the two couples hurried to their waiting carriages, families and friends grouped themselves for an animated review of the morning's work, and then began moving off on foot or by carriage to Longbourn.

If the wedding had placed a strain on Miss Bingley's rather limited self-control, the thought of passing the next few hours at the Bennet home threatened to undo her completely. She hurried through the crowded churchyard to her sister's carriage, with only the briefest of nods and a frozen smile to protect her from inviting outright condemnation from the other guests. She scowled at the footman as he opened the carriage door and flung herself angrily into its plush interior, fuming silently as she waited for the Hursts to affect a somewhat more decorous passage through the crowd.

Heads bobbed and tongues wagged as many eyes followed the retreating forms of the Bingley party. Mr Hurst looked, as was his wont, merely bored, an insult more easily borne than the scornful half-smile of his wife and sister-in-law.

"Insufferable pompous boobs!" hissed Miss Bingley as the Hursts seated themselves.

Louisa countered, "We have done everything possible to prevent this alliance, Caroline. Now we shall have to make the best of it. I have never known Charles to be more determined."

Caroline Bingley's rage at the engagement of Fitzwilliam Darcy to Elizabeth Bennet was no trifling matter. The indignity of finding herself allied to a country simpleton with no social connections was galling enough, but the greater injury of losing her own hopes for an alliance with Mr Darcy was sufficient to catapult her into an hysterical fury that had all but prevented her from attending the wedding.

Louisa settled herself carefully on the carriage seat, caressing the folds of her gown. "You must at least take some pleasure, Caroline, in the dramatic effect produced by Mrs Bennet's joining of feathers and ribbons to adorn her head. I confess myself in awe of the strength of neck required to support such a monstrous display." She smiled happily at her own jest and was rewarded by a snort of approbation from her husband. Caroline, however, was in no mood for wit, and she vented her spleen on her sister, as was her custom.

"I find nothing to amuse me in Meryton, and I never shall! I suppose you are not utterly insensible of the fact, Louisa, that we are ruined by our brother's foolishness." Taking in the despised landscape of Hertfordshire, she cried, "How I wish we had never laid eyes on this wasteland!" She stomped her foot petulantly, heedless of the slight trembling of her sister's lip.

Mr Hurst came to the aid of the conversation with uncharacteristic sagacity, reaching into the heart of the matter. "I don't suppose there will be one decent ragout served at dinner today." His companions momentarily forgot their own anxieties in the vexation of being reminded that stupidity was not at all confined to the country parishes. The remainder of the short ride was accomplished in a silence thick with unspoken recriminations and consternations.

As Colonel James Fitzwilliam escorted his cousin Georgiana through the churchyard, nodding and smiling to all they met, he contemplated with amusement the vexation evident in the receding forms of Miss Bingley and Mrs Hurst. As he handed Georgiana up to his carriage seat, he remarked pleasantly, "Miss Bingley seems a trifle out of sorts today."

Georgiana turned to him with a curious expression. "Why do you say that, James? She has been such a dear friend to us since her brother and mine were in school together. I cannot imagine she would not be sensible of his happiness today. Indeed, I am certain she must have enjoyed the occasion as much as I, for she has been like a sister to me."

"Do you think so, Georgiana?" was his smiling reply.

As he relaxed on the carriage seat, he wondered with amusement what was being said in the Hurst carriage as it rumbled along the road to Longbourn that autumn morning. He was pleased that Georgiana's youth and natural reserve had prevented her from much contact with the society frequented by the Bingley sisters. For his part, he did not mistake the true feelings of those ladies towards any of the participants in the day's merriment.

Chapter Two

Caroline Bingley heaved a deep sigh as the carriage drew up in front of Longbourn. She descended with an elegance and grace that belied the stormy thoughts she was entertaining, and moved resolutely through the crowded garden toward the wedding party, a condescending smile fixed on her face. Mrs Bennet was happily distracted, bobbing and cooing to well-wishers, enabling Miss Bingley to approach Mr Bennet as he stood slightly apart, contemplating the excesses of his wife with equanimity. "My dear Mr Bennet," she began, extending her hand to him, "such a lovely wedding!" He bowed graciously, but before he could make an answer, she continued quickly, "The union of our two families delights me as much as it does my sister."

Mr Bennet smiled pleasantly, thinking to himself wryly, 'That is to say, not at all.' As Louisa and her taciturn husband, Mr Hurst, approached, Mr Bennet graciously included them in his reply. "I appreciate the warmth of your sentiment, Miss Bingley, and entreat your family to think of Longbourn as your home. You will always be most welcome here. In fact, while the wedding parties are away, you must visit us frequently. My wife and daughters will be sorely distressed at the loss of Jane and Elizabeth's company, I don't doubt, and your lively companionship would offer an agreeable change." The sardonic air of his profession was not lost on Caroline Bingley, and as she looked boldly into his eyes she noted that here, at least, was a glimmer of wit in the midst of an otherwise dull assemblage.

Mrs Bennet turned abruptly from the felicitations of a less notable neighbour to attend to Jane's new in-laws. Her normal fluttering servility towards persons of such high birth was somewhat attenuated by the triumph of the day, and she exclaimed happily, "Miss Bingley, Mrs Hurst, Mr Hurst, how delighted you must be! I am sure I have never seen a lovelier bride than our Jane! Such a happy temperament,

13

I daresay, is rarely united with such beauty. How fortunate was the day that Mr Bingley chose Netherfield House as his home."

Miss Bingley and Mrs Hurst managed tolerably well to mask their feelings on *that* subject, although neither could easily form a suitable response. Instead, Miss Bingley turned from her to make a hasty apology to Mr Bennet's invitation, declaring that they were required in London on urgent business immediately following the reception and must unhappily defer the enjoyment of a prolonged visit for another time. Mrs Bennet, momentarily disconcerted by the lofty demeanour of the two ladies, was happily distracted by the arrival of Miss Georgiana Darcy and Colonel James Fitzwilliam.

The Bingley sisters, with Mr Hurst in reluctant attendance, turned their energies to the onerous task of congratulating the brides and grooms. Jane Bingley showed as much willingness as her husband to accept the felicitations of his sisters in good spirits, and, indeed, she did not allow herself to believe that they were motivated by anything other than their brother's best interests. Mr and Mrs Darcy, however, were quite undeceived and received their congratulations in the spirit in which they were given. Darcy's thoughts were masked by a cool reserve, but Elizabeth met Miss Bingley's gaze with a bemused smile.

A few moments of mutual appraisal locked the two young women in silence, but taking the opportunity of seeing Mr Darcy occupied with her sister and Mr Hurst, Miss Bingley spoke quietly, "Little did I imagine when we arrived here last November that within a twelvemonth both my brother and Mr Darcy would have had the good fortune to find the women of their dreams. But I daresay you foresaw the efficacy of the unions much earlier than I." She smiled with the tenderness of a viper.

A slight rise in colour was the only indication that Elizabeth was anything but delighted with the conversation. She replied pleasantly, "That your brother could easily fall in love with my sister was evident to me from the first evening we met at the Meryton Ball. I can scarcely name a soul who does not love her kind and gentle ways. But I must admit that Mr Darcy and I have much more recently grown to esteem one another. I fear my nature is more guarded and my manners less generous than my sister's."

Mr Darcy had not failed to overhear this exchange and turned to his bride, tightening his hold on her hand. "I don't doubt that it required a great effort on your part to fall in love with me, my dear. For my part, it only needed a moment of clear thinking."

That Miss Bingley was not pleased by *this* reflection would seriously understate the case. Her insolent smile tightened into a look that gave away far more than she intended, and she quickly turned to her sister to say, "I fear we are keeping Mr and Mrs Darcy from greeting their other guests, Louisa. Shall we go inside?" With this, she abruptly walked toward the house, leaving her tormentors more amused than abashed.

Mrs Bennet had turned her attention from Mr Bingley's sisters toward Miss Darcy with more than a slight trepidation that she might resemble her brother in manner, but her spirits were soon revived by the shy but gracious demeanour of that young lady. Miss Darcy's eager congratulations were heartfelt if timid, and Mr Bennet forestalled his wife's effusion with an uncharacteristically warm welcome that endeared him to the young lady and was not lost on Colonel Fitzwilliam.

Miss Darcy hastened to introduce her cousin, anxious to have him relieve her of the burden of conversation. "My dear Mr and Mrs Bennet," he exclaimed, "I have been eager to make your acquaintance for many months. I was most fortunate to spend many happy hours with Miss Elizabeth last spring at my Aunt's house while she was visiting her neighbours, Mr and Mrs Collins, and I must say that Rosings Park has rarely had a more fortunate visitation. If I had been asked to choose a wife for my cousin, I could not have recommended any lady of my acquaintance more highly than your daughter."

Mrs Bennet was far too self-absorbed to have much understanding of her daughter's finer points, but she was flattered into speechlessness by the Colonel's compliment. Mr Bennet, far more astute, judged immediately that at least these two members of his son-in-law's family were endowed with a gentility that merited a further acquaintance. His fears for Elizabeth's happiness were relieved at the thought that she had not married into a wholly unfriendly environment. He replied sincerely, "I do not part with her easily, but our separation will be less painful for knowing that Elizabeth will be welcomed in your family. I look forward to the opportunity of furthering our acquaintance, and hope that you will feel always at home at Longbourn."

Miss Darcy was moved by this fatherly tenderness to reply earnestly, "You must come to visit us at Pemberley as soon as we have settled in. I am sure my brother would not want you to be separated long from your daughter."

Mrs Bennet murmured, "You are too kind, my dear, I am sure. We would not like to put you to so much trouble." Her rather limited imagination fluttered about the person of the Colonel, appraising the possibility that he might be induced to take an interest in one of her two unmarried daughters. To this end, she called out, "Kitty, Mary, come here and meet Mr Darcy's sister and his cousin."

Her reverie was cut short by her husband's observation that Miss Darcy and Colonel Fitzwilliam must be allowed to greet the young couples, and that there would be time enough for them to be introduced to his daughters. His wife was sorely vexed by this intercession, but before she could protest, Miss Darcy smiled and nodded her agreement, and taking leave of them she moved quickly toward her brother.

The arrival of Georgiana at her brother's side allowed him and Elizabeth to forget the momentary unpleasantness of their last conversation. Miss Darcy, blushing sweetly, kissed first her brother

16

and then his bride, saying shyly, "I am so looking forward to the pleasure of knowing you as a sister, Miss Bennet... I mean, *Mrs Darcy*."

Elizabeth laughed. "You must begin by calling me Elizabeth - or Lizzie, if you prefer, as my other sisters do. I don't doubt that we shall be the best of friends in no time at all."

Fitzwilliam's eyes shone with pride and pleasure in the little triangle they formed, and he leaned close to his sister's ear to say, "Beware of her power, or she will enchant you as she has me."

Georgiana's eyes opened in surprise at this uncharacteristic levity from her brother, and she replied in a joyful whisper, "I would welcome such an enchantment, for I see its effect on you is pure happiness." Her brother nodded, and then released her hand to reach out to his cousin.

"Good of you to come, James. I detect the absence of other members of our estimable family."

The Colonel smiled knowingly. "I expect that our Aunt Catherine will be venting her formidable displeasure about Rosings today, but never mind that. She has suffered worse affronts than having you defy her wishes, and remains undaunted, I am sure." He moved to kiss the hand of the bride with the most sincere pleasure, playfully declaring, "Since I am denied the pleasure of marrying you, I shall adopt you as my cousin, and I warn you that I plan to make an absolute nuisance of myself by dropping in on you at Pemberley every chance I have."

Elizabeth's eyes sparkled with pleasure, for their brief acquaintance earlier that year had produced between them a warm and durable bond of friendship.

"I should like nothing better than to see you every day, sir, and by your leave, I shall consider you a brother, since I have none."

The arrival of the effervescent Sir William Lucas and his family prevented further discussion of the subject, and Georgiana and Colonel James moved on toward the Bingley sisters who had paused to pay their respects to Miss Darcy. Their addresses to her carried an obsequious air, befitting their sensibility of her superior rank. She was too young and far too happy to suspect that their mild professions of delight were anything but sincere, but her cousin James knew more of the world in general and of these women in particular than would allow him to be taken in by their pleasantries. Of the indolent Mr Hurst he knew little and cared less, but he was too much the gentleman to allow himself the pleasure of snobbishness, and he joined pleasantly in their conversation. It was evident that Miss Darcy's naïve happiness caused the ladies more discomfort than he could have managed, even if he were inclined to attempt it.

The group moved into the dining parlour where an extravagant buffet had been laid, supervised by the gracious Mrs Gardiner, and for a time they were relieved of the effort of conversation by the task of filling plates. Miss Bingley surveyed the room with cool disdain, taking pleasure, at least, in the fact that she was in the company of the only persons worthy of her notice in Meryton that day.

Mrs Gardiner greeted Miss Darcy with the warmest affection, recalling with pleasure their last meeting. She made a valiant attempt to include Miss Bingley and Mr and Mrs Hurst in the conversation but it was evident that they took no pleasure in it. On the pretence of looking for a table, they excused themselves abruptly and moved away, fully expecting Miss Darcy and the Colonel to follow. If Mrs Gardiner was troubled by the intended slight, she showed no sign of it, immediately returning her attentions to the two who remained beside her. Miss Darcy, however, was taken off guard, and ventured a look of quizzical consternation at her cousin. He raised his eyebrows in mock surprise.

Miss Bingley moved toward a table in the corner of the room and settled herself with a flourish. Her brother-in-law grumbled over the fare, while Louisa smiled a trifle nervously.

"Charles would not be pleased to find you alienating his new family so soon, Caroline."

Her sister glanced unpleasantly about the room. "I am not required, I hope, to amuse every merchant and lawyer in Hertfordshire simply because *he* has chosen to do so." She replied in a petulant tone, although she did deign to lower her voice. It did nothing to improve her enjoyment of the day to note that both of their esteemed companions had remained at the buffet in earnest conversation with Mrs Gardiner.

Miss Darcy's good manners came to her aid, and she quickly set aside her vexation to attend to Mrs Gardiner. She shyly confided that from her first meeting with Miss Elizabeth, she had begun to cherish the hope that they would soon be much better acquainted.

"I was disappointed when you were called away so abruptly from Lambton, and when my brother gave me to understand the nature of your urgent business, it distressed me to think of your sorrow."

"How very kind of you to take such an interest, Miss Darcy. I confess that missing the pleasure of dining with you at Pemberley was onerous, but my happiness for my nieces today erases all heavy thoughts of the past," Mrs Gardiner replied.

Miss Darcy turned toward her cousin who stood quietly by. "Forgive me, James. Please allow me to introduce Miss Elizabeth's aunt, Mrs Gardiner. Colonel James Fitzwilliam, my cousin." The two shook hands cordially.

"Both of my cousins have spoken of you with the warmest regard, madam. I hope I shall have the pleasure of meeting Mr Gardiner today. I understand he has honoured Pemberley's excellent trout stream with his expertise, a pleasure I have not had in a very long time," said the gentleman.

Mr Gardiner was already moving across the room to welcome Miss Darcy. The introductions made, the foursome enjoyed an animated conversation on the subject of the beauty of Derbyshire, with particular regard for the hills of Pemberley. While they were thus happily engaged, the wedding party entered the room, and Mr and Mrs Darcy came to join them. The Colonel turned to his cousin. "We have just been longing for your trout stream, Darcy. Mr Gardiner has reminded me of what I have been missing at Pemberley."

Mr Darcy replied pleasantly, "With the addition of Elizabeth Bennet to its treasures, I believe Pemberley will soon be acknowledged as the most desirable estate in Derbyshire. I hope we can count on all of you to visit us there very soon." Elizabeth smiled at the compliment, but took more pleasure in his invitation to her aunt and uncle, whom, she could not fail to remember, he had not so long ago included in a scathing pronouncement on the inferiority of her relations.

Georgiana added shyly, "How lively Pemberley will be, Fitzwilliam. I long to be there again."

He smiled lovingly at his sister. "I have kept you away too long, Georgiana."

Their thoughts were interrupted by a rather loud and lengthy toast to the brides and grooms by Sir William Lucas, the Bennet's nearest neighbour. The next hour was spent by the Bennet family ensuring that everyone ate and drank more than was good for them. Mrs Bennet's loud exuberance could be heard throughout the hall, but even that blemish could not dampen the enjoyment of more than a handful of guests, and those few would have found enough to criticise had her deportment been exemplary. Mr Bennet exerted himself to play the perfect host, although he secretly longed for the quiet of his study, a good book, and a glass of very fine sherry.

Of the four newlyweds, two could be seen to be completely at their ease among the chatter and commotion, for Elizabeth Bennet and Charles Bingley found the atmosphere stimulating and conversation easy. Jane Bennet was content among her neighbours and family, but her quieter nature was more suited to intimate settings than to such a party as this. For Fitzwilliam Darcy, the talent for easy social intercourse was as yet undernourished, but as he hardly strayed more than a few feet from Elizabeth's side, he was for the most part saved the difficulty of speaking much. His quiet reserve on this day could not be mistaken for disdain, for his eyes betrayed an adoration of the woman beside him and a new-found interest in everyone to whom she directed her attentions.

The only discord in the harmony of the gathering came from the table where Mr and Mrs Hurst and Miss Bingley sat in proud state, unmoved even by the valiant efforts of Sir William Lucas who, by virtue of his title and his inability to feel affronted, had placed himself at their disposal as court jester. Had they troubled themselves to notice, the three would have been surprised at how small an effect their displeasure had on the enjoyment of either their hosts or the other guests, although Lady Lucas was heard to remark to her daughter, "I hope I shall never be mortified by any of *my* daughters putting on such airs as those two. An elevated position in society can be no excuse for rude behaviour, in fact, quite the contrary, Maria. It demands a gentility of spirit such as that of their brother. They have made it only too clear that they feel themselves above anyone who is not in possession of connections in London. If the delicacy of my health did not prevent it, I am sure your father would have long since established us in as fine a house as any *they* could lay claim to visiting."

Once a final round of shaking of hands and noisy congratulations, both heartfelt and otherwise, had been accomplished, the two couples mounted separate carriages and with blushing anticipation left Meryton and its inhabitants behind. Miss Bingley and the Hursts finally gleaned their first real pleasure from the day's events by quickly taking a rather unceremonious leave, unleashing in their wake the tongues of the town's most ardent gossips. As for the rest, we may be assured that the hour was late and the refreshments strained to exhaustion before the last of the merrymakers had departed, leaving their hosts spent but happy.

Mr Bennet's pleasant mood extended so far beyond the departure of their last guests as to enable him to sit for half an hour with his wife and youngest daughters, listening to Mrs Bennet prattle on about the manners and dress of this guest and that. He even smiled as she castigated him for diverting Colonel Fitzwilliam's attention from her daughters. "In spite of your interference, sir, I did manage to present Kitty and Mary to him, and I do believe he was happy to make their acquaintance. You do not feel the weight, as I do, of responsibility to our daughters." She finished with a loud sigh.

"I am sure, my dear, that you have managed exceedingly well on your own. You have married off three of our girls in a year, two of them, at least, to advantage, and I am content to allow you free rein in providing for the other two. For my part, I believe I have earned a bit of peace and quiet this evening." He rose and retired to his study, leaving his wife and daughters to continue their review of the day.

It was his intention to lose himself in the pleasure of a good book, but he found himself instead distracted by thoughts of his dear Lizzie. Although the day had done much to relieve his fears on her account, the chilling presence of the Bingley sisters had reminded him of his first impression of Mr Darcy as a proud man of heavy moods. With an air of resignation, he managed at last to turn his attention to the volume in his hand, and before long all grave thoughts were supplanted by the warm glow of sherry and the timeless words of Cowper. It was from his blood, after all, that Elizabeth Bennet had inherited her ability to rise above weighty deliberation, and neither father nor daughter ever wasted much time on useless pining over that which they were powerless to change.

Chapter Three

Jane and Charles Bingley had ardently pressed for a united wedding trip, being perhaps a little nervous to find themselves left to their own devices for so many days. Their regard for one another was of a calm and reserved style, and both could well imagine that they might want a supplement to their conversation before too long. While exhibiting a proper and tender regard for their wishes, Mr Darcy urged them to consider a fortnight's separation, suggesting that they should all be reunited thereafter at his estate at Pemberley, where they could spend as many weeks together as could possibly amuse them. The strain of his brief public courtship had cost him dearly, for he had been forced to spend a good deal of time in the company of people whose regard for him was tainted by the unfortunate first impression he had made in the neighbourhood. The brevity of their engagement, which resulted from that agony of indecision that preceded it, afforded little opportunity for the gentle conversations that may build a tender understanding between a man and woman.

After overcoming so many obstacles to amend his character and gain her affections, Mr Darcy longed for an opportunity to have all of his bride's affections and attentions lavished on him, and his on her. Mr Darcy's nature was such that no detail of their wedding journey had been overlooked. From the finest set of matched horses that pulled their new carriage to the organisation of all accommodations, every thought had been directed toward exciting in Elizabeth a proper conviction of the strength of his devotion and the knowledge that he was to be forever in her debt for the honour which she had bestowed on him by consenting to be his wife.

Elizabeth, having started their relationship by finding Mr Darcy wrong on every matter of consequence, resolved to begin their marriage with the willingness to believe him right, and her passion being not in any way weaker than his, she could well see an advantage to his plan.

But passion is seldom the end of any story, for it cannot long endure if it is not soon supplemented with true affection and mutual respect. Mr and Mrs Darcy, uniting tempers that were both strong and proud, were perhaps more in need of this amendment than those who marry under fewer constraints.

As the couple made their way from Longbourn through the late fall afternoon, they took a northward path that would eventually lead them towards Derbyshire and home. They sometimes admired the passing scenery or commented on the details of the wedding party, but more often gazed into each other's eyes or off into the distance, each harbouring thoughts they were saving for a private audience.

Their final hour in the carriage was spent in rather more silence than the previous ones, as the shadows lengthened toward their wedding night. Their carriage was apparently watched for, as they had scarcely stopped moving before a very gentlemanly man, flanked by two liveried attendants and a lovely young girl, approached them and bid them welcome. The tremor in Mrs Darcy's hands gave less evidence than the slight stammering of Mr Darcy's speech to the tumultuous thoughts entertained by each as they alighted from their carriage and delivered themselves into the solicitous care of the innkeeper and his staff. The armful of flowers handed to Mrs Darcy by the innkeeper's daughter afforded a welcome distraction from her nerves.

This pleasant inn had been honoured more than once by a visit from Mr Darcy, who found in the ministrations of its owner, Mr Godfrey, a right balance of careful attention to detail without the fawning servility that his position was wont to inspire in others of this profession. Falseness of any kind was abhorrent to Fitzwilliam Darcy, and he had a sufficiently high opinion of his own station to disdain flattery from others. Mr Godfrey's pleasure in being chosen for the honour of entertaining Mr Darcy and his new bride was evident in the warmth of their reception. He attended personally to the dispatch of their luggage and then led the couple to his finest suite of rooms, which had been discreetly improved for the occasion with kind attention to the touches that a lady might enjoy on her wedding night.

Mr Darcy approved the suggestion of Mr Godfrey that tea should be served as soon as they had freshened from the journey, and before they had many moments of discomfited silence to bear, a large silver tea tray was delivered into the room and all its accoutrements were quietly and elegantly arranged on a table in the sitting room. The pouring of the tea and filling of plates with delicate sweets and fruits became the focus of their attention for a few minutes, but the thoughts and feelings of neither could long be diverted from the other.

Mrs Darcy's keen delight in the ridiculous ought to have been aroused by the sight that they made. Where it had been feared that the Bingleys might suffer from a scarcity of conversation, it was indeed the Darcys who could not put two words together to form a sentence, whether for their own or the other's amusement. For Mr Darcy, who had often found himself incapable of light conversation, the want was less notable, but fair Elizabeth had rarely been without a witty remark in a quiet room in her one and twenty years, and she found the sensation unnerving.

As to Elizabeth's state of mind, it is not difficult to comprehend the nervous anticipation of a young bride. All of her education had tended towards the arts which proper young ladies require to secure an advantageous attraction, while precious little had been devoted to the skills she might require in maintaining her husband's favour. In her parents' example of matrimonial felicity, the only attribute that could be applied was faithfulness, for they were ill-suited by nature or temperament to please one another. Her Aunt and Uncle Gardiner provided a model of kind attentiveness and mutual concern, but their temperaments were far more like her sister Jane's and Mr Bingley's, being mild and always ready to be pleased. Although she had often

25

tried to practice Jane's forbearance and gentleness, she could see no hope of ever attaining them. Well she knew that Fitzwilliam Darcy's proud nature too closely matched her own. The difficulty of such a relationship was clear, but her thoughts were far from morose for her self-assurance and optimism had taught her that she was rather more than equal to a challenge.

Mr Darcy's reflections were far less suited to the occasion, however, for the long silences of the afternoon coupled with his nervousness had precipitated a disturbing coldness in the pit of his stomach. He was acutely aware that there were parts of his life that he had not begun to share with Elizabeth. The honest and impassioned love he met in her eyes today urged him to open his heart without reservation and he longed to do so, but he could not imagine how to begin to unravel the layers of history that he had carefully avoided for so long; what effect such revelations might have on her feelings he did not wish to imagine.

He was so self-absorbed in this conflict that he sat without speaking for many minutes. It can well be imagined that his mood did not escape Elizabeth's notice, and with her confidence undermined by the novelty of the situation, she could find no words to break the tension. She found herself growing more unsettled with every passing minute.

In this volatile atmosphere, Fitzwilliam was startled by the sound of a teaspoon dropping to the floor, and with a frown for his lack of attentiveness, leaned to pick it up, just as she did the same. Their hands brushed, eyes met, and the thoughts that had distracted them suddenly gave way before the communication of their eyes. The scent of her perfume, the blush that spread along her cheeks, and her nervous smile drove from him every sense but that of his passion, so long repressed. He lifted her to her feet and began to kiss her with such abandon that she could not prevent her body from stiffening in his embrace. Feeling her resistance, his eyes grew dark, haunted, and his grip tightened on her arms.

"Mr Darcy!" she protested with a nervous laugh, pushing away from him to look into his eyes. A jest about his eagerness formed on her lips but she was prevented from speech by the anguish of his countenance, and a startled sound rose from her throat. Her mind raced in confusion as he roughly pulled her to him again. She struggled to free herself, but her efforts only served to intensify his feverish grip.

He pressed himself against her, kissing her violently until he felt her body collapsing into frightened submission. Her tears against his fevered cheeks and the trembling of her body finally reached through his frenzy to find the place in his heart where love cowered. Releasing his hold on her, he backed away in horror and looked into her eyes, and the tempest abated as suddenly as it had begun. His arms fell to his side, and with an oath on his lips and a look on his face of utter contempt, he turned away, snatched his topcoat from the wall hook and fled from the room. Elizabeth stood breathless with shock and incomprehension, then collapsed back into the chair she had been snatched from and released herself to a flood of mortified tears.

Mr Godfrey was just arrived at their chamber door to inquire whether the tea service should be cleared when Mr Darcy burst out of the room with a look of such distress that the good gentleman was tempted to run after him to see what tragedy had occurred. The sound of weeping from within the room caused him to purse his lips and retreat slowly to the lobby. He withdrew with his wife to the staff parlour to prevent any further embarrassment to the gentleman upon his return. They could not bring themselves to intrude upon the lady's sorrows, merely leaving the door ajar in case they were wanted.

After her sobs had subsided into a quieter anguish, Elizabeth remained motionless in her chair for the greater part of an hour. At times she strained for the sound of footsteps, at times concentrated on an attempt to bring some order to her thoughts. Her character would have, under normal circumstances, led her to anger before tears, but on this night she could not so easily rally herself. For the first time in her life she found herself so completely unsettled that she could bring no coherent thoughts together and quite abandoned herself to misery. Her only hope was that he must return at any moment to explain to her something that she could not in any other way understand.

The mantle clock had been striking six when he fled the room, and it was not until the last stroke of seven that she pulled herself from the languor that had overtaken her and began to apply her reason to the situation at hand. To her credit, she managed to presently turn her thoughts from her own pain to his and a tender compassion rose in her breast. The thought that he was suffering terribly overcame her self-pity, and she began to fear he had quite lost his sanity. She rose and crossed the room to the front windows and gazed into the night.

Chapter Four

Mr Darcy had not enough practice in consideration for others to wonder at first about Elizabeth's feelings; his thoughts as he strode from the inn were all for himself, and he proceeded down the lane with such a terrible countenance that it forestalled any greeting from those few persons he met along the way. Indeed, he was aware of no one, so turned inward were his thoughts. The first two miles were consumed with a towering anger that had neither the merits of clarity nor eloquence. They were passed with mutterings of self-condemnation and oaths of rage. Reaching sight of the small village of Highbury, he turned abruptly and retraced his steps, in no mood to enter civilisation's embrace. Having regained the gardens of the inn in quite the same state as he had quitted them, he did not enter, but continued down the road in the opposite direction.

At length his rage dissipated into despair and he turned aside toward a small pond beside the road, dropping down on its grassy bank in utter hopelessness. The months between the first realisation of his love for Elizabeth and the moment of her acceptance had given him many opportunities to examine his faults, and though from the first he had ardently desired to improve himself, he knew not how it should be accomplished. He well understood that his deficiency of sensibility had too long been tolerated, even encouraged, to be easily amended.

Fitzwilliam's mother, a proud and forceful woman, had died when he was only thirteen, but he had formed by then such an understanding of his own worth and position that his father's more gentle influence could not bring about any substantial change in his manners. Among equals, he could behave most courteously, and his student years at Cambridge afforded him many opportunities to form friendships. He was sought after by his peers, especially by Charles Bingley, as a clever and energetic companion with a ready wit. But in mixed parties he always succumbed to a confusion of feelings, for he had never met any woman whom he truly admired, with the possible exception of his younger sister, Georgiana.

That is, until he met Elizabeth Bennet. He was both astonished and dismayed by this attraction to her; she appeared to care nothing for wealth or position, and yet bore herself with a dignity that exceeded that of any woman he had known. She seemed comfortable in any company, capable of speaking sense or absurdities at her whim, and was apparently wholly unconcerned by the effect she had on others.

He could not say when he first began seeing himself through her eyes, but from their first meeting an uneasiness had stirred within him that he could not name. Try as he might to maintain his composure or avoid her, his soul was soon possessed by the notion that he must win her regard to escape her probing, laughing eyes. That she saw and understood too much became soon clear, but the ultimate indignity was that she did not approve of what she saw, and did not care whether he knew it.

From that moment of revelation, he was lost to everything that had previously amused him. After months of solitary torment and struggle, he could see that he would never loose her hold without facing her. He found her as he had left her, cool and indifferent, and though he raged alternately at himself and at her in his thoughts, he found no moment of peace. To be away from her was impossible, but to be near her more agony still. And so he decided he must marry her. He imagined the scene of his declaration again and again, dwelling on the satisfaction he would feel to see her composure finally disturbed. His hopes fell far short of the attainment of true felicity; he merely wished to relieve his pain.

Her refusal of his offer threw him into a terrible confusion because he could not mistake its sincerity. It had so long been his belief that any woman must desire the honour he meant to bestow on her that he could not be easily dissuaded from it. He attempted to blame her, judging that her pride had been offended by his honesty, but his intelligence would not forever allow faulty reasoning. Every word of her lecture on the deficiency of his manners and his insufferable arrogance weighed as a stone on his heart. She had not courted his favour nor exhibited anything but the most civil indifference toward him. If her disdain had been feigned for the purpose of winning his attention, she would not have refused him in so decided and final a manner.

This understanding brought him the beginnings of humility, and although it cost him a great deal to lose his pride, he ended by understanding that he could have her at no less a price. He became, at last, fully resolved to remake himself in the image of a man she could love, using her angry condemnation of his behaviour as a road map. Although he hoped but little for success, he had no other thought but to pursue her, for indeed he could think of nothing else.

Though both partners were said to be gifted with intelligence and common sense in other matters, this affair of the heart, being the first great attachment either had formed, left reason to lag behind passion. It must certainly be attributed to the strength of that passion that they courted and married before reason had any chance to impose itself. Had they spent more time exploring the compulsion that drove them together, they might have formed a better understanding of how it might as easily prevent them from reaching enduring contentment.

With a weak understanding, therefore, of the forces that had brought him to the edge of this pond, Mr Darcy found himself seated there in the dark, clothed in wedding finery, and with no bride anywhere to be found. He examined in every possible light the outburst that had destroyed all hope of happiness, and he could be consoled with no explanation, no excuse, and no reason that would satisfy. Why, when happiness was within easy reach, had he destroyed it so utterly? If he could begin to explain it to himself, perhaps he would find a way to make her understand, but indeed he came to the very same conclusion that Elizabeth was just then reaching - that he had lost his sanity.

Gradually, however, in the midst of his most fervent self-pity, a new thought struggled to the surface, formed and broke and formed again more coherently. Elizabeth in pain, Elizabeth's eyes... Elizabeth! What must *she* be feeling at this moment? He had scarcely given it a thought in these two hours, and his self-loathing reached a new depth as he realised that he had left her in an agony that must surely rival his own. His pulse quickened with a rush of compassion and shame. "Fool... *fool*," he muttered to himself as he leapt up from the ground.

Night had fallen, and had it not been for a rising moon, he would have been quite ignorant of the road back, but surely even in utter darkness the compassionate feelings that drove him toward her would have shown him the way. Before he reached the door he had fully understood at last that in order to secure his own happiness, he must learn how to make *her* happy. Bittersweet were the tears that came to his eyes, for they were among the first he had ever cried for the sorrow of another. He little doubted that they came too late to undo the harm he had done this night, but he had no other thought than that he would spend the rest of his life in the pursuit of this goal.

Chapter Five

As the Hurst carriage moved away from Longbourn on the London road, Caroline Bingley exhaled a long sigh of relief. "I don't believe I have ever spent a day in more tedious company. I expected at least that our charming in-laws and their quaint neighbours might have exerted themselves on such an occasion to dress in this year's fashion, but even that pleasure was denied us."

Louisa rejoined languidly, "It is not so much a case of being behind the fashion as of being totally without fashion!" Caroline laughed loudly, delighted she could at last find humour in the day.

The urgent business that called the party to London was a scheme of Caroline's to hold a soirée for their most intimate friends. She had invited only those members of their circle whose venomous wit might enliven a post-mortem on the subject of the great brought low, and who could be counted on to maintain a discreet silence afterwards. During the darkest hours of the humiliating spectacle she had been forced to witness that day, Caroline had begun to regret her plan, but upon reaching the carriage, she felt as if a weight had been lifted from her. As the miles between her and Meryton mounted, the anticipation of an evening among her peers buoyed her spirits.

Mr Hurst, whose enjoyment of a party was more dependent on the richness of the supper and prospects for serious gaming than on witty conversation, promptly fell asleep in the carriage as Caroline and Louisa entertained themselves planning the final details of their party and deciding in what manner the wedding should be described to give most pleasure to their guests.

"You shall have the honour, Louisa, of testifying to the impeccable manners and dress of the Bennet family, but take care you do justice to Mrs Bennet's monstrous hat. And you must make mention of the absence of dear little sister Lydia, so recently elevated by her marriage to the wicked Mr Wickham. That will be too delicious!"

Louisa laughed gaily at the prospect of such a narrative, for indeed the finery of Meryton and the provincial airs of its denizens left her in no fear of a want of material. Caroline continued, "I reserve for myself the depiction of the brides and grooms, for I could not bear to omit the effect those 'fine eyes' of Miss Elizabeth's had on the noble bearing of Mr Darcy. Did you see how he looked, Louisa? Whatever spell she has cast has quite deranged him for the moment, but I daresay not many days will pass before he awakens one morning to the realisation that the maintenance of the honour of the Darcy name depends on something a bit more substantial." Both sisters laughed maliciously at this image and Mr Hurst's sleep was troubled by frequent outbursts as the Bingley sisters sharpened their wit for the evening's gathering.

By the time they reached their residence in London, Caroline was so fully in control of her feelings that she was in a fair way to anticipating her scheme as a pleasant revenge upon those gentlemen who had so frustrated her hopes for a resplendent future. Truth to tell, she was not so reconciled to her fate that she was able to think with any pleasure of the more distant future, but she wisely chose to confine her thoughts to present pleasures so as not to be disturbed by *that* reality.

The guests that assembled the following evening at the Bingley mansion comprised among their number some of the most privileged idle minds of the fashionable world, and their expensive education and polished speech were soon put to use in ridiculing the fall from grace of one of the most illustrious members of their set. An exquisitely wrought invitation in black with silver inscription proclaimed the occasion as a *Memorial to the Death of Reason*, and it was with venomous delight that the assembled guests delved into the topic.

Although Caroline and Louisa had envisioned the party as a time of reflection on the disaster that had befallen both Charles Bingley and Fitzwilliam Darcy, precious little time was wasted on the fortunes of the former. There was little to amuse them in scorn for Mr Bingley, for his kind heart and good nature rendered him invulnerable to such malice. It was the proud and arrogant Mr Darcy who provided the chief subject for their long-flowing wit; scarcely was there man or woman among them who did not revel in the delicious spectacle he had made of himself.

Caroline Bingley initiated the festivities with an introduction, rising to her subject with all the enthusiasm engendered by her frustrated dreams.

"My dear friends, we are gathered together to mourn the passing of two of our number who are recently descended from the ranks of superior and noble birth into the obscurity of the unfashionable world of Hertfordshire. My sister and I thank you for your attentions to us in our hour of sorrow, for as you know, one of these unfortunates is our dearest brother Charles. We, too, have been called from your midst, forced by our brother's folly to ally ourselves to a family of such humble origin and modest accomplishment that the mere mention of their name is likely to distance us in future from your *own* tender regard." As she paused in mock solemnity, a wave of twittering laughter set the tone for the evening.

She continued, confident that her wit could not fail to promote her standing among such charming rogues as were assembled before her. "My brother Charles is known to all of you for his unfailing generosity of spirit, and if it were his story alone we were forced to tell tonight, there would be little in it to surprise or entertain. His easy nature and the ignorance of his position in society, would, I fear, have suited him more admirably to a life in the colonies, where superiority of birth and connections are seen as matters of small consequence." She paused to allow the suspense to build before thrusting her barb into the heart of the matter. "But our tale of woe is the more shocking because it encompasses *another*, known to all of you for his former unstinting adherence to the social structure that has been the solid foundation from which our great empire rose. The fall of this great warrior, who for the first eight and twenty years of his life so proudly rebuked all usurpers who attempted to rise above their station, has grave consequences for all of us. For if Mr Fitzwilliam *Darcy* has succumbed to the allure of a pair of fine eyes, throwing away in a moment all thought of custom or reason, can the monarchy itself remain firm?"

Caroline Bingley stood basking in the uproarious applause and laughter that greeted her speech, and if she had not managed another witty phrase for the remainder of the evening, her fame - and Mr Darcy's - would have been sealed. But the hearty approbation of her friends inspired her to dizzying heights of malice as the evening wore on, and Charles Bingley was quite overlooked in her lust for revenge. Louisa's amusing narrative on the subject of country weddings was scarcely remembered in the days that followed, for wherever the revellers chanced to meet, the subject of Caroline Bingley's finest hour was sure to be the topic. Her triumph was so complete, indeed, that it was several days before the pleasure it afforded her was supplanted by the gnawing comprehension that the person she most wished to entertain had missed her finest performance.

Chapter Six

The absurdity of sitting alone in misery on her wedding night finally prodded Elizabeth into action. Going into the bedchamber, she hastily washed her face and tidied her hair, and then pulled the bell rope. The Godfreys were thus relieved of the awkwardness of the situation; chambermaids removed the tea service and turned down the bed. The calm bearing of the Madam as she exchanged slight pleasantries with them and ordered a bottle of sherry was a praiseworthy bit of theatre. They were left to infer that newlyweds from the finest families may well have traditions different from their own, for they could little imagine anyone of their acquaintance maintaining such dignity in the face of what appeared to be abandonment.

Only after all preparations had been completed, with the brandy brought in on its silver tray and the maids curtseying prettily out of the room, did she allow herself to return her thoughts to her predicament. The exertion of public presentation had made her feel her normal mental processes returning, and the first faint stirrings of anger brought a bit of needed colour to her cheeks. The sympathy she had bestowed on Mr Darcy was withdrawn and as she paced about the room, her steps quickened with the rise of righteous indignation instead.

"Pity him! Why should I? If he suffers it is by his choice, not mine." In the flush of her anger, she began to recite a litany of every previous example of his incivility. She began with the first night that they had met and the contemptuous look he had worn on that occasion when she had overheard him say that there was no woman in the room whom it would not be a punishment to dance with. One example followed another as she recalled his haughty disapproval of her family and neighbours. On the day she refused his hand, in place of what would have been an appropriate expression of sorrow, he had responded with anger and blame. "Insufferable man!" she exclaimed out loud.

Her anger towards *him* was soon supplanted by reproach for *herself*, that his recent attentiveness should have so easily persuaded her to forget the indignity of those early meetings. "I was such a fool to believe that on the strength of my disapprobation alone his very nature could be overthrown!" she railed.

In the light of this line of reasoning, she was suddenly overtaken with a wave of comprehension that stopped her quite still. If his nature remained as it had been, then he must still harbour the sensibility of her inferiority. Perhaps, as he embraced her, he was overwhelmed by the thought of the dreadful disservice he had done himself and his class in marrying her. That he should be even now pacing the grounds without, searching for a means by which he could extricate himself from her and from his connection to her family, was the obvious conclusion, and it came upon her swiftly. The anger that had buoyed her drained with the rising consciousness of her humiliation and she sat down abruptly, pressing her hand to her mouth.

Lizzie Bennet's experience of debilitating misery was scant, while her anger had often been aroused by lesser injustices, and within minutes a warm flush began to replace her pallor once more. The thought that he should have brought them to this impossible situation, where no resolution could be affected without injury to both parties, rekindled her anger. She stood, stamped her foot in vexation, and resumed her pacing, muttering to herself to punctuate her steps. So totally abandoned to these thoughts was she that when the door was suddenly flung open and Mr Darcy stood inside the room at last, she was for the second time that day rendered speechless.

Having so recently acquired humility, it remained a novel and rather heady sensation for Mr Darcy. He returned to Elizabeth prepared to comfort and console her, and ready to heap abuse upon himself. If any hope could be allowed to lighten his despair, it sprang from the memory of her forgiveness of his earlier transgressions, and he searched for the words to lead them back to where the day had begun. But if he had learned a good deal about humility, he had not yet acquired any clear understanding of the intricacies of human nature, especially the nature of the woman who was now his wife. She stood before him, her cheeks flaming and her eyes flashing a warning. Had Mr Darcy been blessed with the eloquence of angels, he still would have found ample reason to shy away from the formidable indignation of this fair lady. He uttered a strangled moan and collapsed into a chair, holding his head in his hands. The unhappy couple were locked in silence for some long minutes until Elizabeth, grasping the sofa back to steady her trembling hands, spoke.

"Mr Darcy, pray allow me to suggest a remedy for your most evident distress. Since our marriage has not yet been consummated, I believe you would find little difficulty in securing the offices of a good clergyman in the neighbourhood to perform an annulment immediately. It can serve neither of us to continue as man and wife when there are so little grounds to suppose we could offer one another any reasonable hope of future happiness. Indeed, it seems certain that our expectations of one another are wholly irreconcilable."

She was not prepared for the anguish that met her eyes when he raised his head.

"Is that your wish, madam?" he asked hoarsely.

Her suppositions of the past half hour could not hold up in the face of such a countenance, and as the anger drained her knees grew weak. Seeing her waver, he rushed to her side, helping her to sit and then dropping to his knees in front of her.

"My darling Elizabeth!" he cried, with a tenderness that seemed to draw the breath from her and stop the movement of time. His words were scarcely intelligible for the emotion with which they were spoken. He did not know how he could speak, but speak he did, with an eloquence born out of the ashes of his self-pity and spurred to flight by the most unselfish motivation he had ever enjoyed - that their effect might be to lessen her suffering. Without thought for his own happiness, he poured out his heart to her in the most beautiful and gracious language. Haltingly at first, but growing steadier as he saw that the taut lines of pain began to relax, he let his heart guide his tongue. In a hundred lovely turns of phrase, he said, in effect, "Please forgive me."

If there was ever a woman born whose heart could have resisted his ardent profession of guilt and adoration, she must have been very unlike Elizabeth Bennet, whose most romantic sympathies were deeply touched. Lowering his eyes from her gaze, he confessed in such a quiet tone that she scarcely knew whether she heard or imagined his words, "I should have been striving to make your wedding night perfect by expressing my ardent desire to give you pleasure in every way, and instead of that, I have frightened and hurt you. Please be assured that although I see clearly that I cannot love you in the manner you deserve, I doubt that any man could love you more fervently! These words must be impossible for you to reconcile with my actions tonight, but if you will give me leave, I will try with all my power to explain."

With this, he took her hand in his and reverently kissed it, then brought his other hand to rest lightly over the kiss as a benediction. From this pose of humble supplication he did not stir, indeed he hardly breathed, until Elizabeth's heart was breaking from tenderness and pity. She hesitantly moved her free hand toward his, and after an eternal moment, she brought it to rest on his and pressed her consent. Such a sigh escaped him that Elizabeth was completely undone. The moments of tearful silence that followed formed a sweet communion between them that neither hurried to break.

But speak he must at last, for he was utterly sensible that although she may have signalled a willingness to forgive, he must find a way to explain his behaviour, and beyond that to a rekindling of her love he dared not even aspire. As they faced each other, he saw in her eyes an eagerness to be informed, and he gathered strength to continue, although he little knew what he should say.

"When I think back over my life, I see all of the advantages that should have led me to uncommon happiness," he began quietly. "I have had the most solicitous of parents, the best education the world can offer to a young gentleman, and no want of money or position has ever prevented me from enjoying the society of any man or woman of consequence in this land. It is difficult to admit that at the age of nearly nine and twenty I have manners which give pleasure to none, including myself."

He continued with more composure but no less self-reproach, "I scorned you once for not being my equal, and yet it is clear to me that you are so far superior to me in every refinement that may bring happiness, that I cannot contradict your opinion that there is no possibility of my being of any service to you. If you wish to separate yourself from me, I must agree most humbly that you were and are right in feeling that I am the last man to whom you ought to be married. I only beg that you hear from me first that you have, in our short acquaintance, succeeded in elevating me at least to a proper understanding of what is of value and what is not. When you gave your hand to me today, I felt a hope that I could become more worthy of you in time if you perceived some worth in me.

"That I should have failed you so utterly I can scarcely comprehend, but I think I have made a beginning in my understanding, and if you allow it, I will attempt to explain the thoughts and feelings that brought me to my state of mind this afternoon." He asked with his eyes if he should continue and she nodded her assent.

"The first time I left Netherfield House, I determined never to return, so great was my discomposure over my feelings for you. I told you once that I began to love you almost as soon as we met, but I failed to explain that at that time I did not understand the nature of that love. I thought of it as an infatuation, a want that was more akin to pain than tenderness. I had not previously felt such a regard for any woman, and I little understood how to think about what was happening to me when you were near. I continually watched you for a sign that you returned my interest, but so far from finding that, I saw only disdain in your gaze, and most painful of all, I felt that you mocked me."

Elizabeth wanted to explain her own feelings but she dared not interrupt the course of his speech. Although she was eager to hear his words, she could not help but scrutinise his face, his gesture, his voice, for a hint of what she had seen earlier.

The colour rose in his cheeks as he continued, "I was so beside myself with these tormented thoughts that I began to fear for my sanity," he hesitated, closed his eyes and averted his face before adding in a hoarse whisper, "... and for your safety."

The shallowness of his breathing and the tremor in his hands spoke volumes concerning the difficulty of this revelation. Elizabeth, far from being afraid of him now, could only feel the most compassionate tenderness. She reached to turn his face gently towards her and the question in her eyes answered his fear that he had said too much. He knew he must continue, and abruptly stood and began to pace the floor until he could govern the pain that this memory brought to mind. He at length stopped near the window and rested against the ledge, gazing into the brightness of the moon.

"I had begun to fantasise about taking by force what I could not hope to gain any other way. Imagined scenes of seduction became my frequent companions, and I little doubted that I could be capable of *anything*, so strong was my desire for you." Elizabeth shuddered and closed her eyes, reviewing scenes from her memory in the light of this disclosure. Her body tensed in concentration as she tried to block all sensations other than the sound of his voice.

"I left Meryton in a panic, unable to comprehend the depths to which I had sunk. I tried everything in my power to forget you - I devised reasons to hate you - all to no avail. When I heard that you should be staying near my Aunt Catherine's house in March, I was compelled to go there. I could not prevent myself from testing my control - and your resolve - for I had found little peace in those months from thoughts of you. When I called upon you at your cousin's house, I could not detect any change in your feelings towards me, but I felt more in control of myself. You could not have known that I often followed you in your walks in Rosings Park, or contrived to meet you by riding or pacing the paths I knew you to frequent."

He paused, apparently lost in his memories for a few moments and then turned away from the window to face her. "That I passed all tests I set for myself gave me a slight return of confidence. It was but a small step from there to summon my arrogance, and I resolved to marry you. I fancied I loved you, but I came to see later that I was so much enamoured of myself there was little room in my heart to harbour the tender concern and honest affection that love requires. I gave little thought to what you wanted, never considering the possibility that you might have reason to refuse me."

He returned to the sofa and sat apart from her, his face pale but calm, and finished his narrative. "When you did refuse with such an eloquent appraisal of my bad manners and unworthy conduct, it was as if all support had been pulled out from beneath me. I could not think what I should do, and a great anger rose to blind me to the truth of what you had said. My illusion of self-control was shattered and I truly wanted to destroy you at that moment - there seemed no other way to secure my release from you. It was for that reason that I fled the room and quitted my aunt's house the next day."

A brief pause gave Elizabeth time to compare his words to her own memory of these events, and she blushed at the thought of the part her pride and prejudice had played in bringing him to the tormented state he described. After a few moments he spoke again. "I believe you know how much I benefited from your criticism in the following months. When we met at Pemberley I saw that I was calmed rather than tormented by your presence, and I began to hope that time might undo all mischief from the past. I did not speak of and scarcely allowed myself to remember that period of insanity. I think now that I should have been more frank on this subject, but I was afraid to jeopardise my hope for the future with such oppressive thoughts."

The quiet, if pale, countenance that he had sustained throughout this last narration was lost to a renewed agitation as he neared the end of the story. "I pledged to you this morning all that I have and all that I *am*, and I was ready to hope that it would be enough to secure our happiness. But as the day wore on, the weight of my past began to trouble me. Those memories that had been carefully hidden away came flooding back, and I saw myself as I really am, not as your love sees me, Elizabeth. You think me strong and good and honest, and every touch of your hand today, every look, reminded me that you had entrusted your happiness to me." He closed his eyes for a moment to steady himself.

"As we neared the moment of intimacy I most desired, I was gripped by fear. After all of the pain of wanting, the struggle to master my faults… I knew that I could yet lose you… "

His voice had dropped to the merest whisper and his hands clenched and unclenched from the exertion of disclosure. "When I took you into my arms, the force of my passion blinded me to all thoughts of your happiness, to everything but my… need." He lifted his eyes to search her face, and seeing that she waited, her breath held, he confessed, "When you pushed me away from you, such violent thoughts were unleashed… I was afraid I would go mad if you rejected me!" His hands rose to his temples and he pressed hard as if to contain the disorder of his mind. "But I was behaving as if I were

44

already mad..."

Before he had finished, she moved to his side and grasping both of his hands, pulled them to her wildly beating heart, crying, "Stop, Fitzwilliam, *please*, please stop! I cannot bear this grief for another second!" She drew a long, slow breath and then spoke passionately, "You are not all darkness, and I am not all light. Why do you not see the part of the fault that lies with me? You judge yourself by much harsher standards than you do me. Do not think me so angelic that I do not see your faults, or that I have none of my own. My love is not blind, but it is stronger than you credit. I married you willingly, knowing your faults." She paused as colour rose to her cheeks. "My own I am just beginning to understand."

He started to speak but she touched his lips with her hand, saying, "Wait, I must tell you something more before I lose my courage. I have never admitted that I was also drawn to you from our first meeting. I do not wonder to find you mad with my rejection, for from that first sensibility of feeling, *I* began to deny *you* at every turn, even to myself. I called it 'hate' to disguise from myself the indignity of wanting something, some*one*, I thought I could not have. And even when you guessed that to be the truth, I would not admit it."

She went on eagerly: "From the first time you asked me to dance, when I was wounded that you had not asked sooner and that you did not appear sufficiently enthusiastic, I adopted an air of proud disregard to mask my true feelings. Do you not see? We established, both of us, a dreadful comedy of errors from the very beginning. But you must surely blame me for toying with your affections, for I had the advantage of knowing the nature of *your* feelings from the day you proposed to me."

Vexation brought a frown to her forehead, as she struggled to understand and express such novel thoughts as were crowding into her mind. With a shake of her head, she continued, "That I could deny such an intense attraction can partially be blamed on the folly of our times, where a woman is taught to hide behind delicate sensibilities and disown her own passions, even to herself. The careful regulation I have prided myself on has brought us to the very precipice of disaster." Her words quickened with the certainty she now felt. "How close we have come to utterly losing our happiness forever makes me tremble with anger and shame. I would have more safely followed my sister Lydia's example of wild abandon than the course I took, for I am certain no greater harm could have come from facing the truth than that which was wrought by hiding from it."

During the long silence that followed, Elizabeth closed her eyes and wrestled with the mortification of her self-revelation while Darcy studied her face intently, aware that he was seeing her with new eyes. When at last their reverie was broken, it was by a soft sigh from Elizabeth. Shaking her head, she opened her eyes to meet his, then raised her hands to smooth the frown lines tenderly from his brow. He scarcely breathed as her fingertips traced the lines of his face and neck and moved down to his shoulders. With poignant tenderness, she slid her hands under the lapels of his waistcoat and lifted it from him. Holding his eyes in an unwavering gaze, she untied his silk neckcloth and unbuttoned his vest and slipped it off, unafraid of the violent trembling she felt as her hands moved along his torso.

Standing up, she slowly unfastened the buttons on her gown and let it fall to the floor, saying softly as she did, "We have talked enough to understand one thing sufficiently well - that our love must not be denied any longer or we shall both end up quite mad. Teach me to love you as I should," she pleaded with eyes filling with tears, "so that we may never doubt again the steadiness of each other's affection."

A sob escaped his throat as he rose to wrap his arms around her. And indeed, neither could have found another word to say for a very long time, for they were too much occupied for the rest of the night in the belated pursuit of a knowledge that words are powerless to improve.

Chapter Seven

Mrs Elizabeth Darcy awoke at first light to the vague memory of a pleasant dream, and it required a minute's reflection to assure herself that she was indeed lying nestled into the shoulder of her husband, her arm draped carelessly across his chest. Without moving a muscle, she absorbed all of the sensations of the moment and compared them to lines from her favourite love poems, thinking how the words suffered when compared to the exquisite reality.

Elizabeth's temperament, however, was not long captivated by lofty thoughts, and Mr Darcy, lost in well-deserved repose, was gradually brought to wakefulness by the astonishingly lovely sound of laughter. Mirth might have seemed out of place, but the many anguishes of their courtship, their engagement and marriage so speedily concluded, and the fact that she had cried more earnest and painful tears the previous evening than she had in her preceding one and twenty years, might allow for the need to reassert her natural exuberance.

A good while passed before her laughter gave her leave to speak, and Mr Darcy could not immediately decide what to make of it. The sight of his furrowed brow as she raised herself to sit beside him sobered her in a moment and she leaned over to kiss his frown. Her amiable smile quickly allayed his fear and he pulled her toward him to wrap his arms around her, kissing her playfully.

"After such a charming beginning to our marriage," she quipped, "I little doubt that we will soon be as utterly calm and reasonable as Jane and Bingley. I was just thinking how fortunate it was, though rather out of character for me, that I let myself be guided by you on the subject of our wedding trip. I fear the Bingleys would have been frightened half to death had they seen any part of last night's storm."

He smiled at the thought, basking in a feeling of contentment and lightness that was an utter novelty for him. He felt no urgency to speak or move, happy just to lie revelling in these new sensations. Nestling his face into her tousled hair, he closed his eyes to concentrate on the scent and feel of her body in his arms. Elizabeth, however, having lived her first twenty years in a pleasant state of contentment, was drawn to pursue the novelty of discovery and disclosure so recently begun. Raising herself up on one elbow, she studied his face and then continued in a more serious vein.

"Fitzwilliam, you were so eloquent last night, destroying yourself with recriminations and attempting to elevate me to a position too near the angels to be comfortable. I think it only fair to you that I be allowed to be as honest as you have been. Perhaps enough was said last night about passion to allow that subject to rest, but I only want to say that far from reproaching you for a want of control, it does you great credit that if so painful were your feelings from the first, you never gave me cause to fear you. I cannot believe that I was ever in any real danger, for you have shown me in so many ways that your nature is gentle and kind."

This speech heightened the colour in her cheeks and led to a momentary variance of composure, but she soon regained herself to continue, "As for causing me pain, I must admit it is my own wilfulness that is most to blame on that account. The understanding of deficiencies in my own powers of reason should lie heavy on me this morning. Although I dislike admitting it and I am sure you will be too kind to reproach me, I have in fact caused you pain before by hasty judgements that found fault with your character where there was none.

"I feel I must tell you that my reasoning when you left me yesterday led me to conclude that your original contempt for me and my family had been renewed, and that your hasty departure from the room bore witness to your inability to overcome your feelings of distaste for our union."

Mr Darcy frowned in concentration, examining all the pieces of the puzzle they had unravelled the night before. His sister and his friends, especially the affable Mr Bingley, had been always too much in awe of his confidence and strong opinions to force him into such an examination of his words or actions as he faced from the partner he had chosen. While Elizabeth's temperament could be described as mercurial, given to rapid and easy fluctuation, his was of a more leaden composition. Events requiring such abrupt mental and emotional adjustments cost him a very great effort indeed.

He was so much used to thinking alone that he found it difficult to fashion a response; he quietly rose from the bed, found his dressing gown, put it on, and took a turn around the room. Elizabeth refrained from speaking, but watched with growing unease.

When he did at last turn to face her, he spoke deliberately and firmly. "Mrs Darcy, I awoke this morning fully predisposed to be relaxed and in good humour and I now find that you have put me quite out of sorts." For a moment she believed he was making an attempt at levity but as he continued, her hope faded.

"I begin to understand that I have been remiss in some of the duties required of a husband," he said with a tone that conveyed anything but lightness. "This I may forgive myself, for I have not had good instruction from my father on this subject. I understand now that he was so gentle and forbearing with my mother that he did both of them a disservice, for she was, by temperament, a very strong and wilful woman. Without the advantage of being moulded by his judgements, she became a demanding and unsolicitous wife. I shall not make the same mistake, I think, for I see that you are all too ready to assert your opinions and find fault with me at every turn."

Elizabeth was more than a little startled but judged that it might be as well to refrain from hasty conclusions. He continued, "I believe that your father, although of course I greatly admire and esteem him, was as remiss as mine in the management of his wife and, more to the point, his daughters. I shall not continue on this path of error, for it will serve neither of us."

Mr Darcy had been walking around the room as he spoke, but now paused directly in front of his wife and took a masterful pose with crossed arms. She lowered her eyes to maintain her composure, but far from feeling a proper submissiveness, she perceived her old ally, anger, rising to her throat. He paused there for a few seconds, as if challenging her to disagree, and her father's remonstrance to her on the day of her engagement came to mind. He had cautioned her not to marry a man whom she could not esteem, warning her that her temperament would be very dangerous to her if she did. Before she could ponder this thought further, he resumed his pacing, apparently satisfied that he had met no opposition.

"I think it is necessary, therefore, that we come to an understanding from this moment that your actions shall be guided by me on all matters of consequence. I shall begin by making several conditions which I will expect you to acknowledge." His pacing had brought him to a spot behind her and he stopped there. Elizabeth was grateful that he could not see her face at this moment, for she could not have hidden from him the cold indignation that had risen to her eyes.

"First," he began, "you shall always attempt to ascertain my mood before expressing opinions. I shall initiate subjects of a serious nature only as I see they are necessary to our good understanding. Secondly, you will not disagree with my judgements or question my actions." He noticed the growing stiffness of her posture and the crimson wave rising on her neck. "Third," he continued, "you will show respect and humility when I correct you."

Elizabeth's temper was quite inflamed before he had finished his third condition, and she sprang from the bed to face him with burning cheeks. She began to say, in a voice that trembled with indignation, "Mr Darcy... " but he turned away as if he had taken no notice.

"Fourth," he added in a louder and more imperious tone, "you will not interrupt me." He walked deliberately to the other side of the room and stopped with his back to her, leaving her speechless with consternation. He slowly turned around, unable at last to disguise the mirth in his eyes, and said, "And finally, you shall consent never to be out of my sight for more than the space of a few minutes until I am quite content that your judgement has so improved that you will never again be in danger of forming incorrect opinions."

If last night's tears had been the most agonised of Elizabeth Darcy's life, Mr Darcy's present laughter was equally a novelty, for he was unaccustomed to this form of humour, and certainly had no previous occasion to enjoy laughter at his own expense.

"Horrible, despicable man!" she cried, "I'm sure I have never teased *you* so mercilessly! I am reminded," she remarked haughtily, "that my favourite description of you early in our acquaintance was 'insufferable man', but now I see I have never understood the full meaning of those words, or how aptly applied. You may do well to be on guard in future, for I am sure to retaliate. You had the advantage of catching me completely off guard this time, for I had not thought of wit as one of your gifts, but rest assured that I, having had more practice, and being now forewarned, will never be content until I can cause you as much discomfort as you have caused me."

"I am happy to see you have regained *your* wit at last," he replied, still breathless with laughter, "but I will not take the blame for causing you grief, for your own nature has brought this upon you. Did you not confess just a few moments ago that your judgements are hasty and flawed, that you are too inclined to think ill of me? I was merely testing whether you were yet cured of that affliction, but I see that you were as ready as ever to believe me quite hateful."

She replied archly, "I shall withhold my answer for a few more years until I have ascertained whether the fault is in *your* nature or in *my* perception. In the meanwhile, please do me the honour of giving me a signal when you mean to be witty or brutish so that my responses will be more appropriate."

That in the space of less than a day, he should have begun to enjoy both eloquence and wit was no small matter, and he was fairly exhausted with the effort, but altogether pleased. "My darling Lizzie," he said with a jubilant air, "I find myself improving so rapidly under your ministrations that I shall end, I fear, by being flawless in a very short time. You will quite soon have to pronounce me the perfect husband." They now began to laugh together so heartily that the sounds could be faintly heard in the staff parlour on the floor below. The good innkeepers exchanged only looks of satisfaction while the chambermaid shook her head in disbelief at the ways of the highly born.

Levity to tenderness was an easy step. They put aside all troubled thoughts of past and future, and engaged themselves fully with their present happiness. If last night's embraces were passionate, this morning's were sweeter for the laughter they had shared. Elizabeth could not resist one last jest. Feigning a worried frown, she complained, "I still find one impediment to our perfect intimacy, Mr Darcy."

He answered with a gallant bow, "Tell me what it is and I shall remove it at once."

"It is this dressing gown, sir," she replied with a laugh.

At this, he was so overcome with delight and anticipation that he swept her up in his arms and with all eagerness carried her back to bed. It will be left to the imagination of our readers with what felicity the morning was concluded, and how happy an effect a bit of levity may have on a couple's lovemaking. Suffice it to say, not a precious moment was wasted on anything that was not sublimely suited to the occasion, and that when sleep overtook them again, it was untroubled by any restlessness or worry for the future.

Elizabeth awoke with a smile on her face and stretched languidly for a moment before noticing Mr Darcy sitting in a comfortable chair near the bed gazing at her. He moved to her side and gently lifted a curl from her cheek, kissed her lightly then lay down beside her and gathered her into his arms. She nestled her head into his shoulder as a sleepy child might, and they remained quiet and still together. That there was still much to be said and understood neither of them could doubt, but they could look ahead secure in the knowledge that the foundation of their marriage was laid with a strong mortar of love that had withstood its first great storm.

Chapter Eight

If the staff of Mr Godfrey's Inn thought it in any way strange to be called upon to serve breakfast at a time when preparations for dinner were well under way in the kitchen, they graciously betrayed no sign. The young couple paid the highest compliment to the chef in their enjoyment of this first breakfast together, for the combination of exertions, stresses and merriment had left them ravenously hungry. Mrs Godfrey, reviewing the empty dishes that were returned to the kitchen, felt quite alarmed that they might have found the meal insufficient. Her worries were quite unfounded, however, as the Darcys were in no mood to find fault with anything that day. When they finally descended the wide oak staircase, arm in arm, engrossed in light-hearted banter, and came upon their hosts in the great lobby, Mr Darcy bade them good afternoon with a warmth that was quite unlike their previous conversations with him.

"Mrs Darcy and I were thinking of a walk to Highbury. Is there likely to be anything stirring there today?" he asked pleasantly.

Mr Godfrey answered, "Yes, sir, it will be market day today. Highbury is as lively on a Friday as ever you will find it. I daresay you may find it quite crowded on such a fine day as this."

Mrs Godfrey, emboldened by a warm smile from Mrs Darcy, ventured, "If you enjoy embroidered goods, ma'am, you may find a woman named Mrs Arthur who sells the finest needlework bags and table covers as ever there was. She usually has a small table on your right as you enter the square off the road."

"Thank you, Mrs Godfrey. I will look for her," Mrs Darcy answered. "Is that some of her work upstairs? I noticed several beautiful pieces of handwork in our rooms and a lovely table cover in the hall."

Mrs Godfrey was pleased that she had noticed. "Why yes, ma'am, those are her work. I like to have her make things for me from time to time."

"She has an exceptionally fine touch. I will tell her that you sent us."

With a nod from Fitzwilliam, they passed out the door to greet the afternoon sun, already well on its way toward the horizon. The fine weather and pleasant countryside suited the tranquillity of their mood as Mr and Mrs Darcy walked down the lane. Wagons and carriages passed them often on the narrow road and they called out a friendly greeting to each. Had they chanced to meet any who had seen a young man striding angrily this way the previous afternoon, he need hardly have feared being recognised, for Mr Darcy was so much changed today that he scarcely recognised himself.

The conversation was as animated this fine afternoon as it had been subdued the previous one. Perhaps the most remarkable change for Mr Darcy was that, where his thoughts had heretofore been private and his words few, today he found himself expressing whatever ideas came into his mind in confident and fluent language. The sound of his voice, easy and warm, was a joy to his fair bride, and she marvelled at the absence of his customary reserve. It could not be far from the thoughts of either how very differently the day might have gone, but neither was inclined to disturb their enjoyment by speaking of what was past.

Only once did Elizabeth venture a small jest on the subject of their distress. As she remarked on a particularly pretty wood they were passing, she reflected, "Ah, but I suppose you have all the advantage of me, since I believe you have recently walked this way."

With unruffled composure he answered, to her infinite delight, in the same light-hearted vein. "I am afraid I must confess I saw little of the scenery yesterday, for a dark cloud obscured my vision."

She inclined her head in approbation of his response. "Very prettily said, sir. I do believe you have become a devoted student of wit."

He replied, "My eagerness to practice comes from having lived these eight and twenty years in a most abominably serious state of mind, and from my observations of late that beauty is much enhanced by the addition of levity."

"Yes, I do seem to recall," she teased, "that you found my looks punishing upon first observation, and only began to find me pretty after I began to tease you dreadfully."

"My beauty must be far superior to your own, then, as you professed to admire me from the first, even though I had no wit," he replied.

"I believe that the perception of beauty is in the taste of the beholder," said Elizabeth. "I have always been more drawn to the dark tempest than to a gentle spring rain, and so my enjoyment of your looks was improved by their promise of stormy weather."

"If storms are what you require to make you admire me, I fear I must return to my former temperament, or you will soon find me plain indeed," he declared with a frown.

"I thank you for your concern," she replied, "but I think it may be wiser for me to amend my notion of beauty. Upon reflection I must admit that yesterday's thunder was too dangerous even for my taste."

At length, strolling arm in arm through the market crowd, their self-absorption was relieved by the pleasure of focusing on the scene around them. Elizabeth easily engaged herself in exchanging pleasantries with the people they met. Darcy's new-found talent for easy conversation with his wife had not yet extended to social intercourse with complete strangers, but that he enjoyed listening to her was evident from his relaxed and pleasant smile. They provided a very pretty picture to all they met, and those who had seen him on previous visits to the neighbourhood were wont to remark upon the fortunate alliance he had made. In such a quiet community any novelty was enough to stimulate parlour conversations for several days to come. That Mr and Mrs Darcy deigned to make several purchases and appeared to find pleasure in the simple offerings of the market merely added to their fame, and only those predisposed to criticism were disappointed to find nothing wanting in their manners or bearing worthy of mention.

Having before long enjoyed all of the delights of this small village, their steps led them back as they had come. The slight pressure of his wife's hand on his arm was all Darcy required to feel content, and Elizabeth found she began to enjoy silence as well as witty conversation. The afternoon sun was fading before they reached the inn, and they entered it in a most pleasant mood of calm and fatigue. After a few minutes of discourse with their good host, they ordered a light tea in their rooms, and went upstairs to refresh themselves.

The tea was served presently and, as the shadows lengthened in the room, a quiet thoughtfulness overtook the couple. They spoke little, allowing themselves a space to contemplate the feelings and words that had occupied this space just four and twenty hours earlier. If there was sorrow and pain to remember, it was the release from both that was foremost in Elizabeth's mind. She roused herself first, and putting her teacup on the table, went to Darcy's side. Taking his cup, she laid it aside and sat down on his knees. He returned her loving smile with an effort, for his mind had been just then dwelling on the bittersweet memory of her tears. Taking his hand, she raised it to her lips, kissing his palm softly. Then she leaned against his chest and felt his arms encircle her.

Quietly intruding on the silence, Elizabeth said, "I wonder that it is possible for me to feel so at home in your arms when a day ago we had not yet embraced." His arms tightened their hold and he pressed his lips to her dark curls, overcome with gratitude. That she should choose not to mention their first terrible embrace showed a kindness he would not soon forget. At last, he found strength to say, hoarsely, "I feel as though I have come home, finally, after a lifetime of searching."

She raised her head to look into his eyes, and was moved by a trace of tears. She said earnestly, "I pray most fervently that I shall never again give you cause to doubt that your love is safe with me." His throat caught on a sob of gratitude and they reopened the subject of their passion with renewed enthusiasm.

Mr and Mrs Fitzwilliam Darcy supped in their room that night on a feast wrapped in candlelight, talking easily as old friends do. The fragments they had seen of each other's lives began to gather into sketches, with the promise of time enough stretching ahead of them to satisfy each other's desire to know and be known. They spoke of family and poetry, of hopes and memories, enjoying the hearing as much as the telling. And when, at length, they slept, the past was a distant cloud and the future glowed invitingly.

Had Miss Caroline Bingley glimpsed the tragic scene of the previous night, she might have been ecstatic, but the tender reconciliation that followed would surely have plunged her into despair. While his former companions enjoyed the sport of defaming him, they never imagined that the opinions held by Miss Elizabeth Bennet were the only ones of consequence to him at this moment. To be sure, it had required some practice on his part, but once having committed himself to seeing the world through Elizabeth's eyes, he was in a fair way to losing the ability to see it any other way.

Miss Bingley's last thread of hope was that he would certainly come to his senses in time, while *his* grateful prayer was to thank God that he had.

Chapter Nine

The sun rose the following morning on a mood of playful expectancy in the marriage suite. Elizabeth, ever optimistic, had never seriously doubted that she should be content with her life, but the depth of her joy was something more than even her imagination had allowed. With a heavier temperament to manage, Fitzwilliam was constantly being startled to find himself so at ease and so unabashedly happy. Lizzie asked, feigning a worried frown, "Must I always call you *Mr Darcy*, now that we have become such intimate friends?"

After giving the matter serious thought, he answered, "I think not. I believe I prefer to be called Master."

With a slight inclination of her head she acknowledged her acquiescence and then continued with a pretty display of submission, "Then, *Master*, may I speak to you of a matter which has begun to weigh heavily on my mind these few minutes?" Darcy nodded his consent and struggled to maintain the air of condescension wanted in the charade. Her eyes could not conceal her merriment, although she maintained a face all wrought in the timidity of a supplicant.

"You have been teaching me many things on the subject of love that I have earnestly impressed upon my memory, but I fear I want more practice to become a true proficient in the subject. Will you deign to instruct me again?"

"Scandalous want of attention, I call it!" he cried gruffly. "I suppose all of my time is to be taken up with your teaching and I shall have to put off my own studies."

"Pray what do you study, Master?" she asked innocently.

"Why mirth, of course, my dear," was his most amiable reply.

"Then I think we must combine our studies to make the best use of our time," she suggested.

"Happy thought!" said the gentleman. And with no want of enthusiasm for either subject they passed the rest of the early morning very pleasantly indeed, and it could not be easily judged which was the more able teacher or student.

Mr and Mrs Darcy rang for their second breakfast together at a more reasonable hour than the first, and it arrived accompanied by a calling card. Lizzie picked it up and read: "A Mr Robert Alexander, Fitzwilliam. He has sent his regards and requests the pleasure of our company at tea this afternoon at Great Oaks." She looked at him quizzically. "Do you have friends in the neighbourhood?"

Fitzwilliam, to her surprise, was frowning thoughtfully, and he hesitated before answering, gazing out the window as if he might find the answer there. He turned back to her after a few moments and smiled reassuringly. "Mr Alexander was my father's closest friend. He lives on an estate not far from here. I have not seen him in many years, not since my father's funeral I suppose."

Lizzie was perplexed. "Why have you not mentioned his name? Did you not mean to call on him while you were so near?"

Catching her tone, Darcy reached for her hand and said lightly, "I meant to keep you all to myself, my dear. I suppose I should have expected that in a society as restricted as that of Highbury, our presence would not go long unnoticed." This answer sufficed, and Elizabeth and Fitzwilliam soon agreed that, content though they were in their solitude, Mr Alexander's claim as Old Mr Darcy's friend would make it unseemly to refuse the invitation.

As they busied themselves with their breakfast, Lizzie could not fail to notice that Fitzwilliam had grown pensive, and although he attempted to attend to her light-hearted banter, his thoughts were obviously elsewhere. At last she asked, "Is something worrying you, my dear? I hope you are not anxious about what your friends will think of me, for I feel quite equal to appearing at your side in any company. Experience of social pretensions is not so unknown to me as you suppose. I shall treat them as I treated you," she said archly, "with a keen and cutting wit and an unfailing sense of my own dignity."

Her confident laughter drew him from his introspection.

He answered with a smile of contrition. "I do not at all blame you for that thought, Lizzie, considering my former eloquence on the subject of your social inferiority." Taking her hands in his and pressing them fondly, he continued, "I was actually wondering what they might think of me." Seeing her inquiring look, he said, "Shall we send our answer, then, and go out for a walk?"

Elizabeth contented herself that her husband would explain his remark in good time, and went to fetch her bonnet and coat. Alone for a few moments, she acknowledged to herself that if she had any worry, it was that Fitzwilliam, in spite of his protestations to the contrary, might find himself not totally unaffected by the opinions of his peers. The friendly tone of the note left by Mr Alexander led her to believe he held her husband in high esteem, however, and she looked forward to observing him through the eyes of his former acquaintances.

Having dispatched a messenger with a note and ordered the carriage for the outing later that afternoon, they set out on a leisurely walk, taking the path away from the village. They walked in silence, Lizzie waiting with uncharacteristic patience for him to gather his thoughts. When they reached the pond that had been the scene of Mr Darcy's painful reverie two nights before, they turned aside and sat down. Fitzwilliam was reminded of his thoughts on that tormented evening, and the expectation of their visit to his father's friend gave him added cause to reflect on the disparities in his parents' characters and the resulting confusion in his own. He had confided nothing of his troubled childhood to Lizzie, and his habitual reserve inclined him to silence on the subject, but as he turned to face her at last, her trusting smile encouraged him to candour.

"Let me tell you about the Alexanders, Lizzie," he began. "I visited Great Oaks several times while my father was alive, but I cannot say I know the family well. Although Mr Alexander was held in high esteem by my father, my mother thought the family quite unworthy of her notice… their wealth was acquired through trade. She would not deign to stop at their house, although I am sure my father ardently wished to pay them this respect, and so I went alone with him. I am afraid," he said quietly, watching her eyes for a sign of her feelings, "that I took my mother's point of view, and adopted a proud aloofness when in their presence. These five years since my father's death, I have scarcely thought of them, and have not called although I have passed this way more than once."

If Elizabeth was troubled by his words, she gave no indication, answering his gaze with nothing more disturbing than curiosity. He continued by saying that this was not the first invitation he had received from that family. Several letters had been sent to his sister and himself since their father's death, and every one ended with a kind request to visit at any opportunity. He coloured at the thought. He had not answered any after the first letter, and had not encouraged his sister to visit, although it seemed she was fond of the family.

After a thoughtful pause, he said, "I am sure it gave my father great sorrow to see me adopt my mother's attitudes, for Mr Alexander is a man who was very dear to his heart, and very *like* him, I think. I do not doubt that he has formed some opinion himself of my arrogance that I shall have to answer for today."

"I think," Elizabeth considered, "that I would have very much liked your father, my dear." She graciously did not add that she felt herself quite happy to have missed the honour of knowing his *mother*. The omission did not go unnoticed.

"You would have been the best of friends," he assured her, but there was something beneath the surface of his words that troubled her.

Elizabeth waxed thoughtful in turn. "On the subject of your manners, I am sure you are too hard on yourself, for I have never heard anyone speak ill of you outside of Meryton, excepting, of course, myself," she said with a laugh. "I don't doubt that someday I will force you to confess that you were only so very disagreeable in that neighbourhood because you sensed that I would be quite captivated by the challenge of improving you."

She laughed at a sudden intrusion of memory. "I think I must confess that before you found me inspecting your gardens at Pemberley this summer, my aunt and uncle and I had been making very discreet inquiries about you in the house and in town. That your staff found you the most generous and agreeable master could not be denied, and your manners were in every way judged to be superior, not only at Pemberley but in the village of Lambton as well. The worst that anyone could be persuaded to say of you was that you did not rattle on like other young men, for which I should be grateful, as I have a taste for being the centre of attention myself."

Her tone became more serious as she continued. "I must allow I was surprised by the disparity between what I heard of you there and what I had observed in Meryton. It made me doubt myself, and in fact, still troubles me." This admission caused a blush to creep up her face, as she was forced to remember the part her disdain had played in forming the opinions of others against Mr Darcy. Her aunt and uncle, to be sure, were quite astonished on meeting him for the first time at Pemberley to find his countenance pleasing and his manners unaffected, so strongly had she warned them against him.

"You needn't bother to blame yourself for misunderstanding me at Meryton," he said, with an effort to turn the conversation to a lighter note. "I was little pleased to find myself at Netherfield House, I assure you, only having come because I was so pressed by Bingley to admire his new estate and with no excuse ready enough to keep me from it. I expected to find it dull and consequently found it so, and I made no attempt to conceal my feelings from anyone. I am sorry to admit that I mistook this ill-mannered attitude for honesty and was proud of it.

"I may have hidden from some the arrogance of my thoughts, but I cannot allow *you* to excuse me on the grounds of these reports from my servants and neighbours. Having known me from a boy, and holding my father in such justly merited esteem, they would certainly make allowances for me. In my dealings with tenants and trades-people I consider myself fair, as I had only my father's example to follow. My mother, I believe, found them unworthy of any notice or discussion at all."

He persisted on a more sombre note. "My arrogance, I think, was more reserved for those whom I deemed to be pretenders to position or consequence. From my mother I learned always to be on guard, lest anyone not treat *me* with the respect she felt *we* deserved. I was suspicious of the motives of anyone who professed to want my company. I am quite sure that you would not receive such glowing reports from people such as Mr Alexander who well understood my mother's opinions and could observe that I was too much like her to promise well."

Elizabeth was not yet satisfied. "I should wonder, from this explanation, how it should be that Mr Alexander desires to do us the honour of receiving us in his house. I think it unlikely he would risk a rude refusal from you, if he thought you to be so ill-mannered."

Darcy explained, "Mr Alexander, as you will soon see, is a most generous and agreeable gentleman, and little disposed to take offence from others. I do not doubt that if I had refused him, it would merely have confirmed his suspicions and he would not have pressed us again. With our acceptance, he will be quite ready to hope that I am become more my father's son than he had reason to expect."

Elizabeth laughed pleasantly. "Then I look forward to seeing that good gentleman's pleasure and surprise at finding you quite perfect. In fact, I will only be content when I am assured that everyone finds you as charming as I do." Fitzwilliam did not trust himself to continue this line of discussion, for he did not want to tell her how much he doubted that the world would judge him through her loving eyes, or her through his.

Chapter Ten

Such gloomy thoughts notwithstanding, everyone's expectations were rewarded most pleasantly that afternoon at Great Oaks. Mrs Alexander was no less kind and willing to please and be pleased than her husband, and Mr Alexander was everything a good host should be. If he felt any reservation in his feelings toward Fitzwilliam Darcy, it was not evident to Elizabeth, who watched carefully and maintained a becoming air of restraint herself to allow her husband the opportunity to express himself freely. It was a tribute to the effort he was making to secure their good opinion that no awkwardness marred his greeting. He introduced Elizabeth with a glow of pride and thanked them for their kind invitation, stating without ceremony that it had been too long since his last visit to Great Oaks.

The gentleman answered quietly, but with an openness and warmth that indicated his good nature, that the Darcy family would always be welcome in their home. His wife was more effusive, embracing Fitzwilliam as if he were a lost son, and exclaiming over how well he looked and how lovely was his bride. Before they were even seated, she had begun questioning him about his sister and professing an eagerness to see her, for Georgiana had visited Great Oaks often as a child in her father's company.

Elizabeth soon found herself drawn into the conversation and within the space of an hour none could have doubted that they should all quite enjoy each other's company. Mrs Alexander, once satisfied that Georgiana was well and grown quite handsome, turned her attention to discovering Elizabeth. "Mrs Darcy," she asked, "your father's family are the Bennets of Longbourn, I understand. But I do not know of your mother's family." Fitzwilliam tensed involuntarily at this reference to lineage, but he need have feared neither that Mrs Alexander's motive was more than a pleasant curiosity nor that Lizzie would find reason to suspect it was.

Elizabeth answered cheerfully but briefly, keenly aware that this subject must still afford a measure of discomfort to Fitzwilliam. She ended with an affectionate description of her Aunt and Uncle Gardiner, the branch of her mother's family that gave her the most pleasure to acknowledge. Mr Alexander smiled broadly at the mention of their name. "Why, my dear Mrs Darcy, I believe I am well acquainted with your uncle. His residence is in Gracechurch Street, is it not?"

As she assented with surprise that it was, Mrs Alexander interrupted, "Why, then, we have dined at their house, have we not, Mr Alexander? A most charming couple! Bless my soul, I do enjoy the idea that they are your relations, and I see now that you bear a resemblance to your uncle, Mrs Darcy. What a lovely coincidence."

Elizabeth and Fitzwilliam were both delighted at this connection and Elizabeth asked eagerly how they came to be acquainted.

"I first met your uncle when I established an office in London, it must be more than twenty years ago, I believe. I respect and admire him greatly, Mrs Darcy," said Mr Alexander. "He most graciously invited us to stay with them whenever we have business in London, but as we have always lodged at my brother's house, I had no opportunity to avail myself of their hospitality. We did, however, dine with their family on one occasion and I must say I found them most pleasant company indeed."

"Oh, yes," added Mrs Alexander, "we felt as though we were in our own home. Isn't it extraordinary!"

Fitzwilliam rejoined, "I hope I shall have the honour of entertaining both you and the Gardiners at Pemberley one day. I don't doubt that they would be pleased to renew the acquaintance." Mr Alexander was astonished at such enthusiasm from Fitzwilliam for a family that he would once have dismissed as inferior, but he was careful to guard his feelings. In fact, he was finding himself surprised by almost everything about Fitzwilliam Darcy today.

The tea conversation moved on to fond reminiscences of Mr Darcy's father by Mr and Mrs Alexander, and Elizabeth noted that her husband became quiet, his face taking on the mask of reserve that she was beginning to recognise. Mr Alexander did not miss the change in his guest's countenance and seemed to be studying him thoughtfully for a time. He abruptly changed the topic to enquire about their future plans. Learning that the Darcys meant to leave Highbury soon, Mrs Alexander begged leave to arrange a dinner party to include their son and daughters who were all settled within an easy distance of Great Oaks, for she was anxious that they all should meet.

Elizabeth was a little surprised to find Fitzwilliam ready to agree with only one slight objection - that he did not want to inconvenience them. Mrs Alexander's kindly protests to the contrary settled the matter and the Darcys prepared to depart, having engaged themselves for dinner two days hence. Earnestly pressed to stay for supper, Elizabeth made a very elegant excuse, declaring herself quite fatigued, for she guessed that Fitzwilliam must be ready for a rest after the exertion of so much cheerful conversation. They left Great Oaks with the Alexanders' most heartfelt congratulations and felicitations on their marriage, and a happy sense of expectation that the rest of the family, if as generous as their parents, would be very pleasant company indeed.

Elizabeth had not been wrong to assume that Fitzwilliam would make a favourable impression on Mr and Mrs Alexander, and indeed that couple spent a good deal of the evening on this subject. As they returned to the house after seeing their guests to their carriage, Mrs Alexander exclaimed, "What a pleasant surprise, my dear! Our Mr Darcy seems to have shaken himself free of his mother's unfortunate temperament. Did you not find him greatly changed?"

Mr Alexander answered thoughtfully, "I had always hoped that his father's nature would prevail, but his silence these past few years led me to doubt it. I suspect that the *new* Mrs Darcy deserves a great deal of the credit for what we saw today."

"Oh, yes," she exclaimed, "what a charming girl! If he allows himself to be influenced by her I don't doubt he will be a very happy man."

Mr Alexander grew pensive. "I was troubled by his reticence regarding his father. I am sure that Fitzwilliam has a great deal to say on that subject, but I wonder if he will allow me into his confidence. He has always possessed such a stoic reserve, I doubt that he has discussed his troubled family history with anyone. Still, I must try... "

"If anyone inspires confidence, it is you, my dear," Mrs Alexander said, patting his arm. "I don't doubt you will find a way to reach him if he wants to be reached. But perhaps he is able to let the past lie, now that both his mother and father are dead. With Georgiana and now his new bride, he may find himself content and at peace after all." She seemed satisfied - wishing it to be so was sufficient reason to expect that it *would* be.

Mr Alexander smiled at his wife and nodded, understanding that it was her nature to always anticipate a happy ending to every story. He would have liked to share her optimism, but he was more realistic and had a deeper knowledge of the Darcy family than would allow him to hope for such a painless resolution.

Elizabeth left the Alexander home in high spirits, content that they could have found nothing to disappoint them in Fitzwilliam's manners. In her modesty, she little guessed the warmth of their approbation for her. Fitzwilliam, to his credit, was more astute on this point, and he settled back into the carriage with his arm around her shoulder, eager to express himself. "I have never met your equal in making people easy or in improving a conversation."

She protested sincerely, "I? What had I to do with it? If I deserve any credit it is that I was more silent than I am used to be, and allowed you to express yourself, for you were so eloquent you had completely disarmed them in but a few minutes."

He laughed at this thought, but insisted, "I admit I acquitted myself honourably and I feel safe that I have shown myself to be sufficiently improved to merit their renewed friendship. But," he paused, then went on, "I do not mind admitting that the Alexanders were completely captivated by you, my love. And well they should be, if they have any sense, for you are quite astonishingly lovely in every way."

Elizabeth smiled and relaxed against his shoulder, saying, "I will not be so foolish as to argue against such a pretty speech, although I know you give me too much credit and yourself too little. In any case, your Alexanders are such a pleasant couple that I'm sure they would not criticise either one of us. I liked them very much."

"My dearest Lizzie," mused Darcy, "I wonder if, with the exception of my unfortunate self, there is anyone you have not warmed to on your first meeting."

She responded cheerfully, "I agree that I generally enjoy company and conversation, but I am not always as successful in exciting admiration as I was with you." She laughed and added, "And I must confess an unbecoming duplicity at times, for it is often the weakness I observe in the characters of others that excites my interest. If my sister Jane were not so good-natured that she finds it difficult to criticise me, she could tell you terrible stories of my scathing reviews of those I find tedious or unworthy. Fortunately for you," she teased, "my memory is short, especially where injuries to myself are concerned, and I usually finish quite soon by laughing at myself and forgiving all offence. I think I shall one day even look forward to meeting your Aunt Catherine again."

This remark brought hearty laughter from both. They drove a while in satisfied silence, until Fitzwilliam remembered, "You have not settled on a name for me yet, Lizzie."

"Hmm, yes. I suppose I shouldn't call you 'Master' in front of the Alexanders or it will undo all your excellent work," she mused. "Have you never been called by any pet names? 'Fitzwilliam' is so very formal."

"No one but my father ever called me anything but 'Fitzwilliam', for my mother hated diminutives. My friends call me 'Darcy' and my enemies, 'Mr Darcy', as *you* should well know," he teased. "You will insist on knowing, so I will tell you that my father called me Willie."

"Willie!" Elizabeth laughed. "Oh, yes, that is precious indeed. But I'm afraid I would have to laugh every time I said it, and that might interfere with our serious conversations. How about 'Will'? I like the sound of that - solemn enough and yet friendly. *Will*, she repeated. "Yes, I like that."

He tried it out himself a few times and decided that it was not displeasing. "I am, madam, *Will*, at your service." They had reached the inn by this time and walked in arm and arm, very pleased with the day. Mr Godfrey, at his station behind an ancient oak desk, rose to greet them and inquired how they had enjoyed their outing. It was Fitzwilliam who carried the conversation, remarking on the fine estate at Great Oaks and wondering if the Godfreys were acquainted with the Alexander family. They were, of course, known to him, and he owned that they were held in the highest esteem by their neighbours, adding that the children did great justice to the family name. Hearing that they should dine with the family, he ventured that more pleasant company would be hard to meet and that three of the children had married into very fine families in the neighbourhood.

These pleasantries were followed by a discussion of supper plans and the comparative merits of dining in their own rooms or the fine dining room downstairs. A brief meeting of the eyes settled for privacy, and the Darcys went upstairs. When they were alone, Elizabeth asked if Fitzwilliam had ever heard Mr Godfrey say an unkind word, and he answered that he could not recall it. She said, "He and his wife put me in mind of Jane and Bingley, they are so kind and pleasant." She sighed. "Oh, dear Jane and dear Mr Bingley, I wonder how they are getting on."

"I should not wonder if they are thinking themselves the happiest of couples," said Darcy. "I am sure there could be no danger of any disharmony there," he said, drawing her close to him.

Elizabeth lifted her eyes to his and then raised her face to kiss him, saying, "Nor here, Master... or should I say, as the intimacy seems to demand it, *Will*." They laughed as he lifted her up in his arms and carried her into the bedchamber. What was lacking in tension from their loving was well supplied by playfulness, and the exertions of the day were finally rewarded with a pleasant rest. They were awakened by a knock at the door, and Fitzwilliam dressed quickly to admit the supper service. Elizabeth appeared after a few minutes proclaiming herself famished, and they sat down to enjoy another evening of discovery.

By the time they finally quitted the table, Elizabeth had learned a good deal about the habits of the Darcy family, their occupations and travels. All that she learned taught her to respect her husband's father more and his mother less, but she was kind enough to disguise her growing dislike for that woman, preferring to draw him out on the subject of old Mr Darcy. An unpleasant likeness was beginning to form itself in her mind between the arrogant Miss Bingley and the late Lady Anne Darcy, and she disliked the prospect of being thrown into much company with the former, although it seemed likely that she should be. It was fortunate, Elizabeth mused, that Jane was blessed with such a forbearing temperament, for she would certainly be entertaining Miss Bingley a good deal, as well as Mr and Mrs Hurst.

As her husband spoke about his childhood, Elizabeth noticed that his expression became masked as it had at the Alexanders that afternoon, and she assumed his feelings of loss must be painfully deep. To lighten his mood, she turned the subject to his sister Georgiana, knowing he delighted in speaking of her. The death of their mother when she, Georgiana, was so young and then their father, on whom the girl had doted, had made Fitzwilliam most protective and tender towards her. Elizabeth's desire to know Georgiana better, and her hope that she should always be with them at Pemberley, was sincere, for in the little time she had known her new sister, she had formed a most favourable impression of her. Her enthusiasm naturally endeared her to Fitzwilliam, for he judged that with such a confidant and lively companion as Lizzie, Georgiana must overcome her almost painful shyness.

They talked late into the night, with Fitzwilliam finally remarking that he had talked more of himself in the last few days than in his previous eight and twenty years. Elizabeth declared that she would not rest until she had all of his secrets in her hands, which led him to ask whether she was not finding the narrative rather dull. "On the contrary, my dear Will," she exclaimed. "I am just beginning to see how very unremarkable my own life has been by comparison. All of my adventures have come from listening to others or from my imagination."

Taking her hand, he pulled her from her chair onto his lap, and laying his head on her breast, he said softly, "Your gift, I think, is that you draw the very best out of all you meet. I believe you could charm a pleasant tale out of a rock, and find him a very amusing fellow."

Chapter Eleven

Over breakfast the next morning, Fitzwilliam asked Elizabeth, "Do you begin to feel it very dull here in Highbury?"

"If by that you mean more dull now than when we first arrived, I would say that I am glad for this improvement. But if you ask whether it is more dull than any other place, I should answer that I want nothing else but your company to make any location on earth exceedingly interesting," she replied.

"Thank you very much for both the clarification and the compliment," he said with an easy smile and a stretch, "but will you please be serious enough for a moment to help me plan what we are to do, for I am sure the Godfreys have not counted on us living with them until we have grown old. I had thought we might go to London for a week before meeting up with the Bingleys at Pemberley. I am sure you will want to begin plotting and scheming with shopkeepers how best you can rearrange and redecorate the house as soon as you arrive."

She appeared to be gravely considering the proposition for some time, and her eyes betrayed no hint of the mirth she felt at having the opportunity to tease him.

"Yes, I have been giving some thought to that matter these last few days, but I did not like to raise the subject so soon. Since you have mentioned it, though, there are one or two things about Pemberley that I would like to put my hands to, and I am pleased to hear that you would not be distressed by a little change. Of course, I have not your experience of visiting in the finest homes in England and you may well imagine that the limits of my father's estate did not allow for extravagant expenditures, but I feel quite confident that with a little practice and with good advice from friends I could very well be of use to you in improving your house. I had thought I should best begin by asking Miss Bingley for her advice, for if I am not mistaken, she has given a good deal of thought to what she would have done if Pemberley had fallen under her excellent management."

Darcy laughed out loud and relaxing back in his chair, sat admiring his wife.

"I wonder whether I will ever give up attempting to discuss serious subjects with you. It is unfair, I think, that I give you so many opportunities to torment me and you never decline even one."

She retorted, "You must blame yourself, my dear, if you persist in looking for trouble from me at every turn. You must see by now that I cannot break myself of the habit of levity whenever the conversation takes a serious turn. The preservation of Pemberley must be a very serious subject indeed if you could look so worried. It was rather silly of you to think that I, having spent no more than two hours together in your house, should have formed designs on improving it. In fact, I want nothing so much as to explore it for myself, exactly as it has been, to see what light it may shed on your very complex personality."

She could not know that her last sentence, spoken in jest, brought to his mind a painful image which he had been carefully avoiding. With a coy smile, she added, "If you had not so often professed to hate deceit, I would have accused you of attempting to entrap me into betraying a defect in character by opening this subject."

Darcy frowned. "I see you are too clever to be so easily caught out," he declared, recovering himself. "But I am determined to find at least one fault in you before quitting Highbury."

"Unless you greatly improve your skills, I fear we *shall* indeed grow old here," she rejoined.

"Let me try a new subject then," he ventured. "Would you not like to spend some time shopping for yourself? I have not met a woman who could resist the temptation of leading her new husband about London while he is still of a mind to purchase for her whatever her heart should desire, as well as still young and strong enough to carry all of her parcels."

"I see no use in buying adornments for your benefit, for you have never mentioned that it pleases you or displeases you, whatever I am wearing," she said, saucily. "For myself, I am prepared to think my wardrobe quite the most elegant I have ever seen. But if you are worried about the impression I shall make with your neighbours, I will most willingly be outfitted to suit your taste."

"I see I have at last found a nerve, for your face is beginning to flush. Well, I have won the point, but the game goes to you. You do not intend to change my house, nor do you care to spend my money on yourself. I must admit you are quite free from any petty vanities."

With a triumphant smile, she declared, "You give up too easily, sir. I was about to collapse in a moment and tell you all of my faults. Now you shall never hear them from me."

"I am devastated to have missed such an opportunity," he sighed. "I shall have to redouble my efforts to prise them from you. But for now, pray let us return to the question at hand. If you will not be tempted by London, where *would* you like to go next, madam?"

She smiled broadly and took his hands, looking into his eyes to watch his response. "If you really want to know what I would like, it is that we go directly to Pemberley." She was pleased to see the surprise in his eyes, but there was something else there, something disturbing, and she hurried to explain: "If it isn't convenient, of course, or if you prefer to go to London, of course we can wait," she stammered.

He hastened to reply, "No, no, it isn't that. I'm only surprised that you should wish it."

She smiled tentatively. "The memory of our meeting there this summer is so sweet to me. I felt as though I were seeing you for the first time. You have no idea how shocked you looked to find me on your grounds when you came striding up, and I was quite disconcerted myself, having taken pains to assure myself that you would not be at home. I expected that you would be angry to see me intruding there after I had behaved so contemptibly towards you when we last met, but instead you welcomed me with such graciousness that I felt the air must be touched with something magical. I saw you at peace that day, and I have always regretted that we were forced to leave so precipitously, before I could explore the feelings that were raised." She coloured with this admission, but continued with heightened emotion.

"I long to be with you at Pemberley and to see you again in that light."

"I am tempted to tease you now, but I am kinder than you and will not take advantage of your sensibilities. I will even tell you the truth, since you have just paid me a compliment. You could not have asked for anything I more willingly would give you than to take you home as soon as possible." Although his answer pleased her, his face betrayed a gravity that the lightness of his words belied. "I allowed you to mistake my emotions about Pemberley a moment ago. I am not worried that you will cause me any distress by making changes. In fact, quite the opposite, I am worried that the house may change *you*. The atmosphere for me at Pemberley is not what you suppose." He gazed out the window and then turned to her resolutely. "Indeed, until I saw you there, I confess I had no love for it."

"I don't understand, Will. I hold in my heart a picture of you walking beside me in your garden, so relaxed and unguarded. If you mean to tell me this peace did not spring from your homecoming, to what should I attribute it?"

She could not fail to miss the sorrow behind his smile when he answered, "You are so unaware of your power over me, my love, and I should profess myself grateful for that. What you saw at Pemberley was a reflection of the light you carry with you. The moment I saw you walking on the lawn, I felt sure that what I needed to make that house my home was to have you there with me. When you greeted me with such civility, I began to hope that it might yet be possible."

Elizabeth was flattered, but not satisfied by his profession; something remained unsaid.

"But Will, why should Pemberley not give you joy?"

With a shake of his head, Darcy brightened and said, pulling her to him, "That is all in the past, and when we have exhausted all pleasant conversation many years from now, I will darken your brow with my ghosts. For now, be content that I love you utterly, and we shall go to Pemberley and live happily ever after, I am confident."

His embrace was strong and sure, and as it was clear that he resolved to say no more on the subject, she stored her questions away and replied, with more lightness than she felt, "A week alone at home, and I don't doubt that Mr and Mrs Bingley will find us quite the old settled country couple when they arrive."

The faint anguish gone from his face, Darcy smiled and said, "We dine at Great Oaks tomorrow, but we could leave on Tuesday morning, spend a night along the way and arrive in Pemberley by Thursday afternoon. I'll send word ahead straightaway, so that poor Mrs Reynolds does not die of fright to find us arriving unexpectedly with the rooms not aired." With a friendly kiss he released her, and went to find his waistcoat. Returning, he asked, "There is an excellent stable on the road to Langford. Would you enjoy going for a ride this morning?"

Mrs Darcy replied enthusiastically that she would, and he left the room saying that while she was dressing he would order the carriage and send his message home. Within half an hour they were on the road. The weather was exceptionally fine and the road wound agreeably past farms and woods, resplendent with their fall foliage. There was no evidence of uneasiness in their conversation, but unspoken thoughts rose in both of their minds from time to time. He regretted that he had said too much, and she that he had said too little, but both avoided all reference to his earlier remarks for the rest of the morning.

They spoke instead of horses, for Fitzwilliam Darcy was an avid equestrian. Elizabeth's family fortune had allowed them to keep only two very unexceptional animals, and as they were very much occupied in service, she had found little opportunity to ride them. But she shared her husband's enthusiasm for the subject and after he had described and named for her the horses he kept, she said eagerly, "I am not a good rider, but I should love to learn. I hope we shall go riding at Pemberley."

"Every day, if you like," he said, delighted at the thought. "I think I should much prefer seeing you cross a muddy field on horseback than on foot, as you did the day you walked to Netherfield House." They both laughed to remember the picture of her in mud-caked shoes and petticoat as she stepped inside the door that morning.

"I expect that the Bingley sisters, at least, were shocked by the spectacle I made that day," she ventured.

"Hmm, yes, I do believe they made some comment on your appearance," he replied offhandedly.

"And I suppose you joined them in their disapprobation?" she asked with an accusing tone.

He laughed sharply. "No, you will be delighted to know that I observed that the exercise had made your eyes bright. And, by the way, I suffered a most unpleasant look from Miss Bingley for that remark. You are in my debt, madam, for my risking her displeasure on your behalf."

"I am afraid that was not the last unpleasant look you have had from Miss Bingley on my account. She was positively ferocious at the wedding. I felt as if she had daggers in her eyes for me as well as you," Elizabeth said, her playful mood subdued by the thought.

Fitzwilliam took his wife's hand and said gently, "Caroline is a most unhappy woman, more able to find fault than enjoyment. I sincerely regret that I often encouraged her by expressing similar opinions." There was a heavy silence between them, with Elizabeth wishing she had not opened this line of conversation and Darcy uncomfortable with the memories it evoked.

At last, Elizabeth said, "I believe we have taken a wrong turn somewhere."

Darcy looked around him with surprise, and said, "No, we are on the right road. The stable lies just a mile or so ahead."

Elizabeth erupted into laughter. "I was referring to the conversation, Will, not the road." And with his laughter joined to hers, the couple relaxed again into the comfortable banter of a few moments ago. In a short while they turned in at the gate to the Meadows, where they were graciously received by the proprietor, a swarthy man with a quick laugh and friendly manner. He was pleased to choose two of his finest horses for his distinguished guests, and they were soon mounted and away, down a path through dense chestnut woods.

Darcy noticed immediately that what Elizabeth wanted in experience she made up for in a very natural grace and agility. The mare she rode seemed to sense her confidence and energy, and when they reached an open meadow, Elizabeth urged her into a gallop and they surged ahead of Fitzwilliam. He laughed out loud at the challenge and when he was at the point of overtaking her, she turned sharply and eluded him. After an hour's ride, she pulled up at the top of a hill and turned to face him. "Shall we rest for a bit?" she asked, and without waiting for a response slipped easily to the ground. Darcy followed suit and they walked, leading the horses, to the edge of a steep slope from which they could survey the countryside below. They tied their mounts to a tree and sat down.

Darcy put his arm around Elizabeth and urged her closer. With her head resting on his shoulder, she sighed, "I have travelled so little outside of Meryton that every new hillside is a novelty to me. I am afraid you will find me a rather dull companion after a time."

He smiled and answered, "The world is full of exotic sights and sounds, and if you ask I shall take you to explore every one. But as for me, I would have what I want in the world if I never moved from this spot." Taking her face gently in his hands, he stared into her beautiful dark eyes and then leaned slowly forward to kiss her with the reverence of a supplicant kissing the hem of a healer. The hillside and the valley dissolved beneath them as she wrapped her arms around him, and the strength of her embrace and the warmth of her kiss gave him to understand that it was something very *un*like reverence that she hoped to inspire in him.

At length the impatient snort of one of the horses brought them catapulting back to earth and they reluctantly moved apart, glancing about sheepishly.

"You are shameless, I see, madam," said Darcy. Getting to his feet, he lifted his lady from the ground and made a pretence of straightening his coat and brushing off his trousers. "You seem utterly insensible of my reputation as a gentleman."

"I believe, sir," said Elizabeth brightly, "that your reputation was dealt a mortal blow last Thursday by the good Rector of Meryton. It is a bit late for you to be fretting yourself on that account."

"Yes, I had quite forgotten," said he with a laugh. "Since that is the case we may as well ride into Langford for lunch looking like a pair of gypsies who have spent the night on the open road." He put out his hands as she raised a foot to be lifted to her saddle, and they rode towards town in no great hurry to break their solitude.

After a few minutes where each entertained their private thoughts, Elizabeth said quietly, keeping her eyes from his face, "I wonder if the day may come when you regret that you did not marry someone else. We shall not always be so carefree and content to be alone."

84

Darcy did not make the mistake of answering impulsively, but considered the matter carefully before speaking.

"When I proposed to you in Mr Collins' parlour," he said, "I did believe I should be giving up a great deal for your sake. I believe now that if you had accepted me that day, I would have brought to our marriage a mindfulness of my own sacrifice that could easily have undermined our happiness." Elizabeth did not speak during the silent minutes that followed, for it was obvious that her husband was struggling with the expression of his thoughts. The silence soon ended and he went on, with deliberation. "I will not insult your intelligence by declaring it impossible that I should ever revert to my former habits of thought, but it has been many months since I came to understand that position and wealth do not form the foundations of happiness. In fact, I begin to think that they carry with them a predisposition for *unhappiness*, for they separate people unnaturally from those whose love or friendship might otherwise be most valued.

"If I have a fear," he declared, "it is that we may not always be insulated from the contempt of those who still think as *I* did then." He smiled faintly. "I know you will want to laugh at this thought, for you think yourself well able to repel all attacks, but I do not underestimate the strength of such persons' prejudice, and isolated at Pemberley, without family or friends to bolster you... " Darcy left the image drifting before them and Elizabeth considered it carefully, acknowledging to herself the slight coldness in her stomach.

"I was very young and very naïve when I told your Aunt Catherine that my happiness could not be undermined either by her scorn or the contempt of the entire world, for that matter." Darcy smiled. The interview she referred to had taken place less than two months previous. "Since that day," said Elizabeth, "I was forced to acknowledge, at least privately, that my happiness did, in fact, depend on someone other than myself, in truth that *your* good opinion had suddenly become necessary for *my* peace of mind. I shall not pretend that I do not prefer to have people adore me rather than revile me, but I have always found that it was far easier for me to suffer the disapprobation of others than to amend my behaviour in order to find favour with them." Elizabeth turning a smiling face towards her husband.

At this, Darcy's heavy mood lifted in an upsurge of laughter as he realised how little his family and friends, himself included, had been able to daunt this woman's spirit.

"I do have the greatest regret, Lizzie," he said, when he had caught his breath, "that I was not present when you did battle with my Aunt Catherine. I rest my fears in the light of your proven ability to rebuke one of the Empire's greatest tyrants."

The ride, the lunch and the day were concluded with no further reference to intensity of thought, but behind their cheerful banter each harboured a vague uneasiness that stormy weather still threatened the path ahead.

Chapter Twelve

Trevor Handley rode up to the lodge at the entrance to Pemberley like a man who knew where he was going. He dismounted in front of the stone cottage, and as he tied his horse to the iron ring on the hitching post, he looked around curiously, apparently pleased with what he saw. His gait and bearing seemed those of a man younger than his five and thirty years, and he was dressed in a carefully tailored riding suit that was cut to show his muscular build to advantage. He paused for a few moments, running his hand absently over the weathered wood as his eyes took in the contours of the old lodge and the shapes of the ancient plane-trees and oaks that ringed its clearing. The building had a timeless look about it, as if it had grown up in this spot with the forest, and the meticulous hand of its caretaker ensured that it would stand forever thus, guarding the past and prepared for the future.

As he stood lost in thought, the heavy door swung open, and framed in its casing stood a wizened old man with a stern face. The old eyes narrowed as the lodgekeeper scrutinised the intruder, and he asked gruffly, "Have ye business at Pemberley, sir?"

"So you are still at your post, old Thomas!" said the young man, his face registering surprise and delight as he moved quickly toward the frail figure.

The lines of the old man's face deepened in concentration as he struggled to put a name to the familiar voice.

"Do I know ye, then, sir?" he asked cautiously.

Trevor laughed impishly. "Once upon a time I called you friend, when I was little more than a child." He stepped up close and put out a hand to rest on the sloping shoulder. "And many a cold winter's night I spent on your hearth, drinking your tea and listening to your lies," he added, as he saw the glimmer of recognition appear on the old man's face.

A tremulous hand reached up to trace the young man's cheek, and Trevor realised with sorrow that the man could see but dimly.

"Master Trevor? Is that ye, then, come back to us?" he asked, incredulous.

Trevor managed a choked affirmation.

"Lord, Lord, I did not think to see ye again, and that's a fact," said Thomas softly, shaking his head.

Trevor grinned with a boyish charm and recovered his voice. "Nor I you, Thomas. How often I have thought of your cottage and your kindness to me, you and Mrs Hill." Looking toward the door he said, "Where is she, Thomas?"

"Gone these two years, Master Trevor." His voice trembled a bit, but he quickly shook off the sorrow and grasped the younger man's hand. "I wager she'll be stirring in her grave at the sight of ye come back," he said with a chuckle. "Many's the time we wondered what path ye took after quittin' Pemberley, sir. Mrs Hill was in a fair way to be thinking of ye like a son. Her heart was like to break from sorrow when you left us."

With misted eyes, Trevor answered, "I'm sorry, Thomas. It was hard of me to disappear the way I did and never to write, but I could not bring myself to think of this place for a very long time, and I did not want to send letters in bitterness. You must think me ungrateful... hardhearted."

Opening his arms to embrace Master Trevor, Thomas laughed. "Never mind that now, for here ye be. Come in, *come in*, and tell me all your tale," he said eagerly. They moved together, through the doorway into the dim light of the old cottage, and Trevor looked around. He had stepped into his past. He closed his eyes for a moment to take in the warm welcoming smell of the wood fire and to picture himself striding through this very room as a lad of just eighteen, calling brashly to Mrs Hill who promptly bustled out to greet him. She would have water on for tea in a moment; he saw her, in apron and cap, smelling of meat and onions or fresh berry tarts, fretting herself over his thin frame.

Thomas stood by, quietly smiling over his own memories, and then roused himself to offer a chair. "Sit yourself down, sir, and I'll bring us some tea." Trevor moved to help him, but he pushed him back toward the chair and, shaking his head gleefully, he shuffled off toward the kitchen. "I cannot think that ye've come back, Master Trevor," he called over his shoulder.

Trevor called cheerfully after him, "After Mr Darcy's warning that I should not set foot in Derbyshire again, I thought I had seen the last of Pemberley, Thomas. But the countryside has always been in my blood, and as much as I have travelled I have never in the world found its like. I could not be content to stay away, and when I heard that old Mr Darcy had died, I began to feel I must see these hills once more."

Thomas appeared at the kitchen door with a tray laden with sugar and fresh cream, and a plate piled high with scones. Trevor rose quickly and took the tray, setting it on the burnished side table as he noticed the unsteadiness of the old hands.

Thomas smiled wistfully. "Aye, sir, Derbyshire is that beautiful as once seen, a man does not put it soon out of his mind." He returned to the kitchen for the teapot, and could be heard rummaging around for mugs and spoons. Trevor took a turn around the tidy parlour, picking up objects and running his fingers over furniture that glowed with polished care. Everything stood as he had left it, and he felt the moisture in his eyes as bittersweet memories flooded over him.

Thomas, who had returned with the tea things, seemed to read the young man's thoughts. "I am not a one for changing things. I expect ye see the house just as ye left it, sir."

Trevor returned to his chair and took the stout mug offered between both hands. As he cradled it there, letting the sweet smell rise up to him, he asked, "How has life been treating you, Thomas? Are you well cared for since the master's death?"

Thomas settled himself slowly into his favourite chair near the fire. "Aye, sir, when good Mr Darcy left us, I cried like a child, I don't mind saying it. No doubt ye had your reasons to dislike him, but a finer master there never was, I warrant. The young master has not his father's way with people, and some call him proud, but he is as generous as ever his father was with them as depends on him. When Mrs Hill passed, he came straightaway from London as soon as ever he heard, and he left orders at the house that they should send me my meals every day. A girl comes down from the manor every week to see to the cleaning and take my laundering up with her." He paused to contemplate his good fortune. "No, sir, not a day goes past that I don't thank the Good Lord for my situation here. I could not ask for better."

Trevor nodded thoughtfully. "I admit I left Pemberley feeling very ill-used, Thomas, but these many years have taught me a great deal about what a man feels for his family. I bear no grudges. In fact, I mean to call on Master Fitzwilliam this morning, and I hope to be received as a friend. What do you say, Thomas, will he see me?"

Thomas was much relieved at the tone of the conversation, for although he had a powerful fondness for the young man, his loyalty to the Darcy family would have required him to choose their side in any dispute. He was content to leave the past well forgotten, as it could bring no one pleasure to revive those difficult days. He answered cheerfully. "I have no doubt the young master would be pleased to receive ye, although it nearly broke his heart when ye disappeared. His father told him nought of the story, saying only ye were needed at home, but I cannot say as I think he believed that. He used to come to me and ask had I any word from ye, but he was never a one to speak his feelings... " After a pause, he added, "But he is from home just now, and I know not when he is to be seen again. They say he has gone to marry and will bring his bride to Pemberley ere long."

Both men grew quiet for a time with their memories, but at last Trevor spoke. "I heard he has a sister, Thomas. What is she like?"

"The most handsome of ladies she is, our Miss Georgiana, but quiet as a lamb. She was born the spring after you left Pemberley, so that makes her seventeen years old. Ah, a sweeter young thing ye will never meet, sir. It was like to break her heart when her father died, but she is that fond of her brother that I daresay she will be as happy as can be, for she thinks the sun rises and sets on him."

"And what about our young Master Fitzwilliam, Thomas? Is he content?" asked Trevor eagerly.

Thomas smiled, but his answer was touched with concern. "Had ye asked me that a few months ago, I must have said he bore a heavy burden. You knew what his mother was, else I would not speak so freely." The old man paused to struggle with the novelty of such unaccustomed words, for he was not in the habit of judging his masters, and especially not in conversation. "He closed himself up after his mother died. Not a word of complaint, mind ye, but like he had locked something away. And I daresay he did not make his peace with his father, God rest *his* soul, before he died. I think if it were not for Miss Georgiana, we should have seen very little of our new Master Darcy. As it is, he has always been a-roaming, away more than he stays." While Trevor contemplated this information, Thomas suddenly laughed out loud. "But I expect we will see a change in all that, now, Master Trevor, when he brings his bride, for he must be of a mind to settle down after all."

Trevor mused, "I must say that the greatest sorrow I have carried with me all these years was to leave young Fitzwilliam so abruptly, and with no explanation. He was such a lonely boy."

"Aye, sir, that he was, and grew to be a man with that selfsame look about him, haunted-like. Well," his wrinkled face lighting up with the memory of his wife, "if he has the good sense to find a woman half so good as my Mrs Hill, he will be a happy man."

Trevor's jaw grew taut with a memory that shot through him like a knife-blade. He pushed the thought deep into his mind, not trusting himself to speak until he was sure he was in control. He finally sighed and said, "I daresay, Thomas, not a better woman could be found than your Mrs Hill."

The two chatted on for a very long time, over this remembrance and that. Although the young man had scarcely spent a year and a half at Pemberley, and that so long ago, his memories were fresh and clear. At last he rose to leave, promising to return to tell his old companion the story of the intervening years. He teased Thomas with the intimation that he hoped for many a pleasant morning's chat in the weeks to come, but until all details were resolved he must remain silent. As he mounted his horse, he told Thomas that he would ride along and take a look at the manor, being so near. As he rode off, the old man stood musing at his door, and then turned back inside to enjoy private contemplation of this amazing turn of events.

Trevor's thoughts were far from serene as he made his way down the serpentine drive. The memories that had been disturbed quickened his breathing, and before he rounded the final bend in the road, he reined his horse in and dismounted to calm his thoughts. As he walked slowly toward the spot where he had first seen the house so many years before, he could not help but feel a rush of emotion, remembering the day he had been sent away. He had been barely eighteen then, and old Mr Darcy's icy rage had kindled in him an anger and resentment that it had taken him years to erase. The memories returned to him, but as he walked he realised that they no longer brought him pain. His future loomed brightly before him, and with a resolution to lay the past firmly to rest, he raised his eyes to the view of Pemberley Manor rising out of the hills around it, remounted his horse and turned back toward the inn at Lambton.

Chapter Thirteen

Darcy and Elizabeth's final day at Highbury was marked by a mood of quiet anticipation as each occupied their mind with private thoughts of their journey home. In spite of the curiosity that had been excited by her husband's cryptic remarks about Pemberley, Lizzie forced herself to respect his reluctance to elaborate. As they dressed for their dinner with the Alexander family, she wondered whether that visit might shed some light on the subject. As she stood looking at her reflection in the mirror, Fitzwilliam's face appeared beside hers.

"What is the meaning of this enigmatic smile you are wearing, Mrs Darcy?" he queried.

She turned to face him. "I was just congratulating myself on my new maturity, *Mr* Darcy."

"Being married to me for a week has aged you?" he asked in mock seriousness.

She moved closer to him and laughingly caressed his cheek with her fingertips. "I have been restless and impatient as a girl, but I begin to think, given enough time, I shall attain true serenity."

After planting a kiss on her forehead, he said, mysteriously, "May your sorrows be light." Although he wore a smile, his eyes revealed the all-too familiar seriousness that still unnerved her.

She answered cautiously. "I have not yet met with a sorrow that could not be borne, nor with one who's passing did not leave me stronger."

Their eyes remained locked for several seconds as he considered a reply, but suddenly he broke the spell with a broad smile, saying, as he turned away, "Perhaps we should go, Lizzie." With a tiny sigh she checked her urge to question and followed him out of the room.

If anyone at Great Oaks had doubts concerning Mr Darcy's temperament or Mrs Darcy's suitability as his bride, they were all dispelled within a few minutes of the couple's arrival, and the party soon settled into an affectionate discourse. The Alexander children and their spouses proved to be quite equal to their parents in good manners and a general air of mutual respect and fondness.

Although Darcy approached the party with a slight nervousness, in contrast to the aloof air that had estranged him at parties in Meryton, he wore an endearing look of shy pleasure which his wife could not fail to notice. His attentions were divided between observing the congenial interactions of the Alexander family and admiring the effect Elizabeth's affability had on the conversation. Her natural exuberance was loosed in the welcoming atmosphere of Great Oaks, and he found himself envying the easy flow of her thoughts and the quickness of her laughter. More than once, he lost the thread of the conversation as he contemplated the new perspective that was opening his eyes to an enjoyment of pleasures he had once scorned.

Lost in such a daydream, he was startled by a question from Mrs Alexander, who sat next to him at dinner. "Is your dear sister still so fond of music as she was as a child, Mr Darcy?"

Fitzwilliam blushed at his inattention. "She has not lost her enthusiasm, I assure you; in fact it is greater than ever. She has, these past two years, been studying with an excellent teacher at our house in London. She will be joining us at Pemberley quite soon, but I do not know if she will be content there long, given the limited stimulation of country society."

"Ah, yes, it is true that the young often long for more than is provided by the seclusion of village life, at least until they are ready to marry. My youngest son, Edward, returns next month from Vienna, where he has been studying this past twelvemonth. He shares Miss Darcy's enthusiasm for the pianoforte; in fact, the two of them spent a good deal of time together in the music room when she visited us as a child."

Catherine, Mrs Alexander's eldest daughter, seated on Fitzwilliam's left, added, "Edward is so talented, I hardly believe he is related to us. Not a single one of us has any skill at all, although Lord knows our parents were determined we should all play." She laughed. "Do you remember Herr Ludwig, mama? He went nearly crazy trying to make us into serious students, and he ended up putting cotton in his ears when we practised. He did love Edward, though, so he tolerated the rest of us for the pleasure of teaching him."

Mrs Alexander smiled. "Yes, since Edward's departure, we have suffered at Great Oaks from the loss of his music."

"Although I do not play myself, I appreciate the effect of music on an evening's gathering. I look forward to meeting your son." Fitzwilliam added shyly, "my wife has an exceptionally lovely voice."

"Then we must *press* her to sing for us tonight," declared Mrs Alexander happily, a thought which her daughter eagerly approved.

Fitzwilliam's conscience was piqued by the kindly exuberance of the two ladies. He blushed as he remembered the unanswered invitations to Georgiana and himself to visit Great Oaks, and he was moved to an uncharacteristic frankness.

He said, "At times I feel Georgiana's music is an expression of her loneliness. Although she has grown to be a very handsome and accomplished young lady, she does not make friends easily. I am sure she must feel deeply the lack of a lively family. I must confess I have been too distant from her myself."

Mrs Alexander shook her head sadly, saying, "It is indeed a trial to lose one's mother at such an early age. I was so taken with her as a child, my heart went out to her when she came to visit with your father, for she was such a gentle, sweet girl. And then your dear father's death shocked us all. I am sure it must have been terribly difficult for her, as devoted as she was to him." Her eyes welled up with motherly tears, but seeing the discomfort her remarks elicited on Fitzwilliam's face, she hastened to add, "I am certain you have done everything possible to provide for her, Mr Darcy, but you must find it no easy task to supply the guidance and affection that would normally fall to a mother and father. You must not blame yourself."

Darcy replied thoughtfully, "I have always done what I thought best, but I am aware that there were things she needed which I, as a brother, could not provide." He turned towards the sound of Elizabeth's laughter from the other end of the table, and his frown melted into a beaming smile of pride. "My fondest hope is that she will at last have the pleasure of a sister's company… in Elizabeth."

Mother and daughter exchanged a knowing glance, and Catherine said with enthusiasm, "I cannot imagine they will not quickly become the closest of friends, for I already feel as if I have known Mrs Darcy for ages."

Mrs Alexander added, with a nod towards Elizabeth, "She *is* a remarkable young lady indeed. I do hope that the three of you will come to stay with us next time you are in the neighbourhood."

Dinner was concluded on this pleasant note, and while the parents took their leave for a brief rest, the younger group settled on a walk in the garden. Darcy's enjoyment of their easy affection prompted him to quite impulsively invite the entire Alexander family to visit them at Pemberley during the coming winter. In view of the newness of their acquaintance they were surprised by the suggestion, but his sincerity was obvious and they readily agreed. Elizabeth, knowing his natural reserve so well, was more surprised than anyone, and she turned a radiant smile on him, giving his arm a squeeze. Such spontaneity was a novelty to him, and understanding her thoughts, he felt quite proud to have pleased her.

When they rejoined Mr and Mrs Alexander in the house, Elizabeth was noisily pressed to entertain them at the piano, and she laughingly cast an accusing look at Darcy. Professing that her skill was very unlikely to entertain anyone, Elizabeth nonetheless sang and played, blushing prettily whenever she encountered her husband's adoring eyes. Others were enticed to follow her example, and their musical abilities, if not polished, were at least enthusiastic. So lively a party did they all make together, that supper was prepared and laid out before the Darcys had time to protest that they must leave. Pressed to extend their stay in Highbury, Elizabeth and Fitzwilliam remained firm in their intention to travel the next morning, but in their lengthy leave-taking they reiterated the invitation for the family to come to Pemberley, and they parted company in high spirits.

Driving back through the cool night air, Elizabeth and Fitzwilliam found much to comment on in the manners of this fine family. Will ventured, "You have already effected a most agreeable change in Pemberley, my dear; I do not doubt we shall find plenty of company to liven up its rooms during the long winter nights. When I first decided I must marry you, I pleased myself with thinking I would open doors for you to many fine houses, but I see now that it is *you* who shall soon improve *my* social standing."

Her answer was light-hearted but not frivolous. "If I can have a part in showing you to others as *I* see you, they will welcome you with delight."

Mr and Mrs Darcy arrived at the inn to find their trunks packed as requested for the early morning departure, and after a last obeisance to love at Highbury, quickly fell asleep to dream their separate dreams of home.

After the Darcy's had departed, Mr Alexander retired alone to his study, leaving his family to a pleasant review of the day. He poured a glass of sherry and moved his chair close to the hearth, his thoughts occupied, at first, less by today's visit than by the memory of a bond formed nearly forty years earlier.

Robert Alexander met James Darcy in their first year at Oxford. Although their families travelled in quite different social circles, no distinctions of class prevented the young James Darcy from a proper appreciation of the integrity and gentility of his new friend. The admiration was justly returned, and the two were inseparable companions throughout their college years.

Although distance and the claims of family and responsibility separated them after graduation, it did nothing to diminish the strength of their mutual regard. Mr Alexander and his family were not welcome at Pemberley once Mrs Darcy was installed as mistress, but Mr Darcy contrived to find himself in the vicinity of Great Oaks as often as could be, and as the years passed, he portrayed to his friend an increasingly disturbing picture of his marriage. Mr Alexander's strict sense of honour prevented him from sharing the darkest of these confidences even with his wife, and so it was his habit to ponder privately from time to time the sorrows of his friend. After the death of Mrs Darcy, it might be supposed that Mr Darcy would find relief, but in fact, it soon became evident to Mr Alexander that the spectre of his wife would continue to haunt him, tainting, as it did, his relationship with his beloved son Fitzwilliam. With his adoring young daughter forever at his side, he maintained a semblance of contentment to the rest of the world, but Mr Alexander perceived the depth of his anguish, and mourned his inability to bring him comfort.

Mr Alexander reached the point in his reverie that had disturbed his sleep many a night in the past few years. James Darcy, understanding himself to be seriously ill, had summoned Mr Alexander to Pemberley and, in an emotional appeal, begged him to reach out to Fitzwilliam, to help him through the suffering that must haunt a young man who has not made his peace with the dead. Anxious to relieve his friend's fears, Mr Alexander pledged himself to try, but when Fitzwilliam arrived home the following day, that gentleman quickly came to believe that he was quite unequal to the task he had been given. The stony reserve of the young man gave him no opening for speech. Mr Alexander departed Pemberley after Mr Darcy's funeral without broaching the subject and although he had repeatedly sought an opportunity, five years had come and gone without a sign that he would be permitted to explore the path of reconciliation hoped for by his friend.

Upon hearing the news that a *Mr* and *Mrs* Darcy of Pemberley were guests at the Highbury Inn, the seed that had lain dormant for so long took root, and Mr Alexander, with a most uncharacteristic trepidation, had invoked the support of his friend's ghost and taken his carriage to call on Fitzwilliam Darcy. He hardly recognised the young man who had come to tea two days ago, and by the end of the afternoon he allowed himself to hope that a path to the young man's heart might yet be found. Today's meeting had elevated his spirits even further, and his surprise and pleasure were immense when the invitation to Pemberley was offered.

As he stared into the flickering light of the fire, he suddenly laughed out loud at the feeling of youthful vitality that had overtaken him, for he felt he was embarking on a quest. He spoke to the dancing flames, holding up his glass as if to make a toast.

"Well, well, my old friend, I see you have not been slumbering these past few years. If it was indeed your influence that led your son to Miss Elizabeth Bennet, you could not have made a more fortunate move. I do believe it is her hand that will open the door to bring him back to you, for I have seldom met a more lively or sensible young woman. I believe I shall enjoy this visit to Pemberley as much as any I made while you lived. Mind you, I expect you to be there, for I do not for a minute underestimate the size of the task you left for me."

Just then the study door opened, and a very sleepy Mrs Alexander came in, dressed in night-clothes and carrying a candle. She looked around the room in confusion. "To whom were you speaking, Robert? There is no one here but you."

He stood up to take her hand and said with a laugh, "To James Darcy, my dear. I believe he has come back for a visit after so many years."

Mrs Alexander frowned thoughtfully. "I expect he *has*, for you have not stayed up so late drinking sherry since his *last* visit." She smiled. "Do say goodnight and come to bed, will you? I will not sleep a wink if I leave you downstairs speaking to a ghost."

Robert Alexander laughed again, put out the light, and, hand in hand, he and his wife went off to bed.

Chapter Fourteen

Early the following morning, with no pleasantries left unspoken on anyone's part, Mr and Mrs Darcy took leave of the innkeepers at Highbury, taking away with them a wealth of memories, painful and joyful alike. Without damage to her optimism, Elizabeth's new insights allowed for more silence and reflection than she had previously enjoyed. Fitzwilliam carried a profound sense of gratitude, and although Elizabeth made a tentative attempt to reopen the subject of the sorrow he had hinted at, she soon understood that he was resolute in his desire to avoid speaking of it.

The journey to Pemberley was thus accomplished in a spirit of quiet expectation, with Lizzie contenting herself that their present happiness was all that mattered and Fitzwilliam fervently hoping that to be so. By the time the carriage turned in at the entrance to Pemberley, the silence between them grew thick with poignant memories and nervous expectations. Passing the lodge-keeper's gate, Darcy suddenly called for the carriage to halt.

"There is someone I would like you to meet, Lizzie." He climbed down and turned to lift her from the carriage, smiling boyishly. Before they reached the door of the cottage, it opened to frame the wizened form of Thomas Hill, a broad smile lighting his face.

"Good day to ye, Master Fitzwilliam," he cackled, extending his hand, which was taken in a hearty clasp. "A pleasure it is to have ye home at last, sir."

"How are you keeping, Thomas? Are you well?" asked Fitzwilliam, in a tone so earnest and gentle that it brought a quizzical smile to Elizabeth's face.

"That I am, sir, thank ye. Fit as ever, I'll warrant. And your good self?"

"Fine, Thomas. I want you to meet someone," he said, turning and taking Elizabeth's hand to draw her up beside him. "My wife,

101

Mrs Elizabeth Darcy," and to her he said, "meet one of my oldest friends, Mr Thomas Hill. Thomas has been lodgekeeper of Pemberley since the beginning of time, or at least since well before I was born," he joked.

That Thomas was proud and pleased by this introduction showed clearly in his face. He took Mrs Darcy's hand in his gnarly grip and beamed. "It is a great honour, ma'am, to make your acquaintance. If ever there be any service I can render, make haste to Pemberley Lodge."

Elizabeth was charmed by the gallantry of his words, but found it difficult to repress a smile at the thought that his frail appearance spoke more of a need to *receive* than an ability to *give* service.

"Thank you very kindly, Mr Hill. If indeed you have known my husband since he was a child, I expect I shall be in need of your advice from time to time on how best to get on with him."

"Be careful what you say to her, Thomas. She will charm you into giving away all of my faults, and then tease me mercilessly with them," said Darcy.

Thomas hesitated for a moment at such frank and playful speech, but he was rescued from any discomfort by a burst of laughter from his master. With a twinkle in his eye, the old man answered, "If ever I knew of a fault of yours, sir, it must be I have forgotten, for I cannot bring to mind nary a one."

"Spoken as a true friend, sir," said Fitzwilliam with a nod.

"I must be content, then, to hope you will become my friend as well," added Mrs Darcy. This brought a fresh guffaw from Fitzwilliam, and Elizabeth's smile broadened - she had not been amiss in her first assessment of Pemberley as a magical place. In no other setting could she imagine Mr Darcy speaking to a servant as a friend, and indulging in such merry banter.

"It is as good as done, if that be your wish, ma'am," he replied with a stiff bow.

Declining an invitation to come inside, they took their leave and found enough to say on the subject of Thomas Hill to distract them from other thoughts as the carriage made its way toward the manor house. When the carriage pulled up at the front walk, their eyes met in pleasure and relief. Elizabeth found nothing to disturb her in Darcy's gaze, and so she turned her eyes toward the magnificent manor and gave way to her feelings of wonder that she should be mistress of such a house as this.

Their arrival was apparently signalled, as they were greeted by a gauntlet of staff standing in two neat rows flanking the path, waiting to pay their respects. Elizabeth was moved by their timid but enthusiastic welcome and setting aside her own tumultuous thoughts, turned her full attention to Mrs Reynolds, the housekeeper, as she introduced the staff. Mrs Reynolds, whose tenure at Pemberley and affection for its master were exceeded only by that of Thomas Hill, was reassured within a few moments that her new mistress showed promise. A discreet glance at Master Fitzwilliam's glowing countenance added weight to her approval. For her part, Elizabeth noted with pleasure her husband's cordial greeting to each person, and concentrated on committing as many names to memory as possible, although the size of that task made it impossible that she should remember even half of them.

Elizabeth was unaware that the thoughts of more than one of those who stood before her had strayed to a comparison between her and the woman whom many of them had expected to occupy her place, Miss Caroline Bingley. That lady's past visits to Pemberley had prompted an abundance of speculation and, having a thorough knowledge of *her* temperament, their approbation of the new Mrs Darcy was perhaps more intense than was warranted by such a brief meeting. In any case, as Elizabeth was ushered into the massive hall of Pemberley House on her husband's arm, an unmistakable mood of joyful expectation permeated the air and she was tempted to pinch herself to be sure she was not dreaming.

As Fitzwilliam Darcy led his bride on a leisurely tour of the principle rooms of her new home, he was infected with her enthusiasm, and whatever secret fears lurked in the recesses of his mind were locked up for the time being. He wore his pride and contentment like a new coat, and Elizabeth's obvious pleasure enlivened him.

It was apparent that Mrs Reynolds had done everything within her power to assure the new lady of the manor that she should want for nothing in the staff's respect and attention. Fresh vases of flowers adorned polished tables in every room, and more careful preparations had been made than even Mr Darcy, in his meticulous attention to detail, had ordered for the occasion. By the time they reached the drawing room, an elegant tea awaited them, and they sat down to a quiet contemplation of their joy. It appeared that the previous week had been but a prelude to the long and happy story of their life together at Pemberley. The pregnant silence broke at last in a flood of plans for the arrival of Jane and Charles, for Georgiana's return, and for visits and explorations to come, and afternoon slipped into deep evening before an exquisitely poignant meeting of their eyes brought their conversation to a sudden halt.

Holding her eyes fast in his gaze, Fitzwilliam Darcy stood and reached out his hand toward Elizabeth. She laid her own upon it and he raised her to stand in front of him. As he bowed to kiss her fingers, her eyes closed to capture the sensation that rippled through her. He folded her hand over his arm and they moved toward the hall and up the stairs gliding silently as sleepwalkers do, mindless of time and space. At the door to their suite of rooms, he turned to bow playfully. "May I have the honour of conveying you into your chamber, madam?"

She nodded and he lifted her easily off the floor and with her arms entwined about his neck, he stepped, laughing, into the sitting room. As the door closed behind them, their mirth melted into tenderness, and the kiss that followed was a new thing, without tension or sorrow, without laughter or pain. It was an unfolding of petals on a spring flower, the wing of a mother bird around its chick, a stream breaking through to the sea. No words or unspoken thoughts quivered in its wake, for it was the benediction of their union, the pointless, thoughtless manifestation of the force that makes two into one. They retired that night with a soft sweet calm between them that asked no questions and looked for no answers.

In a play, this might have been the fairy tale ending, where the good live happily ever after, and everyone evil is banished from the kingdom. But as real humans are much more intriguing, and their endings are always beginnings, Darcy and Elizabeth rested for a moment at the top of the long stairway they had climbed, little realising that a mountain still lay ahead.

Chapter Fifteen

Mr and Mrs Darcy's first night at Pemberley boded well for the future, and the morning brought with it a desire to begin their life together in earnest. Fitzwilliam, watching his bride with adoring eyes, began to believe that perhaps he had been foolish to worry that the past could reach into his contentment to disturb him. Everything about her presence at Pemberley seemed right. For Elizabeth's part, if she remembered his troubling references to the past at all, it was merely to acknowledge that she had been right to anticipate that time would bring him ease.

Elizabeth's first request was to meet the household staff again so that she could give more attention to their names and positions than she had been able to do the previous day. Mr Darcy was delighted to call them together after breakfast, although scarcely more so than they were to be summoned for an opportunity to have a closer look at their new mistress. None could have been disappointed by her obvious gentleness and her disarming smiles, and after half an hour everyone was well pleased with the interview. As they scattered to their various duties, much was acknowledged between them that spoke of the pleasantness of this change in their lives, and they worked with an enthusiasm that was not lost on Mr Darcy.

As he and Elizabeth walked out into the garden he remarked, "I have never seen such a display before in this house of high spirits and careful attentions. I'm afraid you have quite elevated their hopes and I shall soon find myself competing with them for your attention. You can have no idea of how charming you are, Lizzie."

She laughed. "I will be always content if you deign to remind me of it at every turn. But why should I not be extremely amiable after I was received with such an affectionate welcome? I'm sure the credit for that must be yours."

"The substance of their efforts was ordered by me," he replied, "but the cheerfulness is in response to your easy and gracious manner. I was quite right in my earlier assessment that your presence is what Pemberley required to attain its promise of a happy home."

Elizabeth was indeed aglow that morning, and this veiled reference to his unhappy past was overlooked in light of his obvious contentment. Everything she saw gave her fresh delight, and seeing his estate through her eyes gave Fitzwilliam Darcy a new appreciation for the beauty of the house and garden, and renewed his anticipation of taking her to explore every acre of the grounds and woods without delay. Their wandering brought them to the stables, where he proudly named for her each of the horses quartered there, explaining their relative merits and particular temperaments.

"It is such a lovely morning, Will. What do you say to a ride?" she asked.

He smiled approvingly. "I should like nothing better," he replied, and choosing a mount for her, he ordered it saddled along with his own grey.

The whole of the morning was occupied in exploration of the hills and valleys to the north of the manor. They rode at a leisurely pace, stopping often to admire a pretty view or a winding stream. Darcy brought the scenery to life with stories of youthful explorations and adventures, and Elizabeth proved a most excellent audience, urging him on with questions and exclamations of pleasure at each rounding of a hill or wood. It was soon agreed that they should ride every day while the weather was fine, for the estate was vast and could not be seen in a few mornings' outings.

The morning disappeared in the easy flow of their conversation and they were a long ride from home by the time the sun had reached the top of its arc overhead. The afternoon brought clouds in from the northwest with a chilling wind, and they turned their horses homeward. By the time they reached Pemberley, rain was starting to fall and they raced, laughing, to the door. After warm baths and fresh clothes, Darcy asked that dinner be brought to the pretty sitting room adjoining their suite, and the couple settled in for a stormy autumn evening. The day's explorations had whetted Elizabeth's appetite to know more of her husband's youth, and she followed every answer he gave with a new question.

They exhausted the stories of his childhood friends, including the infamous Wickham, whose name Elizabeth would not have dared mention if Darcy himself had not introduced him into the conversation. In response to his thoughtful portrayal of their youthful camaraderie, she said softly, "I wonder that you can bear to mention him to me, Will, after the way I abused you with his lies. I will always be ashamed that I was so deceived by him and so unfair to you on his account."

Darcy smiled sadly. "If I had treated you with the attention and respect you deserved from our first meeting, Wickham's words would not have fallen on such fertile ground. No, Lizzie, you have nothing with which to reproach yourself. My sister was deceived by him, almost ruined by him. I understand very well how he took advantage of your sympathetic nature. I am only sorry I did not expose him before he destroyed *your* sister's future."

"Lydia chose her own fate, Will. You did everything in your power to repair the damage to her reputation and secure a reasonable situation for them. I will always be grateful to you for that."

"It is I who should be grateful, for it gave me an opportunity to please you." They gazed thoughtfully into the fire, each enjoying bittersweet memories. After a long silence, Darcy asked softly, without turning his head, "Lizzie, tell me truthfully, did you consent to marry me because you felt grateful for my kindness to your sister?"

She thought carefully before answering. At last she said, "When I came to Pemberley this summer, Mrs Reynolds showed us the portrait of you in the gallery. As I listened to her praise of you as the most generous of brothers and the kindest of masters, something stirred inside me that I could not name. When we met on the green, I think I saw you for the first time with my eyes really open, and I was overcome with shame that I had so misjudged your character. What you did for Lydia merely proved to me what I should have known from my own feelings, that you were the man I loved above all men. I only wish I had understood it sooner."

Darcy rose to stir the fire and added another log before returning to sit at her feet. He rested against her knee as she stroked his hair. "You could not have loved me sooner, Lizzie, for I was not ready to be loved. When I saw the indignation you felt at Rosings Park for my interference in your sister Jane's happiness, it awakened in me an understanding of what love should be. But I think it was not until I saw your despair over Lydia's misfortune that I truly felt what it meant to love someone with utter selflessness. Your tender tears that day taught me how kind love must be, and the trouble I took on her behalf was an act of penance. I believe it was the first truly unselfish action I had ever taken, for although I did it for the love of you, I did not want you to know. I did not want your gratitude."

Elizabeth shook her head. "How I wish I were as good as you believe me to be. My first tears for Lydia *were* for her sorrow and shame, but before you had left my side that day at Lambton Inn, I was keenly aware of my own humiliation, and sure that this tragedy would prevent you from renewing your attentions to me."

"And I left you despairing that you must blame me for not having taken steps to make Wickham's character known." He turned to face her and she slipped from her chair to sit beside him on the floor. "We have both had our secrets, Lizzie, and if you wish, I will allow you to have faults," he said with a confident smile, "so long as you promise to never stop loving me."

She took his face in her hands and spoke from her heart, "I would not know how to begin."

Chapter Sixteen

At the end of such a day of uncommon contentment, and following a week of resolution of so many impediments to happiness, Mr Darcy might have expected to lie down beside his beloved wife to a restful sleep, well satisfied that his every wish in life had been thus satisfied. But whether it was some perversity in his nature that would not allow him to reap the benefits of his labours or whether the ghosts of Pemberley were stirred to interference by the sight of such felicity in their midst, Mr Darcy did not sleep.

Elizabeth, nestled in his arms, lay in blissful peace, unaware of the uneasiness that crept into his mind. Shadows danced in the stormy night and the darkened room soon grew crowded with voices of sorrow and unrest until he could be still no longer. With a poignant tenderness he carefully extricated himself from her embrace and, taking up a candelabra from the night-stand, he crept silently from the room to face his torment alone. The rustling of the woods in the wind without could not drown out the confused mutterings inside his mind, and lighting the candles, he walked the halls of Pemberley in search of solace.

As Elizabeth turned in her sleep, searching for the warm presence that had become, in only a week, the firm foundation on which her dreams grew, she was gradually drawn to wakefulness. Finally she sat up, fully conscious of the night, the storm, and the empty bed beside her. She called his name softly, and when she heard no sound in reply but the wind and the rain, rose quickly and wrapped herself in her dressing gown, fumbling in the unfamiliar room for a candle and match. At last her fingers found what they sought and the candle's light confirmed his absence. She moved into the sitting room, calling his name again, but only silent walls attended her.

She listened for a time to the sounds of the storm against the ancient walls and then, candle in hand, ventured out into the dark hallway, straining to hear a sound or see a light. The flickering rays illuminated only faintly the vast expanse of polished floor and the burnished wood of the doors to empty rooms. She moved toward the oaken staircase that led to the floor below and as she descended the stairs caught sight of a reassuring glow from the open library door. With a smile of relief she followed its path, but the sight that greeted her as she stepped silently through the doorway forced a startled sound from her lips.

Darcy was seated in a chair drawn up close to the hearth where a meagre fire had burned down to embers. He was slumped forward, arms resting on his knees, cradling an empty glass in his hands. A coldness gripped her and her brow furrowed in alarm. He looked up, startled by the sound of her voice, and she saw that his eyes were filled with tears.

"Will?" she whispered.

She moved quickly to him and knelt at his feet.

"What is it, Will?" she asked, summoning a voice of calm, but a bewildered sorrow in his eyes was his only reply. She took the glass from his hands and set it down beside her, and then cupped his face in her hands, speaking softly but firmly. "Please, Will... "

He touched her black curls distractedly and his gaze seemed to slip through her to a place beyond sight. She called him back to meet her eyes and he finally asked hoarsely, "Has it always been so easy for you to be happy, my sweet Lizzie?" Her brow furrowed as she puzzled at his question, but he did not wait for an answer.

"There is a darkness in me," he said, struggling for words to express himself, "that is tied to the shadows in this house. I long to be like you, so peaceful and content, but I know not how. If it were as simple as you make it seem, why has it eluded me all of my life?"

His eyes clouded over as his thoughts strayed again into the darkness within. Again she summoned him to her eyes, and he blinked as if just awakening from a deep slumber. At last he spoke, shaking his head to release himself from his reverie.

"In the past few weeks I have known more joy and peace than I had ever hoped to find in a lifetime. While we were staying at Highbury I felt myself a new man, complete and satisfied. But here at Pemberley I am reminded in every room of who I was, and in contrast to your easiness and mirth, the heaviness of my past overpowers me. Instead of being drawn into your happiness, I fear I shall draw you into my sorrow."

Elizabeth was unnerved by the sadness in his voice and she drew his arms around her and wrapped him in her own. She whispered in his ear, "My dearest love, I do not pretend to understand the thoughts that weigh so heavily on you, but I do know that you are kind and good, and your past will not injure me. You must turn your thoughts to the present, to our love."

His arms tightened around her like a frightened child's and he began to cry softly. Her heart opened to take in his sorrow and every fibre of her body reached out to give him comfort and peace in its place. If willing it could make it so, Elizabeth's confidence would have banished all troubled memories forever, but his sorrow sprang from a deep well and was guarded by murky ghosts who would not willingly permit the light of her love to penetrate its depths.

She did not stir until she felt his breathing grow slow and even, and then her brow furrowed in a perplexed frown. She hesitated to disturb the calm, but found she could not prevent herself from asking, "Can you not tell me what causes this grief, Will?"

He thought for a long time, and finally began tentatively, "When I think of my childhood, so many images crowd my mind that it is difficult to form a clear picture. I do not know to what standard I should compare my feelings about those years. My life was very similar to that of other children I knew. We never wanted for activity or novelty, every need we could identify was met, and yet I remember feeling always a restlessness... an emptiness, I think." He paused to reflect, and then looked at Elizabeth pensively. "The day we dined with the Alexander family brought to my mind that I had never experienced such open affection and acceptance as they seemed to enjoy. In fact, before knowing you, Lizzie, I never felt myself capable of truly loving or being loved."

Looking over her head, he spoke softly. "But there is something deeper, something more sinister that enveloped my family," he said, searching for words to describe the uneasiness he felt. "The atmosphere in this house was tainted by it from my earliest memory. As I grew older, I shrank from it and seized every opportunity to be away." Coming back to the present, he studied her face intently. "Your loving touch, your sweet regard, seem to fill a tremendous void in me, and sometimes I think what passed here does not matter. I long to be free of it, but the habits of thought and mood so long established in me are difficult bonds to break." He paused and sighed, taut lines of pain chiselling his face. "My attachment to you is like a lifeline that moors me to sanity. I love you like I love the sun, Lizzie. I cannot go back to the darkness that held me before I met you, and yet its grip is so strong that when I should be basking in your light, I am being pulled away from it." His eyes filled again with tears and he pulled her roughly to him in a desperate embrace. He whispered into her ear, "If I should lose you now, I would end up quite mad."

Elizabeth gently rocked him and said, "Will, think how hard we have struggled for this love. Whatever your life has been, you are something new today, and you must accept that my love is real and strong, as I know yours is. It may be that one day we will come to understand the past - I will help you, I promise - but whatever happened between your mother and father, whatever has hurt you, it cannot alter our feelings for each other, it cannot drive me from your side. Nothing will come between us, I swear to you."

That he fervently wished to believe her could not be doubted, and their embrace grew passionate. But there was a hunger in his kisses that left her feeling troubled and unsure, in spite of her assurances to the contrary, for she had no experience in her life of such a heavy and sorrowful burden. They returned at last to their bed, but the optimism of their first night at Pemberley was replaced by troubled dreams the second, and morning brought with it the realisation for Elizabeth that there were problems that could not be solved simply by light-hearted optimism.

Chapter Seventeen

Mr and Mrs Charles Bingley were passing a very agreeable fortnight engaged in respectful explorations of the delights of matrimony. Jane was, to be sure, a shy bride and Charles a nervous groom, and a little awkwardness marred their first days together, but they were so intent on pleasing one another in word and deed that very soon they found themselves quite easy together. Other than the pleasure of uncovering an ever-deepening sense of mutual respect and admiration, there were no surprises or troubling revelations to disturb *their* days together.

Only one tiny cloud blemished an otherwise perfect horizon for Jane. She would not have troubled her beloved Charles for an instant with any sign of discontent, but in the privacy of her thoughts she sometimes allowed herself to long for an hour to shut herself up with her sister Elizabeth. Although her generous nature and Lizzie's assurances of Mr Darcy's goodness went a long way toward allowing her to hope that all was well with them, she could not be totally insensible of her earlier fears.

One afternoon as they sat at tea in a lovely seaside cafe, Charles was the one to open the subject.

"Are you not wondering, Jane, how Darcy and your sister are faring?"

Jane smiled at him fondly. "I confess I have been thinking of them. I cannot help but remember how it surprised us to learn they were engaged."

"Yes, I had not considered it possible, especially so soon. Not that I did not hope for an alliance between them," he added hastily, "for I think she is just the person he has needed to amend his solitary ways. I admire him greatly, Jane, he has such a fine mind and noble heart, but I confess his nature has been lacking a little in warmth and affection. I hope Elizabeth will not find him too reserved after all."

With a little laugh, Jane answered, "Well, if I know Lizzie, I do not fear she will suffer in silence. I have no doubt that Mr Darcy will find himself drawn out by her liveliness before long, for she always has that effect on people when she chooses." She turned more thoughtful. "Still, he is so very proud, and she can be impatient... I do worry a little."

Charles took her hand across the table and squeezed it affectionately. "Well, I expect they can come to no great harm in a fortnight, and after that we will see if any amendment is needed." Holding tight to his hand, she let her worry dissipate in the blue of his smiling eyes, and a blush soon rose to her cheek as she read his thoughts. Within the half hour they had returned to their lodgings and any consideration of happiness other than their own was set aside, at least for a time.

Miss Caroline Bingley's situation, meanwhile, was taking a decided turn for the worst. The delight she had experienced in mocking the newlyweds had quickly given way to a mood of dour petulance. Even her sister Louisa grew weary of Caroline's obsession and found reasons to excuse herself from keeping company. In fact, Caroline took no pleasure in companionship, preferring to move restlessly about the house or walk alone in the park, nursing her wounded pride. It was in this bleak state that she very nearly collided with Colonel James Fitzwilliam and Georgiana Darcy on a turn about Hyde Park. Finding no way to escape a conversation, she quickly rallied herself to greet them with a display of fawning affection and surprise, declaring that she had intended to call on them that very afternoon. As Miss Darcy showed no sign of feeling neglected, and Colonel Fitzwilliam was courtesy itself, Miss Bingley felt it necessary to propose that they both join her for supper the following evening. Noting his cousin's pleasure at the invitation, Colonel Fitzwilliam set aside his own misgivings and cheerfully engaged himself to escort her to the Bingley house.

Georgiana Darcy was indeed a kind-hearted young woman, with nothing of her brother's pride or suspicion. She remarked to her cousin as they continued their walk through the park, "Miss Bingley seems to have recovered her spirits, James. I do believe she must have been feeling a bit unwell the day of the wedding."

Her cousin was not a man inclined to spread discontent, and as he could see no danger in Georgiana's naiveté, he merely nodded and smiled in apparent agreement. Truth to tell, he rather enjoyed the thought of a closer observation of the Bingley sisters, for it piqued his playful nature to think how difficult it would be for them to feign pleasure in a review of the weddings.

Miss Bingley went on her way feeling desperately unequal to the task of maintaining the blithe facade she had adopted through the length of an evening. Although she would have preferred to face Miss Darcy and Colonel James in the context of a large party, she could settle on no other members of her circle who could be trusted with absolute discretion on the subject of her feelings toward the infamous marriages, and so she contented herself with stopping at her sister's house to insist that the Hursts join in the task of entertaining. This they could hardly refuse, having been guests at Pemberley more than once, and indeed, their own social status was not so fortunate that they would deem it prudent to neglect any members of such a highly connected family as the Darcys.

It was Louisa who brought some cheer into the conversation. "How fortunate that you should meet Miss Darcy in Colonel Fitzwilliam's company, Caroline."

Her sister was not just then in a mood to consider anything about her life as fortunate. "Whatever do you mean, Louisa?" she asked crossly.

"I mean, silly, that he is a most eligible bachelor, and when you have done with mourning the loss of his cousin, I daresay you might turn your attentions in his direction. You could do worse," she answered cheerfully.

Miss Bingley frowned, a bit surprised that she had not had this thought herself. She knew Colonel Fitzwilliam only as a passing acquaintance, and he would not have drawn her attention earlier. His looks were in every way inferior to his cousin's, and being the youngest son of his family, his own personal fortune was inconsequential. But to his credit, he enjoyed a more tractable and social nature, came from a very desirable family, and, as Miss Bingley was handsomely provided for by her father, his present lack of fortune might be overlooked. This idea grew on her throughout the following day, and by the time her guests had arrived that evening, she found herself in a cheerfully expectant frame of mind, greeting them with a genuine warmth that surprised Colonel Fitzwilliam and confirmed Miss Darcy's good opinion.

Georgiana, so naturally reserved, was flattered by the attentions of both sisters, and with Mr Hurst in a slightly more animated state than usual, the evening began well. After a preliminary exchange of pleasantries on the uncommonly fair weather and the news in town, Miss Bingley asked, "My dear Miss Darcy, what do you hear from your brother and his bride?"

As this subject was most welcome to Georgiana, she replied with more animation than usual, "I have not received a letter until now, but I believe they remain at the Highbury Inn. Fitzwilliam mentioned that they might come to London for a few days, but their plans were not firm. It is arranged with your brother and Mrs Bingley that I shall accompany them to Pemberley on Thursday week if my brother and Mrs Darcy do not come to town." Miss Bingley fancied to herself that Mr Darcy might well feel a reluctance to introduce his bride to those whose opinion of her he could not fail to understand, and for her own sake was in no hurry to meet up with them so soon.

"Will you be settled then at Pemberley, my dear?" Mrs Hurst asked sweetly.

Georgiana blushed a little and replied, "Fitzwilliam has entreated me to do so, and I confess I would not be reluctant to quit London. I am more suited, I think, to life in the country."

Miss Bingley was effusive, "Pemberley is so uncommonly beautiful, Miss Darcy, I do not wonder at your eagerness to return to it." She could not resist testing the lady's feelings toward her new sister-in-law. "You must look forward to having the charming company of Mrs Darcy. I expect you have had little opportunity to become acquainted as yet, with such a brief engagement."

Georgiana smiled contentedly. "Indeed, I am eager to know her better, for everything I have seen of her makes me hope that we will be excellent friends. It delights me to see how animated my brother has become of late."

Colonel Fitzwilliam's discerning eye could not fail to notice that his cousin's speech gave no pleasure to their hostess. He took the opportunity of a short silence to remark with a wry smile, "I regretted that we could not have spent more time with you at Longbourn, but as Fitzwilliam's only family in attendance at the wedding, we had a great many introductions to make. You left quite suddenly, before we could have a proper visit. I do hope nothing was wrong."

Prepared to find an ally in Colonel James, Miss Bingley mistook his bemused expression for complicity, and she and her sister exchanged a knowing look as she replied, "Yes, it was most unfortunate that we could not stay longer. The company was most amusing, and I am so fond of the charming simplicity of life in the country. Unfortunately, we were committed to an engagement in town the following day." She hazarded another glance at Louisa, who was dangerously close to laughing out loud at this reference, and continued, "But I expect we will have many opportunities in the future to enjoy the hospitality of Longbourn and to entertain the

Bennet family at Netherfield House, for I believe Charles means to spend a good deal of his time there, at least for the present." She smiled sweetly, thinking smugly that even Charles, with his ridiculous good nature, was going to find such proximity to the Bennets a bitter fruit.

The Colonel smiled, not at all mistaking her words, and said in a pleasantly noncommittal tone, "Mrs Bennet was, I believe, a trifle nervous from so much excitement, but I had the opportunity to become acquainted with Mr Bennet, and I found him a most likeable fellow."

Georgiana added shyly, "I was a little wary, I confess, of being among so many strangers, but I ended by feeling quite at home. I especially enjoyed renewing my acquaintance with Mr and Mrs Gardiner. Perhaps you would like to join me when I call on them," she asked, turning from one sister to the other.

Neither Miss Bingley nor Mrs Hurst, it might be well imagined, was at all eager for that pleasure, and Miss Bingley most especially had begun to grow weary of the entire conversation as she could discern no inclination on Colonel Fitzwilliam's part towards her point of view.

After a murmured response concerning the pressures of preparing for their brother's arrival, she managed to turn the topic to an inquiry about Colonel Fitzwilliam's family, a subject rather more to her liking. He answered her questions graciously, but there was a twinkle in his eyes that she found slightly discomfiting, and she was rather relieved finally to invite them to the supper table, where she amused them with a story of a new play they had recently attended, carefully avoiding any topic that involved a risk.

After supper, Miss Darcy was entreated by the ladies to play the piano; it required a fair amount of coaxing and the proffered arm of her cousin to finally lead her to the instrument. Colonel Fitzwilliam stayed by her side to lend moral support and as he absentmindedly leafed through a packet of sheet music left on the stand, he came across a beautifully ornamented invitation card which captured his attention by its unusual style. His good manners would have normally prevented him from reading something not intended for his eyes, but as the present company inspired unconventional behaviour, he committed the indiscretion of reading its message. A look of bemused surprise came over his face as he noted that the date inscribed on the card was the day after the Bingley and Darcy wedding, and it required no prodigious deductive powers to guess to what cosmic event it alluded.

The inscription read;

On Friday, the 13th of November
Miss Caroline Bingley and Mrs Louisa Hurst
request the honour of your presence
at a private soirée devoted to the
Death of Reason.

With impish good humour, he lifted the card from the pile of music and placed it on top of the piano, meeting Miss Bingley's eyes with a quizzical smile before covering it casually with a sheet of music. A most painful rush of colour rose to that lady's face as she recognised the black paper with white lettering he held in his hand; her obvious discomfort confirmed his suspicion. He turned his attention to Georgiana's beautiful rendition of an Italian ballad without uttering a word. Miss Bingley could scarcely have been more distressed if he had.

At the end of the song, Colonel Fitzwilliam announced with a complacent smile that he had an early appointment the next morning, and begged to be forgiven for breaking up the evening so early. For Miss Bingley's comfort it was rather too late than too early, and she barely managed the civilities called for by their departure. With a promise to Georgiana to call on her soon, she and Louisa saw their guests to the door, and no sooner was it closed than Caroline gave vent to her consternation with a loud exhalation. She spun around and returned to the music room where Mr Hurst nodded in a chair, and walking angrily to the piano, she searched through the sheets of music to find the invitation. Louisa was baffled by her sister's anger, as she had missed the little drama that precipitated it, and trailed behind her asking impatiently what the matter was.

Caroline waved the offending paper before her eyes and as she tore it into tiny pieces she said bitterly, "I doubt that our charming Colonel Fitzwilliam will waste much time in turning our little joke against us!"

Louisa required a little time to comprehend what had passed. "You cannot mean that he read the invitation, Caroline?" she asked incredulously. A line of worry crossed her brow. "But surely it could have no meaning for him. It does not mention Charles or Mr Darcy, and in any case, I am sure he must share our feelings on the subject."

With a snort of disdain for her sister, Miss Bingley threw the pieces into the fire and said petulantly as she began pacing the floor, "If you had seen his face, you would harbour no such illusions, I assure you. What have I done to deserve such humiliation?"

As Louisa could make no suitable reply, she chose quite wisely to remain silent. Mr Hurst had been roused by Caroline's harsh voice, but had no idea of, and very little interest in, what had passed. He gruffly suggested they go home, and indeed Louisa had no objection, as she was puzzling for herself the possible repercussions of this debacle, if indeed Caroline was right. They saw themselves out, leaving Miss Bingley to fling herself angrily down upon the sofa in a fit of pique.

The following two days found Caroline Bingley closeted in her room with an unnamed malady, the visits of her friends politely refused by her baffled lady-in-waiting. Louisa sent a note to ask after her, but did not call, for she had enough experience of Caroline's rages to tempt her to avoid this one if possible. She had worked out for herself that there might be some unpleasantness if her brother were informed of their escapade, but as her position was less vulnerable and her nature more complacent than Caroline's, this thought gave her little anguish.

Chapter Eighteen

Caroline Bingley had moved through rage to miserable self-pity and passed from there to a deep lethargy by the time Jane and Charles arrived in London on Thursday afternoon. It caused her no small effort to greet them with a tolerably believable display of affection, and when they were joined by Mr and Mrs Hurst for dinner, the conversation was as lively as could be expected. If the newlyweds had understood the innuendoes or noticed the exchange of raised eyebrows between Charles' sisters, they would have perhaps been troubled, but as was their habit, they expected no affront and therefore received none. Still suffering from the effects of her experience with Colonel Fitzwilliam, Caroline's sense of humour was much dampened and her ability to find fault with Jane impaired, and their first family dinner was therefore quite comfortable, if a trifle dull.

Jane was prepared by the end of the evening to report that she found the two sisters to be pleasant company, if more subdued than when first they met, and she most earnestly believed that they had decided to like her for Charles' sake. With her heart utterly incapable of harbouring resentments or nurturing misunderstandings, Jane was ready to make a fresh start with his family, and she assumed that in time they would be convinced that Charles had not been injured by his marriage. For his part, Charles understood his sisters as ill as he ever had, and gave as little thought as he had ever done to their opinions.

Although Jane was mistaken about the sincerity of the Bingley sisters, she was near the truth in one thing. While Caroline and Louisa had no intention of admiring their sister-in-law, they were realistic enough to recognise that it was to their advantage to maintain an appearance of respect in order to retain access to their brother's home. Louisa's taciturn husband offered her little in the way of social advantage, having little money and less wit, and Caroline had no immediate option for a better position than that afforded by living with her brother. They were, therefore, constrained to behave pleasantly, which effort was aided by the weight of their fear that their brother should learn of their malice.

With Charles' reputation for amiability and Jane's charming good nature, they found themselves more welcome among Charles' acquaintances in London than Caroline's party might have led one to expect. A more suspicious nature might have sensed a lack of respect in some company, but Jane, in addition to her optimism, had the advantage of being unused to the refinements of London society and Charles the good fortune of a total lack of concern for the subtleties of snobbishness, and so the week passed quickly and agreeably in a succession of wedding visits and an enjoyable sampling of the world of entertainments available in that busy town.

Among the first to pay a call on the couple was Georgiana Darcy, accompanied by Colonel Fitzwilliam. Caroline Bingley, with no time to escape, suffered a few minutes of exquisite anguish before she began to suspect that the gentleman did not mean to expose her before Charles, at least not on this occasion. She was, nonetheless, seriously discomfited by his presence and barely spoke during the entire visit. From Miss Darcy's cheerful manner it seemed obvious that he had not disclosed his information to her, and if Caroline had not been so preoccupied she might have found something to wonder at in his lack of malice.

To Jane's eager questions, Miss Darcy quickly produced from her bag a note addressed to Jane in Elizabeth's hand. Although disappointed that she should have to wait another week to see her sister, Jane's worries were relieved by the cheerful tone of the letter. Miss Darcy added information from a note written by her brother and, with uncharacteristic animation, joined in a discussion of travel plans and hopes for the future.

Miss Darcy's shyness had caused her some anxious moments in anticipation of travelling with the Bingleys, but a few minutes of conversation with them allayed her fears. If her short acquaintance with Miss Elizabeth had led her to hope that they would soon be good friends, her observation of Jane's temperament gave added weight to that expectation.

Colonel Fitzwilliam was in a jovial mood. His admiration for Elizabeth Bennet had been established from their first meeting, and he found in her sister a very different but equally agreeable temperament, and was delighted by the good fortune of both sisters in securing a comfortable future. The affection between Charles and Jane was touching, and he allowed himself to wonder how Miss Bingley could scorn an arrangement that did her brother no material harm and gave him such obvious pleasure. He understood rather better her malice toward Mrs Darcy and would have allowed himself to pity her for her disappointed hopes in that direction had she been possessed of a kindlier nature.

The pleasure that he might have found in exposing her behaviour to her brother was forestalled by the tenderness of his feelings toward Georgiana and his regard for Mr and Mrs Bingley, for he was well aware that those gentle souls would be sorely troubled to know of her malice. It was his fond hope that the knowledge he held would deter Miss Bingley from future outrages against them and he enjoyed observing how uncomfortably she avoided any contact with his eyes.

In fact, the only person who derived no pleasure from the morning's visit was Miss Caroline Bingley herself. As her fear of Colonel Fitzwilliam's intention to disclose her secret abated, the galling scene before her of mutual admiration became insufferable, and she longed to run from the room. The arrival of the tea service provided a momentary distraction from her dark thoughts, but her relief was short-lived.

As Jane presided over the teapot, Colonel Fitzwilliam moved to a chair beside Miss Bingley and remarked casually, "I believe you are acquainted with Mr and Mrs Langley, Miss Bingley."

She replied cautiously, "Why, yes, Colonel Fitzwilliam, I studied with Mrs Langley before she was married and we have maintained a rather close friendship. Do you know them?"

Colonel Fitzwilliam smiled. "Mr Langley and I fence together at the Marlborough Club. He has mentioned your name to me as a most accomplished hostess. He has the highest regard for your soirées, I assure you." Miss Bingley suddenly upset her teacup and he offered his napkin with the most gracious of smiles, satisfied that his meaning had been understood. She apologised and excused herself quickly to change, venturing to meet his eyes briefly as she stood to leave. The look that passed between them conveyed everything that needed to be said, and she did not appear again until she was assured that their carriage was out of sight.

With an invitation to dinner at Miss Darcy's happily accepted for Saturday, the cousins took their leave, asking that their kindest regards be given to Miss Bingley, and extending the dinner invitation to include her and Mr and Mrs Hurst. Colonel Fitzwilliam was well pleased with the impression he had made on Miss Bingley, and as he and Georgiana settled themselves in his carriage, he wore a look of smug satisfaction.

"James," Georgiana said, knitting her brow in a perplexed frown, "I begin to think you were right about Miss Bingley. She does not seem herself lately. What were you talking about when she became so agitated this morning?"

"I merely mentioned that we had a mutual acquaintance," he answered blandly. "It does seem that she is suffering from a nervous condition, for her mood seems to fluctuate quite dreadfully. You have been acquainted with her for so long; surely you must be a better judge than I of her state of mind."

"I confess I have never seen her so unsettled," Georgiana answered thoughtfully, "although, to think of it, when we were together at Pemberley this summer, she passed a day or two in a similar mood. I hope it is not serious - she looked quite pale this morning and she barely spoke."

"She seems a robust young woman. Perhaps it is merely the excitement of her brother's wedding, or a slight nervousness regarding her position in his household, now that he is married," he replied innocently.

Georgiana protested, "Surely she could fear nothing from Mrs Bingley, she is such a gentle soul. And to see Charles so blissfully happy must give her great pleasure. And yet, there is something in her manner of late that is so... I don't know what to call it, James."

"Peevish?" he asked with a laugh.

"Well, yes, I suppose that *is* it," she said, turning toward him with a look of surprise. "But what could be the reason for it?"

James smiled broadly at his young cousin. "You, my dear, are such a guileless child that you always invest everyone with your own pure motives. Has it not occurred to you that Miss Bingley might have had other intentions for her brother and yours?"

"Whatever can you mean, James? Why should she not be happy if she sees that they are?"

"My dearest Georgiana, as your guardian I feel it is my sad duty to inform you that not everyone is motivated by such unselfish thoughts as yours. There are those in the world who are more concerned with their own needs than with the happiness of others." He resolved after a moment that it would do Georgiana no injury to introduce a touch of reality into her life, and so he continued, "Regarding her brother's marriage, she might have hoped for an alliance with a family whose connections might enhance her own position. Although I greatly admire the Bennet sisters, their family brings nothing to this alliance that Mr Bingley's sisters are likely to appreciate. And as far as your brother is concerned, I might hazard a guess that Miss Bingley had entertained a hope of receiving his attentions herself."

Georgiana's mouth gaped open and she leaned back abruptly against the carriage seat. She would have preferred to dispute his words, but as she thought back over her acquaintance with the family, she was forced to admit that his theories could explain a great deal. By the time she answered him, a deep blush of comprehension had risen up her neck.

"I always felt that Miss Bingley's attentions to me were a bit surprising."

James had not anticipated this response. "Georgiana, I'm sorry if I have hurt you - I would not for all the world, you know. It is only that I have a more suspicious nature than you, and I rather expect duplicity than candour from the population as a whole. Perhaps I am mistaken."

She smiled a little sadly and patted his arm. "I do not expect you are, James. Seen in this light, I understand many things that puzzled me before. And it is really a very small hurt, after all, but one that may prevent greater injury, as I shall know how to behave in future."

A silence settled around them that was not broken until they affectionately parted company at Georgiana's door. The young lady went directly to her room, asking that she not be disturbed, for she had a great deal to think about.

Chapter Nineteen

Elizabeth awakened at dawn on her second morning as mistress of Pemberley, having slept but little. Her rest had been troubled by dreams and the moans of the old house under the fearsome winds of the storm. The light of morning was neither cheerful nor warming, for great banks of clouds continued their sweep across the hills, leaving the earth blanketed in a gloomy light. Leaving Fitzwilliam asleep, she moved quietly into the adjoining sitting room and rang for coffee, asking that the fire be lighted against the morning chill. She settled herself on the window seat, wrapping a shawl around her shivering frame and cradling the warm cup in her hands. As she gazed out of the window overlooking the garden, she wondered at how transformed was its prospect on such a heavy day. The old oaks by the trout stream brooded and willows flailed in the gusty remnants of the storm, and the plane trees, heavy with the night's rain, seemed to sag under their burden. The welcoming beauty of the previous morning was quite gone.

After half an hour of meandering thoughts, a small smile crept to her lips. "It is wrong to blame the storm for this mood," she mused, "since I have always loved a tempest." Lifting her shoulders and loosening the embrace of the woollen shawl around her, she stepped over to the fire, giving it a defiant stir. Pouring herself more coffee, she continued the dialogue she had begun in her mind. "Is your contentment such a fragile thing that it cannot endure the sorrow of one night?" she asked herself, promptly answering, "What is needed here is calm and strength. I must not allow his fears to become a prophecy."

As she walked slowly about the room, stopping to sip the strong coffee, Elizabeth felt her confidence buoy and her spirits revive. At last, she placed the cup on the table and crept back into the bedroom where her husband slept curled on his side, and as she slipped silently

133

into the bed beside him, she wrapped herself around the curve of his back like a comforter. She smiled to herself as he stirred and shifted in his sleep to fit himself more snugly to her form, and as she waited for him to awaken she calmly reviewed everything he had said about his past, looking for a key to the agony she had witnessed. She thought of Mr Alexander, remembering the kindness in his eyes. If, as Darcy said, his father was very much like that gentle man, he must have been a loving father. Could he have married a woman so terrible that many years after her death her memory would remain to kindle such a sorrow as she had seen in her beloved's face last night? Perhaps, as with Lady Macbeth, her proud ambition had driven her husband to desperate measures. She grew sleepy with the effort of finding substance in the shadowy forms that troubled his peace, and finally drifted into a fitful slumber.

Darcy moved at last, with the stiff sluggishness of a person awakening from a troubling dream. Elizabeth woke at his first movement and raised herself quickly up on one elbow, leaning over to kiss him lightly on the cheek. She pulled his shoulder gently towards her so that the first sight he had when he opened his eyes was of her reassuring face. His answering smile was wan, but she was content that it was a beginning. She kissed him playfully, and sat up beside him, waiting until the drowsiness began to lift from his eyes before saying, "I woke at dawn and banished your ghosts for the day, Will. I am quite certain it is safe for you to get up now."

He closed his eyes for a moment, blocking out the vestiges of last night's sorrow, and when he opened them again to her serene and confident smile, a trace of tears made them shine. With a light touch, she brushed the stray curls from his forehead as if she could erase all unpleasant thoughts that lay beneath them. He murmured, "Do you fear nothing, my dearest Lizzie?"

She measured her response, a thoughtful seriousness furrowing her brow. "I would be a very foolish creature if I said I had no fear," she answered slowly. "Last night I wondered if my frivolous nature and limited experience would allow me to be of any use to you in driving out this terrible sorrow you carry. I wish that my love were everything to you, as yours is to me, but there is a place in your heart that I cannot reach, and cannot comprehend."

He sat up quickly and took her hands in his, protesting, "Your love *is* everything to me, Lizzie. My only sorrow is remembering how long I laboured without it, and I have no doubt that in time even that shall fade. It is only the light of my present contentment that shows me how morose I have been. If you will bear with me, I swear I will shake off the habit of my restlessness."

Elizabeth laughed, eager to provide a diversion from the grip of last night's scene. "Then let us begin at once, for you have slept half the day away. I want to see every room in your house, and you must tell me what terrors linger behind each door, so we can forbid them to trouble you again."

"I hope you will not force me to do battle with my demons without benefit of breakfast," he declared, trying to match her cheerfulness.

"I will never deny you anything, as long as you wear that smile," she answered. As they dressed for breakfast, she glanced out the window and noticed with satisfaction that although the rain had started again and the wind showed no sign of abating, the feeling of menace was absent from the garden and woods.

After a subdued breakfast, the couple set off on their exploration of the house. As door after door was flung open to their advance, Darcy's eagerness as a guide was gradually restored to that of the previous day. He laughingly described childish antics as they came to mind, and Elizabeth delighted in the obvious pleasure he had in the telling. The house was appointed with elegant simplicity, and she admitted to herself that whatever the previous Mrs Darcy's faults had been, lack of taste was not one of them. She lingered over the fine artwork and delicate curios, searching for clues as to the temperament of her predecessor.

At last, emboldened by her husband's calm demeanour, she ventured to ask, "Is it your mother's hand that so handsomely furnished these rooms, Will?"

"The house was built by my grandparents, Lizzie, and I believe a good deal is owing to their taste," he said thoughtfully. "But my mother undertook massive renovations. I believe that my father gave her free rein to make whatever alterations she pleased. I think he cared very little about any room but his library, and after her death I do not recall anything being done except for the decoration of a suite of rooms for Georgiana as she outgrew the nursery."

Elizabeth refrained from asking many of the questions that rose up in her mind, wary of disturbing the light-hearted flow of his narrative as he led her from one room to the next. At last they entered the old playroom, lovingly preserved as if a bright-eyed child might enter its fairytale atmosphere at any moment. Darcy grew silent here, his smile fading into a thoughtful reverie as memories drew him away from her. She stopped in the doorway, watching as he picked up old toys and books, and ran his hand tentatively down the mane of an old rocking horse. After a few minutes he turned to find her studying him and reached out for her hand. She walked across the room to join him, smiling her encouragement.

"My mother liked to play with me in this room when I was small," he said with a forced smile. "She would send my nurse away and sit on the rug beside me as if we were playmates, her laughter clear and strong as a child's. She was so beautiful when she laughed in this room." His eyes clouded for a moment and Elizabeth squeezed his hand reassuringly.

His head turned toward the door, as if he expected to see someone there, and then he continued in a voice that was strange and distant. "I remember once that my father appeared in the doorway.

She sat singing, unaware of his presence until, I suppose, she noticed that I was looking at him. There were tears in his eyes and I felt afraid, for I had never seen him cry. She stopped and turned slowly to face him, and it seemed as though a light had gone out inside of her. Neither of them spoke, and then suddenly he left, closing the door softly behind him. When I looked at her again, her face was hard and cold. She stood up and walked out of the room without a word, and in a minute, my nurse was back."

Elizabeth scarcely breathed as she waited for his next words. At last, he closed his eyes and then opened them slowly, turning to look into her eyes with a puzzled frown. "I never saw them quarrel, although I often heard their voices raised in anger behind closed doors. The silence between them the rest of the time seemed far more terrible than harsh words. I wonder that I never asked for an explanation, or that none was ever offered."

At last she asked softly, "Were your parents never happy together, Will?"

He did not answer at once, but turned to leave the room, leading her out to the corridor and closing the door firmly before saying, simply, "Not that I can recall." The set of his jaw cautioned her to silence, and they walked without speaking down the long hallway to the stairs. As they turned to go down, he paused and faced her, saying, "I believe they must have hated each other."

Darcy's foray into the past was brief, and before they reached the bottom of the stairs, he had resolved to put an end to it. While Elizabeth was still pondering what she should say, to her great surprise, he motioned towards the drawing room and said, "Since the weather means to make us captives of these walls, will you charm the air with a song?" She hesitated for a moment, studying his face, but all she could see was a pleasant smile that belied the seriousness of the words that still echoed in her head. She smiled and nodded, baffled by this mask, and although her heart told her there was much more that should be said, her head urged her to accept for the moment his determination to change the subject.

She sat down at the exquisite pianoforte that Fitzwilliam had purchased for Georgiana and began to play an Irish tune, singing along in the lilting accent she had gleaned from an Irish maid as a young girl. She watched her husband's studied lightness turn to genuine mirth as he admired her playful rendition, and when she had finished, he asked with a laugh if she had hidden from him her true lineage. She answered him in the thickest Irish brogue that she was, indeed, stolen by gypsies from her parents as a babe, and spirited across the waters in an open boat, where she was sold to an English gentleman who fancied he would bring a playmate home to his lonely daughter, Jane. "Had the gentleman been knowing he would sire three more daughters, he would ne'er have given himself the bother," she concluded, smiling demurely. Darcy erupted into a hearty laugh.

"I daresay you were a good deal of trouble to your parents, Lizzie. Have you no stories to tell me of what a vexing child you were?" he asked.

Elizabeth launched into a cheerful narrative of favourite family stories, leading them ever further from the quagmire of his own memories. Apparently delighted with the diversion, Darcy called for

139

tea, and they whiled away the morning with tales of childish wickedness, the torment of a cranky nurse, and her mother's ever-collapsing nerves. Elizabeth Bennet, as *was*, was adept at mimicry, and as her voice and gesture copied first one and then another member of her family, Darcy listened in rapt admiration.

At last he asked, "Did your father never intervene, Lizzie, to prevent you from tormenting your poor mother?"

She laughed as she pictured her father as a young man. "I believe he was too busy driving her to despair himself to notice how *we* five girls vexed her."

That day and the next, the couple maintained their light-hearted mood, and might have continued on through the week without reference to Pemberley's past but for the arrival of a letter in the afternoon post that catapulted Darcy back into a time he wanted desperately to forget. Elizabeth looked up from her sewing inquiringly as he read the brief message and she grew alarmed by the sudden pallor of his face. "Is anything wrong?" she asked, laying aside her work.

"Good God!" he exclaimed, pushing himself up from his chair and striding about the room. "What can he mean by writing after all of these years?" he asked himself, ignoring his wife's question. He continued to pace furiously until she demanded, "Will, tell me what is wrong!"

He spun on his heel to face her with a troubled look that did nothing to alleviate her anxiety. As he thrust the letter towards her, he saw with remorse that he had frightened her. "Forgive me, Lizzie. I cannot seem to break my habit of being oblivious to anyone's feelings but my own." As she turned her eyes to the brief note that had disturbed him so, he muttered, "I begin to think that by marrying, I have stirred up all of the sleeping spirits of my youth, and they do not mean to allow me any peace."

140

The words he had intended to speak in jest were delivered with such vituperative force that Elizabeth gasped as if she had been struck. "Will, who *is* this man? What has he to do with *you*?" she demanded.

Will drew a deep breath to collect himself and pulled a chair around so that he could face her. As he took the letter from her hand he noticed that she was trembling and he hurried to reassure her. "Darling, I am sorry to have alarmed you. I promise you there is nothing to fear from Trevor Handley. In fact, there might be a great deal gained in meeting him again." While he held one of her hands he reread the letter, searching for something that was not written. The message was simple:

My dear Fitzwilliam,

I do not doubt that you will be surprised to hear from me after so many years have passed. I will be in Derbyshire on business from the twenty-ninth of November and have taken a room at the Lambton Inn. I would very much like to see you if you will receive me.

Please leave a message for me at the Inn.

With fond regards,
Trevor Handley

Finding no new information, Darcy let the letter drop to his knee. He began to explain slowly, finding that the effort of framing the events in a clear, rational perspective calmed him. "I have told you how my father took an interest in George Wickham, his steward's son. It was my father's belief that the advantages of wealth and position carried a responsibility, and he was particularly keen that no one should be denied the opportunity to succeed where ambition was constrained by circumstance. In the case of Wickham, the result was unfortunate, although happily my father did not live to see the level to which he ultimately sank." Elizabeth still found the subject of George Wickham uncomfortable, but was too intent on having Trevor Handley's history explained to pursue that thought.

Darcy continued, "I never mentioned that Wickham was not the only young man befriended by my father. A great friend of his, William Handley, died very young in a tragic accident. He left his wife with a son and two daughters to raise. The management of their estate was taken over by Mr Handley's brother, and whether he was unscrupulous or merely inept, the result was that the widow ended up virtually penniless within a few years. The property was lost, and she removed to her parents' home with her children. The son, Trevor, suffered greatly from the lack of guidance and from the diminished circumstances of his life. When my father learned of the young man's plight, he went to visit Mrs Handley and asked that Trevor be allowed to come to Pemberley for an extended visit, hoping to offer some guidance and to try out his abilities. This she was only too happy to agree to, as she had exhausted her own resources in coping with his restless spirit."

As Darcy paused to reflect, Elizabeth asked, "How old was the boy?"

"I believe he must have been about seventeen years old when he arrived. I was eleven, and to my eyes he seemed a man." He grew quiet again, but at last he continued, "I had by then acquired the habit of reserve that still plagues me, and I did not welcome this intrusion into my life. My father explained the situation to me and asked me to treat him as a member of the family, but I was more inclined to look to my mother for guidance on that subject. She surprised me by her silence. Perhaps she was unsure herself of what his status should be, for in spite of his poverty, both of his parents came from families of some consequence.

"I suppose I expected him to be a rather pathetic figure, reduced to such a dependence on his mother's family when he should have been looking forward to the security of inheriting his father's holdings. In fact, he was quite the opposite, self-assured and even cocky. There was something so engaging about him that I was drawn to be in his company, in spite of my intention to remain aloof. He had all the confidence I lacked, and was as comfortable in the company of my parents as he was with the stable hands. As we sat down to our first supper together, I was conscious that a subtle change had taken place in our household. My mother and father were both as captivated by his easy manners as I, and in the space of an hour, we engaged in more conversation as a family than we had been wont to do in any single week before."

Darcy smiled at the memories that his story raised. "Handley's enthusiasm was irresistible, and within a few days I was trailing after him like a puppy. I was as surprised by my mother's reaction as by my own. She laughed like a girl when he was in her company, and even the silence between her and my father was often broken when he was present. My father took him under his wing and they often spent whole days together attending to the management of the estate. I wonder that I was not jealous of their easy relationship or of the way my mother brightened when he was in the room. I envied him his charm, I suppose, but when I was with him I felt more free and more alive than I had ever done."

Elizabeth was captivated by the story, but increasingly perplexed over his reaction to Mr Handley's letter, for everything he had said until now indicated that he should be delighted to hear from him. As if he had read her thoughts, Darcy's face clouded over. "Within a few weeks, Trevor did indeed seem like a member of our family. When I was occupied with lessons, he was at work with my father or riding with my mother. When my tutor released me, I looked for him and if he was free he would take me fishing or hunting. His skill with horses was beyond comparison for a man of his age, and we rode whenever we had the opportunity. I was content that he should remain with us forever, but something went wrong after his first year with us that I have never understood. I noticed that my father gradually became more reserved around him, and that there was a growing coldness in his voice when he addressed him. They spent less time together, and the old tension between my father and mother returned, worse, I believe, than before.

"One night my father and mother had a terrible argument. I could hear from my room the harsh sounds but not the subject. It was not the first time they had quarrelled, and so I was not much troubled by it until the following morning, when only Trevor and I appeared for breakfast. We were making our plans for an afternoon ride when my father came into the dining parlour and told Trevor that he wished to speak to him privately. His face was pale and angry - I had never seen him so upset. He instructed me to go to my lessons and said he would send for me later. As Trevor followed him out of the room, he looked back at me questioningly, but I merely shook my head, for I had no idea what was wrong." During this last part of the narration, Darcy had slumped down in his chair, and now he frowned deeply. "That was the last time I saw Trevor Handley."

When he did not continue immediately, Elizabeth prodded, "Where did he go? Why did he leave?"

Darcy threw up his hands in a gesture of resignation. "This is the first letter I have had from him in seventeen years."

"But surely your father or mother explained to you the reason for his departure!"

Darcy's smile was rueful. "Of course. My father called me to his study that afternoon and said that Trevor had been suddenly called home on a matter of urgent family business. He said he was not able to tell me the nature of that business, but that I should not expect him to return." Looking at Elizabeth intently, he said, "We both knew that was a lie, but I was so upset that I did not press him for more information. It was clear, in any case, that he did not mean to tell me the truth. My mother stayed in her room that day and the next, and when she did appear again, her icy silence told me that I must not mention the name of Trevor Handley in her presence."

He rubbed his forehead in consternation. "At first I was angry only with my parents. I expected a letter from Trevor at any moment, believing he would not leave without sending me word. As days passed and I heard nothing, my anger expanded to include him, and I began to think that he, after all, must have been to blame for whatever had happened. It was a very long time before our life resumed any kind of normal balance, and when I finally spoke to my father again, it was to ask if I might be allowed to go to boarding school. I think he was hurt by that, which was what I hoped, I suppose, but he agreed that I should go if that was what I really wanted."

Elizabeth sat shaking her head at the picture her husband had drawn of his family, but forestalled her comments. She asked at last, "Will, what did your mother say to your leaving?"

He sighed. "She reacted first with hysteria and then with silence, but I was so angry and hurt that I cared for no one's feelings but my own. I blamed her for my father's distance, blamed my father for her icy moods, blamed Trevor for whatever he had done. Eventually, I suppose, I began to blame myself, for it seemed that anyone I loved ultimately came to grief."

"Will," said Elizabeth, leaning towards him, "you do not still believe that, do you?"

He smiled back at her and replied, "No, Lizzie, not really. But I have thought at times that there was a curse on this house." He asked, more lightly than he felt, "What do you think?"

"I think that if there *was* a curse, we have driven it out with our most amazing love," she teased gently. "Maybe that explains the sudden appearance of Trevor Handley in your life - perhaps he knows that it is safe to approach this house now."

Darcy laughed with genuine relief and pulled her from her chair to sit on his knees. She protested with a giggle - "Will, the servants... " - but made no attempt to free herself of his embrace, and for a few moments Trevor Handley ceased to exist.

Chapter Twenty One

Setting aside the troubles of the past in favour of consideration of the future, Mr and Mrs Fitzwilliam Darcy girded their loins and sallied forth into Derbyshire society on Sunday morning, making their first entrance at Klympton Church. Since the death of the senior Mr Darcy, the family bench had often sat empty of a Sunday, and rumours were wont to fly through the neighbourhood on those occasions to explain why the family had abandoned Pemberley. Each return appearance by Fitzwilliam or Georgiana put an end to the speculation on their disappearance, but engendered a fresh bouquet of whimsy on the reason for their return.

The friends who often accompanied Mr Darcy or Miss Darcy to services were carefully scrutinised, their merits weighed, and their reputations bandied about. Those neighbourhood matrons with eligible sons and daughters decried the fact that the young Darcys seldom arrived unattended by one or more fashionable and unmarried young man or woman, and even when alone they showed no inclination to engage in the churchyard conversations that are a staple of country matchmaking. Some, to be sure, admired their proud silence and took it as a natural consequence of their status, but others, particularly those most nearly equal in rank and wealth, found reason for indignation in the apparent lack of interest shown in the affairs of the neighbourhood.

Georgiana's shyness made it nearly impossible for her to meet the eyes of more than a few, while Fitzwilliam's haughty gaze seemed to weigh everything it met and find it deficient. Their reserve was not calculated to endear them to any but the rector, who by virtue of the generous living bestowed on him by the family, was quite prepared to admire everything about them. He alone was able to elicit from Miss Darcy a few words of conversation each Sunday. Her brother managed perfunctory greetings to those families who had constituted the social circle of his parents, but even on the rare occasion that he paused for a short conversation, they were left with the impression that they were as ignorant of his affairs after speaking to him as before.

Elizabeth Darcy knew little of her husband's reputation other than that which she had gleaned in her few days of visiting in the summer at Lambton, and she had been able to elicit from him only the briefest sketch of the community into which she was about to step, although she eagerly questioned him. It was not that he withheld information from her, for he earnestly desired that she should feel at ease, but that he knew very little of his neighbours. Some few families he knew from his childhood, but he had formed no lasting ties with any of them and could scarcely tell her the names of their children, much less any details of their marriages or occupations.

As the carriage topped a hill overlooking the lovely church in the glen, Elizabeth sighed and gave up her attempt at preparation. "I cannot imagine that you have lived your entire life in this neighbourhood and managed to know so little about the lives of its inhabitants, Will. Were you never curious as to what all of these people were about?"

"I confess it never occurred to me to wonder. While my mother was alive I learned from listening to her conversations with her friends that there was precious little that was worthy of our notice, and by the time I was old enough to form my own opinions, I suppose I had ceased to think about it."

He did not add that for her sake he deeply regretted the indifference he had shown his neighbours, for he expected the result would be a very cold reception indeed for his bride. Elizabeth, however, was accustomed to making her own way socially. Her father's custom had ever been to attend only those functions where his absence would have constituted a serious breech of custom, and, even when guests were invited to Longbourn, he took the earliest opportunity to escape to his study, preferring the rich tapestry of a good book to the coarser fabric of society. Her mother, on the other hand, was entirely too sociable, rarely missing an opportunity to embarrass her in public by too much speech preceded by too little thought. Her younger sisters were only capable of attracting the type of admirer who is drawn to the ridiculous, and although the supply of these was abundant, they held little interest for Elizabeth. With her sister Jane's example as her model, young Lizzie Bennet had early concluded that if she were to have any friends, it must be on the strength of her own merits. Looking out over the crowded churchyard today, she wished as never before that she had mastered Jane's kind forbearance, but with her usual good humour, she braced herself for the challenge. As Darcy reached up to help her from the carriage, his nervousness melted in the face of her smiling confidence. Before releasing his hand, she gave it a tight squeeze, and arm in arm they made their entrance, she serene and dignified, and he content and proud.

The news of Fitzwilliam Darcy's marriage had naturally preceded them to church, and anticipation of their arrival prevented all but the most pious souls from turning their thoughts toward God that November morning. Small groups tarried in the courtyard, feigning earnest conversation, but turning towards the sound of each carriage that approached. Others, fancying themselves above such an obvious display of curiosity, entered the church in dignified silence, but scarcely was there man or woman among them who did not eagerly await a glimpse of the new mistress of Pemberley.

A murmur spread among the courtyard watchers at the first sight of the Darcy carriage. The appearance of royalty would scarcely have generated a more careful scrutiny, for everyone was eager to store away a useful piece of information as currency in the gossip barter that would surely take place the coming week. Elizabeth Bennet had never in her life been subject to such meticulous measurement. They

149

took note of her height and weight, not scrupling to observe the relative merits of each part of her figure. From the ribbons on her hat to the bows on her shoes, no detail was too trivial for notice. The rich black curls that would not be ruled by her bonnet, the shape of her nose and curve of cheek offered to some astute observers clues to her personality. The simple cut of her gown told a tale that some found pleasing and that raised the eyebrows of others. Her light step and the jaunty set of her shoulders bespoke confidence, and her sparkling eyes hinted at an energetic nature. For those members of the country parish whose curiosity was not contaminated by ill will, Mrs Darcy presented a pleasing picture; for those determined to find fault, every feature had its weakness.

Lady Margaret Westby, bosom friend of the late Lady Anne Darcy, turned a disdainful eye upon the young couple as they took their place in the Darcy pew across from hers. Her look contained no hint of curiosity, for she had formed her opinion of the bride the moment she was informed of her name. Her lips pursed into a frown, she quickly turned her attention to the prayer book that she clenched rather too tightly in her hand. Her displeasure did nothing to soften the severity of her face, and the meditation upon which her eyes rested gave her no measure of relief, for her vanity forbade the wearing of reading glasses. Beside her sat a horse-faced maiden who could never be mistaken for anyone but the Lady's daughter, so remarkably did she resemble her mother. Holding a handkerchief clumsily to her nose, the younger woman sniffed and, leaning towards her mother, whispered, "Look, Mama. Fitzwilliam Darcy has come to church with his new wife."

Her mother's face would have screwed itself into an even deeper frown had the overburdened muscles permitted. At this moment, her daughter's enormous stupidity was the only thing that could have distracted her from her irritation towards Fitzwilliam Darcy. She parted her lips a fraction of an inch to hiss, "Will you please be still, Cassandra!"

For answer she received an even louder sniff, accompanied by several rapid blinks of the eyes, as her daughter struggled to understand her mother's anger. Lady Margaret closed her eyes and drew in a deep breath, asking God yet again why she had been given such trials to bear. As usual, the answer was not forthcoming, but as the organ had begun to play she retrieved her errant thoughts and reached for the hymnal, as Fitzwilliam Darcy did the same. As his eyes caught hers he nodded and smiled. Her response was a more delicate sniff than her daughter had produced, but one that carried a more eloquent message.

Standing for the opening hymn, Mr and Mrs Darcy seemed untroubled by the eyes that glanced at them covertly over hymnals in the rows behind. Had they been able to poll the congregation, they would have discovered it rather evenly divided into factions tending to admiration, curiosity, and scorn, the latter group comprised chiefly of citizens of the highest social rank, and therefore nearest the Darcy bench in the front of the church. Those of middle fortune tended more towards approbation, for it was clearly from their ranks that Mr Darcy had chosen a bride. For those of modest means, curiosity alone could be allowed, for they were not permitted the luxury of judging the actions of a person of such consequence.

The rector, mounting the dais in solemn dignity, harboured the tiniest regret that he had not been called upon to bless the marriage, but he was too busy with the effort of calming his fluttering nerves to give it more than a passing thought. Being rather outside of the prevailing winds of gossip, he had only learned of Mr Darcy's marriage and his return to Pemberley a day ago, a misfortune that caused him considerable anguish in rewriting his sermon for the day. His unfortunate wife had suffered a torrent of abuse for not informing him earlier, and she had most wisely chosen to remove herself and her two children from within range of his hearing while he closeted himself in his study to anguish over the perfect text from which to compose a sermon that would form the basis for Mrs Darcy's understanding of his value as spiritual advisor to Pemberley. The fruit of his efforts was a rather laborious treatment of Paul's letters to the Romans, delivered in a voice rather higher than his normal timber, owing to the loss of a night's sleep and exacerbated by the tension of his desire to please.

The object of his enthusiasm, he observed with pleasure, maintained a most properly attentive pose throughout the protracted speech, and as he stepped down from the pulpit, rewarded him with a brief smile as their eyes met. Mr Darcy's thoughts he did not hope to read; in fact he avoided any contact with the inscrutable countenance that had, in previous encounters, generally left him feeling that he might just as well have been speaking to the Great Sphinx itself for all the response his words evoked.

As the congregation filed noisily out of the small sanctuary, Fitzwilliam screwed up his courage for the inevitable introductions that must follow. The first was owed to the rector, Mr Hatfield, and Fitzwilliam found himself relieved of the need to make more than the slightest contribution to the conversation by the onslaught of nervous prattle that issued from that gentleman's mouth. He watched Elizabeth in admiration as she attended to his flattery as if his words were poetry to her ears. She responded with a gracious comment on the beauty of the church and an observation on his astute illumination of the scripture, inviting him to call with his family whenever his duties allowed. They moved on quickly, leaving Mr Hatfield flushing with pleasure, and made their way toward the neighbours clustered at the foot of the stairs.

Lady Margaret and her husband, Lord Westby, flanked by Cassandra and several esteemed members of their elevated circle, were engaged in their usual Sunday morning display of superiority as the Darcys approached. Carefully timing her movement to be assured that it would not be missed, she took her husband's arm and with no gentle force, turned him away from the group and propelled him through the courtyard, saying haughtily, "Come, Cassandra." The bewildered young woman was torn for a moment between fear of her mother and her desire to greet the Darcys, but in the midst of a timid smile, warmly returned by Elizabeth, the commanding voice rang out again and the young lady reluctantly scurried after the receding forms.

Fitzwilliam would have, but for Lizzie, made a path straight to their waiting carriage, but instead, feeling the weight of her hand on his arm, he paused to introduce her to first one group and then another. Their reception among the remainder of the parishioners was as varied as the colours of their autumn plumage. While Darcy masked his nervousness in his accustomed manner, Lizzie's steady gaze met each face in turn with a determination to present herself in a manner that would do him credit. With a becoming blush attending her dignified carriage, she spoke softly but with apparent ease to each person she met, leaving in her wake the impression that she was pleased to find herself among interesting company. All but the hardest of heart were moved by her graciousness to admit that she might indeed prove to be a pleasant neighbour, and more than one acquaintance of the Darcy family observed that she was likely to do Mr Darcy good if she refrained from adopting *his* manners.

As they reached the safety of the carriage at last, Elizabeth Darcy turned a radiant smile towards those who stood in the courtyard waiting to begin the evaluations that must needs follow such a novelty, and her look conveyed not only an earnest pleasure in having made their acquaintance but also a fond hope that they should soon meet again. With this final piece of drama, she leaned back in the carriage, content that she had done all she could to invite the approbation of her neighbours. She found her husband studying her with eyes full of mirth. "My dear Mrs Darcy," he said, "I see that I was quite foolish to trouble myself over your reception among my neighbours. If anyone could find fault in your performance today, they must truly be intent on malice. I regret that Lady Margaret did not stay to enjoy your impeccable manners."

Elizabeth smiled conspiratorially. "Shall I tell you the secret of my success, or shall I allow you to think I am naturally so gracious?"

"Pray do not keep me in suspense."

"The good rector's sermon put me in mind of Jane, for she is the only person I know whose nature closely follows Christ's model of loving kindness. I was imitating her as I moved through the churchyard, for I remembered that even Miss Bingley and Mrs Hurst were captivated by her the first time they met. By the time your neighbours discover my true nature, they may find they have already formed a habit of cordiality towards me," she said with a triumphant smile.

Darcy broke into a laugh that startled the driver, who was unaccustomed to such open displays of feeling from his master. "You shall have need of your sister's patience in the days to come, for I fear your pleasant behaviour will invite a swarm of visitors to Pemberley, eager to test your authenticity," he cautioned cheerfully.

"I shall leave it in your charge, then, to make sure the visits are brief, for I have never been able to master my faults for more than a short interval." She added, "I only wish Jane would arrive before they do, for I would be far better assured of success with her example directly before me."

"There is little hope that they will wait until Thursday, especially Mr Hatfield. You left him in such a state of anticipation that I fear he may be waiting for us at the gate when we arrive home."

She laughed gleefully at the thought of the rector's obsequious form bowing low as their carriage drew up. "As for him, I am not worried. He has something about him of my cousin Mr Collins, don't you think? Even my most outrageous behaviour did not deter *that* gentleman from asking for my hand in marriage."

"I believe you are right. Mr Hatfield is bound to be one of your most ardent admirers, whatever you say or do." Holding hands, they drove in silence for a time, until Darcy remarked in some seriousness, "Perhaps you will come to regret passing up the opportunity for the calm life of a country rector's wife. I'm sure Mr Collins has no skeletons in his closet with which to frighten you."

She studied his face thoughtfully before answering. "I should want a good deal more of Jane's forbearance to be married to a man so intent on pleasing everyone as he is. I much prefer the challenge of improving your reputation to the difficulty of controlling my own faults."

"Then you must take care not to imitate Jane's manner with *me*," he declared, "for with such defects as mine, the wrath of God would serve the purpose better than the forbearance of a saint."

As Darcy had predicted, the neighbours did begin to appear, led the very next day by the inexorable Mr Hatfield and his wife, a plain-speaking, robust young woman who in no way resembled her nervous husband. She declared to Mrs Darcy that she was welcome, as if she were a judge passing sentence. To Elizabeth's well-concealed amusement, she perceived that Mrs Hatfield was to consider herself a protector and ally, against what dangers she could not ascertain, but which were apparently abundantly clear to that lady. While Mr Hatfield fluttered and fawned, Mrs Hatfield's brusque but kind chatter provided a welcome diversion, and Lizzie was pleased to show a cordial interest in her various schemes for the amelioration of certain disturbing conditions among the poorest cottagers. Mr and Mrs Hatfield went away well pleased with themselves, and armed with a promise from Mrs Darcy that she would call on them presently and be guided by their wisdom as to charitable work that she might undertake in future.

In the following days others came, and Fitzwilliam Darcy, though often wishing some catastrophe might present itself to excuse him from attendance, found a source of constant pride and pleasure in observing 'Lizzie's court,' as he playfully dubbed it. There were those who appeared out of a genuine spirit of kindness to welcome a stranger, but they were out-numbered by a less noble entourage of the curious and the supercilious. Elizabeth's honest good nature earned her a warm regard with the former; with the latter she maintained a quiet dignity that afforded little opportunity for criticism. Knowing her propensity for wit, Darcy was forced at times to pinch himself to prevent an outburst of laughter when a sparkle of her eye or a veiled expression intimated to him her true feelings, but she did not allow herself to respond to even the most haughty or foolish of her guests with anything but calm decorum and flattering attention. As the week proceeded, Elizabeth began to feel quite pleased with herself and as Darcy watched her skilful manoeuvres he allowed himself to hope that his fears had been overstated. Even the most formidable of these early visitors, Lady Penelope Arthur and her three impertinent daughters, were not able to break Elizabeth's resolve or Darcy's patience.

As her daughters looked on complacently, Lady Penelope conducted an officious interview which was obviously aimed at ascertaining Elizabeth's credentials for her present post. Fortunately for everyone, the visit was brief, and if it was not concluded to anyone's satisfaction, at least it was concluded quickly. Having failed to find any specific fault with Mrs Darcy and unable to arouse in Mr Darcy any suitable sign of remorse, the lady had to content herself with leaving in rather a worse temper than that in which she had arrived. The Darcys walked the ladies to their carriage and Mr Darcy handed them graciously up while his wife maintained a safe distance without neglecting her duty of attendance to their guests. When the carriage had safely rounded the curve of the drive, Darcy faced

Elizabeth, taking her hands and studying her face. With teeth clenched tightly, Elizabeth stomped her foot as the offenders disappeared around the carriage drive. "Insufferable conceit!" she seethed, her cheeks flaming with released venom. "I wonder that they deign to breathe the same air as the untitled masses. I have never met with such misguided arrogance." Suddenly aware of Darcy's silence, she turned to see him watching her with a wry grin that he hastily attempted to hide behind a mask of attentive concern.

"May I have the honour of knowing what amuses you, sir?" she asked icily.

He could not prevent his mirth from breaking free in a peal of laughter, which further incensed his bride and rendered her momentarily speechless. He sobered at the sight of her wrath, but replied impishly, "Are you quite sure, my dear, that you have never met such 'misguided arrogance' before?"

Her anger floundered on the rocks of a sudden vision of the Meryton Ball, and she replied coolly, before bursting into laughter that instantly restored her equilibrium, "If you refer to your own pride, Mr Darcy, I hope I have never intimated that I found it misguided."

Chapter Twenty Two

On the appointed morning, Jane and Charles Bingley set out from their London home on the road to Derbyshire, sharing an eager anticipation of the weeks to come. When Miss Darcy joined them a few minutes later, it would have been hard to judge who was the most animated of the travellers and who the most anxious to reach their destination. It was certainly Jane, however, who delighted most in leaving London behind, for after a week in such close company with Charles' sisters, even *her* extraordinary willingness to be pleased was strained. While Miss Bingley and Mrs Hurst had taken pains that no direct offence should pass their lips, they showed Jane in an ingenious variety of ways that they neither sought nor valued her company. Her indefatigable optimism assured her that, in time, they would all be friends, but her keen intelligence recognised that the time had not yet arrived. As the carriage drew away from London, Jane leaned back in contentment and turned her full attention to the company of those whose affection could not be mistaken, and not a moment of the day's journey was wasted on unpleasant thoughts.

Anyone witnessing the arrival of the Bingley carriage at Pemberley manor might have thought a separation of years had preceded this reunion, for a fortnight's removal would seem unlikely to engender such affectionate greetings and general exuberance. Their first evening together was taken up with the narratives of the two couples on the events of the past two weeks, with the Bingleys eager to relate all details of the manner in which their time had been spent and the Darcys careful not to. Georgiana listened eagerly, and although her companions often tried to draw her out, she was content for the most part to shift her gaze lovingly from one to the next, revelling in the warm camaraderie about her. Late into the night, finally exhausted, the Bingleys were shown to their rooms and Georgiana tenderly kissed her brother and Elizabeth goodnight.

159

When they had removed to their separate rooms, a private review of the evening kept everyone awake a little longer. Georgiana especially found much to think about, for being by far the most reserved speaker, she had more opportunity to observe than the others. Moved by the obvious affection between Elizabeth and Jane, she entertained the fondest hopes of becoming more at ease with them than she had been with any other ladies of her acquaintance and was utterly released from any nervousness concerning what her position should be at Pemberley with a new lady of the house installed.

The thoughts that kept her from sleep that night, however, were for her brother. Although his previous behaviour to her had inspired her respect and admiration and she had never doubted his kind and generous nature, she had often found herself slightly uncomfortable in his presence. She had been quite unprepared for the change she saw in him tonight. The obvious pleasure with which he joined in the evening's conversation was a novelty, and most astonishing was his lightness and laughter, and the open expression of his delight in Elizabeth. Her timid heart opened joyfully to comprehend the happiness he must be feeling, and she slept at last with the delightful anticipation of further discovery.

The change in Darcy's temperament was not lost on Charles Bingley, and although in his affectionate nature he had found little to complain of in his friend's former manners, he too could not fail to be gladdened by the mood of ease and affability he had seen tonight. Listening to this confidence from her husband, Jane longed to sit alone with Elizabeth as they had always done in the past to compare their thoughts and feelings in minute detail. She found Elizabeth's behaviour little altered, but from their years of close companionship and deep affection, Jane could readily detect a new serenity and maturity in her sister. She looked forward to the coming days to discover by what means Mr Darcy's transformation had been effected.

Elizabeth and Fitzwilliam found nothing to surprise them in the happiness of Jane and Charles, and contented themselves with commenting on the pleasantness of their company and the relative enthusiasm of Georgiana. For many days, no reference to the past had troubled their conversation, and Elizabeth drifted off to sleep contemplating the question of whether or not she would ever see a renewal of his fears. Judging from his obvious delight with Georgiana's return, and buoyed by the presence of the Bingleys, she began to hope the peace was unassailable.

The mood the following morning was relaxed and playful. After a late breakfast, fair weather called the party out for a walk about the gardens, during which plans for future amusements sprang cheerfully from every quarter. Elizabeth and Jane were careful to give no sign of their impatience to be alone, and as if by mutual agreement, earnestly attempted to draw Georgiana into every conversation. As they passed the spot in the garden where Darcy and Elizabeth had happened upon each other the previous July, Elizabeth said playfully, "I wish you could recreate the lovely astonishment on your face when you found me trespassing here last summer, Will."

"I don't believe there was another soul I would have less expected to find greeting me as I arrived home that day." He added shyly, "Or would have been happier to see."

Elizabeth turned to Charles. "This is shocking indeed, coming from the man who pronounced at the Meryton Ball that *you* were dancing with the only handsome woman in the room."

Jane gasped as Charles guffawed. "Lizzie, you are terrible to bring that up!" she chided.

Charles joined in with delight. "Good Lord, Darcy, I had forgotten how abominably you abused the ladies that night."

Darcy smiled complacently and taking Elizabeth's hand, raised it to his lips with mock reverence. "I did not say, my dear, that I found you more handsome when I saw you here. But since our first meeting, I had come to value your wit and overlook your other defects."

"You are most noble, sir. But I must claim the prize for greater charity, for to my great peril I have forsworn any improvement of my defects so as to continue providing you with subjects for *your* wit, while you heedlessly improve yourself with every passing day, leaving me nothing with which to taunt you." Even Georgiana was emboldened to join the laughter, although the light this repartee shed on her brother's character caused her a momentary confusion.

"Beware, my friend. You tread on dangerous ground if you venture to enter a contest of wits with Elizabeth Bennet," said Charles.

Fitzwilliam challenged, "In general, I cannot claim to be her equal, but I must boast that I have sharpened my skills since last we met."

As the others moved on, Elizabeth took Georgiana's arm fondly and held her back a bit. "I'm sorry if I have upset you by making sport of your brother, Georgiana. You must think very ill of me."

Georgiana looked alarmed. "Not at all, Miss Elizabeth. It is only that I am more amazed than I can express, and more delighted, to find my brother so easy. I do not recall him ever enjoying humour at his own expense before."

Elizabeth smiled. "Please call me Lizzie," she said, squeezing her arm, "for I feel as though you are my sister already. I think your brother is altered in some ways, and I hope you will not be troubled by the change. I believe that adding my adoration to what he already had from you has made him feel more relaxed."

This thought was a novelty for Georgiana, for it had never occurred to her that her brother's reserve had been the product of insecurity. She struggled for a moment with the idea, and then seeing Darcy's face lit up in animated conversation, said thoughtfully, "Look at his face. I have not seen him so energetic for many years. You do not give yourself enough credit, Miss... er, Lizzie, as you should, but *I*

162

do, I assure you. I did not think him unhappy before, but I am beginning to think I did not understand him very well." Darcy chose this moment to turn back, and seeing the two ladies so affectionately engaged in conversation, his pride and pleasure showed in a broad smile.

Lizzie laughed brightly, saying, "I only hope you will find such happiness one day, my dear, as your brother and I have found. I am quite astonished myself."

Laughter and liveliness were the order of the week at Pemberley. Even Georgiana found herself joining in from time to time with quiet humour, although it was a very long time before she ventured to laugh openly at her brother. It was not until two days had passed that Jane found an opportunity to be quite alone with Elizabeth. The men had gone off on an errand and Georgiana had turned to practice her music. Taking their cups of tea to the second floor sitting room, the intimate atmosphere of which gave it a more congenial air than the large rooms downstairs, they fell laughingly into each other's arms and opened their hearts to the unfettered confidences they had shared all of their lives.

"Oh, Jane," Elizabeth began, "I have missed you so dreadfully. I have heard of everything you have done, but now tell me about your happiness, although I can read enough in your face to fill a book on the subject."

Jane sighed contentedly. "I am so happy, Lizzie, that I do not know how to begin to describe it. Charles is every day increasing in my esteem, if that be possible, for he is so kind and attentive that I never have a moment to want anything either in material comforts or in companionship. Sometimes I fear I shall wake to find that I have been dreaming, for it does not seem possible that I should be so fortunate."

Elizabeth protested with a laugh, "Your sweetness is always an astonishment to me, Jane. Why should you not be the happiest woman on earth? No one could deserve it more!"

Jane ignored the compliment and earnestly entreated her sister, "We do not need to speak any more about me, for I think you find me very much as you last saw me, but I am dying to be informed what you have done with Mr Darcy. I find him so changed I hardly recognise him, although you did assure me before the wedding that you found him kind and good."

Elizabeth had thought long and hard in anticipation of this interview, weighing in her mind what could be said about the previous two weeks. Clearly there were conversations and events which she should not discuss even with Jane, and yet she had so long been used to sharing her every thought with her sister that she knew it would be difficult not to say more than she intended. She ended up by relating the substance of what had passed between them in the fortnight, only omitting some details of the intensity of their grief and sorrow, and emphasising the resolution of all difficulties. The subject of her husband's lingering pain and sorrow over his past she did not allow herself to open, for she scarcely knew how to explain it to herself.

Elizabeth's narrative was delivered with such a delightful mirth that she soon had Jane beside herself with laughter, and they ended quite content that the necessary separations of their married lives would not prevent them from always maintaining the easy confidentiality of their childhood.

Bingley and Darcy, in the meantime, rode along at an easy pace, enjoying their own opportunity for private conversation. Bingley noted that Pemberley had been well maintained in Darcy's absence and mentioned that his sisters always spoke with the highest regard for the beauty of the estate. "I am afraid that Caroline wishes for an improvement in our situation, as she has not formed a very strong attachment to Netherfield House. She has often expressed the desire that I should use Pemberley as my model for a suitable situation."

Darcy responded playfully, "You may well find that your present home enjoys too great a nearness to Longbourn to suit you long."

Bingley protested amicably, "I very much enjoy the company of Mr Bennet, for he has a wry wit. But," he added, laughing, "I take your point with regards to other members of that household. I do hope to find Mrs Bennet's nerves very much improved now that she has so happily disposed of three daughters in the space of a few months. But tell me, Darcy, don't you find that we have been uncommonly lucky? I confess I have never been so delighted by the company of any woman as I am by Jane's, and I venture to say your life has greatly improved with marriage as well."

Darcy's answer was more serious than his friend had expected. "I have you to thank, Bingley, for this happy change in my fortunes. I confess I little expected to enjoy any of the charms of Meryton when I first visited you there, and with my stubborn pride I came very close to missing what has proved to be the dearest treasure of my life. I had not thought it possible for me to ever feel as content as I do. And although I cannot truthfully say that I have learned to enjoy the company of Mrs Bennet, I must give her my respect for producing two such magnificent daughters."

Bingley was delighted with this speech, and emboldened by the confidence to rejoin, "Yes, you not only nearly missed making yourself happy, you also were in a fair way to preventing me from having *my* heart's desire." If his manner had been less cheerful, Darcy might have felt a sting of reproach, but he understood too well his friend's easy temperament to worry that his words carried any serious censure.

The rest of the ride was marked by a boyish exuberance on the part of both men, ending with a vigorous race to the stables. They entered the house laughing and breathless to find that their wives were still closeted together, quite lost to the passage of time.

Bingley remarked to Darcy, as they burst into the room, that he feared it might have been dangerous to afford them so much time alone to compare their husbands' faults. Jane replied very sweetly that, on the contrary, they had need of a much longer interview to fully describe their happiness. Darcy, enjoying his new-found playfulness, feigned annoyance and said, "I had quite forgotten that Elizabeth has, in the past twelvemonth, seized every opportunity of my absence to form the most dangerous opinions on my temperament and behaviour. I was resolved after we married to never let her out of my sight for more than a few minutes."

Jane coloured, not knowing how to take his jest, but found herself pleasantly surprised by her sister's pert reply. "I am equally capable of poor judgement when you are at my side, my dear, so I fear there is no remedy other than a continued improvement in your manners to impress upon me the error of my previous opinions."

Darcy laughed and responded by clapping Bingley heartily on the back. "I am sure that my good friend will attest to the fact that he has never met a man of more affable manners than I have become of late."

Bingley bowed first to Fitzwilliam and then to Elizabeth, and replied elegantly, "I declare this to be the truth, madam. He wants very little to become quite as pleasant as I am."

"In that case," said Elizabeth archly, "I will cherish the hope that one day Jane may relinquish her claim to being the happiest woman on earth." They all laughed at this, and Jane stood up to take Charles' arm. "I cannot wish you to be happier than I am, dear Lizzie, for I am afraid it could not be borne," she said. And the Bingleys retired to dress for dinner.

Darcy turned his attention to Elizabeth, saying, "I'm sure she is right, my dear. I find myself threatened with the prospect of being quite undone by too much happiness."

She smiled and asked, "Shall I attempt, then, to make you unhappy to save you from this terrible plight?"

He replied, "I cannot imagine how you could accomplish that," and pulled her to her feet, wrapping her in a most passionate embrace. They were so delayed in their own preparations for dinner that they found themselves arriving at the table to find everyone waiting.

Chapter Twenty Three

Reaching the Inn at Lambton on Sunday afternoon, Trevor Handley found the letter he had hoped for awaiting him at the desk. He waited until the porter had deposited his bags in his suite and then opened it eagerly. Its message was direct, its tone guarded.

Dear Trevor,

'Astonished' would better describe my feelings upon receiving your letter. As I prefer a private meeting, I propose to call on you at Lambton Inn on the morning of the 30th November.

> *Please send a message confirming your arrival and suggesting a time which suits your schedule.*

Yours faithfully,
Fitzwilliam Darcy

Trevor Handley frowned thoughtfully, wondering at the feelings of Fitzwilliam Darcy as he penned those words. Considering old Thomas' observations, it seemed unlikely that Fitzwilliam knew much of the circumstances of his, Trevor's, departure from Pemberley. What he should say to him when they met had already caused Trevor more than one restless night, and he contemplated the long evening ahead with little hope of finding a clear answer to that dilemma. Writing a quick note to Pemberley, he rang the bell rope and asked that a messenger be sent to deliver it; he then ordered a bath and a hot meal, temporarily setting aside his reverie in favour of these distractions. As he settled in at last in front of the fire, he poured himself a glass of brandy and picked up Fitzwilliam Darcy's letter again, studying it thoughtfully.

The note was written in a small and meticulous script - the style of a perfectionist, he mused, like his mother. At eight and twenty, it was unlikely that Fitzwilliam Darcy would bear much resemblance to the youth he remembered. He wondered what form his maturity had taken. At eleven, Fitzwilliam had the black curls of his mother and her dark brooding eyes, but no evidence of her teasing wit shown through them. In her presence, his manner mimicked hers in every detail, a contemptuous pride hardening the youthful face into a mask, but once away, alone or riding beside his father, he softened and grew silent, unsure of his role.

Trevor closed his eyes to concentrate on the image of Mrs Anne Darcy, a vision that had not dimmed in these seventeen years. He saw her teasing eyes, the toss of her curls when she laughed, the shape of her back as she whipped her horse and rode on ahead of him at a frightening speed. The sound of her voice rang in his ears, calling out to him, challenging, taunting... He shook his head to rid himself of the picture. Though half a lifetime ago, these images were deeply etched and they carried a disturbing power still. Filling his glass a second time, he fixed his eyes on the flickering tongues of fire, wondering, as he had done a hundred times, if he was mad to stir up the waters that had lain so long at rest.

His thoughts turned again to the youth who had become as dear to him as a brother in the months they spent together. Fitzwilliam Darcy was a lonely child, with deep and serious thoughts that he rarely shared. Trevor had felt drawn to him, protective of him, eager to make him laugh. At first he had envied young Darcy's position for all of the enormous privilege it encompassed, but as time passed he began to observe the restless, brooding undercurrents of the family and he understood that for all the attention lavished on him, Fitzwilliam had been denied the feeling of security. Even as Trevor was besotted with the seductive beauty of Mrs Darcy, he recognised that the dangerous, demanding temperament behind it frightened and confused her son, and emasculated her husband. That gentle soul, who should have been a refuge to his son, was rendered ineffectual by the feline grip in which she held them both, toying with their affections and sapping their strength.

With a shudder of revulsion, Trevor pushed himself up from his chair and paced the floor restlessly, wondering what brought him here. Having so boldly set the wheels in motion, he now briefly considered that there was still time to avoid the reunion; nothing forced him to disturb the dead of Pemberley except the relentless yearning he had never been able to completely still. Since the morning of his forced departure, that drive had not left his thoughts for long. Through the first months of anger and hurt, and into the years of building a life for himself, Trevor Handley had sought to free himself of the influence of the Darcy family. A combination of good fortune and a fierce compulsion to succeed had restored him to a position of financial security and independence. Reason dictated that the time he spent at Pemberley should be relegated to the graveyard of childhood memories, but his heart was never released from the longing to return.

Stopping to rest his arm upon the mantle, he thought back to the day word had reached him of Mrs Darcy's death. He had absorbed the news with a curious lack of feeling. She had captivated him as easily as scooping a hatchling from its nest, but the power of her hold was painful, and although he fluttered about her in fascination, he was tormented at the same time by a revulsion that left him trembling with fear and shame. The surprise was not that she should have died so young, but that she managed to live *so long*, beset by such conflicting powers of giddiness and rage that she scarcely knew whether to laugh or cry. He imagined her soul splitting into fragments as it departed her body, freed at last of the temporal fetters that had bound together forces wholly unreconciled to one another.

It was the death of old *Mr* Darcy that had unnerved Trevor Handley and set him upon his present course of action. While he remained alive, Trevor was tormented by a longing for reconciliation but could not find the courage to seek it; upon his death he began to see that in his obsession with his own pain, he had done the greatest disservice to the one most innocent of any wrongdoing, young Fitzwilliam. Goaded by remorse, he understood he would have no rest until he returned to Pemberley and tried to right that wrong.

The fire had died to ash and the brandy decanter sat empty on the table before Trevor Handley gave up his hope of preparing a speech for Fitzwilliam Darcy, and, determined to let the morning bring him the words he required to put the past to rest, he tried to sleep. In spite of his resolve, the remaining hours of the night were troubled by the relentless workings of his mind and, during brief interludes of sleep, by garbled dreams from which he awoke shaken and exhausted. In a clearer state of mind, he might have guessed that less than five miles away, on the finest estate in Derbyshire, the lord of the manor passed the night with no less anguish and a great many more questions.

Chapter Twenty Four

The knock on the door came promptly at ten o'clock, and Trevor, occupied only by pacing the floor, answered it immediately. Their eyes met and held, each weighing and testing, seeking a foothold from which to bridge the distance between them. After several seconds of mutual appraisal, Trevor's face broke into a warm smile. He said only "Willie," his voice soft with surprise, and stepped back to take in the full picture of the tall, well-built man who stood in place of the boy of eleven he had left behind.

Offering no greeting, Darcy stepped warily into the room, silently appraising Trevor. An awkward silence followed, but Darcy, having come to this meeting determined to leave the burden of conversation on Trevor's shoulders, ventured no assistance other than the observation, "*You* have changed very little in seventeen years, Trevor, but I seem to be looking at you from a different angle now."

Trevor, finally remembering his manners, indicated a chair and said, "Forgive me for staring at you - you look so like your mother... Please, sit down." Trevor sat as well, growing agitated. Darcy maintained a watchful reserve. "I heard of the death of your parents," said Trevor. "I *am* sorry."

With a frown, Darcy answered. "A great deal may happen in seventeen years." There could be no mistaking the coldness in his voice.

"Yes... " After an uncomfortable pause, Trevor added hesitantly, "I understand that you have a sister."

"Georgiana is seventeen. She was born the year after you left Pemberley."

Trevor's expectation that his facility for speech would lead him into the interview began to falter in the face of Fitzwilliam's dogged reticence. He began more than once to speak, but closed his mouth each time without uttering a sound. Finally, rubbing his forehead thoughtfully, he managed to get his feet back under him, and he raised his eyes to look directly into the stern gaze that studied him. With a slight smile, he began softly, "Forgive me. I have struggled for so long, first with the hope and later with the fear of meeting you, and have so often imagined what I should say... and yet I find myself tongue-tied." His pause invited an encouraging response, but hearing none, he squared his shoulders and continued with more energy. "I understand, I think, what you must be feeling. I imagine you were very angry with me when I disappeared so suddenly."

Darcy's tightened jaw gave the only evidence that he had heard, and Trevor nodded to himself as if weighing the case before him. He stood up and walked to the window, finally turning back to face his visitor with a smile of kind resignation. He ran his hand through his hair, and said, "You do not mean to help me, and that is justly so. I have waited too long. Perhaps I should not have come."

In spite of his resolve, Darcy could not prevent the emotion from creeping into his voice. "Perhaps. But now you are here, I see no reason for you not to tell me the purpose of your coming."

Trevor set that question aside in favour of one of his own. "What did your parents tell you about my leaving?"

Darcy's voice was impatient. "My father said only that an urgent family matter required you to go home. My mother never spoke your name again." His tone became accusing. "*I* found no way to understand why I had no word of explanation from *you*."

Trevor turned back to the window, carefully considering his response. When he spoke, his voice was quiet but calm. "I have been a terrible coward, Fitzwilliam. I ran from Pemberley like a whipped dog, and for seventeen years could not find the courage to return as a man, although Lord knows I resolved a thousand times that I should." At last he squared his shoulders and turned back to meet Darcy's eyes. "Perhaps if I had been older I might have chosen another course of action, but I was frightened and angry, and it was a very long time

174

before I came to fully understand what had happened. By then, it seemed too late to approach you. You deserved better from me. I *am* sorry."

Darcy had regained his composure with great effort, and was not about to abandon himself to a further display of emotion. He held Trevor's gaze with brooding eyes, but made no answer. Trevor felt his resolve growing; whatever the outcome, he must finish what he had started. A fire kindled in his hazel eyes as he walked toward Darcy, and his voice grew strong and sure.

"Damn it all, Willie," he said, adopting the familiarity of an older brother, "I have lived for seventeen years with this burden of silence, and it served neither of us. You deserve to hear the truth. Your father threw me out of Pemberley because he believed I was having an affair with your mother."

Darcy's eyes widened and his hands gripped the arms of his chair as Trevor's words penetrated his defences. Trevor plunged into the breach. "He ordered me to leave the house that morning and forbade me to speak to anyone." His voice dropped to a whisper, but it was clearly audible in the breathless silence. "He told me he would kill me if I ever came near Pemberley again." The pallor of his face was mirrored in Darcy's countenance. For several moments there was not a sound from either figure, but Darcy suddenly leapt from his chair with an oath and strode to the far end of the room in great agitation. As he reached the wall and spun on his heels, Trevor sat down abruptly. The words that had echoed in his mind these many years had never before passed his lips, and the speaking brought back the scene as if it had happened yesterday, leaving him trembling.

Darcy opened his mouth to speak, but clamped it shut again and continued to pace the length of the room like a caged animal. After many minutes of this silent drama, he stopped immediately in front of Trevor and demanded harshly, "And was it true, Handley?"

No answer came, and no movement from the figure he addressed. Rage rose up in Darcy's breast, and sorrow crowded against it. He grabbed Trevor by the lapels of his coat and pulled him to his feet. His breathing was ragged. "Tell me the truth, man!" he cried.

Darcy's fury had the effect on Trevor of a tonic, and he felt the weakness dissipate in the wake of a renewed resolve. When he spoke, it was with complete confidence. "I have given you little reason to trust me these seventeen years, and there is no one living who can prove or disprove what I say, so I will not protest my innocence to you. You know better than I the characters of your mother and father. *You* must be the judge. What you believe to be true must suffice for truth between us."

Darcy had released his grip on Trevor's coat, and by the time he had finished speaking his anger had been replaced by a maddening confusion. At last he staggered backwards and sat down, closing his eyes against the conflicting emotions. As he searched for a path through a labyrinth of memories, the last words he had heard echoed again and again in his mind: 'what you believe to be true must suffice for truth...'

The two men remained posed as statues, one frozen in indecision, the other resolutely holding his course. Darcy opened his eyes at last to see Trevor quietly watching him, his gaze compassionate and calm. Trevor took a step closer as if he longed to touch him, but finally, folding his arms, said quietly, "I ask only that you hear me out. I understand that what I have said must raise many questions that will not admit easy answers. You wonder what I want from you, why I did not leave well enough alone. You must certainly be questioning how much truth is in my words. I have not come for absolution nor do I expect you to answer to me for your mother and father's actions. I have long since made my peace with their memory.

"The thought that will not give me peace is that your mother, your father, and *I* all did a much greater disservice to *you* than we did to ourselves. Each of us played a part in this drama and suffered the consequences of our actions or our silence. You were an innocent bystander, and yet I imagine your suffering was not less than ours. I have been haunted these many years by the trust you gave me. I failed miserably to live up to the responsibility of that trust, and while I would not blame you for utterly rejecting my apology, I could find no peace if I did not offer it."

Darcy's vision clouded with tears and he turned his head to fight them back. He had no desire to return to his childhood, but Trevor's steady, reasonable voice drew him helplessly back to the memory of the painful isolation that followed his disappearance. Darcy's only defence, now as then, was a cold anger, and as it swelled in his breast he welcomed it. He rose slowly to his feet, revelling in the advantage of height that allowed him to tower over Trevor. With fists and jaw clenched, Darcy gathered the repressed sorrow, fear, anger and disappointment of his eight and twenty years into a single declaration of independence. This he delivered with all of his strength directly to Trevor Handley's jaw, sending him reeling across the room.

Without a word or a backwards look, Fitzwilliam Darcy turned, picked up his hat and walked out of the room, momentarily empty of emotion but for a curious buoyancy that arose from the novelty of such a free, if violent, expression of his feelings. Striding through the parlour and out the main door, he called to a servant and said calmly, "Tell Mr Wilkins to look in on his guest, Mr Handley. I believe he may require some assistance." Mounting his stallion, he rode slowly out of the village, nurturing the empowering feeling engendered by his action. Before two miles had been covered, however, his confidence faltered and his anger ebbed, leaving him exhausted.

Realising he was unfit to rejoin his family and friends in such a state, he turned his horse from the main road into a winding lane that led him eventually to the bluff overlooking Lambton. There he dismounted and tethered his horse, and, settling himself against a tree, gave himself over to the contemplation of the history he had so long avoided. Trevor's words began a slow, tortuous dance in his mind, and at the end of every path his memory followed, he found the words, 'what you believe to be true... ' Each repetition made it more maddeningly clear that he had not the slightest idea what he *did* believe.

Chapter Twenty Five

By noon, when Darcy had not returned, Elizabeth began to feel uneasy. She sat in the drawing room beside Jane, attempting to occupy her hands with needlework, while Georgiana worked on a new piece of music. Charles had taken advantage of the unseasonably fine weather to go fishing, and Lizzie should have been content with the opportunity to have Jane to herself, but her thoughts wandered constantly to Mr Trevor Handley, and as the morning passed, her attention to present company waned. At last, Jane's voice broke into her thoughts.

"Lizzie, for goodness sake, where are you this morning?" she asked gently.

Elizabeth turned a surprised face toward her sister and blushed. "Were you saying something, Jane?"

"Is anything the matter, dear?" Jane asked.

Elizabeth frowned and looked at the mantle clock for the tenth time in the last hour. "I was only wondering that Fitzwilliam has not returned from his visit."

Jane chided sweetly, "Lizzie, you said yourself he was meeting a man he has not seen in seventeen years. They must certainly have a great deal to say to one another." It was her turn to grow thoughtful. "It is not like you to worry about such a thing. Is there something you have not told me?"

Lizzie noticed that Georgiana had stopped playing and she looked from one to the other, unsure of what she should say. At last she asked Georgiana, "Has your brother ever spoken to you before of this Trevor Handley?"

"I never heard his name before yesterday when Fitzwilliam spoke of his coming at breakfast," she said thoughtfully. "I suppose it is curious that neither he nor my father ever mentioned him to me, if Mr Handley lived at Pemberley for a year and a half."

Elizabeth attempted to lighten the tone of the conversation. "I am sure there is nothing wrong. I only thought they might have returned here together by now, once they had renewed their acquaintance." She picked up her needlework in an effort to appear unconcerned.

Jane knew her sister too well to take her words at face value. "Lizzie, there *is* something you are not telling us."

Elizabeth sighed and abandoned the lightness she had feigned. "I imagine it would not hurt if I tell you that Mr Handley left Pemberley under very mysterious circumstances. The letter announcing his arrival in Lambton left Fitzwilliam unsettled, unsure of how he should understand this visit. It was for that reason he proposed they should meet at the Inn rather than at Pemberley."

While the Darcy ladies knitted their brows over the puzzle, Jane smiled with her usual optimism. "If they parted in confusion, that is all the more reason to assume that they must require a long conversation to explain it. I am sure we shall find out by dinnertime that the misunderstanding has been resolved."

Elizabeth smiled lovingly at her sister, but her eyes twinkled with mischief. "If all the world were as straightforward as you are, Jane, there would never *be* any misunderstandings to resolve. You fail to account for the varieties of temperament in the world, however, that have sometimes led men to start wars rather than reach a common ground." She laughed brightly, as unsuited to sustaining worry as her sister was unable to imagine malice.

The three settled back into their occupations, with Elizabeth determined to occupy her thoughts with something far from the Inn at Lambton. She chose the subject of Christmas, and an hour passed easily in planning the reunion that would take place when the Darcys travelled to Meryton. Mr and Mrs Gardiner were expected to make their usual visit, and Jane felt sure that Charles' sisters and Mr Hurst meant to join them. That news gave neither Elizabeth nor Georgiana any pleasure, but in light of the anticipation of festivities and engagements of the season, they did not dwell on the subject.

Elizabeth had become so engrossed in the conversation that she started at the sound of a man's footsteps in the hall. They proved to belong to Charles, returned from his fishing in high spirits. After a brief greeting, he took himself off to change and Elizabeth's eyes wandered again to the clock. Half past one was about to strike. She stood to walk to the window that overlooked the drive, admitting to herself that she had begun to worry in earnest. Georgiana soon approached and touched her sleeve gently. "Lizzie, do you think there is reason to fear something from this Mr Handley?" she asked quietly.

Elizabeth turned tenderly toward her new sister. "My dear Georgiana," she said, "I am giving you a fright with my foolishness. No, your brother assured me there was nothing to fear from him." She bit her lip as she formed the next sentence. "It is only that the subject of his childhood seems to give rise to such troubling and confused memories. I believe he both hoped and dreaded that this interview with Mr Handley might shed some light on that period of his life."

Georgiana sighed. "I do so wish I could be of some use to him on the subject. Fitzwilliam and I might just as well have had two different parents for the little I understand of his feelings toward them."

Elizabeth Darcy turned her gaze back to the window. "I believe I would like to walk down the road. Perhaps I will meet him coming back. In any case, I am far too restless to sit at embroidery." She smiled confidently. "I am sure Jane is right, and we will know by dinnertime what there is to know." Georgiana nodded, and Elizabeth went to fetch her bonnet.

Elizabeth Bennet had been known in Meryton for her unusual habit of wandering alone for hours about the countryside. She had formed this inclination at an early age, and neither her mother's scolding nor the disapproving frowns of the neighbourhood matrons could deter her from walking out in all seasons, clambering over fences or scrambling through brush, oblivious to the damage she did to petticoats and boots. Walking helped her to think and afforded her a sweet respite from the often tedious conversations of her younger sisters and mother. Once out of sight of Longbourn, her mind was free to transport her to the scenes she imagined of the great world beyond Hertfordshire.

As she stepped into the brisk autumn air, the new mistress of Pemberley paused to look at the vast estate that stretched before her, seeing it as if for the first time. The thought that she had never walked these hills without her Will at her side brought a smile to her lips, for with it came the realisation that she no longer felt the need to be alone. She set out at a brisk pace down the winding drive, so absorbed by the sights and sounds of the forest that all troubling thoughts were soon set aside.

Before she realised how far she had walked, the clearing around the lodge appeared, and with a smile she decided to call on Thomas Hill. Since their meeting on the day of her arrival at Pemberley, she had been eager to know more of the kindly lodgekeeper, and Will had answered her questions with a delight that spoke of his high regard for the man. She approached the door and knocked. She had almost decided that no one was home when the door creaked open on its massive hinges. Mr Hill narrowed his eyes at the unexpected sight of a young woman standing alone before him, and Elizabeth thought for a moment that he might be discomfited by her presence, but as she spoke his name, he realised who she was and welcomed her warmly, opening the door wide to ask her in.

"I was taking a walk and saw your house, so I thought I might stop for a moment," she said tentatively. "I hope I am not disturbing you, Mr Hill."

"Not a bit of it, Missus. I do not often have visitors here, but I am always glad of a bit of company. Ye have walked a fair piece for a young lady. I have the kettle on the fire just now. Will ye not sit down and have a cup of tea to warm ye?" he asked.

"Thank you, yes." He indicated a chair near the fire that she was sure must be his own accustomed place, but she accepted it graciously.

He moved toward the kitchen with shuffling steps, saying, "I won't be more than a minute."

Elizabeth looked around the tidy parlour, trying to imagine Fitzwilliam sitting here as a young boy. He had described the room to her, fondly recalling the welcome he always met from Mr and Mrs Hill, and from his many recollections it seemed that he had spent a good deal of time here. The thought suddenly occurred to her that Mr Hill must have known Trevor Handley as well, and she smiled - she might just learn something useful over tea. As he appeared with tea and biscuits, Elizabeth noticed the great effort it cost him to make his way to her with the tray, but she prudently made no mention of it. Having served her, he settled himself carefully into a chair facing her.

"How do ye find Pemberley, Mrs Darcy?" he asked.

"I should be quite content to never leave it, Mr Hill. I stopped here on a tour this summer with my aunt and uncle and found it enchanting, but I find that each day I discover more to delight me. I have not travelled much, but I cannot imagine there is another house so perfectly situated as Pemberley Manor."

That Thomas Hill felt a personal pride in the estate was obvious by his reaction to her words. "Aye, that is so, missus," he said, "I doubt there is a finer house to be found, nor a family more suited to care for it."

Elizabeth asked, "Have you lived all your life in these parts, Mr Hill?"

His pleasure in the conversation was evident. "Aye, that I have; I was born in this very house. My father was lodgekeeper of Pemberley before ever I saw light, and I stood up in his place when he passed."

His eyes grew dreamy. "Mrs Hill was chambermaid to the manor when first we met, and I worked the stables. Never wandered, never wanted to see further than these hills. A good life, it was," he said softly, as if he had already begun his departure from it.

Elizabeth sipped her tea and let the silence speak between them of mutual contentment. After a few minutes, she asked, "You and Mrs Hill had no children?"

He struggled back from the place his thoughts had led him. Pushing up from his chair, he offered another cup of tea, which she accepted more out of respect for his efforts than out of need. "No, no," he said, shaking his head in puzzlement, "we were never given any, although the Good Lord knows how many a time Mrs Hill prayed for the gift."

"That must have been a great disappointment for you both," observed Elizabeth gently, "for I understand from Mr Darcy that you had a wonderful way with children. My husband is very fond of remembering how welcome he always felt in your home."

Mr Hill cackled happily. "Aye, Mrs Hill was ne'er so bright as when she could set herself to feeding some young lad. Fussed and fussed, she did, over them all, but the young master, he had a special place in her heart."

"Did you know a young man named Trevor Handley who stayed at Pemberley for a time?" she asked, casually.

The question turned his head sharply. "Have ye made his acquaintance so soon, then, missus? Aye, Master Trevor and the young master were like to be brothers, I often said to Mrs Hill. Many's the time they sat right where ye be now, warming themselves on milk and tea and asking could I tell them a tale or so." His voiced trailed off and Elizabeth waited patiently as his memories spoke to him. After a long silence, he shook his head and spoke to the fire. "Strange, his name in this room after so many years. I was near enough to forgetting that lad, and up he rides, grown to manhood, asking where is Mrs Hill."

Elizabeth was startled, and could not conceal it. "Do you mean he came *here*, Mr Hill? When was that?"

Mr Hill grew suddenly wary, narrowing his eyes in a vain attempt to clear the cloud that obscured Mrs Darcy's face. Although his vision was failing, his mind was lucid and he took a moment to remember Trevor Handley as a youth, miserable and alone, stopping at the lodge to pour out his hurt to his friend as he fled Pemberley. Before he left, he had elicited a vow of secrecy, one which Mr Hill had never betrayed. Cautiously, he answered, "Master Trevor came asking after Mr Darcy, it must be two weeks past."

Noticing his discomfort, Elizabeth hastened to reassure him. "Mr Darcy has gone this morning to Lambton, to meet Mr Handley at the Inn." She pondered with a frown how the mention of that gentleman's name aroused such strong reactions, and wondered how best to proceed, but before she could reach a decision, the sound of a rider approaching interrupted her thoughts. Quickly laying her cup aside, she hurried to the door and flung it open, just in time to see Darcy riding past the lodge. With a joyful smile, she called out his name and he pulled the horse up abruptly, wheeling toward the sound of her voice.

Chapter Twenty Six

Darcy leapt down from the saddle as Elizabeth hurried out to meet him. Her eager smile faded as she recognised the tight lines of anxiety that stiffened his features, and he spoke her name in the hoarse tremolo that told her his emotions lay perilously close to erupting. Mr Hill had made his slow passage to the doorway and stood quietly waiting, wise beyond impatience. Looking from his wife to the lodgekeeper, Darcy hesitated for a moment, and then garnered the fraying ends of his self-control. Leading the horse with one hand, he took Elizabeth's hand in his other and walked towards the house. "Good day, Thomas. I see you have been entertaining my wife while I was away," he said evenly.

The old man nodded. He understood, perhaps better than the new Mrs Darcy, the tension underlying that restrained voice. "Good day to ye, Master Fitzwilliam. There's a good fire and a warm cup of tea within, if ye have a mind to set a spell." Darcy looked at Elizabeth and she raised her eyebrows encouragingly. Although she would have denied it vigorously, in her heart she had begun to shrink from the lugubrious scenes that followed any foray into his past, for they left her with a disturbing feeling of helplessness and indecision.

He nodded and said to Thomas, "I would be pleased to join the party." Elizabeth did not realise until she exhaled a quiet sigh that she had been holding her breath.

As he moved slowly towards the kitchen to refill the teapot, Thomas asked them to sit, but Darcy held Elizabeth's hand fast, as if he feared being cast adrift. They remained standing in the centre of the room, uncertainty prickling at Elizabeth's skin like a hair shirt. "I began to worry about you when you were gone for so long," she said hesitantly. He turned his head aside, unable to meet her eyes.

The quiet warmth of the room and his wife's solicitude settled around Fitzwilliam Darcy like a warm blanket. Tears formed in his eyes as he stood gazing dully into the fire. Elizabeth stepped nearer, silently speaking her compassion through her fingers, but asking no questions. His hand tightened around hers as he fought back the confusion that knotted his stomach. As the old man's return interrupted them, Elizabeth felt his grip release and she moved to her chair. Darcy quickly took the tray from Thomas' unsteady hands, the distraction sufficient, after so many years of practice, to allow him to reposition his mask of reserve. As he brought a chair to form a circle at the hearth, Mr Hill spoke purposefully. "Mrs Darcy says that Master Trevor is stopped at the Inn in Lambton. Have ye seen him then, Master Fitzwilliam?"

For several seconds, Darcy sat frozen, only the tightening muscles of his face giving evidence that he had heard the question. His wife watched him anxiously, noticing the slight trembling of the teacup in his hands. At last he spoke, with a strangled voice, "Yes, Thomas, I was with him this morning." The rattling of the teacup became audible and Elizabeth sprang up from her chair and took it from his hands, setting it on the table beside him. He looked at her with the haunted look that had frightened her in the library at Pemberley, and although she waited anxiously for his explanation, silence reigned.

"Tell me what happened, Will," she finally urged impatiently. For a long moment he looked as though the effort of speech required more energy than he could summon. Thomas Hill shook his head with resignation, as if husbanding the strength to face a long-awaited foe. Elizabeth looked from one to the other, her concern for her husband overshadowed by a growing frustration and anger. At last she could bear the tense silence no longer and she rose to her feet, addressing the room in vexation, "What am I to do with all of this silent anguish? Will I be obliged to apply to Mr Handley himself for an explanation of the curious effect his presence - even his *name* - has on the residents of Pemberley?"

Darcy looked up, his face creased with anger. "That will not be necessary, as I do not expect that after today we shall be troubled by either his presence, or by mention of him. I have settled an old account today, and I doubt that we shall see him again."

Elizabeth was alarmed by the hostility in his voice. "What are you saying? What account? And how was it settled?"

For answer, she received only a stony silence, until Mr Hill's sigh startled both of them. Pushing himself laboriously to his feet, he walked to Darcy's side and rested a hand lightly upon the young man's shoulder. The deferential tone he normally used was absent, and in its place emerged a kind but firm voice that commanded their attention. "Master Fitzwilliam," he said, "I am an old man, and my eyes have seen a good many things on this earth that I have spoken of to nary a soul. I must tell ye now that if ever ye had an enemy on this earth, 'twas not Master Trevor, for he has loved ye like a brother. If he gave ye cause for grieving, it was not of his choosing. It will not do for ye to hate him, for it will come to no good." After a dramatic pause, his voice grew tender, encouraging. "Time has come to face up to it, son. Ye have hid your face from the hurtin' since ye were a little lad, but now ye have taken a wife, and she'll be giving ye children of your own."

Darcy's shoulders trembled perceptibly as his emotions fought within him. Elizabeth stood frozen in her place, observing the drama before her incredulously, and as though they were partners in an elaborate dream, time lost its meaning, and identities appeared to shift and mutate before her.

When Darcy looked up into Thomas' eyes, his tears were falling unchecked. He surrendered his position of authority to assume the role of a supplicant, betraying his confusion and sorrow. "You have always treated me like a son, Thomas, and I respect your judgement, but Trevor told me today that he left Pemberley under orders from my father, who accused him of having an affair with my mother.

189

Would you have me believe my own father capable of making such a charge without reason?" Elizabeth gasped and turned pale, but in spite of her confusion she understood that he desperately wanted an explanation that would allow both men to emerge blameless.

Thomas led him gently through the maze. "Son, many's the time I took your father's side when your anger was like to boil over against him. He was a just man and kind, and it does ye credit that ye honour his memory. But no man was put on this earth so strong that the devil could not vex his soul if he had a mind to. Look ye into your heart, lad, and ye will know what weakness it was that troubled your father's soul. Then ye can judge fairly." Indecision furrowed Darcy's brow and he turned his face away as memory of his mother's mocking laugh crossed his mind.

Like a surgeon coaxing a reluctant patient toward a painful amputation, Thomas touched Darcy's face, gently lifting it until their eyes met again. "Do not run from the truth, son. There be nought so hard to live with as a lie."

Thomas dropped his hand to his side and returned to his chair, while Darcy stood and moved to the hearth, leaning wearily against the mantle. In the silent room, the words he spoke next resounded painfully, although they were spoken in a whisper. "I believe I begin to see, God help me." The three remained motionless, fettered by their thoughts, until the sound of a horse at full gallop disturbed the silence. The hoofbeats stopped abruptly outside the cottage and all heads turned as the massive door was flung open to reveal the comely form of the rider, silhouetted in the sunlight behind him. Only Darcy recognised immediately the identity of the intruder.

"Trevor," he said flatly.

For several seconds no one moved. At last, Trevor Handley, his eyes adjusting to the dim light of the parlour, took a step into the room, leaving the door open behind him. He seemed to see no one in the room but Darcy and between his clear hazel eyes and the

190

brooding dark ones a silent reckoning passed, invisible to Thomas Hill's dim vision and inscrutable to Elizabeth. When Trevor finally spoke, the passion of his words was veiled in a measured cadence. "After you left the Inn, I spent a long time looking for a way to ride away from Pemberley, free from the guilt I have carried for these seventeen years. I cannot undo the past, Willie, but I do not want to repeat it. Your father's anger, and mine, came between us once. He is dead, and I have made my peace, but I will not leave again until *your* anger is spent."

Trevor held Darcy's eyes in a steady gaze, and then, inexplicably, he smiled. "If you would care to strike me again, I suggest we go outside," he said calmly. "I should not like to see any of Thomas' furniture damaged."

Elizabeth had been so transfixed during Trevor's speech that she had scarcely breathed, but she gasped at his final words. Her eyes widened as she noticed for the first time the swollen redness of his jaw. Wrenching her eyes from his face to stare at Darcy, she saw a flicker of amusement relax the taut lines of his face. It was enough to release her own tension, and a loud exhalation of relief escaped her, dispelling the heaviness in the room like a rainbow after a thunderstorm.

Darcy turned to his wife sheepishly, and allowed himself a wry smile.

"I have never struck anyone before today, and I must admit it was rather painful," he said, rubbing his right hand with his left. "I don't believe I care to try it again so soon."

Trevor's hand moved up to his jaw and he winced playfully. "Well done for your first attempt, Willie boy."

Shaking his head as if he could not believe the morning's events, Darcy dropped his guard a bit further. "Many years ago you left your mark on me, Trevor Handley. It appears that the score is even."

The two men moved together as Darcy extended his hand. With a glance at Thomas Hill, he said, "I believe I owe you an apology, Trevor."

Trevor answered earnestly, "I do not fault you for your anger. I came here for your forgiveness, not your apology."

Behind his humility, Elizabeth recognised a beguiling confidence and cheerfulness that explained Darcy's youthful admiration for the man. She found herself eager to trust him, especially in light of Thomas Hill's testimony, but a quick look at her husband's face informed her that *his* doubts were not entirely satisfied. As he turned toward her, releasing Trevor's hand, she felt a flicker of impatience before remembering with a blush that she had been misguided before by first impressions. As Darcy stepped to her side and took her arm, she hoped that her face did not betray the mixture of emotions she felt.

His voice disclosed nothing. "Lizzie, I want you to meet Mr Trevor Handley. My wife, Elizabeth Darcy."

If Handley sensed Darcy's coolness, he showed no sign. With a dazzling smile, he stepped closer, his quick eyes appraising Elizabeth pleasantly, and he bowed low.

"I wish I could say, madam, that your husband told me all about you, but I must admit that we were too engrossed this morning in fond reminiscences of our youth to find time for such pleasantries. I hope you will forgive my unceremonious entrance."

"This has certainly been a day for surprises," she said, looking at Darcy quizzically. "You will pardon me, I hope, if I say that I know a good deal about *you*."

Trevor laughed easily. "You must not believe everything you hear, Mrs Darcy. I look forward to the opportunity to defend myself." He turned his attention to Thomas, who had risen from his chair to watch benevolently. Embracing him, Trevor said, "We meet again, friend. This parlour has always felt like a homecoming to me, but more so today than ever before. We only want Mrs Hill to bring in a plate piled with fresh tarts to complete the picture."

Thomas smiled. "Mrs Hill will be sorely vexed to miss such a gathering, I warrant. I will tell her all about it when we meet one of these days."

The circle around the hearth grew with the fourth chair drawn up, and Darcy was gradually stirred from his reticence by the banter that animated Thomas Hill and Trevor. Elizabeth watched with rising hopefulness as his face softened and finally relaxed into a boyish grin. She might have been content to never stir, but the striking of the mantle clock made her start. "Will," she said anxiously, "the others must be terribly worried by now that we have not returned. I had better start back."

Darcy had quite forgotten everyone but the present company in the tumult of emotions the day had brought. He rose quickly, inviting Trevor to come with them to the manor, but the man declined with a twinkling eye. "I have some business to attend to this afternoon, and if all goes well I shall have a surprise for you. May I call tomorrow?"

Elizabeth could detect no emotion in her husband's answer. "You are welcome at Pemberley." Turning to Thomas Hill, he said quietly, "I hope you will be as kind to my sons when they come searching for a refuge from their father's tyranny."

Thomas chuckled. "I doubt, sir, that your children will have the need of my meddlesome ways."

With much jostling and laughter, Elizabeth was seated precariously in front of Darcy on his horse and they headed down the lane toward the manor. As they rounded the first turn, he pulled her closer, encircling her with his arms and leaving the horse to find his way home. She bent her head back for a kiss, and it was in this awkward pose that Charles Bingley came upon them. He roared with laughter, pulling up his horse beside theirs.

"I see that you have found what you were looking for, Mrs Darcy," he said, while they tried vainly to recover some semblance of decorum.

Darcy coloured furiously but Elizabeth straightened up abruptly and assumed an icy hauteur as Charles continued to laugh.

"Young man, I shall have to insist that you cease this ridiculous display at once. If you must know," she said archly, "I was merely demonstrating for your friend that I am a remarkably versatile and flexible person."

"I daresay you have proven that, madam. I should venture to guess that you are the first Mistress of Pemberley ever to engage in romance from the back of a horse." This remark elicited a fresh outburst of laughter from both Elizabeth and Charles, but although Darcy made a valiant effort to smile, he was distracted by a sharp pain that knotted his stomach. He leaned forward involuntarily against it, bringing Elizabeth's laughter to an abrupt halt. She turned to look at his face and saw the flush had drained from it and his breathing came in quick, shallow bursts.

"Will," she said anxiously, "what is the matter?"

He pressed his hand to his stomach and forced himself to take several deep, slow breaths. After a few seconds the biting sharpness ebbed and he straightened up cautiously, forcing himself to smile. Charles had jumped to the ground and held both horses steady as he and Elizabeth studied Darcy's face. Colour returned to his cheeks as embarrassment took hold. He tried to laugh, but the attempt was not convincing.

"I'm fine," he assured them, "really. It was just a cramp." It required a tremendous effort to force from his mind the disjointed images that precipitated his distress, determined that his dark thoughts should not destroy another day's peace.

Elizabeth offered to walk the rest of the way home, but Darcy would not hear of it. Charles remounted his horse and they made their way slowly down the drive, Fitzwilliam engaging them with a forced cheerfulness in a conversation he hoped would restore their mood to its former lightness, and Elizabeth fixing her gaze studiously on the road ahead.

They dismounted at the gate and Charles insisted on leading both horses to the stable, giving husband and wife a moment alone. Elizabeth willed herself to smile brightly as she faced Darcy.

"Perhaps we should send for a doctor," she suggested, studying his face.

"Really, Lizzie, I am perfectly fine," he assured her with a fond smile. "I believe it was a clear case of overindulgence, for I have glutted myself on every possible emotion today."

He kissed her lightly on the cheek. "Let us go inside and see if it is not possible to pass the rest of the day without further incident. We have not been the ideal hosts today, and I fear we shall have to answer to our sisters for our neglect." Elizabeth was clearly not prepared to believe his simple explanation, and her mind crowded with questions about the incident at Lambton Inn, but she was forced to admit that this was not the time for discussion.

They entered the house hand in hand, and after a flutter of almost truthful explanations, the rhythm of the day reasserted itself and everyone retired to dress for dinner. Charles, never one to dwell on troubling thoughts, was soon reassured that his friend suffered no ill effects from the incident on the road, and put it easily out of his mind.

Pleading fatigue, Darcy and Elizabeth retired early that evening, and over a bottle of claret in their sitting room, he filled in for her all the missing pieces from the morning's puzzle. He spoke with a calm composure that stirred in her a hope that the day's efforts would close the chapter on his dark reminiscences. Yet, as she listened quietly, a nagging thread of doubt wove itself into his tale. If Trevor Handley's account of the circumstances of his exile were true, what had led the old master of Pemberley to such a gross miscarriage of justice? She did not doubt that questions still gnawed at her husband's mind, but prudence and experience suggested she accept for the time being his obvious intention to set aside gloomy thoughts.

A movement by her side brought her wandering thoughts back to the candlelit room and she looked up to see Darcy standing beside her, watching her intently. She smiled and rose from her chair, reaching up to caress the unruly curls. "What mystery are you pondering behind those unfathomable eyes?" she whispered.

Enfolding her gently in his arms, he buried his face in her hair. "I am thinking how impossible it is that you love me," he breathed in her ear.

"As impossible as the rising and setting of the sun, and as unlikely to end," she murmured.

Chapter Twenty Seven

Trevor Handley arrived as promised the following afternoon, flushed and happy. His exuberant optimism, with no hint from Darcy to the contrary, led him to assume that the long-standing impediment to his contentment had been removed and within half an hour of his arrival he had laid the foundation for an easy camaraderie with the Darcys and their guests.

At the lodge the previous day, Elizabeth Darcy had been moved by his tenacious pursuit of reconciliation, but was too distracted by the emotions of the day to form a clear opinion of his personality. Today, as they sat down to tea, she was at leisure to observe him more calmly, and she noticed that the effect of his frank good humour and enthusiasm was to render their party even more talkative and jovial than usual. Georgiana warmed to him as she seldom did to a stranger, which in itself would have been sufficient recommendation of his charms, but it was for Darcy's sake that Elizabeth studied Trevor Handley's every word and gesture.

The two men did not often speak directly to one another, but more than once during the afternoon she saw their eyes meet and hold, and she imagined the space between them bridged by a stream of memories. It was the way she communicated with Jane in a crowded room, ever alert to her sister's thoughts and emotions, and with no need of words to explain what was obvious to each. She suddenly wondered how she might have felt if she had been forcibly parted from her sister at a young age, and the thought opened a new perspective for her on her husband's dark moods. She glanced at Jane, as if to reassure herself, and found her sister's eyes resting tenderly on her. She smiled gratefully, then turned her eyes back to Trevor, who was just opening the subject of his business in Lambton.

He asked Darcy with an enigmatic smile, "Do you remember when we rode with your father to Croftwoods to buy that magnificent black?"

Darcy nodded. "Of course. Mr Kingsley was known in those days as the finest breeder in Derbyshire. As I recall, father nearly had to rope you to drag you away from his stable." He laughed. Darcy explained to the others with an indulgent smile, "Trevor was, as a young man, far more interested in horses than in people, I recall."

"I still am, present company excluded," he said cheerfully. "I understand them far better, at any rate. Kingsley died several years ago and his only son has the estate, but his interest in horses always tended more towards betting than breeding. Unfortunately, his enthusiasm was unmatched by his luck, and, as I am sure you know, Willie, he has had to sell off most of his stable in the last few years to settle his debts. I met him a year ago at my cousin's house, quite by chance, and over an enormous quantity of excellent wine, he intimated to me that he intended to sell Croftwoods." His final words were spoken tentatively, with his eyes locked on Darcy's face. "I bought it yesterday."

Elizabeth could not stifle a tiny gasp, as the rest of the group murmured their approval. She attempted to intercept the messages flowing between the two men, but while Trevor's face showed clearly that he asked for approval, Darcy's dark eyes gave no clear answer. "You mean to live at Croftwoods?" he asked evenly. To Trevor's nodded assent, he answered, "I could not be more pleased."

Trevor Handley looked out the window with a contented smile. "Nor could I. In my heart, I was never far from the hills of Derbyshire. I have thought it the most beautiful countryside in England from my first ride to Pemberley."

While the others plied him with questions about his plans, Elizabeth turned her eyes to Darcy's silent face. He wore a pleasant enough look and returned her smile warmly when he noticed she watched him. If perhaps there was a hint in his eyes of sorrow or confusion, she might be pardoned for not seeing it, for having carefully weighed the evidence, she had decided to thoroughly enjoy the company of Mr Trevor Handley. She gave her attention to his description of the neglected house and stables, and it soon became obvious that he intended to stay at Lambton Inn while arranging for the necessary renovations. Whether of his own accord or if prompted by Elizabeth's meaningful look, Darcy cordially declared, "You must move here at once, Trevor. It will suit you far better, and I daresay Charles and I might be able to be of assistance in your work."

Trevor Handley was thus established at Pemberley Manor as one of the family, and in the absence of any evidence to the contrary, Elizabeth concluded that her husband had satisfied himself about any doubts he might have had. For the next several days the three men spent a good deal of time galloping about the countryside or closeted in the library, caught up in a growing web of plans and arrangements. Trevor intended to be settled at Croftwoods immediately, an ambition which required a great deal of energy on the part of all three. In the evenings, they brought a boyish exuberance to the drawing room, and the hours passed pleasantly with music and cards and the enjoyment of intelligent conversation among equals. In a few days time, with work well under way and Darcy's promise to oversee the workmen, Trevor took leave to finalise his affairs in the north.

In the days that followed, a quieter group settled in the drawing room of an evening. The demands of his estate and frequent trips to Croftwoods kept Darcy occupied, with Charles close at his side, and Elizabeth turned a more determined effort to Mrs Hatfield's benevolent schemes, but in the early dark of the early winter days, Trevor's exuberance was missed. Neither Georgiana nor Jane had much enthusiasm for cards, and lacking a foursome, reading, music and quiet conversation became the entertainments of choice.

One evening, in response to Darcy's request that she sing, Elizabeth replied impishly, "I should have thought everyone would be quite weary of my voice by this time. I shall only sing on the condition that all of you join me." With a look of determination that Jane recognised very well, she rose and moved to the library of music and chose several sheets of simple and well-known melodies. Setting them on the pianoforte, she glanced about the room expectantly.

Jane laughed as she set her book aside, saying to Charles, "You may as well leap up with enthusiasm, my dear, for once Lizzie has set her jaw in that manner, she *will* be obeyed."

Charles rose, and with a gallant bow in Lizzie's direction, quipped, "I would not for a moment refuse your sister any wish, but I daresay she may wish another thing once she has heard my voice."

With considerable laughter and protesting, everyone gathered at last behind the pianoforte. Georgiana was commanded to preside over the keyboard and Elizabeth stationed herself beside her husband, holding his arm in a tight grip to prevent his flight. After a long discussion of the relative merits of this ballad and that, the voices of all five were finally blended in song. Bingley was an eager, if not skilled, tenor and Jane, although more reticent than her sister, was induced to rouse herself to a pleasant soprano. The surprise of the evening, as much to himself as to the others, was Fitzwilliam Darcy's contribution.

His voice at first was so soft that Elizabeth had to look at him to be assured he was actually singing, but by the second song, he found himself enjoying the harmony, and unleashed an impressive baritone. Georgiana was so astonished by the sound of it that she made several uncharacteristic fingering mistakes, but they went unnoticed in the general merriment. At the end of the song she turned to face her brother with her cheeks flushed in pleasure.

"In all of my eighteen years I have never heard you sing, Fitzwilliam. Why have you kept this talent so much a secret?"

Embarrassed by such attention, he stammered, "I had forgotten it could be so pleasant." Elizabeth squeezed his arm and called for another song, which began with even more enthusiasm. Mrs Reynolds, passing by the open door of the drawing room, allowed herself the momentary indiscretion of pausing to listen, astonished by what she heard. She smiled in remembrance of Fitzwilliam as a very small boy, his voice so sweet as he sang to himself in the nursery. She could not remember when he had stopped singing and did not permit herself to think about the reason, although she knew better than she would ever have admitted the nature of the sorrow that had dampened his young spirit. She contented herself with a smile of approval for the young lady who had made yet another improvement in the atmosphere of Pemberley. Once having begun, Darcy became an eager participant, and from time to time he could even be heard humming to himself as he moved about the house.

With the dirty weather of winter settled in, Jane and Elizabeth availed themselves of the frequent absence of their husbands to closet themselves together, as Georgiana was often engrossed in her music. One morning, Elizabeth said to Jane with a sigh, "I always wished for a brother, and now I suddenly find myself with two. If only you were to live near us, Jane, we could always have such lovely evenings. Trevor will soon be back. Are you sure you could not extend your stay for a few more days? I would so love you to meet the Alexander family."

Jane smiled in her peaceful way, always ready to find the bright side. "I think, Lizzie, that you and Mr Darcy shall be happy for a little quiet time together before more company arrives. And I do long to see Mother and Father and Mary and Kitty. How quiet it must be at Longbourn now, since you and Lydia are not there to entertain," she said with a little laugh. "In any case, Charles and I must really settle ourselves at Netherfield House. It seems so very strange to think that I shall go there as his wife." There was a quiet space while the two of them contemplated the gains and losses of their married lives. Jane finally said, straightening herself a little, "We must invite Charles' sisters and Mr Hurst to come down as soon as we reach home. I am determined to make them feel entirely at ease with me."

Elizabath looked up at Jane through her eyelashes with a slightly sceptical turn to her mouth. "I don't suppose you care to hear my opinion on *that* subject again, Jane. I shall only say that in spite of your very charming sweetness, I hope you will have the good sense to see them for who they are, not who you would like to believe them. You are not obliged, my dear, to be so good to everyone."

Jane protested vehemently, "Lizzie, please do not think me so foolish as to have forgotten the fact that, at one time, they wanted desperately to keep me from Charles. But people change, and by now they are quite resigned to our marriage, I'm sure. They will see, with time, that he is happy, and I am certain that is what they would wish for him."

Elizabeth placated her with a squeeze of the hand. "You mustn't mind me, Jane. If anyone is able to bring out the lamb in the lion, it is you. I am only glad that I am not the one called upon to be gracious to them. I would not last a week." They laughed together, even Jane being unable to argue *that* point.

Chapter Twenty Eight

Lady Margaret Westby had resolved, upon hearing of Fitzwilliam Darcy's marriage, to make her displeasure known by withholding her attention from Pemberley, and she had instructed her husband and friends to do likewise. Much to her chagrin, she began to hear reports that first one and then another paragon of social virtue had been overcome by curiosity and had called on Mr and Mrs Darcy. More irritating still was the fact that some came away from their visits disarmed by Mrs Darcy's manners and quite prepared, until Lady Margaret prevailed on them to see the error in it, to invite her into their own homes.

With a good deal of indignant sniffing, the Lady decided that it was incumbent upon her to uphold the standards of her class and take a more direct approach in her censure, as it was unlikely, with so many defections, that Fitzwilliam Darcy would have understood the full import of his error. It was not her habit to succumb to impulses, and so she closeted herself in her private sitting room one morning to thoughtfully review all pertinent facts before deciding on her course of action. She could expect no help from her family, as her daughter's dullness bewildered and infuriated her, and her husband was a man, and therefore, by nature, incapable of understanding the subtleties of the social order.

As she paced silently, she was forced to stop at this thought. Fitzwilliam Darcy, of all men of her acquaintance, was the one least likely, in her estimation, to break the ranks of custom. More than any boy in the neighbourhood, he had absorbed his mother's thoughts and made them his own. The memory of Lady Anne Darcy raised a longing still painful in Lady Margaret's breast, for since her death she had suffered under a drought of intelligent companionship that had nearly claimed her will to live. She closed her eyes against the thought of their spirited conversations and hearty laughter, wishing for a moment that she could forget how her life had been enriched by her friend. The thought passed quickly as she realised that those memories were what remained of sanity in her life, and she allowed her mind to rest on the image of Anne Darcy's flashing eyes and insolent smile.

Lady Margaret permitted herself the indulgence of many minutes of reminiscing before she recalled her attention to the task at hand. Her face, softened and almost mirthful a moment ago, recovered its look of indignation. Lady Anne would never have tolerated such a marriage as Fitzwilliam had made, and since she could not speak for herself on the subject, Lady Margaret would have to speak for her. The question that stayed her for the moment was how Fitzwilliam had strayed into such an alliance. Although Lady Margaret had carefully avoided showing the slightest interest in the woman who had appeared at his side in church, she was curiously able to draw from her memory a detailed portrait of the insolent young thing. She was not so unreasonable as to refuse to admit that the woman was handsome. In fact, there was something about her exotic good looks faintly reminiscent of Lady Anne herself.

She contemplated that thought for a moment. It had been her experience that men were sadly lacking in the power to discern true value in women. Only an intelligent woman possessed of a plain face can fully appreciate the truth of that observation. Perhaps she had given Fitzwilliam Darcy too much credit, for although she had deemed him uncommonly intelligent, and more attuned than most men to the importance of good breeding, he was, after all, still a man, and therefore vulnerable to the charms of a pretty woman. That some of her friends, even those to whom she had ascribed strong powers of reason, had found the young lady not totally devoid of charm, attested to the fact that she possessed an uncommon advantage over the average woman of her class.

Pulling herself up grandly, Lady Margaret said aloud, "You shall find, my dear, that your spell can be broken. You have reached too high, and you shall be brought down."

With these heady words still ringing in her ears, the Lady rang imperiously for a servant to order her carriage, for she had resolved to speak to Fitzwilliam Darcy without delay. She would have departed her estate in a mood of complete confidence had she not met Cassandra on the stair, begging to know where she was going. When she informed her icily that she was going to Pemberley, the silly girl asked leave to come along, hoping to make the acquaintance of Mr Darcy's pretty wife. With a snort of disgust, her mother said, "Cassandra, if you are not able to learn some discernment, you will never be permitted to leave the house again." She pushed past her, leaving the poor girl with her customary look of painful bewilderment, and gained the outside air before she paused to heave a sigh of consternation.

It required the entire journey to Pemberley for Lady Margaret to recover her singularity of purpose, but her energy was slightly depleted by the effort and her sense of moral outrage toward Elizabeth Darcy was hampered by the knowledge that she had a daughter herself who caused her to blush with embarrassment.

The announcement in the drawing room that Lady Margaret Westby had come to call raised an uneasy spectre in the mind of Fitzwilliam Darcy. He had begun to hope she would never come, for as his mother's closest confidante, he had little doubt of her opinion on the subject of his marriage. Casting an uneasy look at Elizabeth as he asked the butler to show her in, Darcy wished he had prepared her more fully for this visit.

Elizabeth did not fail to notice the frown on Darcy's brow, and she rose to move to his side, wearing a jaunty smile of reassurance and reminding herself of their laughter after the last difficult visitor. She did not count on their visitor's fierce resolve. Sweeping imperiously into the room, she made not the slightest attempt at civility toward Elizabeth or the Bingleys. She nodded to Georgiana, dismissing her with an abrupt 'Good afternoon, Georgiana' and turned her attention directly to Darcy. As he began some vacuous civility, she interrupted him.

"I should like to speak to you in private, Fitzwilliam." Georgiana's mouth opened in amazement at hearing her brother addressed with such lack of decorum, and Jane dropped her needlework in alarm. Only Charles maintained his characteristically bemused expression and he turned graciously to Jane, offering her his hand. She hesitated for a second, but then gathered her sewing and with a questioning look at her sister, left the room on his arm.

Elizabeth's indignation far surpassed her fear of a scene, and she willed herself instantly into a pose of icy calm and waited for her husband's reaction. Georgiana would have fled like a frightened gazelle had her trembling knees permitted, but since flight was out of the question, she gripped the back of a chair, hardly daring to breathe and look to her brother for guidance. Darcy stiffened and looked directly into the angry eyes before him, and then turned slowly to look first at Elizabeth and then at Georgiana. Coming back to Lady Margaret, he said firmly, "There is nothing that you might say to me that cannot be said in front of my wife or my sister, if they choose to stay. Please have a chair, madam."

She gave her tiny snort of disapproval before answering. "I merely wished to spare you some embarrassment, as I mean to speak frankly, but you may suit yourselves." She seemed to consider for a moment and then took the chair he had indicated. Georgiana stood frozen for an instant and then eased herself soundlessly into her chair while Darcy, with a display of gentle attention, took Elizabeth's arm and led her slowly to a sofa facing the lady. They sat down and waited for her to speak.

Lady Margaret's carefully planned speech was delayed briefly as she adjusted herself to the change of venue. Not easily daunted by impudence, she regained her composure quickly and began speaking directly to Darcy, as if the other two inhabitants of the room were part of the furnishings.

"I have known you since the day of your birth, Fitzwilliam, and I was as close to your mother as a beloved sister, so there is no need for either of us to adopt a tone of false reserve. I have searched in my heart and have come to the conclusion that it is my duty as your mother's friend to express my distress and bewilderment that you have so dishonoured yourself and your mother's memory by not complying with her wish that you marry your cousin, Miss de Bourgh."

Darcy responded with an equally calm determination. "I believe that my mother's concern was for my happiness." Taking his wife's hand in a firm hold, he continued, "She would be pleased, I assure you, to know that Miss Elizabeth Bennet has indeed made me the happiest of men by consenting to be my wife."

Lady Margaret replied coldly, "Do not be impertinent with me, young man. You know as well as I what your mother's response would have been to such an unfortunate alliance as you have chosen to make. You are, to be sure, of age, and are free to follow the dictates of temporal pleasure if you so choose," she looked Elizabeth over scornfully from head to foot, "but I am surprised to see such a lack of regard for the honour and reputation of Pemberley and for the name of Darcy. I am quite sure that the passage of time will arouse in you a proper sensibility of what you have forsaken."

Darcy's face masked the outrage that his grip on his wife's hand betrayed. He was not unaware that his composure would only serve to heighten the Lady's indignation.

"Madam, please do not be troubled for my future happiness. I assure you that I have given this decision considerable thought, and have determined that by marrying Miss Bennet I have done neither a disservice to myself nor to my family. Quite the contrary, in fact, for I think Georgiana would agree that Pemberley is greatly improved by the presence of its new mistress."

Elizabeth remained silent, her eyes fixed unflinchingly on Lady Margaret's face. Georgiana, if she had always been unnerved by this formidable woman, was near tears at this moment. Only her brother's confidence and Elizabeth's stoic composure prevented her from collapse. She fixed her gaze on the two of them, carefully avoiding the face of their tormentor, but had she looked, she might have noticed that the tone of the conversation was giving that Lady as little pleasure as it did the three young people.

"I see, Fitzwilliam, that you do not intend to acknowledge your mistake. I had not expected that from you." She turned her narrowed eyes to Elizabeth. "I imagine, Miss Bennet, that you must be congratulating yourself on attaining a position so far above what your circumstances warrant. I wish to caution you, however, that the title of 'Mistress of Pemberley' cannot and will not be applied to you by those of your neighbours with a proper respect for the natural qualifications required of the bearer of that honour."

As Georgiana's fear began to give way to indignation, Darcy's temper flared dangerously. Only the deep impression of Elizabeth's fingernails on his hand stayed an eruption and he turned his face to study hers. A hint of amusement showed through the blazing in her eyes and with eyebrows raised in anticipation, he ceded her the floor. Looking calmly into the face of her enemy, Elizabeth spoke quietly but with a conviction that reverberated through the room. "You have deigned to judge me without troubling yourself to know me, and I cannot find it in my heart to feel abashed by such unwarranted scorn. I have the advantage of knowing a good deal about your opinions, and I ask that you allow me to state mine, so that you may base your dislike on a foundation of fact."

Lady Margaret drew in a sharp breath and began to rise from her chair, but Elizabeth stopped her with a commanding voice. "You have taken the trouble to come this far. Let us not conclude this interview without reaching a complete understanding of one another." She paused for a moment, and taking silence for acquiescence, continued calmly, "If the standards of elevated breeding require a complete lack of good manners and a willingness to meddle in the private affairs of one's neighbours, I must admit to being ill-qualified."

To Elizabeth's delight, the Lady proved herself a more able adversary than she had expected. With narrowed eyes, she sat back in her chair and allowed the speech continue, carefully scrutinising Mrs Darcy as she spoke.

"In the past few months I have been introduced to the lofty opinions of several persons of consequence whose behaviour makes me blush with shame for the British aristocracy. If it is your intention to facilitate my exclusion from that illustrious company, I must, on the strength of past experience, offer you my heartfelt appreciation. I can only hope that my position as the wife of Mr Darcy does not cause me to forget the standards of decent human conduct with which I was raised. As a good friend of my husband's mother, you deserve my respect and affection, and I am quite willing to begin our acquaintance anew should you wish to enter my home in the same spirit."

A slight flaring of the nostrils gave evidence to the distaste with which Lady Margaret viewed her opponent. When she spoke, her voice was controlled, but she allowed her mouth to twist into an unbecoming sneer. "You may rest assured that I will not trouble you for your respect or affection, as they can be of no consequence to me. Furthermore, I do not wonder that a woman from your background should mistake impudence for good manners, nor do I expect you to understand the responsibility attendant upon the heir to Pemberley to maintain the standards of our society." She shifted her gaze to Darcy. "I do, however, expect more from *you*, Fitzwilliam. I asked to speak to you privately for that reason. My intention, I believe, is clear, and that is to discharge my duty to your mother's memory. Since I find you so utterly insensible of *your* duty, I will say nothing further on the subject." She rose to leave.

Darcy stood up and walked quickly to the door, reaching it ahead of her. He turned to stop her, a terrible anger contorting his features. The Lady stepped back involuntarily, eyes widened in alarm as he spoke in a hoarse emotional voice.

"As much as it gives me pain to admit it, I see that you certainly do speak with my mother's convictions. Her arrogance and utter disregard for the feelings of others has done me a tremendous disservice, and I begin to understand that it nearly destroyed my father as well. If it is my welfare that you seek, you will do me the kindness of taking her memory with you when you leave. It has darkened Pemberley's halls for too many years."

As Lady Margaret blanched in horror at his invective, Elizabeth reached his side and, taking his hand, said his name softly. "Will." At the sight of her reassuring smile his anger abated, and he spoke in a gentler voice, without taking his eyes from Elizabeth's face. "This woman has suffered enough indignity at the hands of my family and friends; I will not allow her to be further maligned in the name of duty or honour or any of the other pitiful excuses that people of our *supposed* station use in defence of their bad manners." He had by this time visibly relaxed. He put his arm around Elizabeth's shoulder and they turned to face their accuser.

Darcy said, "Please excuse my anger - I did not mean to frighten you. Your opinions are your own, but I do implore you to rethink their premise. My mother was wrong in thinking herself above all others, and I was wrong to adopt her principles without examination. I will never allow those sentiments to be expressed at Pemberley again, for as long as I live."

Lady Margaret was rendered speechless, a condition she found novel, to say the least. Mr and Mrs Darcy stepped back to allow her to pass, which she hastened to do, for her nerves were in a dreadful state, and she hurried out to her carriage, not waiting for the butler to reach the door ahead of her.

Elizabeth rewarded Darcy's effort with a kiss and a feeling of giddy relief swept across the room like brush fire. The sound of the door brought Jane and Charles hurrying from the library where they had ensconced themselves. Charles quipped, "Good Lord, man, what have you done to make that woman so angry? I was standing ready to send for the surgeon if needed."

Darcy smiled, never letting go of Elizabeth's hand, "She does not approve my choice of wife."

Elizabeth added sardonically, "With the exception of my last interview with Lady Catherine de Bourgh, I don't know when I have so thoroughly enjoyed the pleasure of being found scandalously wanting in all good graces. I trust once Lady Margaret has reported on my inferiority to our neighbours we shall find ourselves left very much alone, Will."

"That will suit me very well. When I have the opportunity to observe the manners of some of England's finest families, it leads me to wish I had been born a simple farmer."

"I trust that no one could have found fault had I aspired to be a farmer's wife. In fact, judging from our neighbour's appraisal, I would say she would have found me most suited to that calling," said Elizabeth playfully.

Darcy noticed Georgiana's silence. "What do you say, my dear sister? Can you imagine any position to which our Lizzie would not bring a most becoming air of respectability?"

Georgiana was confounded by the apparent easiness of their banter and was pleased to be included, although she was still feeling weak from the scene she had witnessed. "Indeed, Lizzie, you amaze me with your good humour. I would have fled the room in tears had I been in your place!"

Elizabeth smiled at her vexation. "I must confess it did occur to me to do just that, but my bad temper always prevents me from giving satisfaction to any ill-mannered attempt to disconcert me."

Darcy laughed, "I like your bad temper very much, as long as it is directed at someone other than me."

"Yes, I do recollect that I have had the opportunity to withstand a similar confidence from you on the subject of my suitability," Elizabeth answered saucily.

Charles joined in the fun. "Now that you mention it, I recall that Darcy once waxed exceedingly eloquent on that subject."

Colouring at the memory, Darcy said, "Lady Margaret, I hope, will profit as much from your lecture on good manners as I have."

"She has not the advantage, I fear, of being madly in love with me to allow her to benefit from my disapproval," said Elizabeth.

Jane had been standing by in silent amazement, but her curiosity at last urged her to insist on hearing the story in its entirety. With much laughter and posturing, Elizabeth and Fitzwilliam began retelling the terrible tale, interrupting one another frequently to correct errors of pose and elocution, although in unspoken confederacy they omitted all reference to Darcy's angry denunciation of his mother. Georgiana was baffled by their playful references to the past, and deeply troubled by her brother's portrait of Mrs Darcy, but she eventually succumbed to the mood of merriment, grateful to see equilibrium reasserted.

Lady Margaret, well aware that her words had fallen short of their mark, could scarcely have imagined the scene of hilarity that followed her exit from the room. She had found nothing even remotely amusing in her own evaluation of the visit, and arrived home in a most foul temper, with a pounding head that threatened to ruin the remainder of the day. That she was too intelligent to deny that she had been bested was scarcely consolation.

Having spent themselves on the afternoon's emotions, the denizens of Pemberley finally wearied of the topic, and it was formally ended by Elizabeth's pert declaration, "If you will all excuse me for a little while, I will go and repair my shattered self-respect with a nap."

"I shall follow you, picking up the pieces along the way," Darcy declared gallantly.

Chapter Twenty Nine

Once alone in the tranquillity of their sitting room, Elizabeth and Darcy collapsed onto the sofa, exhausted with the emotions of the day. Elizabeth rested her head against her husband's shoulder, held close by his encircling arms, until the last waves of ebullience drained from her body, leaving her weak and trembling. As his arms tightened about her and his cheek rested on her hair, a belated grief was unleashed and she began to weep, her hot, silent tears dropping unchecked onto his chest. His anguish left him paralysed; lacking the words to comfort her, he cradled her to his breast in silent misery.

Darcy finally became sensible of the fact that Elizabeth had fallen asleep. He allowed himself to smile at the sight of her curled against him, breathing peacefully, and inched himself into a more suitable position so that she might rest comfortably. As he breathed the scent of her hair and felt her soft warm frame nestled in his arms, a resolve began to grow within him that while he could not protect her from the rest of the world, she should at least suffer no more from the rampant fluctuations of *his* mood that had marred the first weeks of their married life. Her strength and good humour, he realised, had allowed him to indulge his selfishness and to forget her happiness.

By the time she stirred in his arms, the room had grown dark, but the passage of the afternoon's last light had kindled in Fitzwilliam Darcy a zealous hope that he could yet become the man she loved. She drifted into wakefulness at last, and a sensation of peace flooded over her as she felt the strength of his arms and the calm beating of his heart beneath her head. She turned her face up to his and, with a tiny sob of relief and passion, offered a kiss which he eagerly returned, and all thought of remorse and sorrow fled before their fervent lovemaking.

At last they grew very still, exhausted by the eloquence of their love, allowing lazy thoughts to drift between them. Darcy finally broke the silence with a quiet vow. "If it is within my power, no one shall enter this house again unless they intend to show you the respect you deserve, Lizzie. I should not have permitted her to speak in your presence, for I knew what her opinion would be."

Elizabeth answered thoughtfully, "You cannot keep me safe from the malice of small minds, Will. It was my choice to stay and hear her out, for I thought myself impervious to that kind of attack. The tears I shed were not so much for her scorn as they were for the tremendous burden you carry. I cannot reconcile myself to the harm that was done to you by your parents."

"I am not sure that it can so easily be explained, Lizzie. I cannot free myself of the thought that somehow, in a way I have not yet understood, *I* was to blame for *their* misery," he said. "There are still pieces of the puzzle which elude me, and although I vow to myself again and again to lay the past to rest, it haunts me at every turn. Perhaps old Thomas is right that I must face up to the truth, but I fear there may be parts of it that I do not wish to hear. In any case, I don't really know how to uncover it."

Elizabeth sat up quickly, her face eager and animated. "Will, why not talk to Georgiana? She may know something of your father that you have not seen. In any case, if her face today was any indication, she longs to understand the past - and her mother - as much as you do. I don't believe you have ever really confided in her the depth of your feelings."

Darcy answered in mock seriousness, "Can you blame me for this omission, Lizzie? Georgiana is the one person in my life who has shown me unflagging support. I should not like her to see me as I really am."

Elizabeth's reply was sincere. "I doubt that you credit enough the strength of her affection for you, Will. Surely she has a right to be informed about her parents, and perhaps you could benefit from her perspective. Sometimes it is the quiet observer who sees the most."

216

"I have feared prejudicing her against either our parents or myself. I suppose I am not used to thinking of her as an adult yet," he said thoughtfully.

"Of course, it is only natural that you should feel protective towards her. But she is very eager to know you as an equal, and I believe as her judgement matures, it would be helpful to her to know that you have doubts and confusion too. With her insight added to what you may learn from Trevor Handley and Mr Alexander, perhaps you *will* one day feel that you understand."

Darcy planted a kiss on his wife's forehead, saying as he rose, "I shall try, but it will certainly require some practice for me to speak plainly. We had better go downstairs now or they will be sending an emissary after us."

Later that evening, Darcy did find a quiet moment to speak privately to Georgiana, and he broached, a trifle nervously, the subject of their afternoon visitor. She was eloquent on the topic, especially in defence of her new sister, Lizzie. With a glance to make sure they were not overheard, she said, of Lady Margaret, "That woman has frightened me since I was a child, but I have never heard her speak with such rancour as she did today. How I wish Lizzie had not been subjected to such a display of ill will. Fitzwilliam," she continued, her brow furrowing in thought, "I know you have said she came often when Mother was alive, but I cannot imagine that she was ever welcomed into this house." She carefully avoided mentioning the part of the interview which most troubled her, her brother's angry denunciation of their mother.

Fitzwilliam studied her face carefully and then said, "Georgiana, I think it is time for me to be more candid than I have been with you. Will you come with me to the library so we may speak more privately?"

Georgiana looked slightly alarmed, but nodded quickly. Brother and sister excused themselves and moved silently down the hall, both discomfited by this deviation from their usual roles, but each harbouring an expectation of release. Not sure how to begin, Fitzwilliam Darcy paced the library floor for a few minutes while Georgiana waited. At last, she prodded, "You wanted, I think, to tell me something about our mother, Fitzwilliam."

Darcy was startled by her question, as his thoughts had wandered far from that subject. "I was just thinking," he began hesitantly, "how my own behaviour has caused grief." With growing resolve, he described his state of mind before meeting Elizabeth, not sparing the uncomfortable disclosure that his proud and arrogant thoughts had been disturbingly similar to the words they had heard today from Lady Margaret. Without the benefit of Elizabeth's gentle humour, his narration and her reaction were rather sombre, but although she was surprised by what she heard, it soon became clear to him that he need not have feared any loss of her esteem. Her eagerness to understand and the thoughtful responses she gave made him conscious that he had done her a disservice by not sharing himself more honestly with her, and he was encouraged to reveal more than he had intended.

His confession led him finally to the subject of his mother's temperament, and Georgiana listened intently, eager to hear what had always been hidden from her. Having discerned from a very young age that neither her father nor her brother were predisposed to speak about Mrs Darcy, she had formed her opinion of that lady from the portraits in the house and the information of other relatives. Without disrespect, but with a refreshing honesty, Fitzwilliam now tried to convey to his sister his recent understanding of their mother's pride and arrogance. The portrait he drew was disturbing in its resemblance to their Aunt, Lady Catherine de Bourgh, and to today's unpleasant visitor. Speaking of the deterioration of her feelings toward her husband, he admitted the effect her strong will had on forming his own opinions, and on the distance this had placed between himself and his father, concluding that the restlessness he had previously felt at Pemberley grew from this confusion.

As he finally paused in his narrative, she took his hand tenderly in hers and said, with a strength of feeling and understanding that astonished him, "Dear Fitzwilliam, I am sorry you have been so lonely." The emotion behind her words brought tears to both of their eyes and she struggled with her thoughts before continuing. "I hope you will not be offended by my saying that although I have always been grateful to you for your kind attention and concern, I have never felt able to talk to you about my feelings or your own. I am sure it has been difficult for you to find yourself burdened by the responsibility both for my care and the management of the estate since Father's death. I only hope now that I am grown that you will allow me to share the weight of those responsibilities and the pleasure of knowing you as I think a sister should."

Fitzwilliam was moved by her eloquence, and shook his head sadly. "I have done you great damage. I did not want to involve you in the darkness of my thoughts, but I see now that instead of protecting you from my sorrow, I have burdened you more by withholding my feelings than if I had shared them."

Georgiana shook her head ruefully. "We have been so polite and so distant from one another."

"Yes," he replied. "I am beginning to understand how little honesty this house has known."

"Fitzwilliam," Georgiana said earnestly, "I still do not fully understand something. From your account of our mother and my knowledge of Father, it appears that their temperaments were so ill-suited to one another that they must have had a very unhappy marriage. Was it always like that, from the beginning?"

He grew more solemn and rubbed his forehead, considering her question. After a long silence he looked up at her and his smile only thinly disguised the discomfort he felt.

"There are many things I don't understand myself. Things I saw and heard as a child have begun to take on new meaning for me now that I have begun to allow myself to wonder about them. I confess I have, for many years, avoided thinking about our parents. But now that I am married, I feel I need to make my peace with their memory or risk a recurrence of the melancholy it has often caused me. I cannot bear to have them intrude on the happiness of the present, for all of our sakes, but I cannot see how to proceed to uncover the parts of their history that are unknown to me. I feel as though I have pieces of a puzzle in my hand, but I cannot yet see the picture."

They both remained lost in private contemplation for some time, and then Darcy roused himself to manage a stronger smile. "Let us not be gloomy, Georgiana. We have made a good beginning in setting things to right at Pemberley. I feel sure that with time we will banish all the ghosts, but for today it is enough that we took on Lady Margaret." They laughed together at this thought, and Darcy patted Georgiana's arm. "Meanwhile, we had better take very good care of Lizzie, as we have need of her presence in our lives." Georgiana gave her enthusiastic assent and they said goodnight, but it was a very long time before she moved from her chair.

By the time Darcy opened the library door, everyone had retired to their rooms for the night. He found Elizabeth engrossed in a book in their private sitting room. She looked up and smiled inquisitively as he entered the room and closed the door behind him, waiting to hear the report of his long conversation with Georgiana. He came and stood in front of her chair and, taking her book, set it on the table beside them. Then, to her great surprise, he knelt on the floor in front of her and picked up her hands, kissing each in turn.

"My dear Mrs Darcy," he said tenderly, "you are quite the light of our lives. Georgiana and I both heartily entreat you never to leave us, for we could not bear to be left alone with our neighbours." They laughed together and he got to his feet, pulling her up to him to seal his petition with a warm embrace that soon led to a most passionate renewal of the pleasure that Lady Margaret had spoken of so scornfully.

While that Lady was quite correct in supposing that Darcy's love for Elizabeth blinded him to all other thoughts, she was wrong in thinking anything could or should be of greater importance to him. When they lay quietly together in their bed, Darcy mused, "I hate to admit that you were quite right about Georgiana. I have been adequate as a guardian but remiss as a brother. I am afraid it did not occur to me before that she has been as alone as I these many years."

Elizabeth caressed his unruly locks, engaging his dark eyes with hers. "I know she does not blame you for any omission, Will, but I am sure it will be a great comfort to her to be more in your confidence."

He smiled sleepily and said, "I wonder where my guardian angel lay sleeping before he roused himself to bring you to me, my love."

Chapter Thirty

The departure of the Bingleys was an unpleasant topic for everyone, but with reluctant farewells and plans to reunite at Christmas in Meryton, the couple took their leave. Elizabeth Darcy's frequent letters to her family since the wedding had been filled with descriptions of domestic felicity, and her father especially delighted in the unmistakable evidence of contentment they contained, but they were scant consolation for the loss of his daughters' companionship. The return of Jane and Charles to Netherfield House was an occasion for a renewed cheerfulness on his part and he roused himself to accompany Charles on frequent shooting and fishing expeditions when the weather allowed.

The Bingleys were, in fact, eagerly received by all of their neighbours, and invitations were never wanting to dinners or parties. Jane presided over Netherfield House with her natural cheerfulness and it was not long before their home was accepted as a model of gracious living. Mr Bingley's sisters and Mr Hurst arrived some days before Christmas. Although not much improved in general manners, they were intelligent enough to treat Jane with respect and to confine their criticisms of her and her family to their private conversations. Jane welcomed them for her husband's sake and lived in cheerful oblivion of their continued displeasure with all things pertaining to Hertfordshire.

Darcy need not have feared any despondency on Elizabeth's part from the loss of Jane's company, for her cheerful nature asserted itself and she busied herself with loving attention to him and to Georgiana, and with the preparations for the arrival of the Alexander family in a few days' time.

In a flurry of correspondence, it had been decided that the entire family could manage a visit of several days just before Christmas. Mrs Alexander had begged leave to invite their son Edward, as he had just returned from his studies abroad. Georgiana was particularly delighted by this news, for she had fond memories of him, as well as the greatest admiration for his musical talent.

Before the Alexanders arrived, Trevor Handley returned to Derbyshire with an optimism and enthusiasm for action that soon launched his name upon the sea of neighbourly gossip. That he was well-spoken, well-to-do, and possessed of a rare confluence of good manners, intelligence and wit might have supplied basis enough for fame, but the additional information that he was, apparently, unmarried and had a past vaguely connected to Pemberley Manor assured that his name would be passed from tongue to tongue throughout the county before the last carpet was laid on his polished floors.

Croftwoods Manor welcomed its new master with a flurry of activity which included a very stylish coat of fresh paint, new draperies and carpets, and woodwork polished to a mirror finish. Trevor Handley had apparently no need to economise if his decorator were to be believed, and anyone who crossed his path could attest to the fact that he was pleasant yet decisive, clear in his intentions and instructions, fair-minded but tough in his business dealings. As much attention was given to the refurbishing of the stables as to the manor, and he arrived at his estate accompanied by a small army of grooms and a parade of fine breeding horses that confirmed the seriousness of his claim that Croftwoods' fame would soon be restored.

After supervising the unpacking and personally attending to the placement of the horses in their new quarters, Trevor rode eagerly to Pemberley where he was welcomed with apparently universal enthusiasm. After the departure of the Bingleys, the house seemed large and a little over-quiet, especially to Elizabeth, who was accustomed to a crowded, noisy home, and Trevor Handley was, by all standards, an easy person to like. He swept into the house in boisterous high spirits, infecting the atmosphere with his excitement.

To Georgiana he was charming and gallant and to Elizabeth a tease and a friend. If Elizabeth Darcy detected any reserve in her husband's manner when Trevor was about, she was loathe to break the spell of tranquillity that had settled on Pemberley of late, and so kept her questions to herself.

One topic remained unexplored in the friendly conversations, and that was the subject of marriage. To any question on the theme, whether from one of the Darcys or a nosy shopkeeper, Trevor replied with an elusive vagueness. Even Elizabeth, with her aptitude for reaching around human barricades, could not find an opening in the wall he had built around the matter, and soon abandoned the attempt.

While overseeing the finishing touches at Croftwoods, Trevor spent several nights at Pemberley enjoying an apparently easy camaraderie with Darcy, much to Elizabeth's delight. One chilly morning Handley and the Darcys found time for a long ride; their route ended at Thomas Hill's cottage where the teapot stood always at the ready, and in that quiet setting the affection between them seemed unassailable. Elizabeth, having had no brothers, found the companionship of men and their tales of childhood adventures a delightful novelty, and her admiration for the old caretaker had grown at each meeting. She noted that the now-frequent signs of contentment in Darcy's manner were never more evident than when they sat before the lodge fire, listening to Thomas's memories of his lifelong intimacy with Pemberley.

Carefully omitted from their reminiscences was any mention of Lady Anne Darcy, as if a tacit agreement had been reached that her discordant harmony had no place in this circle of serenity. As for the new mistress of Pemberley, a place of honour had been carved in the old man's heart from their first meeting, and he and Elizabeth shared an unspoken delight in watching Fitzwilliam's gradual metamorphosis.

As Trevor rose to leave he winked at Darcy and announced to Elizabeth that she must come to Croftwoods the following day. She had waited eagerly for the invitation, wishing every time that her husband set off at Trevor's side that she might be asked to join them.

"I would be delighted, Mr Handley. In fact, I had begun to think I should never be asked," she answered with a mischievous smile.

"A thousand pardons, my lady," he said with a bow. "I have only kept you in suspense for so long out of a desire that your first sight of Croftwoods should not be marred by any trace of the chaos that has prevailed there since I began making alterations. Alas, I find I cannot wait for work to be finished – I am so eager to show you what has been done."

"I hope you do not think me so fastidious as to be put off by imperfection," she said wryly.

Darcy quipped to Trevor, "Indeed, if she were of such a delicate nature she would never have married me."

Elizabeth added, turning to Darcy with a grin, "In fact, I claim the credit for helping you to lower your standards, for my own imperfections at one time prevented you from noticing me."

"Only very briefly; I have grown to find them endearing."

The following morning, Elizabeth and Darcy set out for Croftwoods by carriage in a mood of happy expectation. He had spoken with admiration of the beautiful estate and the magnificence of Trevor's stable. They caught a glimpse of the house from a rise in the road before he pointed the driver down a narrow turning through thick woods. The drive wound elegantly through the trees, eventually opening to reveal a softly rolling pasture, meticulously hedged round. Darcy could not resist hinting that he and Trevor had more in mind for the day than an introduction to Croftwoods.

To Elizabeth's repeated questions, he only smiled mischievously and bade her have patience, knowing full well that she had not an abundance of that virtue. Pulling up the carriage finally in front of a carefully tended old brick manor ringed round by fragrant rosebushes still boasting a late bloom, Darcy alighted and helped her down. Before they reached the steps, the door flew open and Trevor stood grinning in delight. He ushered them inside and eagerly paraded them through every room, chattering happily as he pointed out the improvements he had made to the ancient building. Elizabeth obliged him by exclaiming over the pleasant arrangement of rooms and the tasteful elegance of their decoration, indulging him in his boyish pride.

At last he was satisfied that she was suitably impressed, and invited them to the drawing room, where tea had been laid for them. As they lingered over the refreshments, Elizabeth could not prevent her thoughts from wandering to the surprise her husband had hinted at, but she forced herself to attend amiably to the leisurely pleasantries of congratulations and admiration. When the conversation turned to a more lengthy discussion of the weather and farming principles than she felt was necessary, she began to suspect that the men were purposely prolonging her suspense. When she caught Darcy's eye, she saw he was enjoying himself enormously, and made a face at him.

"My dear, if I did not know you better, I would say that your attention has wandered. Are you finding our company dull?" he asked with feigned innocence.

She smiled sweetly and replied, "Not at all, my dear. I cannot recall when I have ever found more pleasure in a conversation on rain and animal husbandry."

Both men laughed and Trevor rose to his feet, addressing her playfully, "Perhaps you would like a tour of the grounds and the stable. I must warn you that I will be more of a bore on the subject of fine horses than I have been on the house."

Elizabeth replied drolly, "You may be many things, Mr Handley, but 'boring' is not one of them." She added sincerely, "I have been hearing more of the magnificence of your stable than the beauty of your house for many days now and it would give me the greatest pleasure to see the animals that arouse such a passion in the two of you."

They began a slow stroll through the garden, stopping at every bed to admire the fading roses and asters and the carefully tended hedges as if they were prize jewels. Trevor and Darcy found it increasingly difficult to hide their mirth, but the more vexed Elizabeth felt at their obvious delaying tactics, the more carefully she concealed her anticipation. Turning the tables, she slowed her pace and insisted on examining carefully the prospect from every angle of the gardens, and extolling the virtues of each weathered bench and arbour. As she suspected, their eagerness to surprise her soon surpassed her own desire to know, and they began to grow impatient with the garden walk.

She smiled indulgently as they steered her around the manor, eventually finding themselves on a path to a paddock behind the house. They stopped there to admire two fine matched greys, one of which was being combed by a groom, and Trevor excused himself to go and speak with him.

The groom presently disappeared into the barn and Trevor returned to renew their conversation with a twinkle in his eyes. Elizabeth was studiously maintaining her pose of disinterest when her eyes were drawn to the sight of the groom emerging from the stable, leading the most magnificent auburn Arabian mare she had ever seen. The horse was willowy and regal of carriage, with a coat that glistened in the sun like a polished chestnut. She snorted and stepped high, drawing everyone's attention to herself imperiously. The superiority of this beautiful mare was evident even to Elizabeth's untrained eye. As the groom led her closer, Elizabeth became breathless with admiration, and did not notice that both Darcy and Trevor stepped back and watched her as she moved up close to the wonderful creature.

She reached out to stroke her mane, and the mare turned to nuzzle her hand, then threw back her head, shaking it so that the silken hair danced in the sunlight. Elizabeth laughed with delight and spoke directly to her, "You are quite the proudest lady I have ever met." The horse whinnied a response and nuzzled her hand again, and Elizabeth exclaimed with delight, "I believe you have something to say to me."

Seeing her pleasure, Darcy could no longer contain his own, and he stepped up beside her to say, "She is trying to say, I believe, that she would like to belong to you." Elizabeth turned quickly to look at his face with eyes open wide in disbelief, and he laughed with the openness of a small boy. He nodded to her questioning look as he declared, "She's yours if you like her."

"The Queen herself would be honoured by such a gift," she whispered, quite overcome.

"The Queen herself could not do more honour to a fine horse," he replied earnestly, and kissed her hand. She turned back to the mare and stroked her, and while the two men exchanged a look of proud delight, Elizabeth spoke to her softly in the intimate tone of a new mother.

"Her name is 'Sweet Felicity'," offered Trevor, "and I do not doubt that the two of you shall be the best of friends. I never give up my beauties to anyone who cannot love them as I do. I see I shall not have to worry about this one."

"Would you like to try her out?" Darcy asked.

Elizabeth laughed, indicating her dress, and said, "As much as I would like to, I don't believe I am suitably attired for the honour."

His eyes sparkled in merriment, but he spoke offhandedly. "I suppose it shall have to wait then." Turning to Trevor, he said, "Let's show Lizzie around the stables, shall we?"

Trevor grinned and led the way, but fell back to give a private instruction to the groom who held Sweet Felicity. He fell in behind them as they entered the building. Hardly able to take her eyes off the mare, Elizabeth tried valiantly to attend to Trevor's proud description of the work he had done on the old buildings and the improvements still planned. Stopping at an empty stall which he identified as Sweet Felicity's, he feigned surprise at finding a parcel neatly wrapped and laid on the fresh hay. "What could this be?" he asked mischievously, picking it up. "There seems to be a card with your name on it," he said, handing it to her.

She looked at both men inquiringly, but they merely smiled, and she quickly opened the card. In her husband's meticulous hand, the note read: "To my Sweet Elizabeth who has given me everything, a token of my love." Her eyes widened as she opened the parcel and took out an exquisite riding costume of red velvet. Trevor quickly moved away, partly to afford them privacy, and partly from a need to control the private pain that rushed into his heart at the sight of their tenderness.

Elizabeth could only manage to say softly, "Oh, Will," before her eyes filled with tears that rendered her speechless.

Embracing her with his eyes, he smiled and touched her hand. "Come and put it on and we shall go for a ride." She nodded and wiped her eyes and they walked in silence to Trevor, who was overseeing the saddling of her horse.

He laughed at the sight of them. "Ah, the sentimentality of young love," he said with an exaggerated sigh. "I only hope you have managed to get the size right, Willie, or this tender moment will be destroyed."

Elizabeth and Darcy exchanged a smile and followed Trevor to the house, where he showed Elizabeth to a room. Her hands trembled as she smoothed the folds of velvet over her lithe frame, and she emerged quickly from her room and ran down the stairs to the drawing room where the men waited, congratulating themselves on the success of the morning. As she entered the room, she laughed at their smug faces. "If I should be thrown and killed today, you may bury me in this costume and write on my tombstone, 'She died in a state of sweet felicity.'"

Flanked on each side by an admiring gentleman, Elizabeth Darcy walked out of the house feeling very regal indeed. They found the horses saddled and waiting for them, and as Darcy took Felicity's bridle to hold her steady, Trevor joked, "By the look in Mrs Darcy's eyes, Willie, you are in danger of being replaced in her affections by this horse."

Elizabeth answered pertly, "He certainly has reason to worry, for although it required the work of a twelvemonth for him to gain my favour, I must admit I fell in love with Sweet Felicity at first sight."

Fitzwilliam Darcy drew himself up haughtily so a comparison could be drawn. "Other than having a sweet, lively temperament, great beauty, impeccable lineage, and an advantage in height, I do not understand that you should favour the mare, my dear," he said.

Trevor laughingly admonished her, "I think you had best choose the man in this contest, as he has the greater wit."

"I'll keep both, by your leave," she answered prettily, "for the man is so talkative that I may seek relief at times in the silence of the mare."

Darcy reached out for her hand and kissed it, bowing low as he did. "I shall hope in time to raise myself in your esteem to a position of preference."

Laughing and boisterous, the three riders were soon speeding across the field, spending the rest of the morning exploring Croftwoods' hilly beauty. Whenever Elizabeth's eyes found Darcy's, she rewarded his thoughtfulness with a look of radiant joy and contentment, and he as often congratulated himself on the good fortune that had made her his wife. Only Trevor Handley experienced moments of sorrow that day, as he found it difficult to shake off the heaviness of his own loneliness, but so strong was his habit of hiding these thoughts that neither Elizabeth nor Darcy noticed any change from his habitual cheerfulness.

At the end of a spectacular day, Elizabeth and Darcy set off for Pemberley at a slow pace, with Sweet Felicity walking behind the carriage. With their high spirits ebbing from fatigue, they grew quiet. At last, Elizabeth said, "Do you mean to spoil me utterly, Will?"

"With every means at my disposal, my dear."

"I have not thanked you properly, but I cannot seem to find the right words," she said seriously.

Pressing her hand, he protested, "You still do not understand that it is *I* who want to thank *you*, for you have given me more than I could have ever hoped for. I can never repay the debt I owe you."

Chapter Thirty One

The days of December stretched out at a leisurely pace for the Darcy family, as the hectic activity of their early weeks together gave way to the establishment of the routines of daily life. Darcy began to feel a pride in Pemberley that he had not known previously, and on Sundays when they set off for Klympton Church, his former reserve was supplanted by a new awareness of the lives of those around them. Inspired by Elizabeth's example of graciousness, Fitzwilliam and Georgiana began tentatively to re-establish their family ties with those neighbours whose warm regard for their father was a vivid memory. Their mother's friends, led by the indefatigable Lady Margaret Westby, at first held themselves aloof, but between the shy sweetness of Georgiana, the new expansiveness of her brother, and Elizabeth's ebullience, the attractiveness of the family began to draw down all but the hardiest defences.

Lady Margaret, wounded and perplexed by her failure at Pemberley, grew ever more distressed by the signs of defection of those she considered her allies. The brunt of her ire was felt most keenly by her husband and daughter as the number of her followers decreased, and she began to sense that rather than presiding over the court of social justice, she was swiftly becoming its victim. In spite of the depth of her convictions, even *she* secretly harboured a growing respect for Elizabeth Darcy, whose composure in the face of hostility remained apparently unassailable.

Far from hiding behind her husband's protection, Elizabeth sallied forth into Derbyshire society with a determination and strength that brightened her eyes and put colour in her cheeks. With Georgiana in tow, she entered quietly but enthusiastically into the benevolent schemes of Mrs Hatfield, improving their effectiveness by a gentle infusion of sensibility and good humour, which effort brought her into contact with many households of the neighbourhood. Once having attained a foothold, she lost no opportunity to disarm the incivility aimed at her by employing her frank good nature. With his fears of her isolation allayed, Darcy allowed himself the luxury of dropping his defences, and with his full encouragement and proud approbation, Elizabeth Darcy took her first important steps toward acceptance as Mistress of Pemberley.

Although Georgiana had taken great pleasure in the company of Charles and Jane Bingley, she was not unhappy to spend a few days alone with her brother and Lizzie. So much had happened in a short time to alter her opinion of her brother that she welcomed time for quieter contemplation. He rarely alluded to the past, but she saw no sign of the moody restlessness that had often characterised his stays at Pemberley. Only Elizabeth was aware that a certain shadow still passed over her husband's countenance from time to time. Sometimes, late at night, she would awaken to find him gone from her side, and she knew he was walking the halls lost in contemplation of a sorrow he could not define.

The interlude afforded Fitzwilliam Darcy and his sister more time together, and Elizabeth enjoyed watching them, marvelling how unlike they were, both in looks and temperament. Though tall and handsome, Georgiana was fine of bone and fair, while Darcy favoured their mother's darker complexion and unruly black curls. In speech they differed even more, for although Georgiana grew more relaxed and more talkative with time, her voice was soft and tentative, and she was little inclined to join into a conversation unless directly questioned, and then not eager to express strong opinions. Darcy spoke with great confidence, and once released from the burden of arrogance, proved an eloquent speaker and an eager conversant. Georgiana was in awe of her brother's knowledge and fluency, and soon found that Elizabeth matched him in enthusiasm for a debate. She was content to observe the animation with which they approached a subject and the flush of colour that was likely to rise to

Elizabeth's face when she felt strongly about her opinion, which was the general rule.

For his part, Darcy ceased to be startled by his happiness, and his fear that it could not endure was replaced by an assurance and pleasure in his present state. If he sometimes brooded late at night, it was less from fear of the future than from a nagging wish to understand the past, to solve the puzzle of his childhood.

One crisp morning, when Darcy had gone off on a tour with his steward and Georgiana had settled in at the pianoforte to explore the delights of a packet of music sent up from London, Elizabeth set off on foot for a visit to old Thomas' cottage. Her husband returned from his ride in high spirits and followed the strains of music to the drawing room, where his sister was so immersed in her occupation that she did not notice his arrival. He stood admiring her from the doorway for many minutes before she sensed his presence and stopped playing, blushing sweetly at his attention.

"Lizzie's gone off for a walk, Fitzwilliam. How was your ride this morning?"

He smiled comfortably. "I believe that I have seriously neglected Pemberley these past few years. We are fortunate indeed that Mr Simmons is such an able manager, or I fear the estate would have fallen into serious disrepair." As he settled himself in a comfortable chair, he asked her to continue playing, and she obligingly turned her attention to her song.

When she reached the final notes, she moved to a chair facing his. "Fitzwilliam," she began tentatively, "I wonder if I might speak to you about something that has been troubling me." He smiled his encouragement and waited for her to continue. "I have enjoyed Mr Handley's visits to Pemberley, but when I hear the two of you speaking of the past, you never mention Mother. I understand that your feelings toward her are equivocal, but... " She paused, torn between deference for his sensibilities and her own desire to

235

understand, and then asked hesitantly, averting her eyes, "Why did Mr Handley leave Pemberley so abruptly, Fitzwilliam? Had it anything to do with Mother?"

Her question startled him and he stammered, "What leads you... why do you ask that, Georgiana?"

The young woman wrung her hands nervously, finding it painfully difficult to speak so openly, but she was determined not to let the opportunity pass. "After Mother died, you know that Father left her room untouched for many years. I sometimes found the opportunity to creep in there alone when nurse fell asleep, for I loved to touch her things and imagine what she was like. One day, tucked under her night-gowns in a drawer, I found a sketch of a young man lying on a blanket beside a small stream. His face was beautiful, with wide, insolent eyes and a teasing look about his mouth. I was so taken by the face that I could not bear to put the drawing back, so I kept it and hid it in my own room. I often looked at it and wondered whose likeness it was, for it was not anyone I could recognise. Finally, I decided to ask Father about him."

She drew in a deep breath to steady herself, unaware that Fitzwilliam's countenance had grown ashen. After a long pause, she stood up in agitation and walked to the fire, speaking quickly, "I had never before seen him look like he did that day. He grew first pale and then livid. He tore the sketch into pieces and threw it into the fire without saying a word, and forbade me to go into her room again. That very day, Mrs Reynolds cleaned out Mother's room, and everything in it was packed up in boxes and taken away." Her eyes glistened with tears at the memory, but she rushed on as if afraid to stop. "I wonder now... that is... I am quite sure the young man in the drawing was Trevor Handley. But why should she hide his picture? And why did it provoke our father to such a rage?" When she finally hazarded a glance at Fitzwilliam, his stony coldness alarmed her.

Afraid of what she had done, Georgiana whispered, "Perhaps I am mistaken."

Her brother leaned forward in his chair and rested his face in his hands, fighting against an urge to flee the room. A sickening wave of confusion destroyed in an instant the hard-won contentment of the past few weeks. The room was filled with the silent wretchedness of the pair when the sound of the front door swinging on its hinges startled them. A moment later two pairs of footsteps echoed in the hall, accompanied by the cheerful voices of Elizabeth and Trevor Handley. They appeared in the doorway to the drawing room, cheeks red from the cold.

Elizabeth said brightly as she stepped into the room, "Look who I've found at the lodge." But her chatter was cut short as she noticed the pale visages of Darcy and Georgiana staring at them. "What has happened?" she demanded.

Darcy stood up slowly, his face contorted with anger, knuckles whitened as he held himself under control and addressed Trevor. "I will have a direct answer from you this time. Did you have an affair with my mother?"

Georgiana's gasp rang like a shot through the stillness of the room. Trevor's face turned hard and his eyes fixed on Darcy's and held in unblinking defiance. "You have already judged me, I see. There is nothing more to be said." Straightening his shoulders, he turned and walked out of the room, his footsteps resounding like a funeral march down the hall.

As the massive door slammed to, Elizabeth said hoarsely, "Will someone please explain to me what is happening here?"

Her husband's eyes blazed. "I do not intend to explain anything. The history of this family is a closed subject and I will not hear that man's name spoken in my presence again." With that he stormed out of the room, striding down the long hall to the library, where he entered and closed the door with a force that set the chandelier rattling.

Elizabeth's wide eyes found Georgiana's face and, alarmed by its pallor, she hurried to her side. In the comforting circle of her new sister's arm, Georgiana gave way to a torrent of tears. At last, holding the frail shoulders at arms' length so she might study the girl's face, Elizabeth, utterly perplexed and dismayed by the scene she had witnessed, managed to say firmly, "My dearest Georgiana, you will make yourself ill. Please come and sit down. Shall I get you something?"

Through her sobs, Georgiana said, "Oh, Lizzie, I had no idea this would happen or I don't believe I would have spoken at all. My brother's anger is so new to me - I am frightened by it." She permitted herself to be led like a child to the sofa and they sat down, Elizabeth holding both of her hands. As Georgiana haltingly told her story, Elizabeth willed herself to stay calm, and her gentle stroking and understanding nods slowly diffused the hysteria that had permeated the air. Georgiana finished with a sigh of longing, saying, "I wish you had known my father, Lizzie. He was so kind, so gentle... I understand that he and my mother suffered from a great difference in temperament, but *is* it possible that... " She paused and then asked plaintively, "Do *you* think it could be true about her and Mr Handley, Lizzie?"

Elizabeth frowned and weighed her words carefully. "Your father thought it was, dear." She shook her head sadly. "I suppose that Fitzwilliam did not want to burden you with the story of Mr Handley's departure from Pemberley, but I think you have the right to hear it." She quietly retold the story of the interview at Lambton Inn and the subsequent reconciliation at the lodge. After a pause, she asked, "Was the sketch you found done by your mother, do you think?"

"I'm not sure, really," she answered. "She certainly was capable of it, judging by the landscapes she left, but I have never seen a portrait by her hand. As a child, I saw nothing more strange about that drawing than the fact that it was hidden in her drawer. But as I remember it now, I feel certain that it was drawn by someone who cared very deeply about its subject, someone who had studied him closely. I only realised it was Mr Handley the other evening when we played cards together. Do you remember? He had beat us all soundly and I looked at his laughing face and suddenly recognised the expression he wore then as the same one I had seen in the portrait - the likeness was so strong I wonder I did not think of it before. Oh, I wish I had never spoken!" she ended angrily.

The two women sat lost in their thoughts. Elizabeth said at last, "I think I shall go and look in on your brother. There must be some way to resolve this question, or at least to go on with our lives." She patted Georgiana's hand. "I hope you don't mean to blame yourself for what happened today, Georgiana. It is as well it all comes out in the open, for there have been far too many secrets in this house for anyone's good."

Georgiana smiled wanly. "You are so calm and sensible, Lizzie, you give me courage."

With a rueful smile, Elizabeth answered, "I feel anything but calm and I have not often been called sensible, but I confess I am not easily frightened. I shall beard the lion in his den."

Elizabeth rose and left the room, pausing outside the library door to take a deep breath. She knocked softly and went inside without waiting for a reply, which was just as well, for her husband did not acknowledge her entrance. He stood gazing out the window, a dark, brooding frown worrying his brow. She walked to his side and spoke softly. "Whatever Trevor has done, Will, I cannot believe he intended any injury to you."

His lip twisted into a bitter smile and he answered venomously, without turning from the window, "You would take no injury from a man who seduced your mother, I suppose. Your forbearance is admirable."

Elizabeth fought back an angry retort, and continued calmly, "You have no proof that he did as he was accused, Will."

"I have his refusal to deny it," he answered coldly.

She began another line of reasoning. "He was little more than a boy, himself. He was only seventeen." When he made no answer, she decided to risk what she knew might be a dangerous path of reasoning. "Did you blame Georgiana for being seduced by George Wickham?" she asked, careful to couch her question in the gentlest possible tones.

He turned abruptly towards her, his anger flaring dangerously. "How dare you taunt me with that?" he demanded. Elizabeth stepped back from his rage. "You only remind me that my father, fool that he was, managed with his tender heart to bring two black-hearted knaves into our lives to destroy our family." His eyes narrowed ominously. "I recall that you defended Wickham's character to me with similar vehemence once."

Elizabeth's stomach knotted and the colour drained from her face as her body urged her to flee, but she held her ground, summoning to her mind saner images to block out the distorted visage in front of her. Her eyes did not waver from his face for an instant as she searched deep within herself for a weapon with which to fight the demon that gnawed at him. At last, angry indignation took hold, and the ice in her veins melted as its heat coursed through her.

"Fitzwilliam Darcy, do you really see yourself as the only injured party in this tragedy? Can you find no room in your heart to pity anyone but yourself? Your mother, your father, Trevor Handley, Georgiana - what torments have *they* suffered? You once extolled to me the superiority of your reason. Is it reasonable that they should have created a world of misery for the pleasure of making you unhappy?"

For a long hanging moment she feared that he would strike her, but his hands remained frozen at his side, his fists clenching and unclenching themselves as he returned her stare. Suddenly, his passionate anger collapsed, opening the path for stinging, bitter tears. At the first sign of them, Elizabeth grew weak and breathed a little sob as she reached up to cradle his face in her hands.

"I love you, Will. Georgiana loves you, and old Thomas, and so, I believe still, does Trevor. Don't let this hurting rob you of everyone you hold dear. Let it go, Will, let it go," she beseeched him.

Chapter Thirty Two

Darcy's brooding subsided sufficiently by the following day to allow him to regain at least the semblance of composure. At his wife's urging he sought out Georgiana and in rational, measured tones, reassured her that he intended to put the past behind him. If she was not completely convinced, she was satisfied at least that he bore her no ill will. The impending visit of the Alexanders gave them a useful distraction, and the subject of the past was declared unbroachable by tacit agreement.

Elizabeth anticipated the arrival of the Alexander family with hope, and although her enthusiasm was tempered by the sorrow of Darcy's estrangement from Trevor, she turned her attention to the subject with eagerness to ensure that the heavy spirits at Pemberley should not dampen their guests' enjoyment. Darcy had less enthusiasm for another foray into his past, but he made a valiant attempt at cheerfulness for Elizabeth's sake. Even Georgiana's shyness of large parties could not prevent her from hoping that their arrival would bring a relief to the strained atmosphere around her. In spite of her nervousness, she remembered the solicitous interest of the family who had welcomed her into their hearts as a child.

Georgiana was astonished to discover that her brother was more nervous than she of his ability to entertain their guests. As she began to understand that she had mistaken his strong opinions for confidence and his proud bearing for self-assurance, she even ventured to tease him a little on the subject. Elizabeth laughed at the two of them as they fretted over the allocation of rooms and other details of accommodation and entertainment. Her own short acquaintance with the Alexander family left her confidant that they would be the easiest of guests to please, and she assured both Darcy and Georgiana that it was inconceivable that they would not be put immediately at ease by the obvious desire of their hosts to make them so.

At last, with every detail laboriously attended to, a commotion at the entrance signalled the arrival of two carriages. Mr and Mrs Alexander drove up to the gates of Pemberley with their youngest son, Edward, and their daughter Catherine. The second carriage brought Augusta and her husband Peter, Catherine's husband John, and Eric, the oldest of the Alexander children.

Edward Alexander was the first to alight from the carriage. He presented quite a picture in his burgundy velvet suit, cut in a dandyish French style that set him quite apart from the more conservative English fashion. In contrast to the genteel conventionality of his family, he was obviously a seeker of novelty. His gait, his manner, his delicate good looks, together with the lace at his throat and cuffs, made it clear that he was cut of a completely different cloth from the rest of his family. As they stepped out onto the drive one by one, the contrast was heightened by the simple dress and unaffected manner of the others.

The spectacle that Edward made in the midst of his kin did not please Fitzwilliam Darcy, but he quickly cautioned himself to suspend judgement until he could have the opportunity to observe him more carefully. Accompanied by his wife and sister, he hurried to greet their guests, and their nervous anticipation was soon replaced by congenial and heartfelt greetings on all sides. Even Georgiana found herself drawn quickly into the pleasantry of the reunion. She was much exclaimed over, particularly by the convivial Mrs Alexander, whose motherly instincts were stirred by the sight of the handsome young woman who had replaced the timid girl she remembered.

They all stood together on the lawn for a few minutes in a jovial and noisy group, often laughing and talking over one another in their high spirits. Darcy felt himself slightly overwhelmed by the commotion, and as the party was led off to the house by Elizabeth, he stayed outside for a few minutes on the pretext of giving directions concerning luggage and the disposition of carriages, quite an unnecessary function as he had already given very specific instructions to his staff in anticipation of the arrival. He soon realised that there was nothing left to be done, and shaking his head in amused disbelief that this boisterous gathering had been his own idea, he followed the party into the house.

Pemberley had not seen such a large party of guests in many years. Darcy's social circle had previously been severely limited by his definition of worthy company, and his protective reserve had led him to disdain large gatherings of any kind. His love for Elizabeth had inspired him to re-examine his assumptions and, having embraced a new perspective, his world expanded rapidly. If he loved Elizabeth, he must accept her family; if he accepted the Bennets, it followed that he must look for signs of intelligence and good nature in everyone, and he was constantly surprised at where he found them. Through Elizabeth's eyes, the world became an increasingly interesting place. Since he no longer looked for offence, he found none, and not being continually offended, he behaved pleasantly, which invited a congenial response from those he met, and so a friendly circle of ever-widening dimensions grew around him.

Entering the drawing room where refreshments were being handed around, he found himself drawn to the agreeable scene before him. He found Georgiana engaged with Mrs Alexander and Edward and he moved toward them to find that the young man was eagerly questioning Georgiana about her music. Within a few minutes he found himself completely disarmed by Edward's cheerfulness. Had he come from a family of less gracious and loving manners, Edward might indeed have been insufferable, but Darcy found his charm was every bit as honest and sincere as the rest, if more flamboyant. The effect of his striking appearance was saved from foppishness by the brilliant warmth of his smile. It was obvious that his family adored him and he them, and Darcy observed complacently that he fitted as a prize stone in a gold setting.

With the initial pleasantries and refreshments out of the way, Fitzwilliam suggested that their guests be shown to their rooms to refresh themselves. The effect of his training asserted itself and Elizabeth noted proudly that his comportment as a host was flawless. Agreeing to gather for supper in an hour, with considerable noise and commotion everyone was finally settled into their rooms to bathe or rest.

Darcy and Elizabeth took the opportunity to retire briefly to their sitting room, where she playfully commended him on his performance. He laughed and remarked, "I must confess that I am as surprised as you to find myself so gregarious."

She commented on the gaiety of young Edward, teasing, "I daresay you were not much impressed by *him* at first."

"I admit I found myself looking at him critically," he answered amiably, "but I decided to forego my usual pleasure in being judgmental, and in our conversation I found much to enjoy. I expect we will be fast friends before long, for it seems that since I learned to love you, I find it difficult to dislike anyone for long."

Trevor leapt into Elizabeth's mind, but she prudently deflected the thought. Instead she countered, "Not even Lady Margaret?"

"I trust that your dislike of her is sufficient for both of us," Darcy said, and with a friendly kiss on the cheek he excused himself to go and see that the coachmen and horses had been properly accommodated. Elizabeth set off for the kitchen to verify supper arrangements. She found Georgiana there ahead of her and after confirming that nothing was wanting, they repaired to the drawing room to await their guests. They were surprised to find Edward Alexander already there, changed into fresh if not less surprising attire. He was looking through a portfolio of music and jumped up when they entered the room.

"I hope you don't mind my presumption," he said, colouring and holding up the music sheets as if he had been caught stealing candy. "I was interested in the new Beethoven you mentioned earlier."

Georgiana hurried to exclaim, "Of course I don't mind, Mr Alexander. I am so eager to hear you play, and I hope you will feel entirely at home at Pemberley. My brother gave me this instrument recently. It would give me the greatest pleasure if, while you are visiting, you would treat it as your own." She walked to the pianoforte and raised the cover, turning back to him with flushed cheeks from the effort of her speech. Elizabeth smiled at such a display of enthusiasm from Georgiana.

Edward was all boyish eagerness. "You do me the greatest honour Miss Darcy, for you must feel very protective of such a magnificent instrument. I would be very pleased to play, but only on one condition."

"What is that, Mr Alexander?" she asked, flustered.

"No, I must make that two conditions, I think," he said with a wide smile. "First, that you promise to chase me away when I become annoying and second, that you call me Edward. There are far too many 'Mr Alexanders' about and we have known each other such a long while, I hope we shall soon feel as though we are all family." His charm was contagious. He moved to the pianoforte and stroked it lovingly, a gesture that widened Georgiana's smile.

"Please play something for us, Edward," she asked softly, and he bowed and sat down. He closed his eyes for a moment and then began a stirring sonata from memory. The passion he felt for the instrument gave him a radiant countenance and it was clear that he was oblivious to everything but the sound and feel of the melody. His hands swept over the keys with a strength and energy that belied their delicate appearance. That his playing was magnificent even a novice would have understood, but Georgiana, herself a talented and devoted musician, watched and listened in awe. Her hands rested lightly on the polished wood and she felt the sound coursing through her. If in speech she felt burdened and anxious, in music her spirit soared.

Her own playing did not lack in skill, but it was tentative and earthbound in comparison to this heavenly sound. When he had finished the piece, he looked up to see a radiant energy in Georgiana's eyes. The rapture she had been feeling spilled over into her speech and she exclaimed that she had never heard anything so beautiful. Momentarily disconcerted by the strength of her praise, he quickly regained himself to spring up and offer her his seat. She declined emphatically, saying she would so much rather listen to him, but his eagerness to hear her was so sincerely and kindly expressed that she agreed to play on the morrow when they did not have an audience, and on condition that he agree to offer criticism. He graciously acceded and they moved to join the rest of the family who had by now gathered in conversation groups.

Elizabeth excused herself from Catherine to intercept Edward as he crossed toward the circle of men. "I hope you enjoy playing as much as we do hearing you, for I am going to insist that you entertain us very often while you are at Pemberley. You have a wonderful gift indeed."

"I love nothing more than music, Mrs Darcy. In fact, I fear I am quite boring on the subject. You shall have more of me than you can easily bear before we leave, I don't wonder."

Lizzie laughed, "For my part, if you should play four and twenty hours of every day as you have just done that Beethoven, it would not be too much."

"You recognised the piece," he said with admiration, for it was a new work, not much circulated in England. "For your pleasure I will perform until my fingers fall from my hands," he said with a bow.

"You are too kind, sir. I will not require such a sacrifice. Now will you have some supper for your work?"

Chapter Thirty Three

Lizzie took up her position at one end of the supper table with Mr Alexander and Edward seated on either side of her. With very little encouragement, Edward proved to be a most amusing storyteller, aided by the fact that his father and his sister Catherine, seated next to him, so obviously enjoyed whatever he said. His father proudly explained that he had been invited to play at St. James' Court for the Christmas festivities that year.

Elizabeth waited for the opportunity to explore the subject of the elder Mr Darcy and so, at a suitable pause, she asked, "What is your first impression of Pemberley after so many years, Mr Alexander? Do you find it much altered from your last visit?"

Mr Alexander answered thoughtfully, "I confess so far that I find everything remarkably unchanged. I had expected that young Fitzwilliam might have put his hand to some alterations, but it appears that he prefers to hold with tradition."

Lizzie was not surprised. "My husband has not, I understand, spent a great deal of time at Pemberley since his father's death," adding, with a scrutinising look at Mr Alexander's face, "in fact, I think he was in the habit of being away from the estate a good deal from quite a young age."

Mr Alexander seemed to consider a response and then changed his mind, simply nodding in agreement. He remarked instead on the superiority of the prospect from the library window, a particular favourite of his, and the topic turned to a discussion of the attractions of the house and grounds.

Darcy was meanwhile engaged in conversation with Eric Alexander, his sister Augusta, and Catherine's husband John Angsley, discussing possible amusements for the morrow if the weather continued to be fine. The consensus was for horseback riding. To include Mr and Mrs Alexander in the day's outing, a plan was forming to route them by carriage to a rendezvous point where they would all meet for a picnic lunch.

"I seem to recall a particularly beautiful spot on a bluff overlooking Lambton," Eric offered, "where the road runs very near an old circle of stones."

Fitzwilliam was caught off guard. "I did not realise you had visited Pemberley."

"It was in the spring, the year before your father's death," he answered. "My father and I spent a fortnight hunting here." Seeing that Fitzwilliam was disconcerted by this answer, he hastened to add, "Your father told us you were sitting examinations and would not be able to come home for some time."

There was an awkward silence before Fitzwilliam recovered himself enough to say, "Yes, I imagine he did not wish to break my concentration." They continued with the subject of the bluff, but Darcy's composure was shaken, and he was greatly relieved when the end of the meal took them away from the dining parlour. Lizzie caught the troubled look in his eyes as the ladies removed, and meeting his gaze, she raised her eyebrows inquiringly. His only answer was a slight shake of the head and an attempted smile as he led the gentlemen off to the library.

Mr Alexander had been observing Fitzwilliam carefully, and when he found a moment alone with him, he remarked quietly, studying his face, "I think I am not wrong in assuming, Fitzwilliam, that our visit here is likely to revive memories which you may find unsettling. I do not wish to intrude on your thoughts, but I offer you what I have, your father's confidences to me as a friend, if you should ever feel a need to talk about the past."

Darcy stiffened, responding with cool politeness, "I appreciate your kindness, Mr Alexander. I am sure in some ways you knew my father better than I." For a brief moment he felt the urge to pour out his thoughts to this kind man, but his habit of reserve checked him.

Mr Alexander nodded sagely, and over cigars and brandy carefully steered the conversation clear of dangerous subjects. With relief, Darcy finally ushered the gentleman toward the drawing room to rejoin the ladies.

Mr Alexander, settling into a chair near the fire, occupied himself with a careful study of the Darcys, seeing through Fitzwilliam's rather stiff attempt at attentiveness and Lizzie's forced cheer. Although he did not know what prompted their departure from the relaxed mood of the afternoon, he sensed that before long he would, for the haunted look in Darcy's eyes must surely signal a crisis at hand. With a silent appeal to his old friend James Darcy, he quietly bided his time.

At a pause in the conversation, Georgiana shyly importuned Edward to play again. He avowed that he had eaten a good deal too much to be lively at the pianoforte and turned instead to Lizzie, professing that he had been longing to hear her sing after listening to his family's praise of her talent. She laughingly assented, for although she had no illusions as to the perfection of her voice, she was eager to keep the tone of the evening light. She sat down, begging for singers to come to her aid, but Edward insisted she must first give him a solo. The song she chose was a lilting ballad that brought a smile to every eye in the room. As Mr Alexander glanced surreptitiously at Fitzwilliam, he noted that the adoration and pride he had observed at Great Oaks was not diminished, in spite of the young man's distracted mien, and he nodded in approval. He mused that if Fitzwilliam could not find solace in *her* affection, his life was indeed lost.

The evening broke up early with plans for the morrow's outing having been concluded to everyone's satisfaction. When the Darcy family finally found themselves alone, Lizzie turned to Darcy with concern. "Something troubled you at supper, Will. What was it?"

He shook his head and smiled, but there was no reassurance in it. "Nothing, really. It was just a comment that Eric Alexander made about visiting Pemberley once. I did not know he had been here with his father." His careful nonchalance did not have the effect he intended.

"Please, Will, I saw your eyes. There was something dreadful on your mind," Lizzie prodded.

He paused and looked first at Lizzie and then at Georgiana. His smile turned sardonic.

"Father told them that I was sitting exams and would not be able to join them. The truth is that I had finished my work months before and was staying with James Fitzwilliam in London that spring." He paused to choose his words, anxious to remain detached from the pain that the story had given him. "He never informed me of their visit or invited me to join them. I should not be surprised, I suppose, for in the last few years of his life we only corresponded out of necessity. My visits to Pemberley had become increasingly infrequent. In fact, he and I were virtual strangers."

The silence that met this seemingly careless confession did nothing to reduce anyone's discomfort. Lizzie sat back in her chair, unable to think of a word to say, but Georgiana looked perplexed and finally summoned the courage to protest,

"But Fitzwilliam, I remember that although you did not often stay with us for long, you and Father were always on the most cordial of terms."

Lizzie watched carefully as he answered, noting the tightening of his jaw as he struggled to maintain his casual air.

"A little trick, my dear, that we all practised at Pemberley long before you were born - never air your differences in public," he said with a smile, but he could not maintain the charade under the probing eyes of his wife and sister. He rubbed his temples as if to clear the confusion in his mind.

The answering silence demanded further explanation from him, and he continued with a valiant effort to speak casually.

"I have been feeling since Father's death that I let him down, that I did not try hard enough to understand him or love him. Everyone spoke so highly of him, but I found him aloof and unreachable. I have always assumed that the fault was mine, but I am beginning to wonder if it was not he who failed me. I think he simply disliked me. Possibly I reminded him of my mother."

As Lizzie turned her scrutiny from her husband to Georgiana, she silently willed her sister-in-law not to back off from the encounter. She felt instinctively that there was something that must be said between them. Georgiana took courage from Lizzie's encouraging look and continued boldly, "That is not true, Fitzwilliam. I know it is not. He always spoke of you with such pride and love."

Tears began to fill his eyes as his armour failed him once again.

"Pride and love? Since you will persist, I will tell you what I gave him to love. The day our mother was buried, he called me to sit with him in the library. I knew he wished to tell me something, but I was so miserable and angry that I could not listen. I understood that he did not love her, but I did, and I wanted him to feel my pain," he said, his voice shaking with emotion, "and so I told him I wished *he* had died instead of her."

Georgiana drew in a sharp breath of disbelief, and Lizzie closed her eyes for a moment against the pain in his eyes. She steadied herself and said softly, "Will, you were only a child. You must not torment yourself with guilt. He surely understood the confusion of your feelings."

Darcy shook his head. "He stood up without saying a word and walked out of the room. I thought I *had* killed him, his countenance was so terrible." While Georgiana sat clutching the arms of her chair, torn between love of her father and compassion for her brother, Darcy battled the urge to give way to his remorse. "We were never really reconciled after that day."

The three of them sat lost in their separate misery for a very long time until Darcy suddenly stood up and announced he was going to bed. He strode out of the room, leaving the two women to stare at each other in disbelief.

Lizzie went to Georgiana's side and embraced her silently, and then shaking her head sorrowfully, said, "I will see what can be done, dear. Try to get some sleep." Georgiana managed a weak smile and nodded her assent, but her sorrowful thoughts kept her immobilised for a very long time.

The comfort of Lizzie's arms could not distract Darcy from his brooding thoughts that night, and after lying sleeplessly for an hour, he rose to keep vigil with his thoughts. By turns he blamed his father, his mother and himself for breaking the bonds of affection that should have held his family together. Examining his memories, he tried to find the place where their sorrow began, but could not fix a time when it was not present. He remembered his mother's face, beautiful, laughing, her rich black curls framing the smooth skin, and suddenly she was transformed before his eyes, an ugly disdain contorting her features, and he knew his father had entered the room.

His thoughts drifted back to the first dinner party when he had been deemed old enough to join the adults. He pictured the radiance of his mother's face, eyes alive and excited, and in the same vision saw his father's benevolent smile at the other end of the table, talking easily, as if this were an ordinary day in their happy family life. The memory brought back to Darcy the cold, stabbing pain he had in his stomach that day. He had wanted to turn over the table, to slap her laughing face, to beat on his father for this terrible ugly lie they were telling, but he had swallowed all of that anger with the soup, and made polite table conversation with his neighbours, just as they had taught him to do.

His memories were pictures in a story, but he had never known the whole story, for the family lived in a maze of secrets - he and his mother, alone together, laughing, playing, singing - he and his father on estate business and visits to old friends. He lived in two circles that could not overlap, and his world consisted of keeping them in balance, stepping between them and keeping the secrets to himself. It had become a way of life.

Lizzie drifted in and out of sleep, waking each time to the empty bed beside her and the faint glow of a candle in the adjoining room. Finally, she arose and went to him. Without a word she moved behind him and began to massage his shoulders, her sure strong hands working the tightened cords, kneading, releasing. He moved his head slowly from side to side as he felt the knots relax, and then reaching back, he took her hands in his and drew her around to sit on his knees. He rested his head against her as her arms held him close, and he felt suddenly too weary to think. Feeling his body release its tension, she stood up and took his hand, leading him back to bed. Cradled in her arms, he wept silently while she kept watch.

Georgiana too kept watch that night. After she had released her own sorrow in tears, she lay in her bed trying to remember her mother's face; it was always the portrait in the hall she saw, a flat canvas textured with oil, black dots where the laughing eyes had been, hands folded in her lap that should have cradled her daughter. She remembered getting out of bed one night, awakened by a troubling dream, and going to her father's sitting room. He sat gazing into the dying fire with eyes that were strangely troubled. He roused himself from his languor to take her on his lap, but as he rocked her gently, he began to cry. She felt the tears on her shoulder and looked up into his eyes, forgetting her dream in the bewildering scene. Seeing her worried face, he forced himself to smile, and as he smoothed her curls, he said in a voice that was not his own, 'Fire and ice, Georgie girl. Your mother was fire and ice.'

That was all. She asked nothing and he offered no more. It had troubled her for a long time, for her father was her anchor, but as time passed with no further incident she began to feel less sure of what she had seen, and in time she set aside the memory, for her father was strong, gentle and kind, and in the portrait on the wall, she could find no trace of either fire or ice.

A weariness that defied sleep settled over the Darcy family. Their separate thoughts were linked by a painful acknowledgement that Fitzwilliam Darcy's battle with his past was far from over. For the brother and sister, the realisation carried with it a feeling of helpless despair from which they eventually escaped into troubled sleep. But for Elizabeth Darcy it engendered a call to action that kept her mind feverishly awake as the clock ticked out the end of her patience with Pemberley's ghosts.

Chapter Thirty Four

As the first rays of the sun cast shadows across the room, Lizzie gave up any hope for sleep. Turning over in her mind each revelation of the Darcy family's troubled history, the weight of their collective sorrows settled over her like a thorny mantle, prickling and agitating her thoughts. The relative calm of the period of Jane and Charles' visit had spawned a hope that Darcy had begun to find a sense of equilibrium, and although he still left their bed at times to wander the silent halls late at night, his heavy brooding moods had been replaced by a more thoughtful, reflective quiet that signalled, she thought, a kind of reconciliation, an acceptance of the past and a hope for the future. The scene with Trevor Handley had devastated that hope, and tonight's angry outburst confirmed that after a brief truce, the battle raged more furiously than ever.

As fatigue added its weight to her burdened thoughts, Lizzie found herself gripped by a feeling of oppressive responsibility. The unfailing optimism and levity of her previous one and twenty years foundered on the rocks of a hostility and grief that surpassed anything she had ever encountered. She began to wonder if such disordered lives could ever be reconstructed. The veiled references Darcy had made at Highbury concerning his fear for the future rose to her mind in a new light and with painful clarity she began to understand the folly of her own naiveté.

Lizzie's thoughts drifted to Longbourn and she pictured her father's bemused face as he chided his wife or daughters for some foolishness. She longed to run to him as he sat in his study, to sit beside him by the fire and pour out her heart to him as she had done as a child when the unfairness of her nurse or a squabble with her sisters had rendered the rest of the house unbearable. The knowledge flowed over her that she had given up the right to such comfort and counsel by marrying Will. The wrongs to be righted at Pemberley were her burdens now, and the wisdom must come from within.

On that painful note, she carefully slipped out of bed. Dressing hurriedly, she left Darcy to his troubled dreams and went downstairs. Stopping at the kitchen, where a bustle of breakfast preparations was well underway, she found the housekeeper.

"Good morning, Mrs Reynolds," she said quietly. "Is there coffee brewed?" She was unaware that she wore her lachrymose thoughts as plainly as an armband of mourning.

The kind woman was alarmed at her mistress' distressed countenance.

"Good morning, Madam. Yes, of course. Shall I send it to the dining parlour or would you be joining Mr Alexander in the library?"

Lizzie was startled by the question. "Which Mr Alexander, Mrs Reynolds?"

"The elder, Madam. I found him up before me, I am afraid, so I've had a fire lit and brought him in some tea."

Lizzie's spirit lifted with the thought of his calm steadiness and her smile erased some of the ravages of the night from her face.

"Oh, I'll join him in the library, if he does not mind the company." She hurried down the hallway, thinking to herself that she was not, after all, without an advisor. She peeked in through the library door and found the old gentleman reading by the fire.

Mr Alexander laid his book aside and rose to welcome her.

"Good morning, Mrs Darcy. I hope you do not mind that I took the liberty of making myself quite at home."

"I am delighted that you should. May I join you?" she asked, coming in to sit by his side.

"I would be grateful for some company. I am usually the first to arise in my family, but today I awoke before the cock crowed."

"I hope your sleep was not troubled, sir?" she asked, just managing to keep her voice light.

"I admit I was a bit restless last night. I have not visited this house since Mr Darcy's funeral, and I found a wealth of memories to keep my mind from sleep last night." With a discerning look at her heavy eyes, he added, "I hope the intrusion of my boisterous family has not upset *your* sleep, my dear."

Her answer was delayed by the arrival of the coffee tray and she busied herself with pouring out a steaming cup. The distraction gave her time to weigh her thoughts and prepare a suitable opening for the subject that lay heavily on her mind, but as her eyes lifted from her cup to meet his steady gaze she found she could not speak for the threat of tears. For several seconds she battled her emotion, but when the cup began to tremble in her hands, he rose from his chair and took it from her in a gesture so gentle and kind that she was quite overcome. She covered her face with her hands and wept.

Mr Alexander sighed and shook his head sadly, and moving his chair around to face her he leaned near her and touched her shoulder, offering his handkerchief with his other hand. Struggling valiantly to control herself, she said, "I am so sorry, Mr Alexander. Please excuse me."

He answered earnestly, "Please do not think you will trouble me with your tears, Mrs Darcy. A man of my age is well acquainted with life's difficulties, I assure you. Perhaps I can be of some help if you will tell me what troubles you." He continued, his voice soothing and quiet, allowing her time to collect herself, "I can guess that your tears are for a troubled young gentleman whom you love very deeply."

She looked up from wiping her eyes, startled. "Do you know something of his sorrow, Mr Alexander?"

He nodded thoughtfully, "I know a good deal more about his parents than I ought to, and enough of his childhood to expect that his memories might render him restless."

Hope brought fresh colour to her cheeks and lifted her sagging shoulders. She looked at Mr Alexander with entreating eyes, "I cannot bear to see the pain he suffers, and yet there seems to be no solace I can offer to ease it. In fact, my very presence in this house seems to provoke memories he had forgotten. He is possessed by the past."

Mr Alexander looked off into the fire and nodded, deep in thought. At last he turned back to Lizzie and said, "Mrs Darcy, since the death of Fitzwilliam's father I have sought an opportunity to open this subject with him. I possess certain insights that I believe might be of value to him, but he has proven reluctant to engage in such a conversation with me. Do you have reason to think he might want to speak of it?"

"He is desperate, I think, to shake this yoke, for it intrudes upon every aspect of his present happiness," she said cautiously.

"Then let us see what can be done. I shall arrange for my children to go off on their outing alone this morning, and you and Georgiana must try to persuade Fitzwilliam to sit down with us." His calm resolve strengthened Lizzie's own determination and she nodded her agreement.

The two parted at the top of the stairs. Enlisting his wife's not inconsiderable powers of organisation, Mr Alexander quickly rallied his family around his plan of action until, with a minimum of commotion, they were set upon the road in two carriages for a day's adventure in the Derbyshire countryside. He returned to the library alone to ponder what the day might bring, silently summoning the spirit of Mr Darcy to come to his aid in the pursuit of the reconciliation that he had died hoping for.

Lizzie, after first assuring herself that her husband still slept, went directly to Georgiana's room and related to her eager ears the substance of her conversation with Mr Alexander. In light of her own confusion and her growing concern over her brother's state of mind, Georgiana immediately agreed to their plan. As she made her way back to her chamber, Lizzie felt a growing sense of urgency, mingled with a slight nervousness that Darcy might not share her confidence in the benefit of Mr Alexander's counsel. When she entered their bedchamber, she found that Will had awakened, but instead of rising, he lay staring at the ceiling. Lizzie sat down beside him and laid a hand on his chest, saying softly, "Good morning, Will."

He turned to look at her with heavy eyes, the smile he attempted slipping into a grimace of remorse. "Why do you not avoid me, Lizzie? Have you not yet grown weary of these endless scenes?" Turning away from her, he added softly, "God knows I have."

With forced brightness she said, "This is a large house, Will Darcy, but not so great that I could find room within it to hide from your temper." She raised her hand to his cheek, and with a gentle touch that belied her anxiety, turned his face towards hers. Her smile radiated a confidence that she scarcely felt, but it evoked from him a surge of tenderness that brought him to the edge of tears. "When we have finished unearthing all of the skeletons and given voice to all of the secrets of Pemberley, you will be at peace, Will, I am certain of it."

Putting his hand on hers he turned his face to kiss her palm gently. "I fear you will grow impatient before we reach the end of this long story," he said quietly.

"You knew well enough when you married me that patience is not my strongest virtue," she smiled, gaining confidence. "But perhaps my impatience will speed the story along." Her smile took on an intriguing impishness.

Darcy pushed himself up to sit facing her. "I mistrust that smile, Mrs Darcy," he said, a touch of lightness creeping into his voice. "What do you mean by it?"

With this sign of his lifting spirits, her ready optimism was unleashed. "I have spent the early morning with Mr Alexander, Will. I believe he knows a great deal about your past, and he is only wanting your approval to open the subject."

The smile faded from his eyes and a perplexed look took its place as he pondered this information, for his mind felt dull and disordered.

As his comprehension grew, so too did his anger, and at last he pushed past her and stood up, wrapping himself in his dressing gown before he spoke.

"What were you thinking of, Lizzie?" he demanded after pacing the perimeter of the room anxiously. "What have you told him?"

Lizzie rose to his challenge, her face flushed with indignation.

"Mr Alexander, or any other sentient observer, may easily read the tragedy in your face, Mr Darcy. If you mean for your family's history to be a secret, you would do well to hide it a bit better yourself." She paused for breath, noting that he made no answer, and continued in a softer tone. "We cannot continue in this manner, Will. You grow more miserable and Georgiana has been affected now so that she almost fears to speak to you. If I am impatient, it is because I feel we need a fresh approach. You have said yourself that Mr Alexander is very like your father, but I see between you no barrier to mutual respect and admiration. He may be able to shed some light on your father's feelings, but even if he cannot reassure you, he will certainly do you no harm."

Darcy had grown quiet and now he walked to his customary place by the window to think. Lizzie approached but did not speak, giving him time to reflect. When at last he turned to face her, anguish had supplanted his anger and he spoke with a quiet resignation.

"I understand that you mean only to help, Lizzie, but I cannot see what will be gained by airing our grief before the Alexanders."

Lizzie smiled weakly, clinging fast to her hope. "I told him nothing of your past, Will, only he seems to know more than you imagine. I believe he has been waiting for this opportunity for a long time."

With a deep sigh, Darcy nodded grimly. "If you are so determined, I will try."

Rising up on her toes, she gave him a kiss and then turned to go before he should change his mind. "Georgiana and I will wait for you in the library."

Lizzie stopped at Georgiana's room and informed her that Will had reluctantly agreed to the interview with Mr Alexander. As they started down the staircase arm in arm, Lizzie noticed that Georgiana was trembling. She stopped to face her, holding her arms in a strong grasp. "Georgiana," she said, smiling with more confidence than she felt, "perhaps we shall learn nothing new this morning, but I cannot help but think that we will benefit from a new perspective. In any case, it can hardly make the situation worse than it is."

"I hope you are right, Lizzie," was her soft reply.

Chapter Thirty Five

The two women found Mr Alexander waiting for them in the library. He disarmed Georgiana's fear by his kindly, confidant demeanour, and they whiled away their time with innocuous conversation about the quality of Pemberley's book collection. Darcy did not keep them long in suspense; in a few minutes he entered the room wearing a studied air of nonchalance and with a nod to Georgiana, greeted Mr Alexander with a pleasant 'Good Morning,' and an inquiry after Mrs Alexander that indicated he intended to keep the discussion light.

Mr Alexander had something else in mind, however. With a last silent invocation of his departed friend's guidance, he rose and spoke in a serious tone.

"I have asked Mrs Alexander to see that we are not disturbed." After a pause, he continued, "You will no doubt see me as a meddlesome old fool, Fitzwilliam, and you must judge for yourself, but I only ask that you hear me out."

Darcy sank back in his chair and shrugged with resignation as the speaker continued.

"I have for several years hoped for an opportunity to speak frankly with you, and my observations of you at Great Oaks and again last night have served to quicken my resolve. During the last days of his life, your father was in a state of bitter remorse over your estrangement from him. Before he died, he begged me to help you make peace with his memory. That charge has lain heavy on my heart these past years, and I despaired of being able to fulfil his wish, for you showed no inclination to continue our acquaintance. When your wedding trip brought you to Highbury Inn, I felt I had one final opportunity to discharge my obligation; indeed it seemed as though your father's hand could be traced in guiding you to that place and in prompting you to invite my family to Pemberley. If you now wish to reject my intercession, I will accept your decision and I will not intrude upon your private thoughts again. But I must tell you that the melancholy state in which I find you prompts me to urge that you pursue every avenue available to assure that the tragedy of your parents does not continue to haunt this house. To that end, I will gladly tell you what I know, if you have the will to hear it."

He returned to his chair and sat down to wait for Darcy's response. That young man's face had grown by turns incredulous, angry and, finally, painfully confused as he listened to the narrative. While it had required the utmost self-control to remain silent at first, in the end he found himself unable to speak. Closing his eyes, he passed a hand wearily across his brow and held it there, as if he could press the troubled thoughts within into coherence. Georgiana's eyes grew large with anxiety, while Lizzie gripped the arms of her chair and forced her energy into a silent prayer that he would seize the opportunity laid before him. Only Mr Alexander maintained a calm demeanour, his face compassionate but serene.

The silence grew oppressive before Darcy finally spoke.

"If my father confided in you, you must know that we were never close, although I admired and respected him." He paused, frowning thoughtfully, but at last discarded his reserve in favour of candour, and continued with quiet resignation. "I will not deny that I have long been troubled by confusing memories from my childhood, Mr Alexander. Until recently, I have not shared them with anyone, and indeed I have endeavoured to forget what I could find no way to understand. I find candour on the subject extremely difficult. Georgiana has, of course, no memory of our mother, and I am sorry to say that neither my father nor I confided in her the depth of the sorrow that ruled their marriage. For my part, I felt I was right to keep from her my dark thoughts; perhaps my father's motivation was similar."

Darcy stood up and moved to the window, and in the moments that followed, silent prayers for his release were offered up by the women who adored him. When he spoke again, a new resolve permeated his voice.

"In the past few months, I have been beset by a renewal of the anxiety that I had wanted to believe was put behind me. Perhaps it is my own marriage that precipitated these dark thoughts... perhaps I do not feel I deserve such happiness... " His voice trailed off and then he turned abruptly to meet Mr Alexander's patient gaze.

"In any case, it is clear that the silence in this house has done no one any good, and I think Georgiana and I must now try to see our parents as they really were, not as we would have wished them to be. If you possess knowledge that will aid us in that pursuit, I should like to hear it." He walked silently to his chair and sat down.

Mr Alexander nodded thoughtfully.

"I have been puzzling how to address this subject and I think it best that you ask me the questions that trouble you. I will answer as faithfully as I am able, but I must ask you to understand that I knew your mother only through your father's eyes, and then only what he saw fit to tell me. I hope I will not offend you if my impressions do not coincide with your own."

There was an uncomfortable silence which Darcy finally broke with a question that had long perplexed him.

"I believe that my mother and father hated each other, Mr Alexander. I want to know how they came to be married."

Mr Alexander weighed his words carefully.

"I knew your father at college, Fitzwilliam, long before he married your mother. She was introduced to him by Lord de Bourgh soon after he married her sister, Lady Catherine. In those days, little thought was given to any reason for marriage other than the mutual interests of the families concerned, but in this case there was a strong attraction between the two. Your father came back to college after spending his term holiday with the de Bourgh's, raving like a lunatic about the woman he meant to marry." He laughed softly at the recollection. "Your father was a kind, soft-hearted man and a good friend, as well as a brilliant student. When he returned that term, he could barely eat or sleep, much less attend to his studies, so obsessed was he by the thought of her. Fortunately, he had only to sit his final exams that spring, and he managed to pass, I think, not so much on the strength of his performance as on his reputation as a scholar."

"As you know, I am sure, our families did not travel in the same circles at that time, and so I had no direct knowledge of her or her family. But from your father's description, she was the most ravishingly handsome woman on the face of the earth. He told us her dark eyes had a fire that burned straight into his heart, while her bearing was all icy composure. Our group of friends teased him mercilessly, I'm afraid, warning him that fire and ice do not mix."

A startled sound rose from Georgiana's lips. When their eyes turned to her she coloured deeply and said, in a quiet, trembling voice, "I was remembering last night something that my father said to me when I was very young. He told me that my mother was 'fire and ice', but I did not understand what he meant."

Mr Alexander cleared his throat and said, "Just so." He took up the narrative again. "I was in no position to influence your father, but as a friend I expressed my fear that such a strong woman might not be the best choice for a wife. He was polite, but the attraction he felt was encouraged by his family's wishes and her own, apparently, for the match was deemed an excellent one on both sides. The marriage was arranged soon after he had finished his degree. You were born within the year, Fitzwilliam, and our paths did not cross for many years thereafter, but your father and I corresponded faithfully. His early letters were full of his happiness and I assumed that my fears had been unfounded. But as the years went on his letters lost their cheerful tone, and although he did not complain, I began to worry that something was amiss." He paused, lost in thought.

Georgiana, emboldened by her anxiety to understand what had been hidden from her, asked, "What could have happened to estrange them?"

Mr Alexander frowned over the memory.

"One day, some years after his marriage, your father appeared at Great Oaks, alone, and asked if he could stay with us for a few days. Of course I was happy to see him, but I could not help but notice that he was deeply troubled. That night, we retired to the library after supper and he began to drink heavily. For the next several hours he poured out his heart to me, telling me more details of his marriage than I should have heard. What he told me disturbed me greatly." A very long pause followed before Mr Alexander began again, and as he spoke he looked sadly into Fitzwilliam's eyes. "I think you must have some memory of the disharmony that was growing between your parents, Fitzwilliam, for his unhappiness concerned your mother's attention to you."

Darcy had been sitting quietly until now, fitting the pictures in his mind to Mr Alexander's words.

"Was it in August that he visited you?" he asked.

Mr Alexander closed his eyes in concentration and then replied, "Yes, I believe it was. Catherine had just been born, and you would have been about five years of age then. Do you remember this incident?"

Darcy nodded, frowning, and spoke as if remembering a dream. "On my fifth birthday, my father brought a puppy to the nursery and gave it to me. When my mother came into the room and found us playing together, her face turned cold with rage and I felt frightened. She stepped out of the room and called for Philip, the butler, and when he came running she told him to take the dog out immediately. She ordered my nurse to give me a bath and then left the room. I looked at my father, who stood by without uttering a sound, and waited for him to explain what I had done wrong, but he said nothing, and left the room. Then I asked my nurse why Philip had taken the puppy away, but she did not answer me, and I saw that she was crying." His frown deepened as his eyes turned to Mr Alexander. "I heard angry voices from their room that night and I did not see my father for the next few days, but I understood that I must not ask my mother either about him or about the dog. I think from that day I began to understand the code of silence in our home."

Mr Alexander shook his head sadly.

"Yes, Fitzwilliam, that fits with what your father told me." A silence ensued and then Mr Alexander asked, "Was your mother kind to you, Fitzwilliam?"

The question struck Darcy as odd, and he carefully considered his answer.

"I always thought she loved me very much, but I was puzzled by her, and sometimes frightened. At times she would laugh like a girl and play silly games with me. We would sing and dance together until she fell on the floor laughing. But her anger was quick, and I suppose I learned very early not to approach her when she was in a dark mood. I also learned not to speak to her about my father. I was either with her or with him - we were almost never together unless there were guests in the house, and it puzzled me to see them laughing and talking in the same room on those occasions. As I grew older, I felt a terrible rage about the deceit we practised." He slumped back in his chair.

Mr Alexander looked at Fitzwilliam questioningly and after a few moments, asked if he should continue. With a glance at Georgiana, Darcy nodded weakly.

"I will tell you what your father believed, and I must say that it seems to me that he was right, but as I have said, I did not know your mother. He believed that after you were born your mother replaced him with you in her affections." He paused for Fitzwilliam to consider this thought and then added, "He felt she needed to possess you, to be constantly assured that you loved her as she loved you. She could not tolerate any sign of your affection for your father, as this threatened her need to be the centre of your life."

Darcy's head was in his hands by the end of this speech and for a long time there was no sound in the room but the ticking of the mantle clock. Finally, he looked up with tears of anguish in his eyes and asked hoarsely, "But why did my father allow this? Why did he never try to explain it to me?"

Mr Alexander stood up and went to Darcy's side, putting a hand gently on his shoulder.

"This thought has troubled me, Fitzwilliam. The day that he came to my house, I advised him that for your sake he must not let this situation continue. You possess a strength of character that your father did not have, son," he added sadly. "I think that he was afraid of your mother in a way. He was certain that if she left Pemberley she would take you with her, and he could not bear the thought of losing you. For her part, I believe it suited her to continue living here, where she could be in control. By keeping her with him, he at least was able to be near you." He walked across to the window and gazed out at the beautiful park below. Then he turned back to study the sorrowing family and said softly, "And I think you should also know that he never stopped loving her until the day he died."

Darcy stood up abruptly, his dark eyes blazing with anger.

"That is not good enough, Mr Alexander! My mother died when I was thirteen. My father had eight more years of my undivided attention, and yet he chose to maintain his silence. He allowed me to believe that it did not matter to him whether I was at Pemberley or not, as long as he had his precious daughter with him." With this he stormed out of the room, slamming the door as he left. With a gasp, Lizzie started after him, but Mr Alexander called her back.

"Wait, Elizabeth," he said gravely. "Let him think about what has been said. He will need some time to understand his feelings," and walking over to take her arm, he turned her towards Georgiana. "I think you are needed here," he said quietly. "I will leave you alone for a little while."

Lizzie's tearful gaze took in Georgiana's ashen face and she saw that he was right, for the young woman had not reached the relief of tears and seemed on the point of collapse. Lizzie ran to kneel beside her, and took her face in her hands, crooning softly to her, "Don't, don't, darling. It will be all right, you'll see. He is so hurt and angry that he does not know what to think. You know he does not mean to hurt you." Finally the tears came. Lizzie pressed the fair head against her shoulder, rocking her gently and stroking her hair. Sobs shook Georgiana and Lizzie's own tears soon mingled with her sister-in-law's.

After what seemed an eternity of misery, Georgiana straightened up, and the first honestly expressed anger of her life spilled out.

"Oh, Lizzie, I hate this house! It has brought us nothing but grief. I wish it would burn to the ground!"

Lizzie sat abruptly on the floor, and to the amazement of both, started to laugh. It began as a tiny giggle that she tried desperately to check, but soon grew into a rolling convulsion that left her breathless, with tears streaming down her cheeks. Georgiana's rage melted into bewilderment. When Lizzie was at last able to speak, she said hoarsely, "Oh, my dear Georgiana, I am so sorry. You must believe that I am not laughing at you. It is only that since I married your brother, I have had to learn a completely new style of living. The cycles of sorrow and joy and rage in this family make me feel I am always struggling to keep up. Is it not enough that one moment I am in a passionate embrace with Will and the next moment a door is slamming or he has broken into tears? Now I have you sobbing disconsolately in my arms and suddenly you want to burn the house down."

Emboldened by the tentative smile that had broken on the girl's face, she drew a steadying breath and added, in a conspiratorial tone, "The first time I watched your brother exit a room in such a rage was the night he proposed to me. The second was on our wedding night. He was gone for more than two hours, and when he came back we cried together for two more. Your cycle of emotions is much shorter, Georgiana. Thank heavens!"

Georgiana's eyes widened in disbelief and she sputtered, "I cannot believe it - not on your wedding night!" Lizzie could not prevent herself from beginning to laugh again, and in a moment Georgiana succumbed to its infectious sound, dropping to the floor into Lizzie's embrace, until they rocked back and forth with mingled laughter and tears.

When they were a little calmer, Lizzie patted Georgiana's hand and confided, "Well, I always expected that night to be the most memorable of my life. I certainly shall not forget it!"

A quiet knock on the library door startled them, and in a moment Mrs Alexander's solicitous face peeked in. Her kind husband had asked her to go in to see if she could comfort the two young ladies, and she had expected tears, but the sight of them huddled on the floor made her knit her brow in confusion.

The ladies rose hastily from the floor and Lizzie, wiping her face and attempting a serious look, said, "Please do come in, Mrs Alexander. I assure you we can account for this extraordinary behaviour." Mrs Alexander came in and sat down, as it seemed nothing else was to be done. Her face wore a kindly, if bewildered, look.

Lizzie and Georgiana looked at each other as if they were children caught misbehaving, but their laughter was too great a relief to regret, and, indeed, rather than feeling sobered, they were in danger of losing all control again. Lizzie could immediately see that Georgiana was going to be of no help, and she turned her attention to

Mrs Alexander, working very hard to maintain some semblance of decorum. She tried to explain.

"Perhaps Mr Alexander told you that he offered to help Will and Georgiana understand the somewhat troubled relationship between their parents. What he told them has sent Will off in a terrible rage and left Georgiana in a confusion of grief and anger. The laughter, I must confess, was my own device for dispelling gloom, as my nature cannot bear the weight of so much sorrow." At Lizzie's explanation, Georgiana was again overcome with giggles, and Lizzie continued, struggling against the urge to join her, "I am afraid that it has worked too well with Georgiana."

Mrs Alexander, a light-hearted person herself, was nonetheless still baffled, but she smiled pleasantly and waited in all patience. Lizzie turned to Georgiana to say, "We must compose ourselves, dear, for if Will should return to find us like this I am afraid of what scene might follow." That was indeed a sobering thought. Mrs Alexander looked from one to the other with concern.

"I am sorry, my dear," she said to Georgiana kindly, "that I did not know your mother at all, and your father very little. I am sure, however, that whatever difficulties they had in their marriage, they both loved you and your brother, and would not want their memory to cause you pain." That the pain she saw was being so oddly expressed seemed not to give her pause, and Lizzie struggled to remain in control.

Georgiana, however, was quite composed for the moment.

"Thank you, Mrs Alexander, for your concern, but you mustn't worry about us. I am sure that when we have all had time to collect our thoughts, we will be able to feel quite at ease."

Mrs Alexander nodded.

"That is very sensible of you, my dear." To Lizzie, she added, "The first year of marriage is always the most trying, Elizabeth, as I told each of my children on the eve of their marriage. But your

274

Fitzwilliam is a wonderful boy, and with you so good-natured and cheerful, you will see it will all be soon set to right." With that she stood up and said, "I will leave you alone now, for you must be wanting to talk privately." As she passed through the door, she turned back to say, "Very clever of you, this laughing cure, Elizabeth. Perhaps we should suggest it to the physicians at Bath, for I am sure it would do more to relieve most complaints than drinking mineral water." She smiled to herself as she closed the door.

Lizzie and Georgiana were too exhausted to be in danger of further collapse either into tears, rage or laughter for some time. The thought of Darcy pacing about alone was disconcerting and they wondered what they should do, and more importantly, what they should say when he returned. They had only a few minutes to ponder before he opened the library door and walked in.

Chapter Thirty Six

Lizzie could guess by the look on Darcy's face that *he* had found no relief in laughter, for sorrow and remorse were written clearly in the lines across his forehead. He went directly to Georgiana and she stood up to meet him, attempting to mirror his serious countenance. He began in all earnestness.

"Georgiana, I am so sorry to have caused you grief. You must believe... " but stopped abruptly, for what he read in her countenance could in no way be taken for grief, nor even for compassion. Lizzie recognised the look in Georgiana's eyes before Darcy did, and her eyes widened in alarm, but she could do nothing more than shake her head hastily before an avalanche of laughter cascaded through the room. Georgiana tried valiantly to stop herself, stamping her foot as if to demand order, but try as she might to focus her thoughts on the face before her, the image of her brother's wedding night defection would not yield its grip on her imagination. Lizzie sat down quickly, covering her face with her hands so that he should not see her own contortions as she tried to prevent herself from joining in.

To say that Fitzwilliam was astonished would have been to understate the case. He dropped onto the nearest chair, waiting to see what would happen next. Georgiana held her breath, but it only caused her next swell of laughter to come out in an explosion. She gasped to Lizzie, "Help me!" but Lizzie was shaking uncontrollably by this time, rocking back and forth in her chair. When she at last took a breath, she started to hiccup, which collapsed them both again, and Georgiana groped for her chair. Darcy looked from one to the other in utter disbelief. Lizzie at last managed to force her face into a semblance of a frown and began to breathe deeply and slowly to control her violent hiccups. When she felt she could maintain a small measure of dignity, she walked to Darcy's chair and sat down on his knees.

"There," she said with attempted seriousness to Georgiana, "that went well, don't you think?" This brought fresh peals of laughter from both of them and they were doubled over again in a moment.

At last, a stitch in her side made Lizzie straighten up abruptly. The pain refocused her thoughts on Will, who she found wearing a baffled smile. She touched his cheek and said sweetly, "Thank you for seeing things as we do, dear."

"I have no idea at all what way you see anything, either of you. I am merely smiling to see that you have given yourself a pain for your incomprehensible behaviour, Lizzie. While I have been cursing myself for wounding my precious sister, you have apparently rewritten our tragedy into a delightful comedy."

Georgiana, finally able to speak, exclaimed mirthfully, "It is only Lizzie's new therapy for grief, Fitzwilliam. Mrs Alexander says she is sure it will serve better than mineral water from Bath to cure what ails us."

"So Mrs Alexander has been laughing with you as well?" he asked incredulously.

Georgiana said seriously, "She only smiled, for she was not nearly as miserable as we were."

"If depth of misery be the key, then I should by now be rolling on the floor," he replied calmly.

Lizzie's pain had begun to subside and she said, "You only want a bit of practice." She stood up with a show of decorum and went back to her chair, smoothing her dress as she sat down and then wiping the last of the tears from her eyes. "There. I believe I am quite serious now," she said, setting her face in a frown.

He answered her with a mocking grin, "Yes, I can see that you are."

"Stop that, Will!" she cried. "I am afraid if I laugh again something will certainly break."

He imitated her frown. "It would certainly serve you right if it did."

"Now then," she began, ignoring his remark, "since we are all friends again, let me explain."

He leaned back in his chair clasping his hands behind his head in an expectant pose. "I am ready to be informed."

Lizzie explained the sequence of events after he had left the room, and when she reached the description of Georgiana's rage, she was forced to dramatise it for him, clenching her fists and stamping her foot petulantly. This brought Darcy upright in his chair. "*You,* Georgiana?"

Georgiana was slightly vexed by his question, and, swinging around to face him, she asked, "Why should you be so surprised? Do you think I have never been angry before?"

His look grew more incredulous, but her anger, rather than sobering him, brought him dangerously close to laughter himself. He tried to murmur an apology, but no sooner would he open his mouth than he felt compelled to close it. The result was a rather foolish grin meant to convey remorse.

Georgiana wavered for a few seconds on the verge of self-righteous indignation, for she was rather enjoying the heady feeling of anger. At last, however, the sight of Fitzwilliam's ridiculous attempt at contrition forced a smile to break through, and she said archly, "It happens that I feel things as strongly as you do; it is only that I am usually less dramatic about it."

Darcy's guffaw could be heard in the drawing room. Mrs Alexander smiled at her husband knowingly and said, "There, you see dear, now she has him doing it too." He merely shook his head, bemused, and as his wife picked up her sewing, she added sweetly, "I mean to recommend her cure to everyone."

By the time calm finally settled over the room, exhaustion reigned. Darcy said, wiping his eyes, "I don't understand how you manage to translate misery into merriment, my dear, but I must say I like it."

"I cannot take credit for what I should probably judge to be a weakness in my character," she replied. "I told you before we were married, Will, that I only remember that part of the past which pleases me. I have tried to be more serious for your sake, but this morning I must concede how little I can control that part of my nature." Looking kindly from brother to sister she said, "I do not mean at all to make light of your pain - I understand that it is very real to you - but sorrowful thoughts simply cannot hold my attention for long."

"They have held my attention too long," Darcy said with a shake of the head. "Lord knows, Lizzie, it is fortunate for us that you *are* able to laugh as you do, or you would never have married me."

"Or, once married, would have been destroyed by your wedding night," added Georgiana with a conspiratorial smile at Lizzie, as she stood up to take her leave. "I think our ghosts have fled to their rest, and so shall I," she said, yawning. "I barely slept last night, and this morning's exercise has quite worn me out." She could not resist turning back to her brother as she paused at the door, "Unfortunately for you, I do not have Lizzie's forgiving nature, Fitzwilliam. You shall still have to answer for your ill-natured remark when I have the strength to take you to task." She smiled to herself as she closed the door behind her.

Darcy was very much amused by this saucy remark.

"While your presence has certainly improved *my* manners, Lizzie, I begin to fear that it is unleashing the beast in Georgiana."

"I believe she has a great deal to say to you, Will, and now that she sees you as more approachable, I do not doubt she will unburden herself completely, given a chance."

"I am sure you are right. In fact, I seem to have quite a bit to say myself. I had no idea that I resented my father's attention to Georgiana until the words came out of my mouth," he said, walking across the room to her. He raised her into a grateful embrace and they stood a long while together, content without words, until, remembering their guests, Lizzie slipped her arm through Will's and they left the library in search of the Alexanders.

Chapter Thirty Seven

As they entered the drawing room, Darcy extended his hand to Mr Alexander, saying as he did so, "I must apologise to you for my childish behaviour. It was inexcusable."

The wise old gentleman held on to Darcy's hand for some time, scrutinising his face with kindly concern.

"You must never regret your own feelings, Fitzwilliam. I was sorry to see you so unhappy, and to be the cause of more pain with what I said, but I believe it is the truth that will free you from your melancholy at last, and you are right to pursue it."

They sat down and Mr Alexander asked if he might say one thing more on the subject. Fitzwilliam nodded.

"You are angry with your father, Fitzwilliam, for not drawing you to him after your mother's death. In your place I would feel the same. But as your father's friend, I understand that the pattern of distance between you was so established by that time that he did not know how to approach you. You are not to blame for that," he said emphatically, "and he did not blame you. No, he blamed himself. But he lacked the strength to begin anew, for you had, by that time, formed rather strong opinions and defences. Your forcefulness, Fitzwilliam, resembles your mother more than your father. He saw, I think, your strength, but not your need, and he had been so wounded by your mother's rejection that I believe he was afraid to seek your love."

Darcy confessed, "While I longed to feel for him what others felt, what Georgiana felt, I suppose I had seen him too long through my mother's eyes."

"He was a very good man, Fitzwilliam, but it does not always follow that good men are good fathers. You must believe that he loved you very much and was proud of you. Some day, I hope you will be able to forgive him his weakness. I don't doubt that you will, for you have his goodness of heart."

"And more importantly," Darcy said, patting Lizzie's arm affectionately, "I have Lizzie to always remind me that love is forgiving, for in spite of my tempers and moods, she seems unable to be driven to hate me." He smiled at her adoringly, "I think that the more difficult task is forgiving myself, but I am learning, at least, to find a reason for mirth where I saw none before."

Mr Alexander relaxed, encouraged by the tone of their conversation. "I am delighted to see that you are aware of how much a man is in need of the love of a good woman. Your father would have been a very great man indeed had he even a portion of your luck on that score."

Fitzwilliam answered quietly, "Believe me when I say that nothing is more important to me." With a tender look at Lizzie, he turned back to Mr Alexander and continued thoughtfully, "What you have told me about my father today I accept as truth; it explains many things. Perhaps in understanding his sorrow I will grow in time to accept my own feelings of loss. I have recently reached my own conclusion as to the damage wrought by my mother. It remains for me to reconcile the love I felt for her as a child with the anger I now have at her duplicity." He grew quiet, staring into the distance as he considered the troubling question that rose up in his mind. At last he asked, steeling himself against the answer, "Do you think she was capable of being unfaithful to my father?"

Mr Alexander took a slow and heavy breath, studying the hands that lay in his lap as if he had not heard the question. His answer, when it finally came, was forthright. "Your father believed her to be, although I must tell you that I chastised him for what I thought was an unfounded obsession." He continued in a quieter voice, "Your mother had a passionate nature, to be sure, and whatever love she originally felt for your father seems to have been extinguished not long after your birth. He assumed he had lost her to another man."

If everyone in the room followed that thought to its logical conclusion, none of them showed a sign of it. The question of Georgiana's birth, eleven years later, was one that even the intrepid Lizzie would not voice at this moment. Mrs Alexander's quiet stitching was all the motion the room contained until Darcy, unable to remain calm with such agitating thoughts abroad, pushed up from his chair and walked to the pianoforte, resting his hand on its burnished wood. After more than one false start, he managed at last to ask, "Did he ever mention to you a young man by the name of Trevor Handley in that context?"

Mr Alexander nodded and cleared his throat to say softly, "Among others."

Darcy's eyes widened and his colour rose. "Others?" he demanded.

Mr Alexander rose and walked to his side, placing a steadying hand on Darcy's shoulder.

"As I said, Fitzwilliam, I believed at the time that his suspicions stemmed from an unhealthy fixation. He could not accept the loss of her affection, and with every change of her volatile moods, he concluded that she had found or lost a new channel for her passion. He watched every man who had contact with them, for so consumed was he by his love for her, he assumed every man alive would find the same fascination." He waited for Darcy to digest this information before continuing. "Do you wish to hear my opinion?"

Darcy nodded in resignation.

"Your mother *was* a beauty, Fitzwilliam, as you no doubt remember, and no one could fail to be moved by her if she chose to be charming. But I believe most other men would soon have been warned away by the dangerous recklessness of her temperament. Your father simply could not free himself from her spell." Noting the trembling of the shoulder under his hand, Mr Alexander gave Fitzwilliam a reassuring squeeze and turned away, indicating with a slight movement of his head to Mrs Alexander that they should depart. As he turned to leave, he noted with pleasure that Lizzie was already moving to her husband's side.

As the Alexanders passed through the door, Darcy found his voice and called hoarsely after him, "But a boy of seventeen might have been powerless to resist if she chose to flatter him... "

Mr Alexander looked into the sad eyes with a steady gaze.

"Quite possibly."

He ushered Mrs Alexander out of the room ahead of him and pulled the door gently to.

Chapter Thirty Eight

The following morning dawned clear and warm. Darcy awoke to an empty room where the sun's rays had already taken the chill from the December night, and he stretched languidly, conscious that for the first time in many days, no fragments of troubled dreams darkened the horizon. Walking to the window, he stood for several minutes gazing absently at the prospect below, his mind curiously empty of its habitual musings.

The young Alexanders had returned late from their excursion the previous day to find a household subdued and reflective. Lizzie and Georgiana had made a valiant effort to enliven the evening for the sake of their guests, but Darcy had only managed a slightly distracted air as his contribution. At a whispered suggestion from Lizzie, he excused himself before supper on the pretext of a headache, retiring immediately to bed. His exhaustion did not immediately offer a release into sleep, but the hour of solitary thought before he closed his eyes did bring a resolution that he must seek out Trevor Handley at his earliest opportunity and make what peace he could there.

A movement in the garden below caught his eye and he raised the window sash to enjoy the unseasonable warmth of the morning. From a lone gardener the sound of a Scottish melody wafted upward. Darcy smiled, remembering how scarcely a year ago he had watched Miss Elizabeth Bennet from a window at Netherfield House on a similar fall day. He was filled with a longing to see her smile, and he dressed quickly and hurried down to breakfast.

His warm greeting and light-hearted apology as he entered the breakfast parlour brought a smile to Lizzie's face and quickly laid to rest any speculation from other members of their party on Darcy's state of mind. Declaring the weather perfect for an outing, Darcy proposed they carry on with their plan to ride to Lambton Bluff. It was arranged that Mr and Mrs Alexander should arrive in the carriage at the rendezvous point, bringing the lunch with them. The rest of the party set off to dress for their ride and Darcy and Eric headed to the stables to settle on mounts. Finally, with a tremendous amount of teasing laughter, everyone was happily seated on a horse and riding off in the same direction.

The novelty of such a warm sunny day so late the year, especially as it had come on the heels of a long stretch of dirty weather, served to elevate the spirit of the party to a childlike exuberance. Challenges were made and races run, with Lizzie most often out front on Sweet Felicity. She seemed to unite her will to the horse's and they moved as one, proud and determined, and very fast, Darcy thought, pushing his grey to move up beside her.

Seeing him approach, her smile turned playful and she urged her horse forward, daring Darcy to keep pace with her. He took up the challenge, and although his stallion had the longer stride, Sweet Felicity was determined never to follow another, and she pulled ahead again. They finally pulled up at a stream and dismounted to wait for the others who had fallen behind. Pulling Lizzie to him, Darcy stole a kiss, saying sternly, "That will teach you not to outrun us!"

She laughed and patted Sweet Felicity, directing her answer to the horse with a toss of her head. "Do you hear that, my dear? This man's passion is aroused by being beaten. Since you refuse to lose, I suppose I shall just have to bear his kisses." He reached for her hand but she eluded him, running away as she called back over her shoulder, "Do foot races have the same effect on you?"

He ran after her, catching up easily this time, and she collapsed, laughing, to the ground. He pulled her to her feet and as they walked back toward the assembling party, he said playfully, "I believe we shall never know if it is the winning or the losing that excites me most, for I seem to want to kiss you in either case."

288

They sat together by the stream, basking in the warmth of the sun and chatting idly. A painter capturing the group arrayed beside their grazing horses, white cloud puffs lazing overhead, might have named his work *Idyll*, for so it seemed. With all sombre thoughts carefully stored away, the pleasure of the moment was delightful to Lizzie and Darcy.

Edward quickly became restless, however, and jumping up, called to Georgiana to leave the old people and come with him. They mounted and set off ahead of the others toward the bluff, which they were approaching from the back side. The sun had moved past midday by the time everyone reached the road where they were to meet the carriage.

The place they had agreed upon was called 'The Altar' by the neighbours, for a circle of mysterious stones seemed to grow out of the thin layer of turf covering the bluff. They were worn smooth by rain and wind and by generations of children clambering over them and travellers taking their rest. The carriage arrived with lunch and the elder Alexanders, and the warm sun, coupled with a heavy meal and several bottles of fine wine, soon rendered the party calm and sedentary. Darcy took the opportunity to ask Mr Alexander to walk with him along the bluff, and they admired the prospect of the sleepy village of Lambton below. As they ambled lazily across the verdant turf, Darcy remarked, "I regret that my pride prevented me for so long from seeking your counsel, sir. The burden of my father's final wish must have been heavy indeed."

Mr Alexander nodded thoughtfully. "I confess that I had some time ago given up any hope of approaching you. But I believe that before now, you were not ready to hear what I had to say. My regret is that *you* have suffered for so long."

Darcy answered candidly, "Until I met Lizzie, I had no standard by which to judge my pride or my unhappiness." Reaching an outcropping of stone, they found a seat and turned their faces toward the carefree picnic party. "I am bewildered by her devotion to me, in spite of all of the reasons I have given her to despise me."

Laying a hand on the young man's arm, Mr Alexander said sincerely, "It is only that she sees more clearly than most the strength of your character, son. She is too wise to love without reason."

Darcy smiled at the compliment to both, and the two sat enjoying the scene before them until Darcy broke the silence.

"I believe I have done Trevor Handley a great injustice, and I am anxious that the sun should not set again before I have made an attempt to right it. Could I impose upon you again to play the host in my stead for a few hours?"

Without asking any questions, Mr Alexander answered with a smile. "You have chosen the right path, Fitzwilliam. Your father's admiration of you was not misplaced."

When they rejoined the conversation at the stone circle, Mrs Alexander was expressing an interest in taking a walk through the village of Lambton, and it was soon agreed that the united party should return by the carriage road. Darcy took Lizzie aside and explained his intention to her, and the pride in her eyes quelled the nervousness he felt about facing Trevor. With the assurance that he should catch up with them for tea at the Lambton Inn, Darcy mounted his horse and set out for Croftwoods, while the party set out at a leisurely pace along the road to the village.

The quiet town was hard-pressed to accommodate such a large and boisterous visitation, but having tied up horses and carriage at the inn, they broke into small groups, agreeing to return for tea at four. Lizzie alerted the innkeeper, and then, taking Mr and Mrs Alexander under her wing, she led them on a pleasant stroll about the green and in the shops.

Darcy urged his horse to full speed, fearing he might lose his resolve if he tarried, and covered the short distance to Croftwoods in half an hour. As he expected, he found Trevor at the stable, engrossed in the work he loved so well. Darcy's face was flushed with the ride and with the sense of urgency his mission engendered; Trevor's eyes betrayed nothing but a mild curiosity. Handing over the mare he was tending to a groom, he walked out into the afternoon sun without uttering a sound, with Darcy close beside him. When they were free of the constraint of being overheard, Trevor stopped abruptly and turned to face Darcy, studying him intently as he waited.

Darcy met his unflinching gaze and spoke with a voice that was taut with emotion, "I believe it is my turn to apologise." He wavered for a moment, unaided by any response from Trevor, and then continued forcefully, "My mother stood between us for seventeen years. It served no purpose. I am just beginning to understand the evil in her power over my life, and my father's." Had he not felt the need to look away to compose himself, Darcy would have seen in his friend's eyes that an aggrieved compassion had quickly supplanted his guarded stare. Instead, he mistook Trevor's silence for stubbornness, and cried out in despair, "Damn it all, Trevor, I am weary beyond belief with fighting my parents' battles for them. They are dead, and we are alive. Let us bury them. Enough damage has been done without my adding fresh injuries."

Trevor's hands grasped Darcy by the shoulders and he spoke with the tenderness of a father to a prodigal son. "Never mind, Willie boy. I should have known better than to take offence at your anger. The past will have no power over us if we give it none." With a weary sigh, he shook his head and said, "Come, let us go inside. You must tell me what raised the spectre of your mother that day."

As Darcy related Georgiana's story of the sketch, Trevor sat plying his forehead with his finger tips, remembering scenes from his time at Pemberley that he had carefully confined to the recesses of his mind. Any thought of Mrs Darcy was wont to lead him along a dangerous path, culminating in a memory that was altogether too painful to see the light of day. A long silence followed the end of Darcy's story.

When Trevor finally spoke, his voice was soft as if from a great weariness. Looking directly into Darcy's eyes, he said, "When we met at Lambton, I told you that I had no reason to hope you would believe me. I did hope that you would come to understand that I never meant to harm you. For what it is worth, I swear to you that your mother did not draw that sketch of me. Before I left for Pemberley, my sister drew it and sent it with me as a gift. In my hurry to quit the house, I suppose I forgot it in my room; I can only assume that your mother found it there and took a fancy to it. Why she should have hidden it is more than I can say, unless your father's jealousy gave her cause to think it wise."

Darcy laughed, a trifle bitterly to be sure, but still it served to lift the gloom from the air. "I have made plenty of enemies in my lifetime, but none has ever done me as much injury as I do myself. My habit of solitary thought serves me ill. I shall try to remember in future to ask questions first and let my anger rise on the wings of fact rather than fantasy."

Once levity had been introduced, Trevor's eternal optimism rendered him cheerful and boisterous in a moment. Darcy required a little longer, but a sudden vision of yesterday's drama reminded him to laugh at himself, which he did, once begun, with enthusiasm. Before an hour had passed, no strangeness remained between them and Trevor had agreed to come for dinner the following day.

As Darcy made his way towards the Inn at Lambton, he forced himself to consider that Trevor had still not directly refuted his father's accusation and he could not say why he had refrained from pursuing that topic. Perhaps because, he suddenly realised, the answer no longer made much difference to him. With a dawning knowledge that his earlier anguish had been replaced by a dispassionate curiosity, he broke into a rippling laughter that made his horse toss his head nervously. Darcy urged him to a gallop, shouting out loud to the wind, "I am free!"

Chapter Thirty Nine

By four o'clock all of the delights of Lambton had been sampled and the Darcys and Alexanders reunited in the parlour of the inn. Darcy arrived within a few minutes of the others, and after an animated greeting, begged to be excused to speak privately with Lizzie. His grin assured her that his effort had been successful, but until he had dragged her, laughing, to an alcove beside the Inn, picked her up and spun her around, she could not have guessed how much so. They exchanged a breathless kiss and in answer to her impatient questions, Darcy answered teasingly, "I will only tell you one secret, Mrs Darcy, and the rest you shall have to win from me later. This one is the best, and I bestow it in grateful appreciation for your miraculous laughing cure of yesterday." After a tantalising pause, he said proudly, "I have stepped out from my mother's shadow."

Lizzie sobered immediately and drew in a sharp breath. "What do you mean, Will?" she asked.

"I do not care if she had a hundred affairs, nor with whom. She loved me as she was able, she lived and died as she pleased. I am severed from her influence to pursue my own happiness." He smiled confidently and continued, "If, God help me, I make as big a muddle of my life as she did of hers, I shall have only myself to blame for it."

The pure, clear notes of Lizzie's answering laughter rang through him like the fluttering of wings, driving the smoky vestiges of bitterness and fear from his mind and fanning his love into a clean, blue flame. "I will tell you all about it later," he said with a smile that promised a great deal. Arm in arm they returned to the dining parlour, flushed with pleasure. To Georgiana's questioning look, Darcy returned a secretive smile, and by way of explanation, announced to his guests that a very old friend of the family, Mr Trevor Handley, would join them for dinner the next day. Mr Alexander nodded sagely and Georgiana could scarcely contain her pleasure at the news or at the sparkle in his eyes.

Lizzie and Darcy sat down to tea with a resolve to focus their attention on their guests, but errant thoughts continued to intrude. Her eyes strayed to his face at every opportunity, as if to reassure herself that he remained as transformed as he had seemed a few moments before. The communication that passed between them, encompassing all the tumult of their courtship and the sweetness of their union, gave rise to an exchange of smiles and knowing looks around them.

Amply fed and pleasantly exhausted, the party that left the Inn was very much more subdued than the one setting out from Pemberley that morning. The sun was down before they reached the manor, and the consensus of the travellers was for baths and early retirement. Only Georgiana and Edward lingered in the drawing room, their thoughts turned to a discussion of his studies in Paris. Having made a valiant attempt at the pleasantries of good-nights, Lizzie and Darcy at last found themselves alone in their room. Without wasting a moment on the questions and explanations that had seemed so urgent in Lambton, they chose instead to finish what the morning's first kiss had started, and all of the emotions of the past two days broke like waves on the stormy sea of their passion. Memories of joy and sorrow, hope and despair swept them along until they lay spent but safe on the shore, drifting into a deep sleep, lulled by the sounds of the receding gale.

Hours later, Lizzie awakened to a kiss on the forehead. She smiled sleepily, the ominous vestiges of her dream slipping away as she nestled into Darcy's encircling arms. He murmured, "What troubled your sleep, my love? You were crying."

She stretched and sat up, frowning with the effort of recalling the disjointed images. A slight shudder passed through her as the vision cleared, and she said, too quickly, "It was nothing, Will, only a dream."

"Tell me about it." She hesitated and he sat up and took her hands. "I don't wonder that you hesitate. I have been so miserable, I know that you and Georgiana have feared for my sanity. But I promise you, Lizzie, the worst is past, I am sure of it. Please."

"I dreamt of your mother," she said tentatively, and seeing he did not flinch from the words, continued. "We were in Lambton, at the Inn, and she came for you. She spoke to you in the sweetest tones, but I was frightened of her. I asked you to send her away... " Her voice trailed off and she looked down at her hands, resting in his.

His grip tightened, but he spoke calmly. "Lizzie, do you remember when you told me that our love was strong enough to overcome my past? I was not sure then, but I am now. She will never come between us again." His eyes, illuminated by moonlight, glowed with a new serenity and assurance, and she rose up to meet his lips, trembling with a reawakened feeling of hope.

The moon set and the winter sky shimmered with the movements of the sentinel stars while Lizzie and Darcy talked quietly of the past and the future. As dawn touched the sky with its first fingers, the nightmarish memories of sorrow and anger had been supplanted by a fresh dream of peace.

Chapter Forty

With a renewed determination to focus on their guests, Lizzie and Darcy rose early, greeted by fair weather and Mr Alexander enjoying his morning solitude. Darcy reached out a hand in greeting and said, "I want to thank you again, Mr Alexander, for everything you have done for us."

"It is you who have done the work, Fitzwilliam. You have not been given an easy path, but you have come a great distance on it."

With a smile at Lizzie, Darcy replied, "I pride myself on one thing, that I had the good sense to marry a woman who improves me at every turn."

Mrs Alexander appeared at the door, and Mr Alexander remarked proudly, "And here is the woman who has made me who *I* am. Good morning, Mrs Alexander."

She smiled her sweet smile and said, "Good morning, sir. And who, may I ask, are you?"

He answered, "Since we have determined that the love of a good woman makes a good man great, I suppose I am a great man."

"Yes, dear, you are," she said, with a slightly baffled look. Then to Lizzie and Darcy, "Good morning, dears. Are we to be laughing again today?"

Lizzie said, "I think we must laugh every day to keep in practice, but I hope with not so much energy as two days ago, for I gave myself a dreadful pain in the side with my levity."

"Well, I must admit I thought it quite the most brilliant method of dispelling gloom I have come across these many years. By your leave I am going to try to get Mr Chester to put a note about it in the Highbury Chronicle."

"I am not certain," said Lizzie, "whether it will work for everybody, and you must be sure to point out that there is some danger involved in case someone in the room has no sense of humour." She looked at Darcy with teasing eyes.

Fitzwilliam added, "I think, actually, that Lizzie herself needs to be present for the cure to work very well. I rarely laughed before I met her, and now I find myself doing it all the time."

As Catherine and John came in, followed closely by Edward, the topic shifted to plans for the day. The young people, with the exception of Edward and Georgiana who had engaged themselves for a music morning, settled on another ride. Mr and Mrs Alexander looked forward to a quiet morning of strolling and reading.

Immediately after breakfast, the musicians excused themselves, wishing everyone a pleasant morning, and retired to the drawing room. Edward's unmistakably passionate style could be heard from the pianoforte as the party separated to dress for riding.

Darcy remarked to Lizzie, "I expect it will take Georgiana a good while to work up the courage to play in front of Edward, she is so in awe of his talent." Before she could answer, the music stopped, and a brief silence was followed by the sound of one of Georgiana's favourite pieces being played in her more reserved style.

Lizzie raised her eyebrows. "If I am not mistaken, she has already overcome her reserve."

Darcy laughed and shook his head. "I think I shall have to suspend all judgements concerning Georgiana's temperament, as I seem to know very little about her."

"Yes, I do believe you have seriously underestimated her strength."

Darcy answered with a grin, "Since you came into my life, Lizzie, I have been forced to re-evaluate my opinions on my entire acquaintance. I haven't decided if you actually affect the way people behave, or if you have simply changed the way I see them."

"That must be very confusing for you," she quipped. "I am quite used to unpredictable behaviour. In my family it is not only considered acceptable, but praiseworthy, for it gives us something to talk about."

"I imagine," he said, "that you and your family found much to amuse yourselves with at my expense."

"Most certainly we did, my dear. I clearly remember one delightful occasion when I imitated your speech to Charles Bingley at the first Meryton ball you attended." She re-enacted the scene for his benefit, doing a very able imitation of his haughty disdain as he professed that it would be a punishment to dance with any of the ladies in the room.

He coloured deeply to remember that evening. "I continue to wonder that you ever spoke to me after that beginning. I have a lifetime of amends to make for my despicable behaviour, not only to you, but to countless others. And now I have managed to offend even Georgiana," he said in mock despair.

Lizzie put her arms around his neck and rose up on her toes to kiss him. "I insist that you continue to make amends to me first, and then, when I am satisfied, you may begin with the others. Georgiana may have a prior claim, but as she did not make it known until recently, she shall have to wait her turn."

Between the kisses that had now become more passionate than playful, he asked softly, "What must I do to earn your forgiveness?"

Her only answer was an enthusiastic murmur of approval for his present behaviour, and without a supreme effort on both parts, they would have failed in their duty as hosts yet again. They dressed quickly and ran downstairs, laughing and a little flushed, but on time for the morning's ride, and the party set off gaily in the crisp morning air.

While the riders revelled in the sunny morning, Georgiana and Edward were thoroughly enjoying themselves at the pianoforte. Georgiana was perhaps more surprised than Darcy to find that she felt no nervousness, so easy and playful was Edward's manner toward her. He listened with sincere admiration, commenting on the lightness and accuracy of her fingering. She protested, "If only I could play with your exuberance and passion, I would be content."

"It is only that you are more reserved than I, Georgiana. You must allow yourself to play from the heart, not the head, for I am quite sure that you have a fire locked deep inside you." She coloured at this reference, but regained her composure quickly. "Choose a piece of music that conveys the mood you wish to express and let your fingers translate it. Pretend that you are all alone in the world and this is the only means of communication open to you." He sat down to wait.

Georgiana frowned in concentration and as she picked through the sheets of music, she tried to see them as emotions rather than melodies. At last she found what she wanted and, with a slight flush of anticipation, sat down at the instrument. She began hesitantly and then stopped, shook her head as if to release her inhibition, and closed her eyes, reaching deep inside herself for the feeling she sought. She began again, allowing the energy to flow freely through her body and willing it to her hands. Waves of notes began to pulse through her, stirring the newly released emotions until they became an eloquent outpouring, and for several minutes she lost consciousness of everything but the music. By the last note she was breathless and flushed. When she finished, Edward jumped up from his chair, applauding, and said with surprised admiration, "When were you ever so angry as that, Georgiana?"

"The day before yesterday!" She laughed happily, shaking her arms to relax them. "I understand you now. The music has such power when it comes from inside." She stood up and indicated that he should take her place. "It is your turn - I need to rest!"

He gladly obliged, and as she watched him play she observed how his posture and facial expression illuminated the sounds of the instrument. She stood up eagerly when he had finished and said with a laugh, "How would the sweet release of laughter after sorrow sound?" They sorted through the collection of music until she found the right piece and she sat down to try the magic again. When she finished playing, she found him looking at her with admiration.

"Magnificent!" he said, with boyish enthusiasm.

"I feel as though a weight has been lifted from me. Two months ago I would not have even owned such feelings, and now you have given me a means of expressing myself that I have never found in words. Thank you for this gift!" she said with shy pleasure.

"You had the gift already. I only helped you unlock it," he answered. "Shall we go out for a walk?"

They found his parents out in the garden, admiring the view of the surrounding hills, and the four of them set out to explore the delights of the sun on the trout stream below. Georgiana felt she was seeing familiar sights with new eyes, and in her heart she stored the sounds of birds and running water and the leaves rustling in the wind to take back to the pianoforte.

The riders returned in the early afternoon in a most festive mood, well pleased with their adventure, and by the time Trevor Handley made his exuberant entrance for dinner, an air of jovial familiarity was well established between the two families. Darcy stood to greet his guest with a warm handshake, introducing him to the Alexander family as a lifelong friend, and from all appearances it had never been otherwise.

The following day brought more typical December weather, but spirits were not dampened by the change, and the week passed more quickly than anyone would have wished. Trevor became a frequent and welcome guest at evenings of cards and music, and Fitzwilliam and Georgiana took advantage of several opportunities to continue their discussions with Mr Alexander, their further exploration of the past unmarred by the sorrow and anger of the first. As each night gave rise to a peaceful morning, Lizzie's heart soared with a mixture of contentment and anticipation.

It was with great reluctance that the Alexander family took their leave at the end of their visit. Edward, with no responsibility to call him home, was easily persuaded to stay a few days longer, until the Darcys' departure for their Christmas trip to Meryton. Lizzie wrote to Jane with the praises of that young man, along with a description of Georgiana's continuing metamorphosis.

Even more delightful to Lizzie was the flowering of the relationship between Georgiana and Darcy. The two seemed never to tire of their conversations together, for although they had shared the same house and parents, the stories of their lives were very dissimilar. Darcy began to better understand his father through her eyes, and Georgiana her mother, and their discussions brought them enlightenment with little pain. In addition to forgiving his father, Darcy made the more important step of forgiving himself. The healing laughter that had begun with Lizzie rang often through the halls of Pemberley, and even Mrs Reynolds eventually stopped being startled by it.

Lizzie, inspired by the beautiful performances she was hearing, engaged Edward as a piano teacher for herself. She was by no means as gifted or devoted a student as Georgiana, but she was enthusiastic and brought a playful style to the instrument that was all her own. Edward enjoyed imitating the manner of his beloved teacher, Mr Ludwig; his impersonation of the man's speech and bearing frequently sent Lizzie into gales of laughter, and the more sternly he tapped his baton and frowned, the less able she was to contain her mirth and maintain her concentration. Her playing did improve under his keen eye, however, and she began to practice more regularly, professing to live in fear of his terrible rage.

Lizzie and Darcy also found in the quieter days an opportunity to pursue a calmer study of each other. He soon found that there was much in his memory that gave him pleasure. Lizzie was always willing to produce an amusing story of her own family when their mood was light, and they spoke comfortably of their interests and aspirations. One day Darcy confided in Lizzie, "One thing still puzzles me about my parents. Everything I heard from Mr Alexander confirms my own perception that their affections were irrevocably alienated when I was very young. But then Georgiana was born... "

"Yes," she mused, "I have also had that thought. I suppose they might have had moments of reconciliation, if your father's love was as strong as Mr Alexander suggests."

"From my father it does seem possible, but from my understanding of my mother's disdain, I find it hard to imagine her welcoming his attentions. I suppose we shall never know the answer," said Darcy, with a composure that evoked a private smile from his wife.

Trevor Handley had by this time regained his status as a constant companion of the Darcy family, and as they prepared to depart for Meryton, Lizzie attempted, without success, to persuade him to join their Christmas party. He professed his reluctance to leave his stable, begging leave instead to take Sweet Felicity home to Croftwoods in their absence to see personally to her care. After fond farewells, Trevor rode away with Sweet Felicity in tow. Lizzie turned to Darcy and said, "You were right, I daresay, when you said that Trevor prefers the company of horses to people. I expect he will take Felicity a gift on Christmas morning and feel more content than if he were having a feast with his family."

For her part, Lizzie quickly forgot every other attachment in anticipation of the coming reunion at Longbourn. As she dressed for the journey, she paused to study herself in the mirror, reflecting with satisfaction that she would carry home with her a more perfect contentment than she had ever known. With so many obstacles overcome, the horizon stretched clear and bright before her and the storms of the past were relegated to the deepest recesses of her memory.

Chapter Forty One

When the Darcys and Edward Alexander set off on their Christmas journey, the four formed such an easy, congenial group that a casual observer would have taken them all for brothers and sisters. Edward left them at the road to Highbury, at their insistence promising to rejoin them at Pemberley as soon as he was able after their return. Lizzie could hardly sit still on the carriage seat as they neared their destination. She especially looked forward to the reunion with her father, for she understood only too well from his uncharacteristically regular correspondence that he felt the loss of her company most keenly.

Even Darcy found that his spirits were not at all dampened by the prospect of spending a fortnight in Hertfordshire, for besides the anticipation of visiting with Jane and Charles Bingley, he had developed an affectionate interest in knowing Lizzie's family better, especially her father, of whom she spoke with such high regard. He had set for himself the goal of being so pleasant with her family that they would wonder at themselves for ever having disliked him. With the Gardiner family expected at Longbourn, the Darcy family would reside at Netherfield with the Bingleys. Darcy found solace in the unspoken thought that, should he prove unequal to the task of endearing himself to Lizzie's family, he could escape as often as need be to Charles' side; both anticipated that they might need a refuge from too close a proximity to Charles' sisters.

As Lizzie could not bear to keep her father waiting, their carriage stopped first at Longbourn. Their welcome was touching. Even Mrs Bennet's nervous prattling was lovingly met, for Lizzie could readily see that she was frightened by the prospect of being hostess to such a formidable man as Mr Darcy. Darcy succeeded more easily than he had imagined in putting himself and his hosts at ease with his warmth. Mr Bennet's fears had been much relieved by the cheerful letters he had received from Pemberley, but it required the proof of his own eyes to fully convince him of his daughter's happiness. This pleasure he had within a few minutes of their arrival, and indeed he was astonished to observe the depth of their affection. As they retired to the sitting room, Darcy chose a chair at Mrs Bennet's side, causing her to colour nervously, but he applied himself to such charming conversation and flattery that it was not long before she had forgotten herself completely and was in a fair way to thinking him the most pleasant of men.

In fact, he had decided to like her himself, and soon found that he was amused by her childlike exposition of the news of Meryton. If he had not found pleasure enough in their conversation on his own account, the happy approbation he saw in Lizzie's eyes when they turned toward him was reward indeed. As for Mr Bennet, it required little effort to cultivate an easy friendship with him, for the two were united by the bond of their affection for Lizzie, and Darcy's close observation of that gentleman soon led him to understand that Lizzie had him to thank for her wit. Having become in the past few months a student of mirth, Darcy found himself before long a co-conspirator with Mr Bennet in wry comments and whispered jests, and their chief delight was in teasing Lizzie at every opportunity. With the spirit of camaraderie upon him, Darcy soon began to press the Bennets to visit them at Pemberley, for he could well imagine that life at Longbourn had been rendered very dull indeed, especially to Mr Bennet, by the loss of Lizzie's lively companionship.

When Mr and Mrs Gardiner arrived with their brood, they were a little surprised and very much pleased to discover a scene of most touching domestic felicity in their sister's house. Mrs Gardiner needed little more than a few minutes to see what she had hoped, that Lizzie was radiantly in love. Of Mr Darcy's adoration for Lizzie she had been well informed before Lizzie herself understood it.

The days that followed flowed with a commotion of laughter and talk, with parties and dinners and all manner of entertainments in the neighbourhood. Even Caroline Bingley expertly covered her true feelings by adopting a light and amusing demeanour, determined that she should retain access to Pemberley. Although Elizabeth harboured no illusions as to that lady's character, she was too happy and too busy to spare time for ill feelings. Even faced with the expectation that the Bingley sisters should accompany their brother to Pemberley after Christmas, Lizzie was optimistic.

Darcy cautioned: "You must know, Lizzie, that Caroline Bingley holds you in no great esteem."

"I should judge *that* to be an understatement of enormous proportions. But if the daggers in her eyes are not loosed, I doubt that she can do me real harm, unless, of course, you mean to fall in love with her," she teased.

"Please, Mrs Darcy, be sensible of the fact that I have not yet attained your facility to laugh at an enemy. Even at the height of my arrogance, I found her scathing wit daunting, but now that you have removed my armour, I quake in fear of her razor tongue," he said dramatically.

"You shall have to manage as best you can," she replied in the same spirit, "but as for me, the task of winning Miss Bingley's esteem will present an even greater challenge than I enjoyed in winning yours. I shall learn to be civil and forbearing, or die valiantly in the attempt!"

As the date of their departure approached, Mr Bennet's sorrow in parting with both Lizzie and Jane was eased by the repetition of Mr Darcy's invitation to Pemberley, and although Mr Bennet doubted that his wife's nerves would easily accommodate such a strain, he agreed that they would try when the weather improved. Caroline Bingley, who had arrived at Netherfield House with the fond apprehension that by now the allure of those 'fine eyes' that had so besotted Mr Darcy would have faded and he would be in a fair way to regretting his hasty marriage, began to feel horribly out of sorts. She had carefully studied his demeanour at every opportunity, and had afforded him ample opportunity to hint at his disappointment, but all she had managed to discover in the end was that he was more hopelessly in love than ever.

As preparations were made to set out for Pemberley, the thought of entering what had previously been her favourite estate as a guest of the new Mrs Darcy began to raise a bitter taste in her mouth. It was too late for a graceful escape, however, and so she was forced to enter the Hurst carriage with a display of feigned pleasure, and to seek solace in arguing with her sister and being rude to her brother-in-law. The latter had not the good grace to be vexed by her acerbity, but promptly fell asleep and was soon snoring loudly. At their first rest stop, she complained so of the noise that Elizabeth sweetly suggested that she join Mr Darcy and herself in their carriage. The offer caught Miss Bingley off guard and she needed a little while to decide whether it would be more vexing to sit closeted with the reason for her discontent or to continue her peevishness in private. At last her curiosity got the better of her and she decided that there might yet be some sport in a close observation of the spectacle of the formidable Mr Darcy brought low by his adolescent infatuation.

Darcy gave Lizzie a private look of feigned terror which she acknowledged with an amused nod, and on the way to the carriage she whispered to him, "She is in such a foul temper that I wonder if it might not serve to introduce her to the laughing cure."

He rolled his eyes and said, "I fear that even *your* powers are not equal to such a task, my dear."

Miss Bingley's mood brightened immediately on entering the carriage, for she had found little opportunity to exercise her wit of late, and the thought occurred to her that she might amuse herself by testing Mr Darcy's interest in their mutual acquaintances, knowing that he could not be insensible of their opinions on his marriage. As she prattled on about this or that event or couple, she was slightly disconcerted to see that Mr Darcy was staring at her with those dark, appraising eyes of his. She was very much aware of how her references to the ridiculous in behaviour and dress imitated his own former opinions, but if he was sensible of the irony he showed no sign, other than a slightly amused smile. Although he rarely joined into the conversation, she was encouraged to continue, happy to be entertaining herself, if no one else.

Since Lizzie, having met none of the subjects of this witty narration, was specifically excluded from the conversation, she had ample opportunity to ponder the shallowness of its content. That the chief exercise of a rather prodigious intelligence should consist of finding fault with every taste not her own seemed to Lizzie a terrible waste. She was quite lost in this entertaining reverie when she realised that Miss Bingley had spoken to her.

"Forgive me, Miss Bingley, I'm afraid my mind was elsewhere," she said pleasantly.

Miss Bingley flashed a condescending smile at Elizabeth. "It is I who should apologise, for I must have been boring you, talking only of people you do not know." With a meaningful glance at Mr Darcy she added, "But I daresay before long you shall meet them all. When do you go to London? I suppose you shall want to shop for the summer," she said, with an amused glance at Mrs Darcy's simple frock.

As Elizabeth leaned forward attentively, Darcy saw with amused anticipation that her keen sense of the ridiculous had been aroused. He had been listening to Miss Bingley's gossip attentively, fully aware of her intention to mock him, and equally aware of the effect her style was likely to have on Lizzie. While he did not underestimate the power of Miss Bingley's invective, he understood better than she that Elizabeth Bennet was unlikely to be injured by it, and he waited in bemused silence to hear how his wife would turn the conversation to entertain herself.

Lizzie addressed herself to Miss Bingley in a conspiratorial style. "You know, I have so little experience of the delights of London, I confess I am a bit reluctant to venture into society there. I am afraid Mr Darcy's friends will find me quite naive and countrified." She added softly, "I am sensible that some may even see me as quite an unsuitable wife for a man in his position. I hope I will be able to avail myself of your kindness, for I am sure that an introduction from someone in your position would open doors that otherwise might be closed to me." She settled back against the bench wearing a smile of contentment, and Darcy found that he required the aide of a rather violent attack of coughing to control the laughter that was threatening to undo his composure.

He dared not venture a look at Miss Bingley for a long time, but he did not need to see her face to guess her reaction to Lizzie's speech. The last thing that lady could have wished for was to become a chaperone and confidante to his wife, but having accepted their invitation to Pemberley, she had placed herself in an untenable position to refuse Elizabeth's request. He studiously gazed out the window with his arm resting on the sill and his hand poised thoughtfully against his mouth, feigning disinterest and waiting to hear how Miss Bingley would extricate herself from this situation.

Before she could recover herself to make a suitable reply, Lizzie continued, emboldened by the lady's obvious discomfiture and by the ridiculous sight of Darcy's efforts to control his amusement. "As to summer clothes, I am afraid I am sadly ignorant on the subject of fashion." She smoothed her dress with a rueful smile. "Mr Darcy has been kind enough not to criticise my wardrobe, and in fact I think at times he barely notices what I am wearing," she said, patting his arm, "but I am sure *you* must appreciate that a woman in my position cannot be too careful about her attire. I fear that people are often all too willing to judge a person by their appearance."

She paused, allowing Miss Bingley time to regret nearly every moment of the last few minutes, and then loosed her final arrow: "Would it be too presumptuous of me to ask that you recommend me to your own tailor, Miss Bingley, for you are always so exquisitely dressed." Darcy's cough had suddenly returned with renewed force, and Lizzie hit him on the back a bit harder than necessary, he thought. He had just about managed to suppress his laughter, fervently hoping that she was going to be merciful enough not to continue the charade, when she said with annoyance, in a voice that was an unmistakable imitation of her mother, "Will, please stop that coughing. My nerves are in such a state!"

Convulsions of laughter shook the carriage bench and Lizzie felt very pleased with herself indeed. If Miss Bingley had been speechless in the face of Lizzie's appeal, she was agape at Darcy's laughter. She managed a nervous laugh, but it was evident that it gave her no pleasure to be excluded from the joke. Lizzie smiled complacently, waiting for Darcy to regain his composure. When he had become a bit calmer, she confided in Miss Bingley, "Please excuse Mr Darcy, Miss Bingley. I do not know to what I should credit it, but ever since our marriage he has been wont to find amusement in even the most serious of subjects. I think you may even find Miss Darcy similarly affected at times, although she has a good deal more self-control." She gazed out the window, the image of serenity, while Darcy suffered another attack of discomposure. Miss Bingley was bewildered and unhappy, fearing that she was somehow the object of his laughter, but she at least had the relief of the distraction to excuse her from replying to Elizabeth's appeals. She admitted grudgingly that there was more to Elizabeth Bennet than she had expected to find.

Mr Darcy did not trust himself to attempt to explain his laughter, and Lizzie was apparently satisfied with her work, and so the three rode in silence, all attention to the passing scenery and their own private thoughts. Darcy smiled to himself at the flawless performance of his bride. She had said nothing that could be construed or reported as offensive, instead choosing flattery as her weapon, and with it had caused Miss Bingley an agony of consternation. He respected that lady's intelligence enough to believe that she could not fail to appreciate Lizzie's wit, even if she did not enjoy being the object of it. Miss Bingley had by now resigned all hope of a pleasant journey, for she could not soon enough be removed from this carriage, and the third, carrying Charles and Jane Bingley and Miss Darcy, did not offer promise of much improvement, for she had long since ceased to be amused by the sweet affability of that couple, and her affection for Miss Darcy had cooled considerably with the loss of the prospect of having her for a sister-in-law. She began to look forward to Mr Hurst's snoring as a relief from the Bennet sisters and their ridiculous husbands.

Chapter Forty Two

With the notable exception of Miss Bingley, for whom the torments of the journey only increased as it neared its end, a mood of gaiety and anticipation reigned as the party alighted at last at the entrance to Pemberley Manor.

Darcy's success in ingratiating himself to Lizzie's family did not prevent him from feeling a tremendous relief at being home, and he sent off a messenger directly to Croftwoods to invite Trevor Handley to wait upon them at his earliest opportunity. The answer that was speedily returned by Trevor's secretary delayed that felicity for a week or more, for Trevor had but two days ago embarked on a trip to the north, combining attendance at an auction in Leeds with a visit to his mother, who resided in the county seat of Matlock.

Miss Bingley, for her part, suffered from a most painful fluctuation of feelings, the nearest one to happiness being a sort of sighing resignation. She was, to be sure, still capable of scathing wit, but with no encouragement from her long-time ally Mr Darcy, she found little opportunity of employing it, excepting when she was alone with her sister and Mr Hurst. Charles and his wife had no appreciation, nor had Miss Darcy, for sarcasm, and Mr and Mrs Hurst, although ready to enjoy a jest at anyone's expense, were not themselves clever enough to maintain the conversation to her satisfaction, and she soon grew tired of performing for their amusement.

She became by turns morose, restless, angry, and petulant, and could fix on no amusement about the house that could engage her long enough to be deemed a pleasure. The weather was not her ally, for she might have found some relief in a long walk in the garden, but constant gloomy rain kept the party confined to the house, and although it was a very large mansion indeed, she could not find room to escape from the cheerful laughter and amiable conversations of the rest of the party except by retiring to her room. The pleasure to be found in retreat was seriously diminished by her observation that the company left behind suffered very little from the loss of her presence.

As the first week drew on to a close, Miss Bingley had grown weary herself of her usual objects of contempt, for the subjects of the Bennet sisters' clothes, manners, hair, speech and family offered little new to interest or amuse. All of her attempts to embarrass Mrs Darcy or unsettle Mr Darcy had been met with charm or indifference. She had, in fact, never known that gentleman to be so content to pass an afternoon in the quiet of his home, and his behaviour in general spoke eloquently of a peaceful satisfaction with the status quo.

It did not improve Miss Bingley's mood that she was thus forced to reflect on her own feelings, for the obvious happiness of her companions heightened her awareness of her own miserable state. She knew not how to join into their easy laughter and was tormented by the suspicion that far from finding her an object of envy for her superior status and education, the Bennet sisters were somehow mocking her. And yet, neither Jane nor Elizabeth ever treated her in any manner that could be considered less than cordial. Lizzie was far too happy to find pleasure in tormenting her, and noting the diminished power of Miss Bingley to cause her more than mild annoyance, she had found herself following Jane's example of kind forbearance towards her. In fact, there was something about the gentleness of the two sisters that suggested that what they felt for her was neither awe nor discomfort, but rather pity. To be sure, this thought excited in Miss Bingley a most terrible rage, and her sister Louisa was forced to play the confessor, as usual.

That Louisa was beginning to tire of her sister was evidenced by her announcement at the end of a week's time that she and her husband would be leaving Pemberley the following day for their home in London. With little of her sister's morbid fascination with the Bennet and Darcy families, and her relationship with Caroline severely taxed by that lady's obsession, she had come to the conclusion that the society and liveliness of London would be a welcome relief. Her husband, moody by nature, had grown more than indifferent to the company by this time. Miss Bingley heard the news with a momentary vexation, but found, to her surprise, that she was soon feeling relieved to be freed from their companionship. It was generally expected that she would take the opportunity to escape as well, for her behaviour in the previous few days left little doubt that she found no pleasure in either the society or the surroundings, but she surprised everyone by announcing that instead of travelling to London, she had written to a friend in the north and only awaited a reply to be on her way.

In fact, no one was displeased by the planned departure of Mr and Mrs Hurst, and the prospect of a timely end to Miss Bingley's visit made it easier for everyone to bear the thought of a few more days in her company. Even Charles, who thought very little about such things, found himself troubled by the vexing manners of his sister. It was Georgiana, however, who finally gave voice to the general displeasure. Her own fondness and regard for the Bennet sisters drove her to seek Fitzwilliam out after breakfast one morning as he retired to his study to attend to some correspondence. Closing the door behind her, she walked resolutely up to his desk and drew a chair near enough so that she could speak without raising her voice.

"Fitzwilliam," she began, frowning, "how are you able to countenance the manner in which Miss Bingley behaves? I am quite out of patience with her moods and tempers, and I fear if her ill usage of Lizzie and Jane continues, I shall soon find it impossible to hold my tongue."

Darcy sat back attentively in his chair, and although he had no inclination to mock her seriousness, he could not fail to be amused by the novelty of her strong opinions. He considered thoughtfully before asking, "Have you spoken to Lizzie of your feelings, Georgiana?"

"No, I have not," she replied, surprised at such a question. "You certainly know of my affection for her. Lizzie is too kind to suspect the malice behind Miss Bingley's behaviour, and I have no wish to draw her attention to it."

Darcy was forced to betray his feelings with a laugh. "You are the one who is too kind, my dear. If you were speaking of Jane, I believe you would be correct in your analysis, for I have never known a less suspicious nature than hers. But Lizzie is well aware of all of the faults of that lady, I dare say. Allow me to tell you what happened on the road from Meryton last week when Miss Bingley joined us in our carriage."

He proceeded to relate the details of the conversation between Lizzie and Miss Bingley, describing the pallor of the latter's countenance when she understood what a dreadful error she had made in her attempt to unsettle Lizzie. Georgiana's eyes grew wide with surprise. Darcy continued, "If I feared for a moment that Lizzie was suffering, I would not hesitate to banish Miss Bingley from Pemberley forever, but I have too much respect for Lizzie's intelligence to make such a move without her express approval. You have always been so blinded to my own faults, Georgiana, at least until recently," he said with a smile, "that you do not realise how my former behaviour mirrored Miss Bingley's."

He laughed out loud at the impatient frown she wore. "Georgiana, dear," he said, leaning forward to take her hand, "the first thing that attracted me to Lizzie at Meryton was her astonishing disinterest in my disdain. I am afraid you would have been seriously distressed by my bad manners on that, and on subsequent occasions, but Lizzie's confidence and good humour allowed her to answer my insolent behaviour with dignity and mirth. Although I cannot seriously hope that Miss Bingley will benefit as much as I from her association with Lizzie, I doubt very much that Lizzie will be injured by *her*."

Georgiana had been listening intently and when he had finished she leaned back in her chair thoughtfully. "Perhaps you are right, Fitzwilliam. I suppose Miss Bingley's bad manners pose no real threat."

"Yes," he replied, "it constantly astonishes me that she is able to find amusement in offensive behaviour. I wish we had been able to witness her interview with our Aunt Catherine, Georgiana. From Lizzie's account and what my Aunt told me afterwards in an attempt to turn me from my intention to marry her, I must judge that even *that* formidable woman met her match in Lizzie. Although I heartily agree that Miss Bingley's manners are insufferable, I am beginning to learn from Lizzie that the best defence against misguided arrogance is a keen sense of humour. Lizzie's wit is more tempered than mine by kindness, however, and since their encounter in the carriage, I believe she has begun to take pity on Miss Bingley and has forsworn her inclination to make sport of that lady's miserable prejudices."

Georgiana was persuaded to agree upon reflection that her anger with Miss Bingley was motivated more by her own discomfort than by any evidence of Lizzie's distress. She confided to her brother her own confusion of feelings toward Miss Bingley and ended by repeating the speculations of their cousin James on the subject of her frustrated hopes. He nodded serenely.

"I was myself puzzled at her previous attentiveness to you, Georgiana, for it is not in her nature to bestow her favour without a self-interested motivation. I came to the same conclusion as James some time ago, and I regret that I did not confide in you." Looking intently into Georgiana's eyes, he added, blushing deeply, "I must confess to you that there were moments when I seriously considered the efficacy of such a plan." To her wide-eyed stare, he explained, "I had so little understanding at that time of what a happy marriage should comprise that I am afraid I was in danger of referring to my mother's standards."

319

Georgiana could not prevent herself from a shudder of revulsion at the thought of Miss Bingley as a sister-in-law. Darcy laughed at her consternation and said, "Well, fortunately, we have been saved from that indignity, and I believe we shall have our reward in heaven if we can manage to show charity to poor Miss Bingley. She no doubt feels herself to be grievously abused by the events of this twelvemonth."

His sister smiled benevolently. "I am sure you are right, Fitzwilliam. In light of what you have told me, she deserves our pity more than our anger. I will try, whenever I find myself vexed by her, to remember my own good fortune." She patted his arm tenderly. "I shall leave you to your correspondence." She rose to leave the room, but turned back, frowning thoughtfully.

"May I ask you, Fitzwilliam, how close we were to the disaster you mentioned?"

He shook his head ruefully, "Too close for comfort, Georgiana." With a slight shake of her head, she quitted the room, leaving her brother to such unsettling remembrances that he was unable to attend to his business for a very long time.

Chapter Forty Three

Lizzie's chief preoccupation in those days had nothing to do with Miss Caroline Bingley. Indeed, she gave very little consequence to any of the events that took place at Pemberley, for although she maintained the appearance of an appropriate interest in her guests, the thought that constantly occupied her mind was that she was carrying a child. She had begun to suspect the likelihood during the Christmas holiday, and as the days passed her excitement grew, until finally she confided in Jane.

Jane's delighted anticipation matched her own in almost every way save for Lizzie's insistence that she not tell anyone. She begged daily to be released from the burden of secrecy, for it was not in her nature to hide anything from her beloved Charles, but Lizzie laughingly turned aside her entreaties, professing her desire to wait until she was assured she was not mistaken. In truth, she was troubled by her own reluctance to include Darcy in her joy, but with each opportunity for private speech with him, she found herself curiously unwilling to open the subject. Finally, the interference of a stranger prompted her to disclose her news.

After his conversation with Georgiana regarding Miss Bingley, Darcy had just managed to turn his attention back to his business when an urgent letter arrived. Calling Lizzie to the library, he explained that he and Georgiana were summoned to meet with their solicitor in Matlock at their earliest convenience on a matter concerning the disposition of certain holdings that remained from their father's estate. He suggested that she might enjoy the trip, especially if Jane and Charles could be persuaded to join them, and that it seemed likely they might find Trevor Handley still in attendance upon his mother.

Lizzie grew thoughtful for a moment and then quickly decided that this was the moment for disclosure. She sat down near him and reached out to take both of his hands in her own. "As much as I dislike the thought of spending so much as an evening away from you, darling, I am afraid that I am not inclined to travel at this moment." She laughed as his brow furrowed in concern. "There is no cause for worry, Will. It is only that I am feeling a little unwell because I am going to have a child!"

The look on his face as he struggled to comprehend her news sent a slight chill through her. The reluctance she had felt to tell him was justified by the mixture of emotions that showed only too clearly in his eyes. Struggling with his thoughts, he gripped her hands tightly and said, at last, "Are you sure, Lizzie?"

She laughed with more lightness than she felt, the tightness in her throat preventing her from answering with more than a nodding assent. After several moments of a most painful silence, he looked away and stood up, walking to the window in the pose she had come to recognise as his manner of collecting his thoughts. She waited in silence, a knot of anxiety forming in her stomach by the time he finally spoke.

"Of course I expected we would have children, only I had not thought it would be so soon." Her eyes began to fill with tears, but she angrily fought against them, determined to feel only her own joyful anticipation. The calm contentment of the past weeks had led her to hope that he would rejoice with her, but she admitted to herself that his response was not unexpected.

She stood up and walked to his side. As he turned to look at her, the worry in his eyes filled her with a tenderness that made her want to cry out, but she spoke softly, willing herself to remain calm.

"Look at me, Will. I am not like your mother. You must not fear that this child will come between us. He will be the expression of our love for one another." She smiled with all of the confidence she could summon.

His hands reached up to cradle her face lovingly. "Lizzie," he said sadly, "I thought I had finished giving you pain. Although I cannot comprehend why it should be so, I do not doubt for a minute that your love is beyond corruption, for I have put it to the harshest tests. But I have been so severe upon my own father that the responsibility of taking on that role fills me with fear."

Lizzie felt her heart lighten and she replied with assurance, "You will be the kind of father that you dreamed of having yourself. You must not doubt that. You will see that our joy will only increase."

He picked her up in his arms, laughing, and kissed her. "I only hope that by the time this baby arrives, I have completely given up my own childish behaviour. It will not do for you to be teaching us both good manners at the same time. I believe you should be enjoying my heartfelt congratulations at this moment, and instead you are drying my tears." When he finally set her back on her feet, he teased, "I believe you have already begun to gain weight, Lizzie."

"Will you love me any less when you are unable to lift me off my feet?"

"I cannot imagine that I will ever be able to love you more," he replied earnestly, and their tension dissolved in the laughter that followed. "We must go and tell this baby's aunts to begin sewing."

Lizzie's face took on a very serious expression and she said, "Will, would you mind if we did not make an announcement just yet? I know it is a foolish wish, but I dislike the idea of having our happiness spoiled by Miss Bingley's sulking. You may, of course, tell Georgiana, but I would prefer to wait until after Miss Bingley's departure to make it generally known. It will only be a few more days."

Darcy was more agreeable to her suggestion than he cared to let on, for in spite of her confidence, and his swift recovery, he recognised in himself a need to quietly ponder this new vision of the future. "I shall write immediately to Mr Long and tell him I must defer our business to a later date. But should we not send for the doctor, Lizzie?"

Lizzie laughingly assured him that she was in no way ill, and that the separation of a few days would only increase their affection for one another. "Jane will delight in mothering me, you can be sure, Will, and as the baby will certainly not arrive until August, you had better take the opportunity to see to your business now."

Satisfied with her reasoning, Darcy went off to speak to Georgiana, while Lizzie returned to the drawing room to rejoin their guests. As the Hursts were to leave the following day, Louisa had gone to her room to direct the packing of their trunks, and Mr Hurst was nowhere to be found. Miss Bingley had taken advantage of a reprieve in the weather to take a turn in the garden, and so Lizzie was delighted to find that only Charles and Jane occupied the drawing room when she entered.

Jane looked up with a question in her eyes, as she did each time she saw Lizzie in those days, and the flushed cheeks and moist eyes she observed caused her to put down her needlework rather abruptly. Lizzie smiled with a radiant glow and asked Charles sweetly if he could part with Jane for a few moments. Charles stood up, and with a gallant bow, offered her his seat, declaring that he would accompany his sister on her walk. Lizzie thanked him warmly, and when she was sure they were alone, said to Jane in a conspiratorial tone, "I have just told Will, Jane, but I begged him to say nothing until after the Hursts and Miss Bingley leave. You may tell Charles, of course, but he must promise not to mention it to his sisters just yet."

Jane laughed happily. "Oh, Lizzie, you are the silliest thing, but of course we shall do as you wish. I will be so relieved to unburden myself at least to Charles that I shan't mind another few days passing before I can twitter endlessly on the subject."

"I cannot wait until I can stop pretending to have an appetite for food or an interest in any other thought than that which so occupies my mind!" She had quite forgotten Darcy's letter, but it suddenly came to her mind and she explained the matter to Jane. "Perhaps Charles would like to accompany Will and Georgiana to Matlock. I remember them speaking of college friends in that area."

Jane agreed to suggest it, and by the end of dinner that day, everyone's plans had been made. Georgiana, Darcy and Charles would leave together the next morning, expecting to return in two days time, and the Hursts would set out for London. Miss Bingley waited only her reply to speed her on her way, and Lizzie and Jane were in a fair way to enjoying the prospect of relative solitude for the opportunity it would afford them for private discussion of the intricacies of motherhood. They little doubted that Miss Bingley would be a good deal in her room until her departure, as she had become increasingly withdrawn over the past few days, and there was no reason to suspect that the changes at hand would improve her mood in any material way.

Chapter Forty Four

In fact, a change did take place the following day that improved Miss Bingley's mood a hundredfold, investing her with a new animation and a hope of diversion. The Hurst and Darcy carriages departed after an early breakfast, leaving Jane and Lizzie standing arm in arm at the gate. The sisters hurried into the house out of the chilly January air and, asking for tea to be sent upstairs, retired to their favourite sitting room on the second floor, pleased to be at their leisure for some hours. Miss Bingley had ever been a late riser, and in the past days had formed the habit of taking breakfast in her room; she rarely appeared downstairs much before dinnertime.

Lizzie was immediately enjoined by Jane to give a thorough account of Mr Darcy's reaction to her news, which she faithfully rendered. To Jane's perplexed questions about his hesitation to share her joy, Lizzie at last opened her heart to disclose the substance if not the details of his tumultuous history.

While Jane listened in amazement, Lizzie unfolded the story of the Darcy family, including the roles of Mr Alexander and Trevor Handley in bringing to light all that had previously been hidden. Confident at last that Darcy's quick recovery the previous morning bespoke a resolution of the conflict that had marred the bliss of their first months together, to Jane's gentle probing, she was able to answer with complete confidence that no further obstacles remained to a blissful future. Her laughter rang out frequently as she gave full rein to her happiness.

While the two sisters were thus engaged in animated conversation, Caroline Bingley finished her solitary breakfast and moved gloomily to stand at her window, the prospect of which overlooked the front garden. Her attention was drawn from her private musings by the appearance of a handsome stranger alighting from his horse. He walked inside with the confidence of a frequent visitor, and her curiosity roused her from her dark mood and encouraged her to rather hastily finish her preparations for an appearance downstairs.

When Jane was satisfied at last that she understood everything pertinent to her sister's and Mr Darcy's future happiness, and they had just begun a perusal of the novelty of her pregnancy, they were interrupted by a knock on the door. A maid came in to say that Mr Handley waited upon her in the drawing room. Jumping up happily, Lizzie exclaimed to her sister, "What a shame he has missed Will, but perhaps he has brought Sweet Felicity with him. Do come down with me."

Miss Bingley was about to open her door when she was stopped by the animated voices of the Bennet sisters in the hall. With an ear pressed unabashedly to the door, she could just make out their conversation, and the spark of her curiosity kindled into a flame at Jane's words: "I will be down presently, Lizzie, but I doubt that you shall mind half an hour of private conversation with him after a month's separation. Shall you tell him your secret?"

Lizzie laughed. "Yes, I believe I shall. I am sure he shares my feeling that there have been secrets enough at Pemberley. I begin to think I do not care who knows."

As Elizabeth hurried downstairs to greet her visitor, Miss Bingley was experiencing a sudden revival of her wit and found herself for the first time in many days eager to be included in the society of Pemberley. She opened the door cautiously and followed Lizzie down the stairs, being careful to remain unnoticed. Standing outside the parlour door, she heard Lizzie greet her visitor with obvious delight.

"Trevor, we have been so impatient for your return. Will and Georgiana have only this morning left for Matlock, where they had hoped to see you."

With a gallant bow, he kissed her hand. "I am sorry to have missed them, but I confess it was *you* who was foremost in my mind this morning."

Before Lizzie could ascertain the reason for this enigmatic greeting, she became aware of a presence in the open doorway. As if Miss Bingley's sudden appearance was not surprising enough, the animation of her countenance and the amiable and gracious manner in which she responded to Lizzie's stumbling introductions was nothing short of mystifying. By the time Jane entered the drawing room, Miss Bingley had charmed from Mr Handley the history of his family and their connection to Pemberley while Lizzie watched in quiet amazement.

As the conversation turned to a review of the more recent past and inquiries into news of their families, Miss Bingley sat back to peruse the morning's work. She had not failed to notice Lizzie's loss of composure when she interrupted her conversation with Mr Handley. The obvious affection between them seemed surprising considering the brevity of their acquaintance, and no mention had been made of Lizzie's 'secret'. Mr Handley's particular purpose in coming ostensibly concerned a mare who was ailing. Each of these thoughts served to fire her already active imagination, and she began to think that Mr Handley was just what was wanted to upset the cloying happiness that rendered Pemberley unbearable. The humiliations of the past were quickly forgotten as her mind raced down first one avenue and then another, exploring the possibilities for sowing seeds of discontent in the Darcy household.

After a brief flirtation with the idea that she had discovered an affair between Lizzie and Mr Handley, Miss Bingley rejected it as implausible. Even *her* jaded eyes could not seriously picture Elizabeth Darcy as an unfaithful wife, but with a wry smile she mused that if she could not uncover evidence of impropriety, she might as easily invent it. Her intimate knowledge of Mr Darcy's pride gave her reason to anticipate that it would not be beyond her powers to stimulate a bit of jealousy with a well-timed hint. Her wit had previously taken her on similar excursions into intrigue with amusing results, but never had the prospect of the success of such an adventure brought so sweet a hope to her breast.

Miss Bingley was delighted when Mr Handley consented to stay to dinner, and smiled benevolently as Lizzie offered to show him to a room to refresh himself. Left alone with Jane, Miss Bingley had the opportunity to take advantage of her guileless nature, plying her with questions concerning Mr Handley's intimacy with the household. Finally, she remarked offhandedly, "The easiness and affection between your sister and Mr Handley is charming. He seems to feel himself quite at home here."

Jane smiled happily at her sister-in-law's uncharacteristic enthusiasm. "Lizzie has certainly had a hand in making him welcome. I sometimes envy her affectionate nature. I am sure Mr Darcy is delighted with the amiability between the two, as he looks upon Mr Handley as the nearest thing to a brother."

Miss Bingley's smile was sardonic. "To be sure, one hopes to have harmony in one's home." As Lizzie returned to the drawing room Miss Bingley excused herself to dress for dinner. In blissful ignorance of the delightful hope they had excited in Miss Bingley, Jane and Lizzie followed suit. When the foursome reunited for dinner, each of them brought to the table a cheerful enthusiasm for company, although motivated by very different expectations.

Neither the dinner conversation nor the coffee after provided Miss Bingley with any fresh insights into the relationship between Lizzie and Mr Handley, other than that they shared a rather curious admiration for an old man named Mr Hill and a fascination with horses. The former, it seemed, was quite frail, and the ailing horse would remain in his stable for observation.

Having no interest in either subject, Miss Bingley happily occupied herself with her own thoughts. Caroline Bingley must be forgiven for the malicious joy with which she contemplated the upheaval that must ensue should she succeed in dividing the affections of Mr and Mrs Fitzwilliam Darcy. Her happiness in the last twelvemonth had been so sorely undermined, and the particular pain of the charming domestic scenes she had been forced to witness of late was so fresh, that she was of a mind to hug herself at the prospect of mischief. Even the possibility that the adventure might end in a failure which could estrange her forever from that gentleman's friendship did nothing to daunt her enthusiasm, for the present state of his felicity was unbearable.

As the travelling party was expected back the following day, she felt a sense of urgency and spent a good many hours that night testing out various schemes, finally falling asleep with a malicious smile fixed firmly on her face. She rose much earlier the next morning than she had been wont to do, and went downstairs hoping for still more material on which to build her case.

Lizzie and Jane had also been occupied with a review of the previous day's conversations. Lizzie remarked at breakfast, "I have not witnessed such animation in Miss Bingley since the earliest days of our acquaintance. To what, I wonder, do we owe this sudden *joie de vivre*?"

"I believe she has decided to try to enjoy our company, Lizzie. Surely she has become resigned to Charles' marriage by now. I will welcome her friendship."

Lizzie laughed. "Dear Jane, you are so eager to believe that Miss Bingley wants only a minor adjustment in attitude to render her contented and pleasant. I, on the other hand, have concluded that the only possible explanation is that she sees Mr Handley as a possible suitor, and hopes to excite his interest."

331

Both sisters agreed heartily that whatever the cause of her transformation, its effects were to be encouraged. Fortunately their conversation moved on to other ground, for the lady in question arrived at the breakfast table a few minutes later, much to their surprise.

Miss Bingley greeted Lizzie and Jane warmly. "May we expect the pleasure of Mr Handley's company again today?"

With a knowing glance at Jane, Lizzie replied, "Mr Handley mentioned that he expects to be very much occupied with the preparation of his stable to accommodate several new horses he recently purchased at auction." She watched Miss Bingley carefully but could not read her reaction to the news. She continued, "Perhaps we might all make an outing to Croftwoods one evening after the travellers return. Surely Mr Handley cannot plan to be at work both day and night."

"I would very much like to see his estate," she replied pleasantly.

The post arrived just as they moved to the drawing room, bringing a letter from Darcy which informed them that his return would regretfully be delayed at least another day or two. Lizzie shared this information, but did not mention his earnest inquiry concerning her health and comfort, nor his report of Georgiana's happiness at the news he was able to impart to her.

Miss Bingley, to Lizzie's surprise, seemed rather pleased than otherwise at the delay, and sat down at the writing desk, humming quietly to herself. Had Lizzie or Jane had the slightest notion of what she so happily wrote, the mood in the room would have taken a decided turn for the worse, but as it was, they smiled at each other and occupied themselves with the contents of a letter that had arrived from Mr Bennet.

Caroline Bingley's creative mind was taking wing. The plan that had been taking shape in her mind over the past four and twenty hours revolved around the rather delicate task of seeking a private interview with Mr Darcy upon his return to Pemberley. With the news of his delayed return, she had the sudden inspiration that a letter sent to Matlock would have the decided advantage of giving him time to brood over its message before arriving home. As she sat at the desk, penning the first draft, the fact that Lizzie sat only a few feet away, unsuspecting, added to the delicious pleasure that her thoughts occasioned.

Lizzie gathered up her mail and stood up. "I think I shall go and call on Thomas Hill. I had thought to wait for Fitzwilliam's return, but as he will be delayed, I may as well go today."

Her sister glanced at the brooding sky. "Must you go out in such threatening weather, Lizzie?"

This brought a broad smile to Lizzie's face, for she could see that between Darcy's worrying and Jane's mothering, she would, before long, be lucky to leave the safety of her bedroom. "I promise to bundle myself up and, if it will make you happy, I shall take the carriage, although I would much rather walk." She hurried off to avoid any further interference, leaving Jane shaking her head fondly.

Miss Bingley very sweetly excused herself as well, as she did not want to be interrupted by any intrusion from Jane on the thoughts she was so enjoying. Rather dreamily, she positioned herself at the window of her suite, picturing the dark brooding brow of Fitzwilliam Darcy as he returned home with a recently-planted suspicion growing like a canker in his mind.

She even smiled benevolently as she watched Lizzie, wrapped in a long woollen traveller's cape, descend the garden path toward the waiting carriage. As the carriage turned the curve of the drive, she thought of how smug its occupant must feel to be mistress of Pemberley and her smile twisted a trifle. Suddenly her reverie was interrupted by a sight that gave rise to a flutter of nervous excitement. A horse approached at a gallop, pulling up abruptly at the sight of the carriage, and its rider leapt to the ground to speak to Mrs Darcy. The carriage door was flung open and as the two spoke together in obviously animated speech, the man reached out and took both of her hands. After a few more minutes of earnest conversation, the carriage door closed, the rider remounted, and both horse and carriage headed down the lane at a brisk pace.

Caroline Bingley stood with bated breath until the two disappeared behind a curving in the road, then threw back her head and laughed. She glanced down at the pages still clutched in her hand and then gleefully tore them into pieces, throwing them onto the fire before setting herself down at the writing table to compose a new letter to Mr Darcy. Her imagination, overworked in the past four and twenty hours, could allow for no explanation for the scene she had just witnessed other than the one she wished most to believe - that Mrs Darcy *was* engaged in a liaison with Trevor Handley. She paused for a moment to entertain the possibility that there could be another explanation, but concluded that the facts could have led any disinterested observer to the same conclusion, and the truth was therefore immaterial.

Stimulated by the excitement of creating a scandal with no risk to herself, she needed no rewriting of the thoughts that flowed eloquently from her pen. She laboured enthusiastically over the task, producing exactly the letter she wanted, comprising a perfect balance of regret, outrage and solicitous concern. The letter was written, blotted and sealed with a flush of victory still full upon her cheek, and she stole quietly from her room in search of a servant to dispatch the letter by urgent post for Matlock.

For Miss Bingley's purposes, the day continued to progress in a manner that gratified her at every turn. The storm that had threatened began in earnest, and as she had no desire to miss the entrance of Mrs Darcy, she stationed herself in the drawing room with a book, her chair chosen to offer an immediate view of anyone entering the hall. Jane had evidently retired to her room, but at such a moment of triumph, Caroline Bingley did not mind in the least sitting alone, for she was amply amused with her own thoughts. When Jane did appear, her face immediately grew clouded with worry at finding Miss Bingley alone.

"Caroline, have you seen Lizzie? She is not in her room."

Miss Bingley smiled condescendingly. "She has not returned from her visit as yet, my dear."

Jane crossed quickly to the window, where the sleet, driven by a forceful wind, clattered against the panes. "That cannot be. She has been gone for hours, and his cottage is just down the road."

"Perhaps her friend is ill and she dares not leave him alone," Caroline answered innocently.

Jane turned fretfully from the window, her concern growing rapidly into anxiety. "If that were the case, I feel sure she would have sent word with the driver. I will ask that a rider be sent out to find her at once," she said decisively, starting toward the door. At that moment, a breathless servant appeared, saying a messenger had arrived from Croftwoods and begged leave to speak with her. With a glance of alarm at Caroline, Jane hurried off, with Miss Bingley following behind in state. The man, wretchedly wet and cold, brought a message from Mr Handley to say that Mrs Darcy had gone to Croftwoods with him on an urgent matter and was prevented by the storm from returning. To Jane's breathless inquiries, he answered that her horse, Sweet Felicity, was taken with a fever and Master Trevor feared she may not live.

Miss Bingley raised her eyebrows in a quizzical smile. "It appears that there is a good deal for your sister to attend to in the neighbourhood."

Her sarcasm was wasted on Jane, whose thoughts were already uncomfortably occupied with the image of Lizzie tending to her horse in a draughty barn. The more immediate concern was the messenger, however, and she instructed the housekeeper to see that he had dry clothes and a warm drink immediately. Miss Bingley started back toward the sitting room, her amusement tempered by a tiny twinge of conscience over Jane's distress.

"Do not be so fretful, Jane. I am sure Mr Handley has the good sense to assure himself that your sister is not injured by the weather. No doubt she is sitting in his library before a blazing fire right now, sipping on tea and reading a book while she waits for the storm to abate." She could not prevent herself from adding with a smile, "It appears to be one of Mrs Darcy's particular missions in life to traipse across country in dirty weather to visit those who are ill. I would not have expected her ardour for such missions of mercy to extend to sick horses, however."

Jane reached out to clasp her arm. "Sweet Felicity was a wedding gift to Lizzie from Mr Darcy, and is as dear to her as a friend. It does not surprise me that she should go to her, but in her... " She broke off abruptly and turned away, then continued, "That is, with the weather so very bad... " Miss Bingley might have wondered at Jane's stammering had she not been so preoccupied with harnessing her glee. It required all of her concentration to keep her mirth in check.

The afternoon felt endless to Jane, and Miss Bingley exerted herself to be good company, feeling she could be magnanimous in light of her secret pleasure with the day's events. She went so far as to pity Jane for the shadow that would pass over her life when Lizzie's indiscretion came to light. Although she had no love for Jane, Miss Bingley admitted with grudging respect that she *was* a sweet girl, and had none of her sister's impertinence or pretensions. It was a shame that *her* reputation should be so blemished by first one sister and then another. She even felt a pinch of sorrow on Charles' behalf, but it was of short duration and easily forgotten.

Chapter Forty Five

The ride to Croftwoods seemed interminable to Lizzie. Since their return from Longbourn, she had anticipated her reunion with Sweet Felicity so eagerly that more than once she had urged Fitzwilliam to send a rider to bring her home, but the continuation of wet, icy weather made the plan seem foolhardy even to her, and she forced herself to be patient. As the carriage bumped across the winter ruts, she began to feel more than a little uncomfortable, partly with the motion of the carriage and partly with the fear that she was going to lose her precious mare. Trevor's gravity had frightened her when they met on the road, and although he did not intend for her to return with him, it was soon evident that she would not be persuaded to stay away.

It was fortunate that the distance was not great, for by the time the carriage entered the paddock of Croftwoods, it was obvious to Lizzie that she had done herself no good by the trip. She put her own discomfort out of her mind, however, insisting that she see Sweet Felicity before entering the house to warm herself. In spite of Jane's fears, the stable, built originally with luxurious care for the comfort of England's finest breeding stock and meticulously restored by Trevor Handley, was neither draughty nor cold. She found Sweet Felicity in a partitioned room, lying on sweet straw and warmed by a hearty fire in the blacksmith's hearth. It took no great expert to understand the seriousness of the situation, for the heavy breathing and trembling of the great mare bespoke no trifling ailment. An elderly veterinarian huddled over her, applying a poultice of some foul-smelling concoction to her heaving chest. Lizzie gasped and hurried to her head, dropping down beside the beloved creature to murmur in her ear and caress her face.

At the sound of Elizabeth's voice, the mare raised her head and made a gentle blowing sound that prompted Trevor to smile. "I daresay she has missed you, Mrs Darcy." Lizzie's eyes filled with tears as she looked into the huge brown eyes, and she remained huddled over her, speaking close to her ear in a tone of intimacy that startled the veterinarian, unaccustomed as he was to finding great ladies on the floor with his ailing patients. Within a few minutes, the trembling of the horse's body diminished and the doctor pulled a packet of powders out of his bag, handing it to Trevor.

"Mix this is some warm water, Mr Handley, and we shall see if she can get some of it down, now she's more quiet."

Elizabeth did not trust herself to meet their worried eyes or ask any questions, but concentrated instead on her soothing ministrations. With a great effort, they managed to administer the draught so that at least a portion of it was swallowed, and within half an hour Sweet Felicity appeared to have fallen into an uneasy sleep. Only then did Lizzie quit her post reluctantly, and at Trevor's insistence she was escorted into the house and shown to a room to refresh herself. Within a few minutes she rejoined him downstairs, anxious to hear his opinion on the mare's condition.

Trevor's indefatigable optimism, aided by the effects of a warm fire and a hot cup of tea, soon revived Lizzie's spirits. When Trevor excused himself to return to the stable, she declared that she would go with him. He frowned and moved to the window, peering into the garden, where the storm's gathering gloom had rendered the morning a dusky grey. The first heavy drops of rain slapped the window pane and he turned back to Lizzie and said firmly. "The storm has opened up. You will be soaked through if you venture out in this weather, Elizabeth. I assure you, if there is a grave change in her condition, I will bring the carriage up to the door for you." Although she protested, it was to no avail, and wrapping himself up against the wind and rain, he quickly went out the door.

Left on her own, Lizzie felt suddenly tired and she settled herself on a sofa to wait for Trevor's return. In the still room, the noise of the storm grew ever louder, the heavy rain turning to sleet that beat upon the house with awesome force. A gnawing discomfort began to grip her, for she knew it would be impossible to return to Pemberley under these conditions. A look at the mantle clock told her that Jane would begin to worry soon. She had little time for fretting, however, for the front door was soon flung open and she hurried out to the hall to find Trevor shaking off his wet coat. "I fear you are the one who is soaked through, Trevor. How is she?"

"She is still resting easy. The vet will stay with her and the groom has instructions to bring us a report every hour. Her breathing is, I believe, a bit less laboured. We can only wait and hope for the best, but I assure you, Tom Howard is the best vet in the county. If there is cause for hope, it rests on him."

Lizzie forced a smile and replied, "I suggest you go and change your clothes if you do not wish to be the next to need the services of a doctor."

As she glanced anxiously toward the window, Trevor seemed to read her thoughts. "I sent a rider to Pemberley to assure your sister and Miss Bingley that you are safe. I am afraid there will be no question of your carriage braving the roads under these conditions. I should not have allowed you to come out in such threatening weather."

Lizzie's face showed first relief and then distress. "I thank you for your trouble, for I am sure Jane will be beside herself with worry, but I fear your man will be drowned before he reaches the manor."

Trevor laughed heartily. "You need not trouble yourself about him. I asked for a volunteer to make the ride as soon as the storm showed signs of letting up, and young James stepped up and declared himself ready to set out straight away. He is courting your chamber maid, Mary Williams, and I expect he would brave a hundred storms for the chance to spend the night at Pemberley. If he has any luck at all, he will catch cold and be forced to stay in bed for several days, with her keeping vigil at his side."

Their laughter erased all tension for the moment, and as Trevor went to change his clothes, Lizzie returned to the drawing room and settled herself in for a day of waiting. The groom was prompt with his reports, but the first few hours brought no very welcome news. Although the mare's condition did not worsen, neither did it show any signs of improvement, and as if to remind them of the seriousness of the case, the storm continued in gale force throughout the day. Twice more, Trevor braved the icy rain to spend an hour in the stable, and at last he returned with the news that although the danger was not entirely past, the mare's fever had broken.

Lizzie's relief brought a fresh animation to their conversation, and over supper she decided to share with Trevor the news that she was expecting a child.

"Our Willie is going to be a father? That will make me just about an uncle! When should we expect the happy event, Madam?"

"Perhaps the middle of August," she replied.

Trevor looked grave. "If I had known, I would never have troubled you with Sweet Felicity's illness. I hope this day's work has not over-tired you. Should you not be lying down?"

Shaking her head in mock vexation, Lizzie declared, "I wonder why it is that everyone makes such a commotion about this condition. If my mother with her nerves could bear five children, I am quite sure I will manage at least one. I am perfectly well, I assure you," she said with a laugh.

Relaxing into a wide grin, Trevor began describing for her amusement the outfit that he would order for her son's first riding lessons, and they talked on easily through the evening.

"You would make a wonderful father, Trevor. I wonder that you don't think of starting your own family," Lizzie ventured, but the expression that passed fleetingly over his face told her she had made an error in raising that subject.

"I am sorry, Trevor. I see I should not have said that."

Trevor carefully scrutinised the coffee cup in his hand and an uncomfortable pause ensued. Finally he spoke with a carefully casual air. "Not at all, Elizabeth. It is natural that people should expect me to marry. I am afraid my reticence on the subject of my marriage has given rise to a vast deal of speculation in the neighbourhood. I *was* engaged at one time to a woman of my mother's choosing, but fortunately, before any real damage was done, I felt compelled to disclose to her a fact which I had hidden from everyone else for my entire life." His words hung on the air like a heavy cloud on a still day and Lizzie experienced what was for her the rare sensation of speechlessness.

Chapter Forty Six

Georgiana and Fitzwilliam spent their first afternoon in Matlock in their solicitor's office, and it soon became evident that the work before them would require more than the space of a day to complete, as one of the parties would not be available until Friday evening. Charles Bingley, although he experienced a pang of regret at the thought of prolonging this first absence from Jane, had more than one acquaintance in the area, and professed his willingness to stay another day or two if need be. Darcy was uneasy, but Georgiana comforted him with the thought that Lizzie would be well tended by her sister, and she suggested quite reasonably that if they left Matlock without completing the business at hand, their presence would be required again in the coming months. Resigning himself that this was the most sensible course of action, Darcy sat down to write to Lizzie. He felt it necessary to suggest she call for a doctor at any hint of trouble, and ended with the entreaty that she must send a letter off each morning to assure them that all was well.

That evening, Darcy also sent a note to the home of Trevor Handley's mother inquiring whether her son was still in town and requesting permission to call on them. A speedy reply informed them that Trevor had quitted Matlock only the previous day, but that Mrs Handley and her daughter would be honoured to receive any member of the Darcy family at their convenience. With their departure fixed for Saturday morning, Darcy and Georgiana engaged themselves for tea on Friday afternoon with the Handley family.

Mrs Handley and her youngest daughter Meredith had lately taken up residence with Mrs Handley's eldest brother. As he had no family and suffered from poor health, his time was chiefly spent in Bath, and he gladly left his sister to supervise the estate in Derbyshire. Mrs Handley was a handsome woman, intelligent and dignified, but possessed of the same lightness of spirit that endeared her son to all he met. As closely as their families had once been connected, Fitzwilliam had never met Mrs Handley, but it was not long before Georgiana and Fitzwilliam understood the strength of her esteem for their father, for indeed she spoke of little else for half an hour. Georgiana hazarded more than one glance at Fitzwilliam before feeling assured that he experienced no discomfort from such lavish praise. For her part, Mrs Handley's description of Mr Darcy's generous and kindly nature moved Georgiana nearly to tears, and she was drawn out of her customary reticence to encourage the lady's reminiscences.

Brother and sister were both surprised to learn that their father's interest in the family's affairs had continued until the time of his death and that it was to his wisdom and guidance that she attributed her son's success in life. No hint intruded of the rift between their father and Trevor. Fitzwilliam glanced at Miss Handley, who sat quietly listening, looking for a sign that she knew something of Trevor's history that might contradict such hearty praise, but he found only a smiling serenity there. While he quietly assimilated this new information, Mrs Handley shifted the topic to Fitzwilliam himself.

"I can assure you, Mr Darcy, that it was with the greatest pleasure that I received your letter yesterday. Although we have not met, it has been many years since my desire to know you was first formed through the information contained in Trevor's letters from Pemberley. Having no brothers of his own, he delighted in relating to us every detail of the time he spent in your company. I have often entreated him to invite you to visit, but I fear his time was too often consumed by his enthusiasm to make a name for himself." She paused and then added, with a wistful smile, "He has borne heavily the burden of re-establishing our family fortunes since the death of his father and the mismanagement of our estate by his uncle. Having no brothers to aide him in providing for me and for his sisters, he took the full responsibility upon himself. Without the assistance and support of your family, I do not believe he could have managed as he has."

Feeling vaguely discomfited, Fitzwilliam turned the conversation to the present, extolling the beauties of Croftwoods and Trevor's enthusiastic renovation of its famous stables and until tea was poured the conversation offered no new surprises. A very reticent Miss Handley presided over the teapot and was drawn into the discourse at last by Georgiana asking about the young woman's special interests. The novelty of hearing his sister speak willingly and easily to a stranger brought a smile to his face.

Hearing Miss Handley's demure assertion that she could boast of no special talents, Fitzwilliam rejoined, "I have heard my sister speak of an exceptionally fine drawing of your brother that she discovered at Pemberley. Trevor informed us that it was the work of one of his sisters. Either you have a talent that you refuse to acknowledge, or it was the work of your older sister."

Meredith laughed lightly and shook her head, blushing slightly.

"Unless my mother has kept secret from us a third sister, I fear there has been a mistake, for neither Alexandra nor I have the slightest aptitude for drawing." Her mother confirmed with a benevolent smile that although she might boast of her daughters' accomplishments in many other spheres, neither of them, to her knowledge, had ever shown an interest in portraits.

Fitzwilliam managed an offhanded reply and abruptly changed the subject, inquiring whether they were not planning to visit Croftwoods in the near future. Georgiana sat back in her chair, fighting to still the icy foreboding that crept over her. Mrs Handley did not miss the change in the room.

"Miss Darcy, are you feeling unwell?" she asked with concern.

"Excuse me, Mrs Handley. It is only that I am a little tired. We have been much occupied for the past few days," she stammered.

Fitzwilliam, grateful for the diversion, rose from his chair and addressed his sister.

"Forgive me Georgiana. I was not thinking." Turning to Mrs Handley he explained that they were anxious to return to Pemberley as soon as possible, and had engaged themselves for an evening meeting with their solicitor to complete their business. She accepted their explanations graciously but remained perplexed, reviewing the conversation for the source of their sudden distress.

Scarcely knowing what they said as they took their leave, Fitzwilliam and Georgiana were finally seated in the privacy of their carriage, and in the half hour that was required to see them back to their hotel, not a word was spoken by either. Until they reached the safety of their sitting room, neither could bring themselves to put into words the discomfiting thoughts that occupied them both. At last, as she removed her bonnet and cape and hung them in the vestibule, Georgiana ventured to intrude upon Fitzwilliam's private contemplation.

"Is it not possible, Fitzwilliam, that you misunderstood Trevor's meaning about the portrait?" she asked, although the sternness of his features told her it was not.

"He spoke with complete assurance," he replied unhappily.

After a few moments she tried again. "I am sure father felt an obligation to his friend to continue his support for the mother and sisters' sake and was unwilling to punish them with his accusation concerning Trevor."

"Yes, I suppose that might be the case." He paused and then added, almost to himself, "But the portrait is another matter entirely... "

As brother and sister sat in front of the fire, a long silence ensued during which Georgiana nervously plucked at her dress and Fitzwilliam stared vacantly into the flames. It was from this pose that they were startled by a knock on the door. Fitzwilliam started up quickly to open it and received from a servant a letter which, he informed them, had been delivered immediately after their departure from the inn.

A note contained in the outer envelope expressed their solicitor's regret that the letter enclosed had been received in his absence the previous day and had inadvertently escaped his attention until now. He hoped Mr Darcy would be in no way inconvenienced by the delay, etc. Without bothering to finish reading, Darcy tore open the enclosed letter, which was dated Thursday morning and sent by urgent post from Pemberley.

His hands trembled as he saw that the handwriting was that of Caroline Bingley, for he could in no way imagine that anything other than disastrous news should be sent with such haste, and in her hand rather than Lizzie's. He read it through once, comprehending little at first but that it spoke of no harm or danger to his beloved. It required a second and third reading to make him fully sensible of its meaning, and even then he required more time to decide which emotion he should apply to its contents, so bewildered did he feel. Georgiana sat frozen in her chair, equally afraid of the letter's import, and she scarcely breathed while she waited for him to speak. After an interminable wait, the hand holding the paper dropped to his side, and he looked at Georgiana with a baffled frown. The worry on her face aroused him to say, "Lizzie is fine, Georgiana, but beyond that I do not know what to make of this." As he thrust the letter into her hand he stood up and began pacing the room, muttering under his breath, "Am I never to have peace...?"

Georgiana read the letter with increasing agitation.

My Dear Mr Darcy,

It is with the greatest reluctance that I intrude upon you in this manner, but the intimacy of our long acquaintance and the esteem in which I hold you as my dear brother's friend urges me to bring to your immediate attention a matter which I believe seriously threatens your happiness and that of your dear sister.

A man with whom I believe you are well acquainted, a Mr Trevor Handley, arrived at the gates of Pemberley only hours after your departure yesterday. I am given to understand that his arrival was not unexpected and he was met with a most unusual display of affection by Mrs Darcy. Understanding as I do Mrs Darcy's lively temperament, I was persuaded at first that her attention to him was evidence of a general affection rather than a particular regard. By this morning, however, I am most painfully disabused of such a notion, as I happened to observe something that left me in no doubt that their feelings for each other bespoke an intimacy impossible to impute to disinterested friendship.

I have carefully weighed every evidence, searching in vain for an interpretation that would be less painful to all of us. Finding none, I have been tormented by the awful responsibility attendant upon the possession of such information, knowing too well the disastrous effect my disclosure must have on your trusting nature. I would have sooner doubted the evidence of my eyes and ears than give credence to the possibility that Mrs Darcy's affections could ever be turned from you. And yet, remembering as I cannot fail to do the unfortunate incident this summer involving her younger sister and Mr Wickham, I am forced against all my wishes to fear that the standards of acceptable behaviour in that family are at a variance with those espoused by society in general.

It is therefore with the deepest sorrow that I take pen in hand, finding myself unable to be a party to such a deceit. Although I dare not assume you will thank me, I am persuaded that in such a case it must be the lesser evil to immediately uncover such reprehensible behaviour, lest silence cause an even greater harm. I intend, having thus resolved myself, to make known to Mrs Darcy and Mr Handley my understanding of their indiscretion, so that you may be assured that no further harm will be done before you are able to return and intercede on your own behalf.

With my deepest regrets, etc.,
Caroline Bingley

Georgiana read through the letter a second time with colour rising to her cheeks as she comprehended the seriousness of its content.

"This is the most monstrous fabrication, Fitzwilliam! I can scarcely believe even Caroline Bingley capable of such a lie, angry or hurt as she may be. What does she propose by this outrage?" As tears of vexation filled her eyes, her brother walked slowly to the window and stood lost in miserable reflection for several minutes before speaking.

"Georgiana, Caroline Bingley is no fool. She rarely plays a game she cannot win. That is the reason for her being in such a temper of late - she cannot tolerate losing. This year has brought her nothing but defeat," he continued, calmed only by his wish to appear rational for his sister's benefit. "By now she had hoped to be married to me and mistress of Pemberley; I don't doubt that she hoped you might marry Charles as well or at least that she would have persuaded him to find a more suitable house. Her prospects would have been nearly perfect in either case, but now they are impossible. Her sister has begun to lose patience with her, and in any case she has no hope for happiness in sharing the Hursts' home. Her brother is married to a woman she does not admire, and lives in a town she despises. She is completely miserable at Pemberley, as we have all too clearly seen."

He paused, frowning as he thought more deeply about Caroline Bingley than he had ever done. "I know of no other immediate prospects, which leaves her with the alternatives of living alone in London or spending her time moving from one house to another as a guest. She must indeed feel she is ill-used by everyone at this moment."

Georgiana objected, "But surely she cannot blame Lizzie for all of that!"

"No," he said quietly, "but perhaps she can blame me. I believe she is jealous of Lizzie, but her hatred must be reserved for me. She is certainly aware that it would destroy my happiness if I were to lose Lizzie."

"But, Fitzwilliam, you made her no actual promise, did you?"

"No, Georgiana, I never spoke to her of marriage, but I am guilty of allowing her to hope, for her aspirations were clear to me and I did nothing to discourage her."

"Do you believe her capable of destroying Lizzie and Mr Handley to take revenge on you?" she asked incredulously.

"I believe she is desperately unhappy and I know she is capable of retaliation when vexed, but I am unsure of the lengths to which she might go," he answered miserably.

"But could she be so foolish as to imagine that we would believe either of them capable of committing an indiscretion in front of her eyes? It is too ridiculous to even consider."

Fitzwilliam paused to consider before answering. "I can think of two possibilities. The first is that her intention is to expose all of us to public scorn and ridicule, in which case it matters little to her whether we believe or disbelieve her charges, for there are many who would be only too eager to accept them as true. The second possibility is that she honestly misunderstood whatever she saw and that she believes she is telling the truth. That she would like to believe Lizzie capable of such a thing is obvious, and she would certainly hope that I might be grateful to her for her intervention."

It was Georgiana's turn to lose herself in thought, and she finally said with a deep frown, "But if she believes it to be true, what could possibly have happened between them to suggest such an idea?"

Neither brother nor sister would put words to a third possibility although they were too intelligent not to think of it: that Caroline Bingley might be telling the truth. The accusation, coming as it did on the heels of their confusing visit with Mrs Handley, took on a most ominous character.

Fitzwilliam was the first to speak, shaking his head to clear it of *that* thought.

"The final question is, what are we to do now?" He glanced at the mantle clock and saw that it was just past five o'clock. The evening meeting with their solicitor, Mr Long, was scheduled for eight. "I could send a written reply immediately, but I have no idea what I should say, or to whom. Or we could set out for Pemberley now, but I am loathe to leave our business unfinished when so little is wanting."

Georgiana's brow furrowed in concentration. "If this letter is a cruel hoax, as seems likely, Miss Bingley will be biding her time in silence, waiting for our return, for it would serve no purpose to give Lizzie notice of her intention to do her harm. But if she is sincere, then a dreadful scene will have unfolded by now. Lizzie should not, in her condition, be so upset." Her eyes filled again with tears of compassion for the woman who had become as dear to her as her brother.

Darcy replied firmly, "I cannot take the chance of delaying another moment. If we leave immediately, we will reach Pemberley yet tonight. We must send word to Mr Long that we are called away."

Georgiana took a deep breath. "Fitzwilliam, you could make far better time if you went alone on horseback. If we were to summon Mr Long immediately, you could sign a power of attorney allowing him to act on your behalf in tonight's negotiations. I believe I understand very well the conditions which you intended to propose to Mr Pope, and with Mr Long's assistance, I feel sure we could manage very well in your absence."

Her brother forgot his troubled thoughts for a moment as he turned to Georgiana with a startled expression. A smile of pride spread over his face as he read the determination in her unblinking gaze.

"I see I shall have to stop thinking of you as a child, my dear. You possess an uncommon amount of good sense. Are you quite sure?"

"Yes, of course," she said, managing an answering smile that belied the nervousness she felt. "I will be the better for knowing that you are on your way to Lizzie's side. Mr Bingley and I will follow you tomorrow morning." But another disturbing thought had just entered her mind. "Only, what shall I tell Charles? Should I show him the letter or make some other excuse?"

Fitzwilliam's thoughts were racing ahead to Pemberley, and he paused only long enough on his way out the door to say, "I shall leave that decision to you, Georgiana, as I am not as capable as you are of reasonable thought at this moment. I shall send for Mr Long at once and arrange for a mount."

Within the hour, Mr Long had arrived, been persuaded against his better judgement to accommodate the unusual request, and had completed the necessary paperwork. Leaving a message for Charles to contact Georgiana immediately upon his return that evening, Darcy left Matlock for a long cold ride, the approach of nightfall spurring him on to cover the miles as speedily as possible.

Chapter Forty Seven

On Friday morning, Lizzie awoke under the spell of a night of troubling dreams. Several minutes passed before she was able to orient herself to the unfamiliar bedroom and sort out which of the unsettling images in her mind pertained to the events of yesterday and which were remnants of her uneasy sleep. As she stretched lethargically, a slight discomfort reminded her of the future, but the thought did not bring its customary surge of joy this morning. She sat up carefully, swung her feet to the floor and walked over to the window.

When she pulled back the heavy drapes, sunlight spilled into the room and bathed her in warmth. The sodden ground, littered with scattered branches, testified to the strength of yesterday's tempest, but the morning sun rekindled her spirit, and she dressed quickly and hurried downstairs to find Trevor. A pang of tenderness came with the memory of their conversation last night, and the recollection of his tear-rimmed eyes as he poured out his story eclipsed even her anxiety for Sweet Felicity. The Trevor Handley she had met last night seemed a distant kin to the confident, grinning gentleman who had enlivened the drawing-room conversations of Pemberley in the past few months. Meryton's bucolic society had offered little training to Lizzie in understanding the morass of treachery and tragedy she had encountered since her marriage, and as she approached the drawing room, her brow was furrowed in contemplation of this most recent chapter.

The drawing-room was empty. As she stood hesitantly in the hall, the butler appeared to conduct her in to breakfast, but until she could be satisfied that Sweet Felicity was in no danger, she had no appetite. She asked for her cloak, and over his protestations that the master would be returning immediately, started for the front entrance. Before she could reach it, the massive door swung open and Trevor

Handley stepped inside. He smiled broadly at the sight of her worried countenance and she was relieved to see that he had recovered his jaunty bearing.

"Good morning, Mrs Darcy. I hope you have not been fretting, for our beauty is up on her feet this morning and I daresay she will be quite herself in a few days."

Lizzie laughed with relief. "That is welcome news, indeed. I had just resolved to go and see for myself."

"Have you had your breakfast yet?" he asked, and finding that she had not, he offered her his arm. "If you will join me, I'll tell you all about it and we can go to the stable directly after."

She consented willingly and as they moved toward the breakfast parlour Trevor explained that he had risen at dawn and hurried to the stable to find both mare and doctor sleeping peacefully. Having awakened Mr Howard, he had stayed to watch while the veterinarian examined her, and within a few minutes Sweet Felicity had struggled to her feet, impatient to be fed. Although the congestion in her lungs was still evident, it appeared that her youth and strength would speed her to a complete recovery.

With her anxiety thus relieved, Lizzie concentrated her thoughts on Trevor's jovial banter. He made no reference to last night's conversation, and before long she began to wonder if she had dreamt up his confidence. In any case, his manner clearly signalled that he did not wish to reopen the subject. They completed their meal and went quickly to the stables. As he had said, Sweet Felicity had taken an amazing turn for the better, and contenting herself that all was well, Lizzie declared that she must return immediately to Pemberley.

"I can only imagine that Jane must be beside herself fretting about me."

"The rain will have done the roads no good, Elizabeth. I think it safer that we should wait, at least until later in the day. I can easily arrange for a letter to be delivered to your sister."

Elizabeth could not be persuaded, however, and Trevor reluctantly agreed. "Then I shall accompany you as far as Pemberley lodge and have a visit with Old Thomas." The carriage was ordered and Trevor's mount quickly brought round, and they set off on the short journey. Their progress, painfully slow, was marred by several violent jolts of the carriage, as a wheel clattered over a wash-out or slid into a muddy rut. At the first difficult spot in the road, Trevor suggested that they turn back, but Lizzie was determined; a vague worry urged her toward Jane and home. He cursed under his breath at every bump, urging the driver to be more careful, and at more than one difficult spot, halted the carriage and descended to walk ahead, guiding the horses by hand through the morass.

Although Lizzie carefully maintained a light-hearted banter, the discomfort that the swaying and jolting caused made her wish she had not been so obstinate. By the time they reached the lodge and Trevor alighted to untie his horse, she was happy for a moment's pause. From that point, the distance to the manor was short and the road better maintained than the public lanes, and she at last reached home with a heavy sigh of relief.

Jane, keeping a restless vigil in the drawing room with her sister-in-law, had started to the window in response to so many imagined carriages that Caroline Bingley began to feel irritable, in spite of her eager anticipation of what the day might bring.

"My dear Jane, I do wish you might be a little more calm. You are making me quite nervous."

Jane sighed and picked up her sewing. "I *am* sorry, Caroline. I am sure the roads are barely passable after that storm, but knowing Lizzie as I do, I fear she will attempt to return this morning," she answered, hardly knowing whether she wished more for her sister's arrival or a sensible delay.

"You cannot hope to influence her from here, I daresay," replied the other, raising her book and feigning an intense interest in its contents. Her own thoughts were no less occupied with imagining Lizzie's entrance, but she harboured a secret hope that it might be preceded by the arrival of a troubled Mr Darcy. She did not doubt that he would hurry back to Pemberley upon receiving her letter, and the prospect of him bursting in from an anxious night on the road to find that his blushing bride had spent the night with Mr Trevor Handley was too delicious to bear. The intensity of last night's storm made that imagined scenario unlikely, as he would have, in all probability, been forced to take shelter until it passed, but she was nevertheless amusing herself with the thought when the unmistakable sound of carriage wheels jarred her from her reverie.

Jane dropped her sewing with an excited exclamation and hurried to the door, throwing it open to observe Lizzie being handed down from the carriage. She hurried outside to meet her and gravely studied her sister's face before enfolding her in a welcoming embrace. As they walked toward the house, Jane admonished in hushed urgency, "Lizzie, you frightened me to death. Are you all right?"

Lizzie's laughter was more reassuring than the pallor of her cheeks. "I am sorry to have worried you, dear Jane. Did you not receive a message that I was safe at Croftwoods before the storm began?"

Jane nodded, but continued to complain, "You are not allowing for the delicacy of your condition. The carriage ride cannot have been good for you, Lizzie."

She was prevented from continuing by the appearance of Caroline Bingley in the doorway. Miss Bingley raised her eyebrows in amusement at the sight of Lizzie walking arm in arm with Jane. "My dear Mrs Darcy, what can you mean by going out in such dreadful weather? You will catch your death of cold. Surely your horse could have been counted on to recover without you forfeiting your own health."

Lizzie laughed gaily, "Such a pair of mother hens. Dirty weather has never brought me any harm. Jane, if you would just ring for some hot tea, I will warm myself by the fire for a moment."

Miss Bingley led the way into the drawing room, and feeling herself on high moral ground, she adopted a pose of bemused condescension. "I hope that your sister and I are to be soon entertained with all of the details of your escapade."

Lizzie disliked the tone of Miss Bingley's voice, but chose to ignore it, addressing her response instead to Jane, who settled herself next to Lizzie in a chair near the fire. "It was thoughtless of me to run off as I did, but when Mr Handley met me on the road with the alarming news that Sweet Felicity was dangerously ill, I could not bear to waste a moment." She related the story of her arrival at Croftwoods and spared no detail of the vigil of the previous day, ending on a note of flushed excitement with the news that the crisis had passed.

"And you returned unescorted this morning?" Miss Bingley asked slyly. "I wonder that you did not wait for confirmation that the road was passable."

Lizzie turned an unsuspecting eye on Miss Bingley. "Mr Handley saw me as far as the lodge, where he stopped to look in on Mr Hill. I expect his arrival shortly."

Miss Bingley smiled. Nothing had been said to dampen her hopes, and in fact, she looked forward to an interview with Mr Handley.

"Ah, yes, I had forgotten your friend the lodgekeeper. It was for him that you left the comfort of your home. I trust Mr Handley will find him as healthy as the mare."

Lizzie felt a rising consternation, but catching sight of Jane's peaceful countenance, she smiled and quelled her irritation.

"I think I shall go and have a bath and put on fresh clothes. Keep the tea warm for me, Jane." She hurried out of the room before the insolent Miss Bingley could begin again.

Chapter Forty Eight

Jane smiled fondly as her sister hurried from the room. "I was foolish to worry so. Lizzie has a hardy constitution." Miss Bingley smiled, thinking to herself that a greater test would soon be required of that lady's resilience, and settled herself back on the sofa with her book. She had not long to wait for the next chapter of the story to unfold, for within the quarter hour there was a knock on the door and Trevor Handley was admitted, aglow with the brisk air and marked with the evidence of his gallant battle with the muddy road. With the help of an attentive butler, he was soon cleaned up and outfitted with a pair of Darcy's shoes to replace his muddy boots, and he joined the ladies in the drawing room. After a warm greeting, Jane excused herself to check on Lizzie, and Miss Bingley took her place at the teapot, eyeing her prey with amused condescension. Lizzie and Jane could not have been more mistaken about Miss Bingley's designs on Trevor Handley. The only thought she had entertained on the subject of his suitability was whether Mr Darcy could be compelled to feel jealous of a man so obviously inferior to him.

Her delight at the opportunity he had afforded her drove her to speak impertinently. "Forgive me for being so bold, Mr Handley, but do you not feel that your presence in this house today is inappropriate?"

Lizzie, returning at that moment to the room with Jane beside her, was stopped at the door by Miss Bingley's brazen tone. If Mr Handley paled in astonishment, Lizzie's cheeks flamed in indignation. "Miss Bingley, what can you propose by this?" she said, just managing to control her voice.

Miss Bingley turned slowly to face her wearing a smile of amused disdain. "I believe you understand perfectly well what I mean, Mrs Darcy." She thought pleasantly of Mr Darcy winging his way to

Pemberley on a swift horse, and the nearness of her ultimate triumph emboldened her and gave her countenance a radiant glow.

The fact that Lizzie had maintained her sense of humour and dignity in the last several weeks in response to Miss Bingley's unpleasant moods and behaviour did nothing to improve her tolerance for this new imposition. Taking a deep breath to calm herself, she turned to Trevor and said, "I wonder if I might have a private word with Miss Bingley, Mr Handley."

Trevor, so taken aback by the thinly disguised animosity of Miss Bingley who only two days ago had appeared utterly gracious and civil, reluctantly bowed his acquiescence and hurriedly left the room. Jane turned to speak quietly to him as he moved into the hall. "You will forgive me, I hope, Mr Handley, but I feel I must stay with my sister." He nodded curtly and, shaking his head, walked toward the library, sorely troubled but unable to decide on any other course of action for the moment.

Jane turned her attention back to the two women who stared at one another with fierce animosity. Elizabeth rose to the occasion, for she had the advantage of more than a twelvemonth's restraint in the face of Miss Bingley's haughty impudence to prepare for just such an opening. Indeed, she relished the thought, as she walked slowly across the room to take a seat facing her nemesis, that the time had finally come for Miss Bingley to answer not only for this present insolence, but also for her insufferable behaviour of the past. If Lizzie had borne Miss Bingley's previous insults with an amused equanimity, she could not countenance this insult to a guest in her home with equal forbearance. She sat down with controlled dignity, looking directly into Miss Bingley's mocking eyes, and even the colour raised by her initial shock disappeared in the wake of the icy rage that overtook her. Miss Bingley felt an equal share of anticipation, so assured was she of triumph. The prudence that had previously caused her to veil her animosity was quite overturned by her present smug belief that she was acting on behalf of Mr Darcy himself, for she had not the sense to doubt that he would soon be persuaded to see Mrs Darcy through her eyes.

A young maid, arriving at the door with a fresh pot of tea, took such fright from the expressions of these two ladies that she backed silently away and hurried off to ask Mrs Reynolds what she must do. The room was charged with such an eloquent, if unspoken, communication of mutual animosity that even an intrepid observer might well have taken flight. When Lizzie finally spoke, her voice crackled with indignation.

"I must ask you to explain the purpose of your remark, Miss Bingley."

"It is you, I fear, Mrs Darcy, who has much to explain. As a long-standing friend of the Darcy family, and with their happiness a subject most dear to my heart, I believe it my duty to intercede on their behalf in any matter which so deeply concerns their well-being."

Jane, unlike her sister, had little experience of anger and less propensity to comprehend evil. She walked silently to Lizzie's side and sat down beside her, saying, with a quivering voice, "I believe what you have to say concerns me as well as my sister, Miss Bingley."

"Just as you like," Miss Bingley said scornfully. "What I say here I will gladly say to all the world. Since the first day of my acquaintance with you and your family I have suspected, and indeed observed, a fault in breeding and a laxity in morals that led me to fear that a closer connection would be undesirable and indeed dangerous. When I perceived an inclination in my brother to pursue your acquaintance, I strongly protested against it, firmly believing that such a connection could only lead to a tragic conclusion."

Jane and Lizzie, well apprised of these feelings, were nonetheless astonished to hear them given voice. So eager were they to hear what prompted such frankness that they did not make a sound, Jane's voice stilled by a bewildered sorrow, and Lizzie's by the knowledge that if she ventured to answer at this moment, it would be by slapping the lady's face.

"Mr Darcy shared my concern and added the weight of his disapprobation to my own. What trick of entrapment led him to lay aside his own inclination, you know better than I, Madam, but for the sake of our friendship and in deference to my brother's decision to marry your sister, I have kept my counsel since the engagements were announced, hoping to be proven wrong in my assessment. The events of the last four and twenty hours have caused me to most painfully recall my misgivings, and indeed I am persuaded that I had rather underestimated the danger than otherwise."

Lizzie could no longer maintain her silence, and although she did not lose the dignified pose she had adopted, her voice could not disguise the contempt she felt.

"Excuse me, Miss Bingley. I am most eager to hear your account of the events to which you allude, but before I have the pleasure of understanding your present motivation, allow me to say that I have suffered your insults and insinuations for too long not to return your candour with an observation of my own.

"Before meeting your party in Meryton, I had not had occasion to keep company with families of your social elevation or financial advantage. I believe it was quite natural for me to assume that I would find in their manners and habits an improved understanding and dignified bearing suitable to their position in society. What I have found, however, is that no one of my previous lowly acquaintance has ever behaved with the wilful arrogance or utter disregard for human decency that I have observed in you and others of your standing. For incivility and a contemptible lack of manners, I must rank you with Lady Catherine de Bourgh and Lady Margaret Westby, in whose company I do not doubt you would be pleased to find yourself. I fear that my recent experiences of such uncivilised behaviour may lead me to forget the kindness which I was taught to practice in my humble family.

"If you feel you are justified in your present behaviour, I shall listen most eagerly to your explanation, but I can in no way excuse your conduct during the last fifteen months, for neither I nor my sister Jane have ever treated you with other than the utmost respect and kindness, in spite of our clear understanding of your attempts to do us injury. For you to insult a guest in my home is beyond all boundaries of acceptable behaviour."

Miss Bingley here abandoned her haughty condescension in favour of a sneering rage. Her flashing eyes brought to Lizzie's mind a thought of Darcy's mother. She hissed, "Do you dare sit in judgement of my manners and those of others who are so far superior to you? Do you consider it a mark of your excellent breeding to accept the attentions of a lover before your marriage is six months old?" She watched triumphantly as Mrs Darcy's face spread with a rising tide of crimson, mistaking her incredulity for guilt.

Jane's gasp of disbelief was the only sound in the room for several seconds, but Lizzie was suddenly released from her speechlessness by a wave of comprehension. She asked evenly, "May I assume you refer to my friendship with Mr Handley?"

"Even you, Mrs Darcy, cannot be so brazen as to hope that your behaviour these four and twenty hours could be interpreted as the natural consequence of *friendship*," Miss Bingley replied loftily.

It was soon her turn to wax scarlet, for Lizzie turned quickly to meet Jane's eyes and then began to sputter in laughter. Lizzie's old ally, her keen enjoyment of the ridiculous, had come to her aid, and the torrent of laughter that ensued quickly eased her sense of injury. Jane's gentler nature impeded her immediate comprehension of all that had been said, but she was heartened by her sister's laughter to believe that there was yet some hope of reconciliation. Turning from Lizzie, whose mirth left her unable to speak, she looked at Miss

Bingley to find her face contorted with anger and was moved to wish Lizzie would soon regain her composure in favour of a sober explanation of the facts. Miss Bingley, in spite of her already low opinion of the two women, was amazed at the impertinence of levity in the face of so serious a charge. Lizzie, however, was enjoying herself too much to stop before tears streamed down her cheeks.

Miss Bingley, for her part, took no pleasure in the turn the conversation had taken. The exquisite moment of triumph and the pleasure of her censure were lessened by the comprehension that these women were beyond shame. She rose imperiously to her feet and moved toward the door, which gave Lizzie the motivation to regain her composure. She rose too and called to Miss Bingley to wait, but the lady only deigned to pause long enough to remark haughtily, "I daresay you may see this matter in a more serious light when Mr Darcy is apprised of it."

Her words had the desired effect of removing every trace of levity from the room, but she was not prepared for Lizzie's response.

"Miss Bingley, forgive me for saying it, but you have made a most dreadful mistake. Please, please do come and sit down again. I apologise for my laughter, but the idea of my having an affair with Mr Handley has taken me quite by surprise." Miss Bingley was torn between her curiosity and her malice, but ultimately decided that there was nothing to be lost by continuing the conversation; the thought that Mrs Darcy was about to entertain her with protestations of innocence or an appeal for her silence struck her suddenly as amusing.

The three ladies assumed their previous positions with Lizzie rubbing her forehead thoughtfully before she spoke. "In our very brief acquaintance I have come to feel towards Mr Handley the love of a sister, and I greeted him with the same affection that he would have received from Mr Darcy." Released from her angry indignation by laughter, Lizzie felt growing within her a genuine concern for Miss

Bingley's welfare. The recognition of how pitifully tormented this woman must be in her disappointed hopes led her to speak without rancour, her generosity aided by the assurance that she had nothing to fear from such a pathetic figure.

Miss Bingley clung desperately to her conviction of Elizabeth's guilt, but her face assumed a taut pallor as doubt crept in, for nothing in that lady's demeanour suggested anything but the conviction of truth. Jane hastened to add to Lizzie's explanation with guileless fervour.

"I assure you that my sister speaks the truth, Caroline; Mr Handley is a frequent visitor to this house and is as near to a brother as Mr Darcy could wish for. Your distress on Mr Darcy's account was motivated, I trust, by your perceived duty, but I assure you that my sister's regard for him would never allow her to behave in any manner that would threaten either his happiness or her own."

Her offensive weakened, Miss Bingley fell back to her defensive position: that anyone might have reached the same conclusions and that, in fact, the behaviour of the two of them was still to be considered scandalous. As if he read her thoughts, Trevor Handley suddenly appeared in the doorway. He spoke with obvious discomfort.

"I am sorry to admit that I have been listening for some time outside the door; I fear that my presence is required to clarify matters." To Lizzie he added, "I appreciate your discretion, but I feel that a few words from me will resolve all confusion." He then turned and addressed himself to Miss Bingley, speaking with complete candour, "My presence of mind is to be faulted for allowing Mrs Darcy to return to Croftwoods with me, but I assure you that in my company she faced no danger greater than that afforded by the weather and difficult roads. It has been many years since I came to the realisation that I am incapable of feeling a romantic attraction to any woman."

With this speech, Miss Bingley needed very little time to comprehend that she had no further options. Trevor's revelation rendered her delightful intrigue a farce and a quick glance at Elizabeth proved that his confession was not a surprise; surely Mr Darcy would be aware of the facts as well. In full retreat, she rolled her eyes heavenward in a most uncharacteristic sign of defeat. The sound of Jane's incredulous gasp was over-reached by the guttural moan that issued from Miss Bingley's throat, and at last she began to weep, covering her face with both hands.

Lizzie, far from enjoying the scene, was overcome with pity, and moving quickly to Miss Bingley's side, she laid a kindly hand on her shoulder. She then said, intending comfort, the only words likely to increase Miss Bingley's distress: "You need not fear, Miss Bingley, that the details of this conversation will ever pass beyond the walls of this room."

To the amazement of all three, Miss Bingley reacted to these words as if she had been struck a blow, and her tears increased to uncontrollable sobs. Mr Handley decided he had outstayed his usefulness and quietly excused himself to retreat to the safety of the library once more. Jane and Lizzie looked at one another in bewildered concern, for the grief before them seemed all out of proportion with its cause. Her own injury forgotten, Jane went to kneel beside the miserable form, but if Miss Bingley found any comfort in the gentle ministrations of the two sisters, it was not evident for a very long time. At last Lizzie said softly, "Perhaps you would like to lie down for a little while."

Miss Bingley suddenly uncovered her face and looked at Elizabeth, then Jane, her brow furrowing in concentration. The comprehension of their sincere good will opened a door in her heart to feelings of shame and remorse that she had never before experienced. She was, in fact, enjoying the sensation that Mr Darcy had explained as seeing himself in the mirror of Lizzie's love, and although the sight was not pleasant, its novelty distracted her from her self-pity, and she found herself compelled to pursue the vision. She nodded weakly and allowed them to assist her to her feet.

"I will walk up with Caroline – you must see to Mr Handley, Lizzie," Jane said softly, taking Caroline's arm.

Lizzie hurried off, still shaking her head in perplexity. She found Trevor pacing in the library, and, dropping into a chair, smiled weakly.

"I cannot find words to express how sorry I am that you had to be a party to such unpleasantness, Trevor. I must thank you for your gracious intercession."

"I am utterly to blame for shrouding my life in so much secrecy."

She laughed kindly, "No one, not even I, could have foreseen this turn of events, although Miss Bingley and I have a long history of unfortunate conversations. This one was slightly more venomous than the others, however, and I am very sorry that you were forced to hear it." She added with a grimace, "You must wish at times that you had never heard of the Darcy family. Such conflagrations!"

"I hope I shall never wish that. I confess I feel more relief than distress. It is just as well that I have been forced to acknowledge who I am. I have struggled too long with my silence." His face broke into a smile. "After all, I have only been accused today of one particular sin, while you and Mrs Bingley have been condemned for a general failing of character. If you can bear up so cheerfully, I am sure I cannot do less."

Lizzie rubbed her forehead, suddenly overwhelmed by the combination of emotions and exertions of the morning, and conscious that the discomfort she had experienced several times in the past four and twenty hours had returned with greater force.

"Well, perhaps some day I will entertain you with a full history of our relationship, but right now I believe I must go and lie down. I hope you will not mind entertaining yourself."

Trevor's confidence had returned. "It is time I went home, Mrs Darcy. I have work to do, and I imagine you and Miss Bingley will have more to say to one another before the day is done." As he reached for her hand, he looked into her eyes with a frown of concern. "Are you unwell?"

Jane appeared just then at the library door, and, with a quick look, appraised the situation. She said sternly, "Lizzie, this will not do. You are going to make yourself quite ill if you are not careful."

Now Trevor *was* truly distressed, but Lizzie laughed at the expressions they both wore.

"Please don't look so miserable, you two. Jane has been waiting patiently for several weeks to make a public display of fussing over me, and I am quite prepared to indulge her, but I assure you that I am only a little tired."

In spite of her protestations, Trevor insisted on taking her arm, and with Jane on her other side, Lizzie allowed herself to be helped up the stairs. He left Jane to help her into bed and continue her remonstrance against over-tiring herself.

"You owe it to Mr Darcy and to the baby to take care of yourself, Lizzie. This morning's work has done you no good and you must not allow yourself to be so upset again."

Lizzie smiled. "Jane, you know that I am fit and strong. I am sure that having a child cannot be so difficult as you want to make it. I shall promise you, however, not to go into battle again until I am rested," she said sleepily. Jane sat by her on the bed until she was sure that she was resting comfortably and then went out into the hallway, shaking her head sadly as she thought over the angry words that had been said that morning. With nothing more to be done for Lizzie, her thoughts turned to Miss Bingley, and with a heavy sigh, she moved down the hallway toward her room.

Chapter Forty Nine

Left alone in her room, Caroline Bingley lay down to think. Memories crowded her mind and she allowed herself to drift from one to another, examining them in the light of the new vision she had of the Bennet sisters. What she had deemed ridiculous behaviour now took on a kind of nobility; her own witty disdain began to seem childish and ugly. The image that kept replaying itself was of two pair of hands reaching out to comfort her. Try as she might, she could understand nothing from these gestures but that they were the work of kindness and generosity where none was merited.

The thought of the letter she had dispatched with such hope and anticipation now produced a cold gripping pain when it came to her mind. She allowed herself to grasp at possible antidotes to its poison, but in the end she could find no relief. Its contents could not be explained away in any manner that would make her appear less stupid or less spiteful. How Mr Darcy would react she could scarcely imagine. And Charles—she had only valued his acquiescent and trusting nature inasmuch as it suited her own desire to manipulate his actions and thoughts. Would even *his* generous and happy temperament allow him to overlook such despicable behaviour?

Lizzie's description of her as arrogant and ill-mannered taunted her. Her own wit and intelligence, which once she had prized so highly, now appeared as shallow and ineffectual tools that benefited her little in attaining any real happiness. Her disdain for Mr Darcy's infatuation gave way to envy and finally admiration as she began to understand that he had learned something she had never grasped— how to love and be loved.

Leaping more and more quickly from one enlightenment to the next, she began to see the group of haughty and insolent people she had proudly called her friends as miserable and weak when compared to her present companions. Lizzie's stinging appraisal of their bad manners and incivility came back to her, and her shame redoubled, for held up to the light of her new reasoning, she could not argue against its validity. It was in this state of miserable self-revelation that she heard a knock at the door, and she turned away from the sound, wishing herself spirited away beyond the reach of human voices.

Jane knocked softly a second time, and hearing no sound, ventured to open the door a crack. Her whispered "Caroline..." brought only the sound of crying from the huddled form on the bed. Jane sighed and stepped into the room. Having no idea what could be said in comfort or what should be said in remonstrance, she chose instinctively to communicate with her hands. She sat behind the trembling body on the bed and lightly touched her shoulder. When that gesture was not shaken off, she began to gently rub Caroline's back as if to smooth away the sorrow.

After a few minutes, her ministrations brought a measure of relief, and Caroline Bingley sat up to look into Jane's eyes. Finally she said in a hoarse voice, "Why do you wish to offer me comfort? What can you mean by it?"

Jane smiled weakly, "My dear, I mean you no harm. I understand, I have understood for a long time, that you are terribly unhappy. I am sorry to see you so and I want you to know that Lizzie and I bear you no ill will. Please believe that."

Miss Bingley, indeed, could not find any sign of either hurt or anger in Jane's gaze. On the contrary, she was forced to acknowledge that in return for the abusive language she had employed, and in spite of her proud admission of her interference in their happiness, the Bennet sisters were intent on repaying her only with charity. She had suspected their kindness, had mocked it from her first observance, but she could no longer pretend that it was insincere or the result of weakness or stupidity. Lizzie's anger had required the work of fifteen months to arouse, and once expressed had dissipated at once, replaced by pity. Now Jane sat in front of her offering only comfort and kindness, and Caroline Bingley had no idea how to respond to it.

At last the questions on her mind pressed her urgently to speak. "After everything I said today, you still cannot find it in your heart to be angry, can you Jane? I cannot comprehend your nature."

Jane frowned thoughtfully. "I was greatly troubled by your words this morning, Caroline, but seeing your pain, I remembered how many things I have to be grateful for."

Caroline shook her head in confusion. Jane began again, feeling an urgency to be understood. "You spoke from your own anger and disappointment today, not to hurt me or Lizzie, but to relieve your own pain. When I remember that, it makes me only wish there was something I could do to give you peace of mind."

Caroline again betrayed her disbelief at these words. "I have wanted to believe you and your sister cunning or stupid. I have hated you because I could not enjoy the simple happiness I saw in you. Today I have begun to see myself as shallow and petty, and I wonder why I have been unable to recognise sincere goodness when it is all around me. What Lizzie said is true, you have only repaid my insolence with kindness, and I wonder why that should have aroused my contempt rather than my admiration."

Jane's quizzical smile encouraged her to frankness; hesitantly she began to unfold the tale of lies and interference that she had earlier alluded to, sparing no detail of her attempts to disparage the Bennet family and convince Charles of their unsuitability as relations.

The tale ran long, and Jane allowed her to speak without interruption, and when she had finished, all of the sins that she could readily call to mind lay confessed. Although the substance of her actions was known to Jane, the details forced her to admit to herself what Lizzie had once tried to make her see, that Miss Bingley had behaved very badly indeed. If in her confession, Miss Bingley had harboured a hope of putting Jane's nature to the test, she was soon forced to admit that this woman before her was incapable of rancour. Jane maintained her pose of bewildered compassion throughout the narrative, registering nothing more alarming than an occasional look of surprise, and Miss Bingley ended her speech at last without the relief that an angry response might have given her. Jane's reaction, in fact, was to reach out her hand in comfort, and Miss Bingley felt her very soul being shaken by it. Her tears renewed with vigour as she struggled to comprehend the baseness of her own motives.

"I have done everything in my power to make you and your sister unhappy, and yet you sit before me offering love and forgiveness."

Jane spoke at last, sadly, but with calm composure.

"Please understand that it is not in your power to make me unhappy, Caroline, except in the sorrow it brings me to see your distress. Had Charles' love for me been insufficient to overcome your interference, I would have blamed neither him nor you. I would have wished it otherwise, but I would have gone on with my life, content in the knowledge that I had loved him. You believed I would not make Charles a good wife, but you were mistaken. I cannot hate you for that. As much as I regret that you have chosen a path of unhappiness for yourself, *I* choose to be happy, and you have no power to change that."

Miss Bingley was shattered by the novelty of that thought. At last she regained enough composure to ask, "And your sister?"

Jane thought carefully before answering, "I see things as I wish them to be, but I think Lizzie sees things as they are. While she has certainly been angry with your actions and words, she shares my belief that happiness is a choice we make for ourselves. You need not fear that you have injured her." After a pause to reflect, she added, "There is one thing that does perplex me, Caroline, and I do not know that you have the answer yourself. I do not understand why it seems to give you pleasure to speak ill of others. I have thought long and hard about the pleasure that Lizzie has in teasing people when their behaviour is ridiculous. Your wit is as eloquent as hers when you mock, but the intent, I believe is very different. Lizzie's laughter comes with a love for the frailty of humanity, while yours seems rooted in abhorrence."

She stood up to take her leave, saying, "I will leave you to rest now, and we will speak no more of this matter unless you wish it."

Miss Bingley sighed deeply. As she lay down, she wondered how she would find the strength for the apologies and explanations that would be needed before the subject could be laid to rest, for the final ugly secret of her letter left her in no doubt that whether she wished it or not, much more must surely be said. She had comprehended a great deal this day, but she doubted that she would live long enough to understand or feel the serenity she saw in Jane's countenance. One thought remained clear in her mind, that she would not venture to speak in future unless she was sure that no harm would come from her words. As to the attainment of happiness for herself, she could not imagine how that could come to pass.

After half an hour of silent reverie, Miss Bingley shook off her lethargy. In her haste to defame Mrs Darcy in her husband's eyes, she had spared no thought for the harm that might be done to Mr Handley. Setting aside the difficult subject of the Darcys, she chose the easier first step of making amends to him, and, hoping to be spared from meeting Jane or Elizabeth at this moment, went downstairs to look for him.

Although he had intended to return to Croftwoods, Trevor's concern for Elizabeth had stayed him, and Caroline found him sitting, grim-faced, in the drawing room. Miss Bingley began speaking rapidly, her face flushed with the novelty of humility and the effort of making herself coherent.

"Mr Handley, I have done too much harm today for a simple apology to suffice, but let me only say that if I could reclaim my words of this morning, I would be the happiest of women. Since that is not possible, I am resolved to make amends as I can and live with the consequences of my foolishness."

He formed a gallant acceptance, but before he could speak she raised her hand.

"Pray let me continue. I have yet one more error to confess. It weighs upon me so heavily that I must tell someone, for I fear that more mischief will be done if something is not attempted quickly to set things to right."

She paused uncomfortably and Trevor rubbed his forehead, beginning to feel that the day had aged him, and that it was far from finished. What more Miss Bingley might have to say, he was loathe to hear, but he was certain that there was no escaping it. Judging from the agitation of her appearance, it was a matter of no small import, and he shook off the urge to run from the room, waiting silently instead for her to compose her confession.

She began at last, "I, that is, yesterday... " and paused, looking up at Trevor as if hoping he would supply the words she needed. He motioned her toward a chair and sat down facing her in a pose he hoped expressed a willingness to listen. She took confidence from this encouragement, and, taking a deep breath, said quickly, "I sent a letter yesterday morning by urgent courier to Mr Darcy in Matlock to warn him of the threat I perceived to his happiness. I can only hope that he had the presence of mind to dismiss it as preposterous, but... " She broke off, fighting back tears.

Trevor's composure shattered. He leaned back in his chair, feeling as if he had been struck a hefty blow. Miss Bingley, her misery complete, dropped her head. She had harboured a faint hope that Mr Darcy already possessed the information that would make her charges absurd, hoping against hope that the only damage that would be done was to her own credibility. But seeing Mr Handley's reaction, she could not doubt what she already suspected, that it was by far the most serious error in this unfortunate day's foolishness. It was Trevor's turn to draw a slow, steadying breath, and finding that insufficient to relieve his agitation, he stood up and began pacing the room. At last he asked shakily, "At what time did the letter go, Miss Bingley?"

"At about 10:30 yesterday morning. Just after you met Mrs Darcy's carriage on the road."

"It will have reached him yesterday afternoon, then." He resumed his pacing, but as he pictured the faces of Mr and Miss Darcy as they opened the dispatch, he turned abruptly to ask, "What exactly did you say in this letter?"

Her speech waxed fluid with the relief of her confession and she gave him an accurate account of its contents, colouring deeply as she recalled her haughty pleasure in its writing. Stunned by her words, it needed some little effort for him to speak again, but this time his tone was icy.

"Why did you not mention this before now?"

Her eyes filled with tears of mixed shame and release. Here at last was the anger she had expected.

"I could not bring myself to admit it."

Mr Handley was indeed angry. As he resumed his pacing, he thought of the fragile trust that had grown up between him and his friend, and realised far better than Miss Bingley, what effect her letter might have on Fitzwilliam's mind. As he sought to formulate a plan of action, he glanced at the mantle clock and entertained the possibility that if Fitzwilliam had believed her charge, he would have most likely departed Matlock in a towering rage, and would have reached Pemberley by this time. Remembering the impossible weather of the previous day, however, he was forced to acknowledge that he might yet be on the way.

Miss Bingley, her poor mind exhausted from its day's work, sat quietly waiting for Mr Handley to think through the problem. At last he stopped moving and said, "I think I must ride for Matlock. If, as I fear, they have resolved to return immediately to Pemberley, I will meet them on the road. I may be able to offer some relief from their distress." He hesitated. "I have been waiting for a report from Mrs Bingley on Mrs Darcy's condition."

Miss Bingley was alarmed. "What do you mean?"

He looked at her with appraising eyes.

"Jane insisted that she go and lie down. Perhaps you did not know that she is with child." A small gasp escaped Miss Bingley as she assimilated this information. The ugliness of the morning's scene took on a new and more terrible dimension and she rose abruptly, her face ashen.

"I shall go and find Jane immediately and bring you word." She quitted the room in a state of the utmost agitation and hurried upstairs. She looked for Jane in her room but found it empty. Approaching Lizzie's door with a feeling of dread, she garnered her strength and knocked softly. Jane opened the door, her face drawn into a frown of tender concern. To Caroline's frightened inquiry, she replied that Lizzie was sleeping, and seeing the evident distress on Caroline's face, hastened to add that she hoped a rest would restore her completely. She promised to bring a report when Lizzie awoke, and Caroline turned from the door to deliver this message to Trevor Handley as he paced in the drawing room below.

Having nothing further to do, she quietly wished Mr Handley a safe journey and retired to her room to await the final scene of the drama she had spawned. She could not tell whether she wished for a speedy conclusion to her anguish, or a period of respite, but of one thing she was sure, that she had not yet paid the full price for her meddling.

Chapter Fifty

Fitzwilliam Darcy scarcely saw the road in the fading light, so desperate was he to make sense of the conflicting voices that argued in his head. It must be said on his behalf that he started out with only the earnest desire to assure himself that Lizzie was in no distress and to trust that answers to all questions would be forthcoming.

His first diversion from this purpose was to curse the day he had met Miss Caroline Bingley, and this he did out loud and with great energy. He had to admit that he had once admired her power over a gathering, her easy speech and tireless witticisms, but this brought his thoughts to his own culpability, for although his nature was more kind, he had never discouraged her outspoken contempt for others until she had begun to criticise Miss Elizabeth Bennet.

Two years ago, he had harboured no great expectations of contentment, but he had reached an age where he began to think he must sometime marry, if only to produce an heir for Pemberley. Of the women with whom he was acquainted, only Caroline Bingley was sufficiently amusing and, with a pride matching his own, unlikely to embarrass him. His aunt's increasingly vocal wish that he should marry her daughter had urged him to think of marrying someone else, if only to silence her on the subject. He smiled wryly as he thought of how much more graciously she would have conceded defeat to Miss Bingley, for their temperaments, at least, would have been well suited to one another.

This thinking led him to remember what he had said to Georgiana: that he still judged Miss Bingley an intelligent woman, one unlikely to spread rumours that might come back to embarrass her later. If she indeed believed she had written the truth… As quickly as it came, he banished the idea that there could be a basis for her accusation, and soothed himself by dwelling for a time on the happiness Lizzie had awakened in him and her unshakable faith in their love. He tried to imagine her sleeping or reading by the fire. Did she know that the letter had been sent; had she been confronted with Miss Bingley's allegations by this time? Shame crept up his spine as he wondered if Lizzie would think him capable of believing such slander.

Darcy shook away that thought and turned his mind to Trevor Handley, reviewing the day's conversation with Mrs Handley and her daughter. Although he forced himself to search for a calm and rational explanation for Trevor's lie about the drawing, none presented itself. His avowal to Lizzie that he was freed from tormenting himself about the past was undermined by this evidence that Trevor did not trust him with the truth.

He thought again of Lizzie, remembering how her compassion had led her into sympathy with George Wickham. Doubt gnawed at the edges of his mind, and an icy pain grew in his stomach as he gave in to the anxiety he had often felt that her love was too good, too perfect, and his happiness too complete to last. Tears rose to his eyes and he tormented himself with the contemplation of the intolerable emptiness of life without her. His contentment was still too new to allow him the luxury of complacence. He had more than once given himself over in the privacy of his mind to the nagging doubt that her affection for him could endure and now he derived a kind of perverse pleasure from giving his fear full rein, hoping that the torment would spend itself long before he reached her side.

His mind drifted unexpectedly to a particular memory of his mother: she wore a riding habit and carried a jaunty hat in her hand, a black leather whip tucked under her arm. Darcy thought he must have been about ten years old, and he remembered clearly how beautiful he had thought her. He had asked if he could ride with her, for he loved her most of all in these moments when she was possessed by a mood of reckless gaiety. His father was not at home, and the troubling discord of their strained interactions was put out of Darcy's mind for the moment. She had considered his request with an enigmatic smile, and then said with a laugh, 'Not today, my love. I have commissioned Trevor to give me a riding lesson, and I am determined to have all of his attention for myself.' She had walked away from him with a look he had long understood signalled the end of a conversation, and he did not venture to protest, but went instead to his room, from whose window he could watch her step out onto the front walk.

He pondered her words. She was a superb horsewoman—why would she feel the need for a lesson from their young friend? Young Fitzwilliam, although his pride would not have allowed him to own it, was more than a little daunted by the self-assurance of his new friend Trevor Handley, and awed by his confident, slightly flippant manner with his mother. It was evident that she found Trevor amusing, and she often condescended to watch as Trevor instructed her son in riding or fencing, engaging in a playful teasing that left Darcy feeling confused and uncomfortable. He remembered the view from the window that morning, his mother's step light and prepossessing as she approached the horses that Trevor held waiting. Trevor greeted her with his jaunty laugh, and Darcy turned quickly away from the window, troubled by the scene but unsure why.

The implications of this memory were suddenly clear beyond doubt. Darcy began with urgency to explore other memories of Trevor's stay at Pemberley, looking for confirmation of his conclusion, forcing himself to review every scene, every word that he could recall of that year and a half. The teasing banter, the flushed excitement, the light-hearted laughter of the early days paraded before his eyes, followed by ugly scenes of rage in the house, muffled arguments behind closed doors, and ending with an icy silence hanging in the halls. That his mother contrived to be alone with Trevor was clear; equally certain was that Mrs Darcy's disdain for her husband would not allow him to imagine that she would permit him intimacy.

If Trevor lied about the portrait, perhaps he was lying about everything. Perhaps he was, after all, Georgiana's father. He had never actually denied it. Who would blame a woman like Lizzie with her zest for life for being attracted to a man as self-assured, as optimistic and carefree as Trevor. *And as capable of deception.* Had it not been Fitzwilliam's fear from the beginning that he would drive her away with his morose moods?

He reined in his horse abruptly, unable to ride for the trembling that had overtaken him. He covered his face with both hands and his horse shied nervously at the sound of his anguished groan.

Chapter Fifty One

Lizzie awoke after a long, troubled sleep to find the late afternoon shadows darkening her room. At her first movement, Jane appeared in the doorway to the sitting room where she had been watching her sleep. She sat down on the bed and took her sister's hand, a line of worry creasing her forehead. Lizzie smiled complacently and sat up, saying, "Jane, please do stop worrying about me! I feel perfectly well, I promise you." But even as she blithely protested Jane's concern, a pain startled her that could in no way be mistaken for mere discomfort or fatigue, and she cried out involuntarily, bending forward.

Jane took hold of both of her shoulders, insisting that she lie down again, and said, more calmly than she felt, "I am going to send for a doctor. Do not try to get up, please, Lizzie. I will be back in a moment." Lizzie had no intention of moving, for she too was beginning to feel frightened, and she nodded her assent. Jane returned to her side in a few moments and seating herself on the bed next to Lizzie, offered what comfort she could until the doctor arrived. Neither spoke more than a few words, for there was little that could be said to appease the fear that something was going dreadfully wrong. The pain abated at times, only to return after a few minutes with renewed vigour. After an anxious hour of waiting, a kind elderly man was shown into the room by Mrs Reynolds, and was introduced as Doctor Andrews.

Jane waited anxiously as he conducted his examination, and the serious demeanour of the old gentleman did nothing to alleviate their fears. Before the sun had set that night on Pemberley's hills, Lizzie had lost the child she carried.

Doctor Andrews was wise in the ways of human suffering. He had seen enough sickness and sorrow to understand that the latter was sometimes the greater danger, and he realised the limitations of his skill in dealing with it. He assured Lizzie and Jane, devoting a long and kindly speech to nature's way, that as she was young and healthy, there was no reason to assume she should not bear many children in the future. Neither sister was ready to be comforted by this thought, and although Lizzie made a valiant attempt to answer him in a spirit of optimism, when he left the room she allowed herself to give full vent to her grief. Alone together, they lay down on the bed, Jane tenderly cradling her dear sister in her arms, and they wept.

By the time Dr Andrews returned, Lizzie had dropped off into a fitful slumber, and Jane relinquished her post for a few minutes to deal with the matter of sending a message to Mr Darcy.

From the moment of Mr Handley's departure, Miss Bingley had retreated to her room, maintaining a prayerful vigil over the empty hallway. When she heard the doctor called for, she was frightened to distraction by the thought that it was her behaviour that morning that had precipitated Lizzie's distress. Dr Andrews, as he emerged from Lizzie's room, confirmed her worst fear, and she fled again to her room, more wretched than when she left it, if that were possible. Her quiet hours of tearful self-pity, shame and remorse gave way to a raging anger. She paced the floor, giving vent to every manner of invective she could summon upon herself until in utter exhaustion she threw herself into a chair. With the door ajar, she settled in for a night of sorrowful watching.

Jane had barely stepped into the hallway when Caroline Bingley sprang from her chair. She almost wished for an outpouring of anger and blame, but instead she was met with the tenderness that swelled her shame more than harsh words could have ever done.

"Oh, Caroline," Jane said, blinking back her tears, "I am so grateful to find you awake." Caroline reached out awkwardly and took her hands. "I think I must send word to Mr Darcy that Lizzie has lost her baby, but I cannot think what to say."

Caroline Bingley turned a whiter shade of pale. "Is she in any danger?" she stammered.

"Doctor Andrews assures us that all will be well," Jane hastily assured her, "but I feel Mr Darcy would wish to be informed."

Caroline Bingley suddenly felt quite ill from the knowledge that it was time for her confession. Pressing her hands to her abdomen, she spoke quickly, fearing she might collapse before she had finished. The letter, her confession to Trevor Handley, and his departure for Matlock were covered in minutes. While Jane stood frozen, assimilating this information, Caroline's mind raced to formulate a plan. "I fear he may be already on the road, and I can only pray that Mr Handley has found him by this time. It can do no harm, however, to send a messenger to Matlock, in case he is still there. May I see to it for you?"

Jane, too stunned to think of a response to Miss Bingley's disclosure, nodded silently and turned away to resume her watch over Lizzie. Concern for the distress of anyone but her beloved sister was beyond her at this moment, and fatigue and sorrow dulled all thought concerning the implications of what she had just heard.

Miss Bingley rang for a servant to order a rider, and then sat down to pen a note with trembling hands. With mind and body so disturbed and exhausted, she toiled over the words, looking for a way to express concern without undue alarm. She fought back every thought of the last letter she had written, lest she should find herself unable to write at all, and soon she had a tolerable message penned and sealed.

The doctor, content that Mrs Darcy was sleeping and in no immediate danger, left Jane to her vigil and went to lie down. Mrs Reynolds had anticipated his stay and had a room prepared and aired for him long before it was needed, and she led him there herself before going to prepare some tea for Jane. It was clear that Mrs Darcy's sister meant to keep watch through the night, and as Mrs Reynolds had no more desire to sleep herself, she stationed herself down the hall from her mistress' room and waited in prayerful anticipation. Her initial regard for Mrs Darcy had grown into a powerful affection, and she well knew that she was not the only member of the Pemberley staff that would sit up through that long night hoping and praying for relief for their beloved mistress and her gentle sister.

If Caroline Bingley drifted off to sleep from time to time, it must be admitted that she had faced that day a gamut of emotions that covered quite the full range of human misery, and with the promise of yet another high drama when Mr Darcy should return to Pemberley, she needed to rest.

Chapter Fifty Two

A sudden weariness overtook Darcy as he stood by the road. The rising moon gave no illumination to his muddled thoughts and the long ride ahead of him seemed suddenly unbearable; he longed to disappear into the cloak of night. He mounted his horse and urged him on until lights signalled an inn. There he stopped abruptly, handed his horse to a groom and went inside with no plan in his mind other than the certainty that he could not go home in this state of mind. Presenting such a picture of forbidding bad temper that no one ventured to bother him with pleasantries, he sat down at a table near the fire and asked curtly for food and wine.

As chance would have it, it was during this interval that Trevor Handley, scanning the road for a familiar carriage or rider, crossed Darcy's path. Had he been able to read his friend's thoughts at that moment he might have felt fortunate to delay their meeting. While he could scarcely doubt that Darcy might have reached an unfortunate conclusion, his optimism taught him to believe that the truth would ultimately prevail. With several hours of reflection behind him, he felt a growing sense of relief that the burden of secrecy had finally been lifted from him and resignation concerning the direction his life had taken.

It required the effect of several glasses of wine for Darcy to force himself back onto the road. While his thinking was none the clearer for it, the pain eased and he attempted to focus only on the soothing rhythm of the horse and the pattern of the stars overhead. Peace could not be so easily purchased, however, and before an hour had passed he opened a dialogue with himself, scarcely aware that he spoke out loud:

"Why have I not taken my father's temperament as my own? He was steady and calm, not subject to the swinging moods of my mother. Would he not have applied logic to such a question?"

"But let us not forget the portrait Mr Alexander has painted – a man who was overcome with jealousy and suspicion."

"And yet, if his suspicion was based on good cause, it would not be a failing…"

The now-familiar knot in his stomach tightened and he could not prevent his mind from taking the inevitable next step: "Can there be any basis for me to suspect that Lizzie would be unfaithful to me, even if Trevor Handley were the devil himself?" The horse grew skittish when Darcy pounded on the saddle.

"Fool!" he shouted to the wind. "Two months have passed since I declared myself free from the interference of the past and yet I am still driven to distraction by these ghosts! I won't have it - I *will* be free and I *will* be happy. Lizzie has shown me the way-I need only follow it!

It was indeed fortunate that this monologue brought him to the crest of the a hill that overlooked Pemberley and before he could stray from the enlightened path he had attained, he spurred his horse to a gallop and raced against what now seemed to him a ridiculous propensity both to think too much and to consistently reach the wrong conclusions.

The faint glow of moonlight endowed the manor's granite face with an illusion of safety and peace that made him want to cry out in longing. He pulled his horse up, threw the reins over a post and ran up the steps to the house, little imagining that the day's grief had just begun.

The silence in the halls of Pemberley gave no clue to the turmoil that had echoed through them in the past four and twenty hours, and Darcy ran up the stairs with only one thought, that Lizzie would bring him relief. As he entered the sitting room that led to the master suite, he was startled by the sight of Jane, wrapped in a shawl and looking exhausted. She started up at the sight of him, an exclamation of surprise and relief on her lips. Darcy's enthusiasm wilted and dread took its place.

"Where is Lizzie? What has happened?"

Jane nodded toward the door to the bedchamber and whispered, "Thank God you've come, Mr Darcy. She is sleeping." Her mind filled with questions and explanations, but he turned abruptly away and went inside. She waited for a few moments, unsure of what she should do, and then retreated quietly to her room, leaving the door open in anticipation of a call. Darcy understood nothing from her presence save that it was troubling, but went quickly to Lizzie's side, sitting down on the bed and touching her face softly. Her eyes opened in bewilderment to the touch of his hand, and seeing him sitting beside her she was suddenly filled with such an overwhelming combination of relief and sorrow that she immediately began to cry. Her thoughts were as disjointed as his and drowsy from her troubled sleep, but the distraught look on his face spoke eloquently, and she believed that his suffering for the loss of their child must surely equal her own.

"Oh, Will, I am so sorry for causing you such pain," she said through her tears. Darcy had come to Lizzie with the hope that she would guide him, as she had always done, to a path out of the twisted maze of his thoughts; he was stunned into silence by her apology and her tears and it required but the work of a moment for the knife to twist itself in his gut.

She wiped her eyes, rallying her strength to comfort him, but the expression on his face seemed curiously wrong for the sentiment he should have been feeling. Furrowing her brow in concentration, Lizzie looked toward the window, confused by the faint glow of moonlight. "What time is it, Will? How have you come so soon?"

He replied in equal confusion, "I left Matlock as soon as I received Miss Bingley's letter."

"Miss Bingley's letter?" she asked, trying to focus her thoughts. "What do you mean?" Her sorrow and the sleepy stupor of a moment ago disappeared, supplanted by a wave of foreboding that gave her new energy.

Darcy's chest tightened as he recalled the torments of the long night's ride. His mind was working slowly, as if a blanket of fog muffled her words and clouded his thoughts. He stared into Lizzie's face, but the image that rose to his mind was of his mother, scornful, haughty, and as he now understood, capable of the grossest deceit. He worked to make sense of Lizzie's remorse, and rubbing his forehead, tried to concentrate on the words she was saying.

She repeated her question, her voice edged with tension, "What was written in the letter, Will?"

He looked up and met her gaze, studying her eyes as he spoke in a voice devoid of emotion. "She did not tell you, then. She wrote to me yesterday that she had evidence of... that you and Trevor... " His voice trailed off, his stony face masking the sickening fear that had returned to his stomach.

Lizzie sighed and closed her eyes. "Oh, Caroline... No, she did not tell me," she said wearily. Taking a deep breath, she raised her eyes to his, and a menacing chill stole over her as she tried desperately to read the shrouded thoughts behind them. As comprehension dawned, colour rushed to her cheeks. "Is that what brings you home so quickly?" she asked at last, forcing her voice to remain calm.

Struggling with his fatal honesty, he left her question hanging in the air for too long before answering. "I hoped the report must be either false or the result of a mistaken understanding on Miss Bingley's part," he said evenly, praying that she should relieve his anxiety, frightened that she would not.

"But you considered that it might be true," she replied coldly.

The strain overturned his self-control and he said in a terrified voice, "Tell me that it is not, Lizzie."

The angry pride in her voice pierced him. "If you believe me capable of such deceit, Mr Darcy, I wonder that you look to me to relieve your fear. You had better seek your reassurance from someone in whom you have total confidence, although I can scarcely imagine that such a person exists."

"What can you mean by that?" he asked harshly. His face had grown suddenly ugly and hard as fear and pain gave way to anger.

Lizzie's eyes as quickly narrowed as her own anger rose to meet his. "Have you been waiting for an opportunity to prove to yourself that I too must fall short of your expectations? Why must you live your life as if you were always expecting the next injury?" With the acrimony of her words hanging in the air, choking her, she turned her head away from him, praying silently that he would contradict her or move to touch her.

His cold reply startled her. "My willingness to be offended is exceeded only by your own, madam. If you will permit your reason to intercede, I believe you must allow that you have given me reason to suspect you capable of sudden changes in affection."

Her mouth flew open in outrage and she turned again to face him, her eyes alight with a fire that would have startled even the former Mrs Darcy. "You rushed to my side," she flung at him angrily, "to accuse me of unfaithfulness and you dare to wish I had not taken offence! Mr Darcy, if you do not yet believe in my love, I fear you never shall."

A most terrible confusion supplanted his anger and he cried out, "What is the meaning of your apology, if you have done nothing wrong?"

She answered bitterly, "I assumed wrongly that the distress you brought into this room was for the loss of our child. I did not imagine there could be another cause for it."

He staggered as if dealt a blow, a low groan escaping his throat, and he chose, as was his habit, the path of least resistance. Fleeing the room before she could make another sound, he raced down the stairs and out of the house, blinded by tears and struggling to breathe.

Chapter Fifty Three

Caroline Bingley had risen, startled into alertness, at the sound of Mr Darcy's entrance, reaching her door just as he entered the sitting room. She sighed and took a chair, waiting with a strange feeling of calmness for his angry denunciation. She took some comfort from the knowledge that his arrival would at least bring solace to Lizzie and Jane. His sudden reappearance forced a gasp from her lips, for even her most painful expectations had not prepared her for the raging countenance she saw before her. As his eyes met hers, she stepped back instinctively, but instead of the confrontation she had envisioned, he grimaced in pain and continued past her door, stumbling as he fled down the stairs. She heard the massive door flung open and then slammed shut, leaving her in a stupor of incomprehension. The sound of Lizzie's sobs and Jane's running steps came through to her as elements in a dream, and she covered her face, unable to move.

Darcy stopped in the garden for a few seconds, grasping at the pain in his stomach, and then straightened up and made way for the stables. He gruffly awakened a groom and commanded, "Saddle the grey at once!" And when the poor man stood frozen in incomprehension, he shouted, "Be quick, man!" and turned on his heel to pace angrily outside the stable door while he waited. The groom fairly leapt into action, emerging with Fitzwilliam's stallion on a rein in a matter of minutes, and trembling at the tormented visage of his Master. Darcy bounded into the saddle, calling back to the groom to see to the weary horse in front of the house.

Urging the grey to racing speed, they were lost to sight around a bend in the road in moments. The miserable groom, fearing the worst, ran to the servant's entrance to hear what news there was. He found no answer to his question, for confusion had turned to chaos, and no one within those walls had any clear understanding of what had passed.

As Darcy rushed from the room, Lizzie suddenly understood what her injured pride had prevented her from understanding in time: that he had come to her with no knowledge of her miscarriage. Her mind raced through the tangle of misunderstandings and recriminations until, remembering the look of horror on his face as he fled, she abandoned herself to moaning sobs. Jane, listening for every sound, came running to find Fitzwilliam had gone as mysteriously as he had appeared, and she wrapped herself around Lizzie to try to still her keening wail, rocking her and murmuring as if to a distraught child. Mrs Reynolds reached the room moments after Jane and her eyes widened at the scene on the bed. Jane looked up and said urgently, "Please wake the doctor, Mrs Reynolds. Hurry!"

The doctor, startled from his sleep, hurried to Mrs Darcy's bedside, but neither he nor Jane could calm her or prise from her a coherent word. For the better part of an hour, she succumbed to a despair that was wordless and chaotic. Disjointed images drifted in and out of her consciousness, but she could make no sense of them. Glimpses of the past year and a half, of Rosings Park, Meryton, the Inn at Lambton, of passionate lovemaking, anguished tears, and laughter, tumbled over one another, but the thread of love that held them together seemed broken, and Lizzie felt, for the first time, utterly without hope.

When her sobbing finally abated, she lay spent in Jane's embrace, listless and detached. She could not bear to confess, even to Jane, the things she had said. Dr Andrews shook his head sadly and mixed for her a powerful draught to help her sleep, then settled himself in the sitting room to wait for its effect, while Jane rocked her gently, mouthing words of comfort but feeling only incomprehension at the behaviour of Mr Fitzwilliam Darcy.

Although Lizzie slept at last, it was not a restful sleep, and as she tossed and muttered, Jane's anxiety increased. The doctor kept his vigil in the sitting room, gravely watchful, and although he said nothing to alarm her, Jane understood that he was troubled by what he observed. She was entreated by Dr Andrews to get some sleep herself and she lay down beside Lizzie to try, but the fear that gripped her and the stirrings of a very real anger taking shape within her towards Mr Darcy would permit no more than fitful dozing. She tried again and again to make some sense of his disappearance, but could see no way of excusing him for his behaviour. Through the long hours that followed, the walls of Pemberley stood guard over the muted sorrows of its inhabitants, upstairs and down.

Fitzwilliam Darcy rode as a man possessed, and with no intention but to put distance between himself and his despair, he urged his mount forward. His isolation loomed before him as he desperately sought a direction for his thoughts and his movement. With burning eyes and pounding head, he surveyed the wreckage of his life and found nothing to anchor him, and nowhere to go. If he had grown up a lonely man, he had been insensible of it until he met Lizzie; now, the thought of life without her left him so empty he felt he was collapsing into himself. He urged the horse on as long as he dared, creating for himself the illusion of purpose, but at last the futility of his ride stopped him and, tying the panting horse to a sapling beside a stream, he dismounted, dizzy with exhaustion and sorrow.

His mind twisted and turned like a netted fish, caught between her accusations and the thought of her grief and loss. Bitterly, angrily, he berated himself for being such a fool, and, when he had tired of repeating to himself her recriminations, he found yet another cause to heap abuse upon himself: the thought that he had not once in that endless night remembered the child she carried. And finally he allowed himself to recognise his own bereavement, for in the past two days he had come to think of this baby as a seal on the promise of a contented future.

Drifting from pain to pain, he knew he could never repair the damage he had wrought. It was inconceivable that Lizzie, even with her forbearance, could ever welcome his presence, and if she could not, then who? 'You had better seek your reassurance from someone in whom you have total confidence, although I can scarcely imagine that such a person exists.' The truth of her words was inescapable: he lived his life as if always looking for an injury. There was no one for him to turn to. He had no doubt that even Georgiana's steadfast love could not endure if he confessed to her the anguish he had caused Lizzie.

Weariness finally stilled the tide of acrimony and he sat empty and adrift, dully watching the sun rising over the verdant hills. Unbidden, an image of his childhood came to mind of a night he and Wickham had escaped from the house to sleep in a favourite hiding place in the woods near Pemberley Lodge. Their boasts of fearlessness and a crackling fire had not prevented them from being startled by every noise the forest offered to stay their sleep, but as neither could be the first to suggest they return home, they talked and laughed loudly to warn off any predator that might be lurking in the circle of trees. Just before dawn, as weariness battled with nervousness, a breaking of twigs bespoke an intruder nearby and their eyes met in unmasked fear. As the silhouette of a man emerged from the woods, a startled cry rose from their lips and was answered by a low, rumbling laugh. In a moment, Thomas Hill stood before them, hands on hips, presenting such a welcome picture of safety that the boys whooped with delight.

The memory of Thomas' voice in the dark brought a wan smile to his lips. 'Your father will be of a mind to flay ye over this prank, young master, when he finds ye missing.' He laughed pleasantly. 'If the two of ye have had your fill of the savage life, ye'd best come home with me and warm yourselves.'

After a few moments of irresolution, he mounted the grey stallion and began a slow, melancholy ride to the one house where he had always been met with compassionate acceptance, Thomas Hill's lodge.

Chapter Fifty Four

Trevor Handley, unaware of the drama unfolding in his wake, rode through the night with little thought for anything but his hope of remedying the distress of his friends. Since he met no one on the road, he began to trust that their response to Miss Bingley's letter was to discount its veracity. Whatever discomfort it had cost them he felt sure could be easily remedied with his assurances, and all damage would be speedily undone save to the reputation of Miss Caroline Bingley herself.

It remained for Trevor to find the inn at which the Darcys were accommodated, which he did quite easily, knowing as he did the preferences of his friend. Although the hour was late, Georgiana answered his knock quickly, as if she had been anticipating it, but her exclamation of surprise showed that Mr Handley's was not the face she expected to see. Recovering herself, she ushered him into the parlour. The etiquette of a proper greeting was forgotten in the emotion of the moment, and Trevor reached out to take her hands, looking into her eyes for a sign of her feelings. "My dear Miss Darcy," he said, "I regret troubling you at such a late hour, but the urgency of the situation bade me come without delay."

"Oh, Mr Handley, I am so glad you are here," she said breathlessly. "I have been so consumed with thoughts of Pemberley that I could not think of going to sleep. Have you come from there?"

"Yes. I came as soon as Miss Bingley informed me that she had written to you, fearing that you and Fitzwilliam would have been alarmed by her letter. The proprietor told me he left… where is he?"

"He left for Pemberley several hours ago. Did you not meet him on the road?"

He frowned thoughtfully. "I watched for him as I rode, but I passed no one."

"How did you leave Mrs Darcy?" she asked quickly. "I hope she

397

is well."

"I believe so, although she was a little tired," he replied.

Now her brow knotted in concern for her brother as she offered him a chair and then sat facing him.

"I cannot imagine that you did not meet Fitzwilliam on the road," she said nervously. "But forgive me-you must be cold and exhausted from your ride, Mr Handley."

"That is of no consequence. I am sure I missed Darcy either when I stopped to rest my horse or he did the same. It is unfortunate, because I feel responsible for the misunderstanding that has occurred and hoped to be of service in alleviating his distress. Miss Bingley, it seems, made a grave error in interpreting the affection she observed between me and Mrs Darcy." He paused to compose himself, noticing the colour that flooded her cheeks as she stared down at her hands. Although she had clung to her belief that Miss Bingley had misrepresented the truth, she admitted to herself that unanswered questions concerning Mr Handley's own trustworthiness still clouded her thoughts.

He began by explaining in detail the events of the past two days, and finished with the disclosure that had ruined Miss Bingley's hopes. By this time, having practised this speech first with Mrs Darcy and then with Miss Bingley, he found it brought him but little discomfort to reveal the secret he had held for so many years. Georgiana's hands flew to her face and her eyes grew wide in disbelief and then quickly relaxed into a smile.

"Please do not think me unkind, Mr Handley," she said with compassion. "I am sure it has not been a pleasant day for you. You must have been reluctant to open your private affairs to so public a scrutiny. I was only feeling the relief of so many hours of tension. You can appreciate, I am sure, that Fitzwilliam and I were at a loss as to how to interpret Miss Bingley's letter, but I confess I did not expect our fears to be relieved in this manner."

Trevor nodded, touched by her openness. "Do you mind if I ask you what Fitzwilliam's reaction was to Miss Bingley's letter, Miss Darcy?" Georgiana was slightly unnerved by the question, for she understood only too well her brother's ambivalent feelings. She hesitated for a moment and then decided that Mr Handley's generous gesture merited complete candour on her part. She did not answer his question directly, but instead told him of their meeting with his mother and sister that morning, ending with the question concerning the portrait.

"Miss Bingley's letter arrived at the moment when we were discussing the implications of that information, and you can well imagine, I am sure, that taken together, the evidence was unsettling. I believe that my brother left Matlock with an open mind, but I cannot truthfully say that he had no doubts concerning your character."

Trevor shook his head in consternation, rising to walk about the room. "I blame myself, Miss Darcy, for not being completely honest with Fitzwilliam before now," he said. He turned to face her and spoke with new resolve. "The portrait was done by a man whose affection for me I could not bring myself to explain to your brother. I thought it harmless to say it was done by my sister, never imagining that it would be of any importance. I sincerely regret that my pride has caused discomfort to you and to Fitzwilliam."

Georgiana sighed, moved by his sorrow.

"Mr Handley, I have come to think of you as a brother, as I know Fitzwilliam does. I hope you will believe me when I say that, if any apology is necessary, it should come from us for mistrusting your intentions at every turn. My mother and father bear the responsibility for planting the seeds of this confusion, but Fitzwilliam and I have allowed it to grow. I confess I do not understand my mother's motivation, or the part she played in your life, but I believe my father was as much a victim as you of her intrigues. I pray that once everything is understood, we shall all finally find release from the turmoil that began so many years ago."

With an affectionate, if melancholy, smile, Trevor took Georgiana's hand.

"May I say, Miss Darcy, that you are wise beyond your years. With your kind and reasonable nature and Mrs Darcy's sensible good humour, I begin to hope that your brother and I might yet form a permanent basis for a friendship unencumbered by the shadows of the past." He rose again, and with a bow, declared his intention to return without delay to Pemberley. Over her protests that he must rest first, he insisted that he could not sleep until he was assured that no further injury should result from any omission on his part. "I will take a fresh horse and provisions for the road. Please do not concern yourself, Miss Darcy."

As she was bidding him a reluctant farewell, assuring him that she would follow at first light in Mr Bingley's company, a loud knock startled them. Georgiana went to open the door and found Charles Bingley standing there. He had just returned from a day with friends and had been informed at the desk that Miss Darcy urgently required his presence and that a visitor had been shown to her room earlier.

His surprise at finding that the visitor was Mr Handley was evident, and when that gentleman departed after a hasty greeting, he looked even more perplexed. Georgiana welcomed the opportunity to unburden herself to Charles Bingley, for she was growing very tired.

"It has been a day of long stories, Mr Bingley. I do not wish to alarm you, but I believe you must hear everything that has happened so you may form your own opinion." Georgiana walked to the desk, picked up Miss Bingley's letter, and handed it to Charles, standing quietly by his side. When he had finished, he groaned, letting his head fall into his hands. Georgiana touched his shoulder lightly, saying softly, "I am sorry to upset you."

Charles looked up sadly, shaking his head.

"I cannot believe that even Caroline would have the audacity to

400

write such a letter. It is unthinkable that she should fabricate such a serious charge, and yet I cannot see how there could be any truth to it. But Mr Handley... how does he come to be here, and where has he gone? And where is Darcy?"

Georgiana explained everything that had been said and done by the two men since Miss Bingley's letter had arrived. It was a very long time before Charles could assimilate all of the day's events, and he finally threw up his hands in consternation.

"Good Lord, I wish I had not gone out today! What a dreadful confusion!" As he sat lost in woeful contemplation, Georgiana was forming a plan.

"Mr Bingley, I begin to think that we must leave for Pemberley at once," she finally said. "Lizzie and Jane must be distraught by the day's events, and I cannot bear to sit here and worry about them. I am sure I would not sleep at all tonight in any case."

Charles frowned. "Of course, Miss Darcy. But are you sure that such a journey would not be too difficult for you?"

She answered firmly, "I will rest better in the carriage, knowing that we are on our way to Pemberley."

He nodded. "I shall go and order the carriage at once and prepare my bag. Someone will be up directly to help you with your things."

Georgiana thanked him and hurried to pack. Charles Bingley, for all his easy-going affability, showed a remarkable intensity in making the necessary arrangements for their departure. In spite of the lateness of the hour, he soon had the staff of the inn and the coachmen bustling about under his direction, and in less than an hour all preparations had been completed, and the two travellers and their luggage were packed into their carriage and wheeling through the deserted streets of Matlock. Far from the rest she had envisioned, Georgiana found herself fretfully alert and throughout the long hours of the night and early morning she and Charles talked on, by turns hopeful and despairing of finding their families at peace upon their arrival.

Miss Bingley's second letter passed them on the road, arriving at the inn when its intended recipients were well on their way to Pemberley. It was forwarded to Mr Long's office by the harried innkeeper, who could in no way understand the rapid comings and goings of his guests since the previous afternoon. Mr Long found the letter on his desk when he stopped in on Saturday morning, and owing to its urgent address, took it upon himself to read it. It said:

My Dear Miss Darcy and Mr Darcy,

The urgent purpose of this letter prevents me from making the explanations and apologies that are due to you following my letter of Thursday morning. I trust that upon your return to Pemberley there will be sufficient opportunity to pursue that subject. I must say quickly that I hope Mr Handley has reached you in Matlock by this time and apprised you of the true facts of the matter, and that you will accept my most sincere apology for any unhappiness I have caused.

I write, however, of another matter of which Mrs Bingley and I agree you would wish to be immediately informed. Mrs Darcy has, this evening, lost the child she carried. She is being attended by a Doctor Andrews, with whom I believe you to be acquainted and in whom I trust you have every confidence. He has assured us that there is no reason to fear any permanent harm will come to Mrs Darcy, but, as you can well imagine, the situation has deeply affected her happiness, and indeed that of all of us.

Although I do not wish you to be unduly alarmed, I believe your speedy return to Pemberley is very much desired by both Mrs Darcy and Mrs Bingley.

Please accept my sincere wish for a safe journey,

Yours, CB

Its contents were baffling, and not knowing what else to do, he enclosed it in a new envelope and posted it back to Pemberley.

402

Chapter Fifty Five

Trevor Handley's return journey was accompanied by a greater sense of urgency than the first. In spite of his optimistic assurance in front of Miss Darcy, he was filled with a sense of foreboding. Although he did not doubt that order would be restored finally at Pemberley, he knew Fitzwilliam Darcy too well to imagine that the resolution would come without pain. When he had exhausted all of the possibilities that might await him, he turned his thoughts back to the year of his arrival at Pemberley. For the rest of the night he struggled with the shadowy possibilities of the path his life might have taken had he remained at home. Although he was not a man given to remorse or despondency, he understood how his own weakness and confusion had contributed to the entangled relationships at the Darcy home.

His dark thoughts lifted with the rising of the sun and a growing resolve took their place: whatever the outcome of his meeting with Fitzwilliam he would live the rest of his life honestly. As the hills of Pemberley came into view, Trevor rehearsed again his explanation to Fitzwilliam. The exhaustion of the hours on the road was relieved by the prospect of an end, at last, to this chapter of his life.

Trevor approached Pemberley Lodge with the thought that he would pay a visit later in the day to old Thomas, for throughout the complicated threads of his life, that man stood alone as someone in whom he had been able confide his innermost hopes and fears. As he glanced fondly at the ancient circle of chestnuts, he noticed a horse standing in the tiny paddock behind the house, his saddle hung on the fence rail. He pulled up his horse and frowned in concentration, then rode back for a closer look. There could be no doubt that it was Fitzwilliam's grey stallion. He dismounted and tied his horse to the post in front of the house, and striding to the door, knocked loudly. Through the casement he saw Thomas Hill struggle to his feet from his chair near the fire, and the door soon opened.

Hailing his old friend with a warm greeting, Trevor peered over his shoulder into the dimly lit room, asking, "I saw Darcy's grey in the paddock, Thomas. Have you seen him?" The old eyes wrinkled with pleasure, although his face bore the mark of fatigue and sorrow.

"Come in, come in, Master Trevor. Ye have come at a good time, I warrant. Master Fitzwilliam lies sleeping inside, but when he wakes, he shall be in need of stronger shoulders than these old ones for the burden he looks to bear." He stepped aside to allow him to pass. Trevor sat down, suddenly weary beyond words, for Fitzwilliam's presence here could not be taken as a good sign in any light, and the thought of the struggle ahead seemed overwhelming. He ran his hands through his hair distractedly, and then with a sigh, turned his full attention to Thomas.

"You had better tell me all your news, my friend. Then we shall see what we can make of it."

Thomas explained how he had been awakened just after dawn by the Master, whose state of anguish exceeded anything he had seen before. He had wrapped him in a blanket and set him down by the fire, trying to make sense out of his incoherent rambling. What he came to understand at last was that Mrs Darcy had lost the child she carried, and that Master Fitzwilliam had destroyed his only hope for happiness. He seemed convinced, in spite of Thomas' protestations, that she would never be able to forgive the injury he had caused her. Finally, unable to persuade him to calm or rational thought, he had prevailed upon him to sleep.

Trevor shook his head sadly. "I have been such a fool, Thomas. I let my pride prevent me from being honest. If Willie had known the truth about me, all of this misery might have been prevented."

The kind old gentleman put his gnarled hand on Trevor's shoulder. "Ye must not take on so, Master Trevor. The devil himself has been at work at Pemberley these many years, and ye have suffered from his tricks as much as any. There is no such easy thing as hindsight to drive a man to sorrow. There is nary a one of us who has not kept his counsel when the telling looked to cause more trouble than the silence. If it comes to that, I am as much at fault as ye are." He pushed himself slowly from his chair and started for the kitchen. "We shall have a cup of tea, for ye look to need one, and then ye may tell me what devilment brings the two of ye to this state."

The smell of the hearth fire and the rich milky tea evoked in Trevor the feeling of coming home. He spoke softly, unburdening himself to Thomas as if he were a lad of seventeen pouring out his heart to a kindly father. Thomas listened as he always had, without interrupting and without judging, merely nodding as the chaotic pieces came together. At the end of Trevor's tale, he smiled and leaned back in his chair, apparently satisfied with what he had heard. Trevor looked at him questioningly.

"Why do you smile, old friend?"

"There is trouble and then there is trouble. Now, what the old Master had with his wife was real trouble, like to kill him, it was. There was no reasoning with the woman. Her crazy doings hurt people more than she ever knew, hurt you and hurt young master something terrible, and still to this day, she haunts these hills. But Master Fitzwilliam's young missus, she has the heart of a thoroughbred. Nothing broken here that cannot be repaired. As for ye and the master, ye be brothers more than some born of the same mother. What brought ye back together after these many years will not be so quickly forgotten." He chuckled softly. "No, Master Trevor, ye have only a spot of trouble here blocking the path and then the way will be clear ahead."

Trevor closed his eyes over a deep sigh, smiling to himself at the simplicity of the old man's wisdom. They sat side by side in a mood of confident contentment, watching the fire die to embers before a sound behind them alerted them that Fitzwilliam had arisen. Trevor rose and turned to face him, his features composed and still as he waited to see what mood his friend would be wearing. Thomas Hill kept to his chair, fingertips pressed together in his lap and his rheumy eyes fixed on the fire.

In spite of the fact that Fitzwilliam Darcy had lain down in Mr Hill's bed wishing he could die, his broken heart did not stop beating, and he could not avoid waking, disoriented and stiff, to a bright morning sun and the fragment of a dream where Sweet Felicity was nudging him and urging him to arise. Remembering the beautiful mare and still groggy from sleep, he suddenly thought of the look of delight on Lizzie's face when he told her she was hers. He allowed himself to remember other moments of joy, and the peace he felt as, time after time, her laughter broke through his barriers. He thought back to the moment when her eyes had first met his, and how the unsettling directness and honesty in them had captivated him. Her outspoken anger at his first proposal, her first touch on his skin, the moments of learning and loving together, were integrated into a tapestry of love, and he began to feel again the exquisite longing he felt whenever they were apart.

This effusion of warmth was short-lived as shame and remorse swept over his body, chilling him through. He thought back to the day she had told him she was to have a child, remembering with a blush his selfish reaction to the news. How could he explain last night's suspicions when only a few days ago he had pronounced her love incorruptible? Her words of censure repeated themselves over and over in his head and he could make them no answer. With the clarity of the morning, he understood that if he had not met her armoured with his own misgivings, his heart would have been open to seeing her suffering. The thought of how utterly he had failed her brought a low groan from his throat, and unable to support his loneliness, he rose wearily and walked to the parlour.

Finding Trevor Handley in front of him gave the room a surreal quality and he stopped to orient himself. So preoccupied had he been with the horrible scene with Lizzie, he had not thought of Trevor for many hours, and at first he could not make out what he should feel toward him. With a great sigh, he finally stepped into the room, saying only, "Trevor... " He walked past him to stand in front of the fire, and as he stared into its glowing embers, he felt nothing but a deadening weariness. At last he broke the pregnant silence with a voice scarcely more than a whisper. "Am I correct in assuming that you are Georgiana's father, Trevor?"

Trevor thought he had prepared himself for every possible direction that his interview with Fitzwilliam might take, but he was taken utterly by surprise by this question. After a long silence, broken only by the sound of the faint hissing of the dying fire, Trevor answered, "If your mother had had her way, I might have been, Willie."

Turning slowly to face him, Fitzwilliam stared into his unblinking eyes. There was no anger left in him. "Please explain yourself, man. I have no energy for riddles."

Trevor nodded calmly. "Your mother had a most desperate need to elicit attention from every man she met. She was not content with your father's adoration; from almost my first month at Pemberley she teased and tormented me. As I came to realise much later, she must have sensed more clearly than I did my ambivalent feelings and amused herself with planning my seduction. I cannot claim any high moral victory; I was fascinated by her and even wished to be able to love her, if for no other reason than to prove to myself that I could." He paused uncomfortably, but the painful confusion in Fitzwilliam's eyes spurred him to finish saying what had to be said. "In spite of the high regard in which I held your father and my fondness for you, I believe if I had been capable of loving any woman, I would have responded to her approaches."

"For the love of God, Trevor, what are you saying?" Darcy cried.

Trevor took a deep breath to steady his nerves. He had not

worried about the reaction of Mrs Darcy or Miss Georgiana to his confession, and he cared nothing for Miss Bingley's censure, but broaching the subject to Darcy was an entirely different matter.

"The only person I ever loved was a man." As his words hung in the charged air, Trevor hung his head and Thomas Hill closed his eyes in silent benediction. At last, the end was in sight.

Fitzwilliam sat down with his mouth agape, struggling to comprehend what he had heard. After a long silence, Trevor continued. "I might as well tell you about the portrait, so we can make an end to this subject. Georgiana told me about your visit to my mother."

Fitzwilliam was baffled. "How can it be that you have spoken to Georgiana?"

Trevor explained briefly about his ride to Matlock, and then, taking a chair, he continued in a quiet, reflective tone. "As a young man, I led a solitary life, for I found as I grew to manhood that I did not share the interests of most of my childhood friends. There was one man, my tutor, in whom I found I could confide the confusion of my feelings, my sense of being different. He shared many of my interests, and between the time spent on my studies and our long rides into the countryside, I formed an attachment to him and a reluctance for the society of others that troubled my mother. It was for this reason that she wrote to your father, hoping that a change of atmosphere would be beneficial.

"I must admit that I agreed to her plan with some eagerness, for I myself found my feelings toward my tutor disturbing. Although he did not attempt to interfere in my decision to leave, I understood that he was deeply affected by it. On our last ride together, he produced two sketches that he had done of me, and asked that I carry one on my journey to remind me of our friendship. The other he kept. It was from that day that I understood clearly his feelings. I was not then ready to acknowledge or accept my own, but I was moved by his pain, and I took the drawing with me to Pemberley. During my months here, I struggled continually with the question of my feelings, and your mother's advances only served to heighten my confusion and pain.

"One day I finally found the courage to unequivocally reject her flirtation, and I believe that in her fury she took her revenge by telling your father that I had attempted to seduce her, for it was the next day that he dismissed me from Pemberley. So great was his rage and so deep my own shame that I made no attempt to answer his charges. I suppose I knew, in any case, that I could not stay. I did not want to risk your finding out the truth, and it was for that reason that I dared not say goodbye to you."

The atmosphere in the room was oppressive with the sorrow and remorse of both men. After several long moments of reflection, Trevor continued quietly.

"It was true when I told you that I left the portrait behind. I left Pemberley with the conviction that I must begin my life anew, and I wanted no remnants from the past to interfere with my resolve. I forced both my tutor and your mother from my mind, and when my mother insisted that I must marry to secure my fortune, I seized upon the hope that I could make myself into the man that she wanted me to be. I made a valiant attempt, but I could not change what I am."

Fitzwilliam clutched his head in his hands. He had neither Lizzie's nor Georgiana's ability to rearrange his thoughts quickly and so several minutes passed before he experienced the release of compassion. To his credit, he did not speak until he had carefully weighed Trevor's words, and then his answer was tentative and cautious.

"Why did you never tell me this before, Trevor?" he asked, raising his head to meet Trevor's eyes.

"I regret that I did not," he said evenly, "for it seems that it would have saved all of us a good deal of anguish. I suppose I did not trust you to believe or understand me, and I had no wish to defame your mother's memory. I felt you had suffered too much already for things that were not your fault."

Steadying himself with a long, slow breath, Fitzwilliam stood up and walked to where Trevor sat. He laid a hand on his shoulder. "You have been kind and patient, and for your trouble I have answered you with abuse. You have done nothing to merit the injuries you have sustained at the hands of the Darcy family. I apologise, for all of us."

Trevor smiled through tear-rimmed eyes. "You bear no responsibility for the actions of your parents, Willie. I told you when first we spoke at Lambton Inn that I have made my peace with them. As for mistrusting me, I am as much at fault as you for my failure to be candid. I pray that at last we may both take solace from one another without further reference to the past."

Fitzwilliam turned away in painful silence, and stood lost in thought. The habit of unspoken thoughts and hidden emotions that had darkened his childhood had prevented him from reaching out to Lizzie when he first became sensible of his love for her, and when he had finally overcome that obstacle he found that he still remained fettered to his past. Throughout his struggle to free himself, with each faltering step he felt that he had learned something of love and trust, had understood more deeply the need for forthrightness and honesty, and yet here he found himself again, separated from his heart's desire by a gulf that seemed impassable. He spoke, at last, more to himself than to anyone in the room.

"There is one part of the story which I am powerless to rewrite. I have, through my foolish pride, destroyed the happiness of the woman I thought to be my salvation."

Thomas Hill, whose presence the two men had forgotten entirely, now stirred in his chair and, as if he had just awakened from a dream, spoke to the heavy silence.

"It comes to my mind how I quarrelled with Mrs Hill one day,

410

just after I brought her here to the lodge as my wife. I took out of the house and was gone all day, but then I got to feeling pretty low, and I came back with my tail between my legs, ready to say I was a fool. Well, she was not sitting and weeping over me like I had expected. She was gone, and not a sign to tell me where and how. Wild with my grieving, I went to the old Master, your grandfather, Master Fitzwilliam, and I begged use of a horse to find her. I rode about all that night, first to her parents' cottage, then to her sister's over Klympton way, and then I sought out her friends, but no one had seen her. I came home, tired out and sick at heart, only to find Mrs Hill at the parlour window, waiting and watching for me. She spoke no word of reproach, only welcomed me with open arms. A man cannot easily understand the ways of a good woman."

At last, and, as usual, very late, Darcy realised that he had again left Lizzie alone while he indulged his own misery. He had quitted her side believing that she would never want to see him again, knowing that he had so far overstepped the bounds of decency that he could not face her. Repeating the mistake that had prevented him from intimacy with his father, with his sister, with his friends, he continued to erect barricades of distance between himself and his problems. The futility of this lonely path suddenly loomed before him. He turned to look at Thomas with grateful tears in his eyes.

"Do you think Lizzie is waiting for me, Thomas?"

"That I do, young master," he cackled, "that I do."

Answering the look of flickering hope in his friend's eyes, Trevor Handley smiled and said, "Take my horse, Willie boy, and I will saddle the grey and follow."

411

Chapter Fifty Six

Charles and Georgiana were so preoccupied with reaching the manor that they passed the lodge without noticing either Trevor's horse tied out front or the stallion in the paddock. They arrived to find the house shrouded in silence. Seeing no one in any of the downstairs rooms, they hurried up the stairs, Charles calling Jane's name. Caroline Bingley, ensconced in her room, heard his voice first, but could not force herself to venture out to greet him. As the misery had mounted during that horrible night, she was left beyond tears in a deep lethargy, passing the hours in watchful contemplation of the wreckage of her life and the sorrow of her companions.

Jane emerged from Lizzie's room almost instantly, her nerves tense from the long hours of waiting and watching, and in relief, she fell into Charles' embrace and gave in to the tears she had been holding back for so many hours. Georgiana and Charles were frightened by her misery, and as he held her close, murmuring words of comfort, they waited anxiously for her to find her voice. At last she stepped back a bit to look into his sweet, steady eyes, saying, "Oh, Charles, I am so glad you've come. I am so afraid for Lizzie."

Georgiana gripped Jane's arm. "What is it, Jane? What has happened?"

Turning tearfully to Georgiana, Jane asked, "Did you not receive the message Caroline sent? Lizzie has lost her baby." The impact of her words left Georgiana breathless and tightened Charles' embrace, but Jane struggled to compose herself. "That is not the worst of it. She was weak and unhappy, but the doctor assured us that she would recover. When Fitzwilliam arrived last night I hoped his presence would bring her solace and strength. But Charles, the most dreadful scene occurred between them, I know not what... " and her voice broke as tears overwhelmed her again. Charles could not concentrate on anything but Jane's distress, for she seemed in danger of collapse.

413

Holding her tightly against him, he led her to a chair and then pulled another up close beside her so she could lean against him. Her eyes darted wildly to the door of her sister's room.

Charles asked quietly, "Jane, please tell me if you can, where is Darcy now? What happened between them?"

She breathed slowly and deeply to calm herself, and then turned her frightened eyes to Charles and eventually managed to relate what had taken place, ending with Lizzie's hysteria and the fact that she had not spoken a word since Fitzwilliam's departure.

"The doctor has given her a strong draught to help her sleep, but it seems to give her no peace. She tosses and moans, awakening at times to look around the room like a frightened fawn, and she only grows weaker." The tears began again, but anger gave her the strength to continue. "I cannot think what he could have said to her. Why, in God's name has he run away when she needs him so? There is no excuse, and yet, there must be an explanation!" she added, with a plaintive look at Georgiana.

Charles looked thoughtfully across the room, creases of concentration deep on his forehead. Georgiana stifled the sob that welled up in her throat but could not speak.

"I do not see how this riddle can be solved until we have spoken to Darcy or until Lizzie is able to explain. Has anyone been sent to look for him?" he asked. Jane answered that she had not left Lizzie's side. Standing up, he said firmly, "I will see what can be done." He leaned over and kissed her cheek, patted Georgiana's arm and then hurried down the stairway.

Georgiana's was nearly undone by grief for the two people she loved so dearly, but the past few months had given her a strength and confidence that now came to her aid. "Jane," she said, holding her voice steady, "we must trust Mr Bingley to find my brother, and hope that in time everything will be clear, but in the meantime there must be something we can do for Lizzie."

Jane rallied her flagging strength and wiped away her tears. She looked at Georgiana gratefully, managing a weak smile. "Come in with me. Perhaps your presence will calm her." They entered the bedchamber and Jane sat down in the chair near Lizzie's head, gently caressing her hair. Lizzie's eyes opened but she appeared not to focus. Jane bent close to her face, and spoke softly. "Darling, Georgiana is here and Charles has gone to find Fitzwilliam."

She reached for the water glass beside her and offered Lizzie a drink, but she turned her head aside wearily without a word. With a plaintive look at Jane, Georgiana took Lizzie's hand and said soothingly, "I am so sorry about the baby, Lizzie. You will grieve that loss for a long time, but I think you are suffering from an even greater sorrow. Jane tells me that Fitzwilliam was here and something happened between you. Please try to tell us what troubles you so."

For a moment, Lizzie's eyes met Georgiana's and then she turned away. Her voice when she finally spoke was as small and miserable as an injured child. "I hurt him so very badly... " she whispered, and silent tears spilled onto the pillow.

Georgiana and Jane exchanged worried looks, and then Jane had an idea. "Lizzie, you must try to find strength to help me understand your grief, for I am so worried I can neither eat nor sleep."

Lizzie turned quickly to look at her sister. "Oh, dearest Jane..." She reached for her hand and Jane moved to sit on the bed beside her. "I am so ashamed of what I said... and what I felt. I have driven him away from me forever." She choked on her tears, but Jane was determined that she should not sink back into silence, and she continued to press the opening.

Gently but insistently, Jane said, "Please, Lizzie, for my sake, tell us what happened." With a deep sigh, she began haltingly to describe, in a voice they could barely hear, his words and actions and her own, colouring them with the belated understanding of hindsight.

Agitation brought a flush to Georgiana's face as she struggled to work through the layers of confusion of the past few hours. She brushed the curls from Lizzie's forehead.

"Lizzie, my dearest Lizzie, I can scarcely believe that all of us have been locked into such a drama over mistaken meanings. Such agony, and such pain, and each of us angry or hurt for nothing!" Lizzie closed her eyes wearily, exhausted by the thought of how many times she and Darcy had lost precious moments in the pursuit of such folly.

Jane carefully considered what she should say, and with a look at Georgiana to ask for her indulgence, she leaned anxiously toward Lizzie. "But my dearest, why do you insist on blaming yourself? It was not unreasonable for you to feel hurt and betrayed by his lack of trust. I begin to think very badly of him myself."

This was the trick that won the hand. Lizzie was aroused by this criticism of Darcy to raise herself up on one elbow. "Jane, you must not speak ill of him! Just when he had begun to learn to trust, I allowed my own pride to step between us. It was the same fault of pride that led me to believe Wickham's scandalous lies. He was right when he said I am as apt as he to find offence." Her agitated speech brought colour to her cheeks and her voice strengthened as the passionate words gave her new energy. Jane smiled, and with a sigh of relief, leaned back.

Disconcerted by this response, Lizzie snapped, "How can you smile?"

Jane answered gently, "I am pleased to see you have recovered your anger, Lizzie. It suits you much better than despondency." Lizzie's mouth gaped open at the realisation that Jane had tricked her and in a moment she began to laugh. Weak as she was, the tiny sound was scarcely audible at first, but as the answering laughter of Jane and Georgiana swelled around it, the curtain of gloom that had darkened the room was rent as if struck by a bolt of lightening.

Chapter Fifty Seven

Edward Alexander was eager to return to Pemberley at the earliest possible moment, for as the days of Christmas festivities passed, he became increasingly aware that a novel sensation of incompleteness had overtaken him. His sleep was disturbed by a restlessness he had never known and his appetite suffered from a lack of interest in food. His attendance at St. James Court, where he had been invited to entertain, had been exhilarating, but even in the midst of the excitement of the moment, he found his mind wandering back to Pemberley, and whenever he had a free moment, he allowed himself the pleasant diversion of thinking about Georgiana.

He knew exactly the moment when he had first realised that she was as much a part of his destiny as was his music. It was the day of their outing to the circle of rocks on Lambton Bluff. As they stopped to rest by a stream, he had noticed she sat a little apart from the group, enjoying their conversation but not eager to enter it. In spite of her youthfulness, she had a dignity of carriage and a reserve that bespoke a serious nature, and her thoughts seemed to be planted more firmly in the clouds than on the grassy bank. So unaware of herself was she that she took no notice of Edward's gaze, though it rested on her for a long while as he tried to guess her thoughts. Suddenly he noticed that she was moving her fingers where they lay on her skirt and when her eyes drifted closed in concentration, he realised with delight that she was practising a piece of music in her mind.

He jumped up and walked over to where she sat, startling her from her reverie, and asked her if she would ride on ahead of the group with him. As they set off across the meadow, he asked what song she had been playing, and she laughed, surprised to have been found out. She replied, teasing, that with his astonishing musical talent he should have been able to guess. With this merriment, his heart began to open to her as it had only done before to an exquisite melody. He saw nothing of the painful shyness that worried her brother, for in his presence she was warm and natural, joyously at ease.

In his weeks at Pemberley, an easy rhythm arose between them, a kinship of the soul, more perfect than earthbound love. They engaged in none of the ordinary motions of courtship, no blushing or sighing, no sleepless nights or longing looks across the room, for they were so united in spirit that they needed no intrigue to capture each other's attention. He was quite certain that she would be surprised to hear him speak of marriage, for no hints of it had ever been exchanged between them. But the weeks of his absence from her felt an eternity, and he had come to the conclusion that he had desires for her that dwelt on the earthly plane. He fervently hoped he might in time inspire a similar feeling in her.

Amid the rush of Christmas festivities at Great Oaks, Edward had managed to hide his growing impatience to rush back to Pemberley, but at last he could bear it no longer. He asked to speak to his father privately, and they retired to the old gentleman's study. At the first mention of Miss Darcy, Mr Alexander understood what was on his son's mind, but he allowed him to reach the point in his own way, circling about it with a studied air of nonchalance. Edward expected some resistance from his father to his profession of regard for Georgiana Darcy, for she was undoubtedly young for marriage, and his own position as the youngest son did not allow him the means to offer her the style of living to which she was accustomed.

His father surprised him by pouring each of them a glass of sherry. Handing one to his son, he raised his glass in the air, a twinkle in his eye, and said, "Let us toast your uncommon good sense, my son. May you be as fortunate in love as your father has been!"

Edward laughed and drank, relieved and touched by his father's words, but then he waxed serious. "Thank you, Father. It gives me great pleasure to have your approval. I must confess, however, that I expected some reservation on your part, and as for Mr Darcy, I feel quite overwhelmed by the prospect of asking him for his sister's hand."

His father smiled benevolently. "Perhaps your first concern should be for winning the heart of the lady in question, for I take it from your declaration today that I am privileged to hear of your intentions before you have made them known to her. From my observations, I would venture to guess that she will not be averse to receiving your attentions, but I would advise you to seek her opinion on the subject before approaching her brother."

Edward laughed. "It is certainly presumptuous of me to be planning our future without reference to her wishes. The strength of my feelings for her leaves me no recourse but to assume that she will return my affection, for I cannot imagine what I would do if she did not. In any case, I must speak to her as soon as possible, for I can think of little else."

"What do you think, Son, if I were to accompany you to Pemberley? We could leave as early as we like on Saturday morning. Your mother means to spend a few days at Catherine's house, and I would not be adverse to another conversation with Fitzwilliam and Georgiana myself. I have something from their father that I have been waiting to show them."

Edward was delighted with this suggestion. They finished their sherry and went off to speak to Mrs Alexander, who received her son's information with as much enthusiasm as her husband had. Her sweet optimism further buoyed Edward's hopes, and he passed the next few days in a state of blissful anticipation.

The elder and younger Mr Alexanders set out on the road to Derbyshire in high spirits, little guessing what chaos reigned at Pemberley House as their carriage bounced along the wintry roads.

Chapter Fifty Eight

Charles found in activity a temporary relief from the distress around him. Hurrying off to the stable in search of information, he quickly found the man who had saddled Darcy's horse. The groom answered Charles' questions concerning his master's words and actions warily, torn between loyalty for Mr Darcy and concern for the mistress. In any case, there was little to tell that shed any light on Mr Darcy's whereabouts, except for the direction in which he had ridden and the speed with which he had departed.

Charles frowned in concentration, finally asking, "How many men have you that can ride? I want everyone available sent out to locate Mr Darcy. It is important that he return as soon as possible." The man scratched his head at so unusual a request, but there was not a man on the staff of Pemberley who would have hesitated to ride through a hurricane if it would help either the master or Mrs Darcy. The groom assured Mr Bingley that every able rider would saddle up immediately, and after working out a search plan together, Charles headed back to the house, satisfied that there was nothing more to be done there.

Once inside, he cast about for a sense of direction, content that there was nothing for him to do in the sick room. His thoughts turned reluctantly to Caroline, and drawing her letter out of his pocket, he read it through again, shaking his head in disbelief. With regret, he understood that the difference in their temperaments had always kept them from enjoying a true affection for one another, and at this moment he felt more distant from her than he had ever done. He felt a pang of remorse that he had so long ignored her inappropriate behaviour towards Jane and Lizzie. His easy nature and her strong opinions had combined forces to encourage him to pretend ignorance of her anger and disappointment over his marriage and that of his friend. It crossed his mind that if he had interceded with her earlier, he might have prevented this tragic day, but it was not his way to regret the past. Bracing himself for the unpleasantness of his duty, he mounted the stairs slowly and went to his sister's door, sighing with resignation as he admitted there was little hope that the interview would bring any real understanding to either of them.

Caroline opened the door and stepped aside to allow him to enter her room, her eyes cast down and her countenance grim. Taken aback by her uncharacteristic posture of humility, he opened and closed his mouth several times before he decided how to begin.

"I have here the letter that you sent yesterday to Mr Darcy, Caroline, and I would like you to explain to me your intention in writing it. Could it be possible that you intended to precipitate the tragedy that has ensued?" he asked at last. For a few moments, Caroline fought for composure, stunned by the novelty of his anger, but when she attempted to form an answer, she suddenly burst into tears and collapsed into a chair, burying her face in her hands. Charles stood forlornly scratching his head. He had rarely been in either the mood or the position to censure his sister, but if he had ever entertained such a thought, he could scarcely have imagined that his words would create such an effect.

It was not long before Charles desired fervently to be elsewhere, for his anger had wilted in the face of her tears, and he was left with no clear idea of what more should be said. He cleared his throat as sternly as he was able and said, "We will speak of this later, Caroline." Thus resolved, he quickly turned and left the room, shaking his head.

Outside of her door, he stood frowning. He still felt it incumbent upon him to take some action to ameliorate the suffering that reigned at Pemberley, but he was quite at a loss as to how that might be accomplished. His musing was interrupted by noises coming from Lizzie's room, and as he walked nearer, he began to think it sounded for all the world like laughter. Before he reached the door, it suddenly opened and a very astonished Dr Andrews came into the hallway.

"Are you Mr Bingley, sir?" he asked. At Charles' nodded response, he indicated Lizzie's chambers and said, "I believe that the crisis has passed. You may go in if you like." The tired old gentleman moved down the hallway towards his room, shaking his head, while a very confused Charles Bingley ventured into the sitting room and peeked in through the open doorway.

In place of the miserable visages he had left not half an hour before, he found a weakly smiling Lizzie flanked by two very giddy ladies, holding hands and catching their breath. Lizzie saw him first, and with the warmest of smiles, urged him nearer. She struggled to sit up but Jane firmly pushed her back onto the pillow.

"Do come in Charles. My wounded pride and near-fatal remorse have taken me nearly to the gates of Hades, and I am a bit tired, so I hope you will not mind if I do not rise to greet you. Jane is apparently determined that I shall not."

Charles smiled broadly. "I will overlook your informality if you do not take offence at my visiting your bedchamber uninvited. I am so pleased to see you are feeling better," he declared earnestly, turning to Jane for an explanation.

Lizzie answered his quizzical look before Jane could speak. "I must tell you, Charles, about a serious defect in your wife's character. I myself was unaware of it until now."

Charles' look of bewilderment increased with Jane's vehement interruption. "Good Lord, Lizzie. Have we not had enough of accusations and deceptions to last a lifetime? Let us talk of the weather if we need further stimulation!" Although he could make no sense of their conversation, he was more than happy to join in their renewed laughter as Jane moved to embrace him.

In the midst of this merriment, Caroline Bingley suddenly appeared in the doorway, drawn in disbelief to the sounds of laughter that echoed down the hall. Seeing her, Jane quickly stepped away from Charles, and reached for her trembling hand, her gentle heart moved by the lines of misery etched on that handsome face. With an encouraging smile, she said kindly, "Do come and see Lizzie, Caroline. She is so much improved that I am sure we no longer need fear for her."

The room was hushed as Caroline Bingley was led like a penitent child to Lizzie's side. Lizzie sobered and reached out to take her free hand, and looking from one to the other, said, "I am very sorry to have given you all such a fright. Miss Bingley, we have just agreed that the topics of deceptions and accusations have been quite overworked of late, and we were about to have a pleasant conversation about the weather. Won't you join us?"

Before Caroline Bingley could begin to comprehend what was happening, a maid appeared to announce the arrival of gentlemen, and Charles left the room to investigate. He returned presently, followed by the solicitous figures of the elder and younger Alexanders, their faces drawn into confused concern at the hasty explanation Charles had made.

Greetings were in progress and a pleasant hubbub filled the room when the very dishevelled and totally mystified form of Fitzwilliam Darcy appeared in the doorway. All conversation ceased abruptly as Lizzie paled and sucked in her breath at the sight of his forlorn countenance. That he could not easily take in the general merriment was evident from the furrowed lines of his brow, and no one ventured a word for several long seconds. Lizzie broke the silence at last. Smiling through a mist of tears, she said with quiet tenderness, "I am so glad you are here, Will. We were just about to discuss the weather. Don't you agree that the most precious moments in life come in the calm that follows a great storm?"

Darcy was transported by her words out of the clouded abyss of remorse and sorrow he had been occupying to a lofty peak, where the light of hope and love shone full on him. As if there was no one in the room but Lizzie, he walked to her side, eyes locked on hers in a silent embrace. The rest of the party dispersed quietly, leaving the couple alone together, their eyes communicating all that was needed to ease the anguish of the recent past. Without a sound between them, Darcy sat down on the bed next to her, enfolding her gently in his arms. As her head found its familiar resting place on his shoulder, she allowed the healing tears to come. He held her close, softly kissing her tousled curls, his tears falling in unison with her own. Neither could have said how long they rested together in this exquisite homecoming before Darcy realised she had fallen asleep in his arms. With the tenderness of a father with a sleeping child, he eased her down onto the pillow and soundlessly moved around the bed to slip in beside her. Wrapping himself around her like a cloak, he lay feeling the rise and fall of her chest and revelling in the sweet scent of her body. No thoughts troubled his blissful repose save the assurance that it would require the furies of hell to ever drive him from her again.

Chapter Fifty Nine

The group that filed silently out of Lizzie and Darcy's room reassembled in the hallway and, in hushed but exuberant tones, continued their conversation, their happiness made complete by the knowledge of the tender reconciliation that was taking place within. As they moved toward the stairway, Trevor Handley arrived on the scene, spawning a fresh round of introductions and explanations. Caroline Bingley took advantage of the chaos to quietly move off in the direction of her room. With a solicitous look toward Charles, Jane followed her and took her arm, halting her flight. "Please come downstairs with us, Caroline. You have scarcely left your room these two days."

Caroline shook her head sadly, speaking in a hushed tone. "I do not believe Charles would welcome my company, Jane, nor do I expect as much forbearance from the others as you and Lizzie have shown."

Jane replied kindly, "You know better than I, I feel sure, how unlikely Charles is to harbour ill feelings. He will be pleased to put the entire subject to rest, as I am sure everyone will. I cannot guess Mr Darcy's feelings, but at any rate, he is not likely to come downstairs for some time."

With a deep sigh, Caroline reviewed her options and realised she could not stay forever in hiding. She spoke earnestly to Jane, "From our first meeting, I understood the sweetness of your temperament, but I did not choose to place a high value on it. I have learned that no other quality is more important to my brother's happiness, and I most sincerely beg your forgiveness for behaviour that I now recall with abhorrence. I hope in time that you will be able to look upon me as a sister and believe me capable of wishing you every happiness as I should have done long ago."

Jane answered simply, "I welcome your friendship and will hope to gain your affection in time."

"You have my affection now," Caroline answered, in a voice that bore no trace of her former hauteur. It took no great discernment to see that the new Caroline Bingley was so materially changed from the old as to render her nearly unrecognisable. Her bearing and her voice were softened, and as she entered the drawing room a few moments later, arm in arm with Jane, she seemed to occupy a smaller space than formerly.

The tumultuous conversation ceased as the two women entered the room and all eyes turned inquiringly towards them. Jane quickly dispelled the tension with her warm smile, setting the tone for reconciliation by announcing, "I persuaded Caroline that it is time to leave the past behind us."

Charles readily took her cue and came forward to extend his hand to his sister. She met his eyes reluctantly, but once engaged she found herself drawn to the kindness of their expression as if she had never really seen it before. She said quietly, "I have had many hours to reflect on my behaviour, not only of these few days, but of the past year and a half, and I do not find much that brings me pleasure. I once scorned your gentle forbearance, but I have come to treasure it, Charles. I am sincerely sorry for the grief I have caused." Turning her eyes to face the rest of the group, she added, "My actions were founded on a most malicious intention to do harm to those who deserve rather my love and esteem. I beg your forgiveness," she said, her eyes filling again with tears.

Jane stepped back to admit Georgiana to Caroline's side. "Please be assured, Miss Bingley, that your apology is accepted. No material damage has been done, and I, for one, am eager to close the subject."

Caroline stammered, "But the baby... "

Jane protested vehemently, "Caroline, you certainly must not blame yourself for that! I do not, and I am sure Lizzie agrees with me. It was a most unfortunate coincidence of timing, that is all, and Dr

Andrews assured us that in all likelihood it could not have been prevented. I am sorry if you have been tormenting yourself on that account."

Caroline's eyes moved quickly around the circle to see nods of agreement, and Trevor hastened to add, "If anyone is to blame for that, it is I, although I had no idea of Mrs Darcy's condition when I brought her word of Sweet Felicity's illness."

Miss Bingley was so much relieved that the tears that had threatened were now released unrestrained. Charles put his arms around her and she leaned against him until they subsided. Then, for the first time since her humiliation began in this room, her face broke into a weak smile. She could not be persuaded to sit down with them, however, for the release of her anxiety had rendered her utterly exhausted. Charles took her arm and saw her to her room before returning to the drawing room, where the conversation had returned to the exchange of stories of each person's part in the movements and vigils of the past few days. For the Alexanders, speechless at first in their bewilderment over such a commotion, it required a good deal of interrupting and clarification for the tale to be told in any way that could make clear to them what had passed.

At last, everyone was quite satisfied that they had heard and told their story, and they agreed to resume the normal course of life by dressing for a belated dinner. Mrs Reynolds had distracted herself from the day's anxiety by arranging a bountiful meal. A quiet watchfulness grew as they lingered at the table, for the day's events could not be properly closed until the final player took the stage. Each person in the room had a keen interest in the appearance of Mr Darcy, some to hear his story and others to tell theirs, all of them anxious to know that Lizzie was truly out of danger. Jane scarcely touched her food and finally consented to be led upstairs by Charles, who insisted that she looked exhausted. After assuring her that he would awaken her if Lizzie needed her, he watched her fall quickly to sleep, and then rejoined the party, which had shifted to the drawing room.

Chapter Sixty

Lizzie slept on as the light of afternoon gave out and stars appeared to illuminate Darcy's vigil. When she awoke at last, it was to the sound of the calm beating of his heart where her head rested against his breast. She lay without moving and without thought of past or future, imprinting on her mind the sweetness of this moment. Detecting the slight change in her breathing that wakefulness brought, Darcy tightened his embrace and Lizzie nestled closer to him.

When he broke the silence, his voice was a hoarse whisper, choked with emotion. "I cannot breathe if the air be not sweetened by your scent. I cannot see without the illumination of your smile. I have been so lost, and so alone, my dearest love. You bring me home to myself."

Lizzie turned to face him and raised her hand in the darkness to trace the lines of his face, smoothing the furrowed lines etched by so many hours of grief. "My love," she breathed, "if I give you aught, it is what you have awakened in me." They clung to each other, allowing the eloquence of silence to speak the feelings of their hearts, but it was not long before Lizzie's remorse drove her to speak. "You were right to say what you did about my pride, Will." He began to protest but she stilled him with her fingertips on his lips. "I have criticised your pride without owning my own. You have given me too much credit for bringing happiness to Pemberley. Today I nearly destroyed it."

Darcy replied softly, "Your anger was wholly justified. It was unthinkable that I should doubt, even for a moment, your love for me. I am so sorry about the child, Lizzie. It will forever give me pain that I was not a help to you in this sorrow. You have never backed away from *my* need."

Her eyes filled with tears, but she spoke with composure. "I imagined you holding your son, Will. His first smile would have filled you with peace and drawn your eyes away from the past toward a new beginning for the Darcy family. I wish I could have given you that gift."

"My sweet Lizzie," he breathed, "what have I given you to deserve your love?"

"You are my anchor, Will. Your heart has weathered my indifference and my rebukes. I do not ask for anything more." After a long and poignant silence, she added with an impish smile, stroking his stubbled cheek, "Except that you bathe and shave." As he broke into relieved laughter, he felt a wave of admiration swell within him, for as usual her levity forged the final link in their reconciliation.

Disentangling himself from her, he sat up to stretch. "I was remembering today your preference for Sweet Felicity over me, and I thought it might elevate my standing with you if I returned smelling of horse."

Lizzie erupted into peals of laughter which Darcy soon echoed. Rising to light a lamp, he smiled ruefully at his rumpled clothes. "I will return presently, a better man. Shall I call someone to sit with you, my dear?"

She laughed happily. "If you wish to make me truly happy, you may call for supper. I am ravenous!"

He bowed, "At your service, Madam."

As he turned to leave the room, Lizzie called, "You must find Dr Andrews, Will, and release him from his vigil. I have been a most irksome patient, and I am sure he has had enough of Pemberley to last him a long time."

Darcy rang for Mrs Reynolds and, happily assuring her that Mrs Darcy was much improved, he ordered his bath and Lizzie's supper and asked her to send the doctor in to Lizzie.

As Darcy stepped out of his room bathed and shaved and feeling that the last vestiges of his ordeal had been washed away, he was greeted by a very stern Dr Andrews. He felt himself wilt under the look of disapprobation that the gentleman wore.

"Fitzwilliam, I have attended you from the moment of your birth, and so I believe I may speak frankly." The young man nodded. "Your behaviour today gravely endangered Mrs Darcy's health. For a woman, the loss of a child is a sorrow that is felt more deeply than most men can imagine."

Darcy looked away to hide the tears welling in his eyes. "I cannot justify my behaviour in any way except to say that it is as incomprehensible to me as it is to you. I am afraid I have an unfortunate tendency to run away from difficulties." Darcy frowned in thought and then turned to search the doctor's face. "But perhaps you understand the legacy of this house more than I credit..."

The doctor hesitated for a moment, cleared his throat and finally answered, "You have my congratulations, Fitzwilliam, on a most fortunate marriage. I trust you will not take offence at my saying that Mrs Darcy is an exceptional woman and I sincerely hope that you appreciate what she brings to Pemberley."

Darcy answered slowly, "I believe I do, sir."

Dr Andrews nodded, satisfied, and the two shook hands. As he took his leave, Mrs Reynolds appeared in the doorway carrying Lizzie's supper tray. Darcy smiled his greeting, saying, "Has Mrs Darcy eaten?" He was surprised when she hesitated and cleared her throat nervously, a crimson blush creeping up her neck. "What is it, Mrs Reynolds?" he asked. "Is anything wrong?"

"I know it is not my place to speak, sir, but I feel there is something... that is, I... " she stammered, and the dishes rattled faintly on the tray.

He took the tray from her hands and set it on the table, turning attentively back to face her. "Please sit down, Mrs Reynolds. Are you unwell?"

She wrung her hands uncomfortably. "No, sir, not at all. It is only that since the mistress has come to Pemberley, sir, well, there has been such new life about the house. And," her blush deepened, "I thought a miracle had happened when I heard you sing for the first time since you were a young lad. If anything were to happen to Mrs Darcy, sir... I just could not bear seeing her so sorrowful."

Mr Darcy winced at the poor woman's distress. He cleared his throat. "I have behaved abominably, have I not, Mrs Reynolds?" he asked quietly.

Her eyes grew wide. "No, sir, I did not mean to suggest such a thing!"

He smiled ruefully. "You have known me since I was four and you have always shown me the greatest kindness, Mrs Reynolds. Pemberley is your home, and it is right that you should care about what happens here. If it is my power, Mrs Darcy shall never suffer another moment's distress on my account."

With a quick curtsey, Mrs Reynolds picked up the tray and said, "God bless you, sir."

"He already has, Mrs Reynolds," he said, opening the door for her. He smiled fondly at her receding form and then, shaking his head, went into the bedchamber and sat down next to Lizzie.

As he leaned over to kiss her forehead she inhaled deeply and said, "You certainly do have a more pleasant smell than when last we met."

He responded with a grin, "So you admit, then, that you do prefer me to Sweet Felicity?"

"Hmm, it is so difficult to decide. May I give you my answer in the morning?"

"Take as long as you need, my dear," he answered graciously. His face turned serious. "How are you feeling? Dr Andrews assures me that you will mend, but he was very stern with me about my behaviour. Mrs Reynolds as well."

Lizzie's eyes grew wide. "It is only that they don't know how abominably I behaved, Will, but if it is any comfort to you, Georgiana and Jane have heard the truth from me."

"We shall have years to debate the relative merits of each of our failings, but I believe there may be some guests downstairs that are going to require an immediate explanation from me for this day's work."

"When they have finished flaying you I will be here to salve your wounds," she laughed.

"Since you have laughed at my fears, I shall not tell you what Mrs Reynolds has had to say to me." She opened her mouth to protest but he shook his head resolutely. "Shall I go call Jane and Georgiana, my dear? They will be anxious to see you for themselves."

"Oh yes, do, if they are still awake," Lizzie answered happily. "Mrs Reynolds says cook has some supper waiting for you too, if you have an appetite."

In the drawing room, conversation had begun to languish out of sheer weariness when the sound of Dr Andrews' step on the polished floor brought new life into the room. He carried his bag and topcoat, and to their eager questions replied that Mrs Darcy had recently awakened, much strengthened and clearly out of danger, and that she had just finished her supper. As Georgiana hurried up the stairs to Lizzie, the gentlemen's conversation grew animated. Georgiana met her brother at the top of the stairs and smiled broadly at the change in his appearance. "Fitzwilliam, Dr Andrews told me that Lizzie is doing well, and I can see that you are much improved."

Reaching for her hand, Darcy said, "I was just coming down to see if you were still about. Lizzie insists she is feeling fine and I am sure your company would do her good, Georgiana."

She smiled at him fondly and then stood on tiptoe to kiss his cheek, "We can talk later. The men are waiting for you downstairs."

Darcy walked down the stairway slowly, wearing a thoughtful frown as he pondered the humbling conversations he had just had. Before he reached the drawing room, however, his thoughts turned to a consideration of what his friends might wish to add to his burden of guilt; he did not doubt that their censure would be even more pointed. As he entered the room, the looks that greeted him ranged from compassion to perplexed concern, and in the face of so many pairs of inquiring eyes, an exhausted bewilderment came over him.

Bingley plunged directly into the heart of the matter, as was his manner, saving the moment from awkwardness. Clapping an arm around his friend's shoulders, he exclaimed, "Good God, man, what in the devil happened to you today? I arrived this morning to find Jane in hysterics and Lizzie collapsed, and learned that you had left the house in a demented state not half an hour after arriving."

Darcy smiled wanly. "I suppose I have you to thank for the search party, Bingley. I was just leaving the lodge when they fell upon me. I was nearly frightened to death by the sight of them, but they could tell me nothing except that I was needed at the manor. I arrived at the house fearing the worst, only to find Lizzie presiding over a festive party from her bed."

Charles laughed. "I felt some action was required, considering the state of distress in this house."

Darcy coloured at the memory of his melodramatic exit that morning. Under ordinary circumstances his reserve would have prevented him answering such a pointed inquiry into his private life, but the events of this week had upset all conventions and as he looked around at the circle of friends assembled there, he recognised the kindness in their eyes. With no great fluency he gave them an abbreviated account of the misunderstanding that had occurred and the quarrel and flight that followed, finishing with the story of his rescue at the hands of Thomas Hill and Trevor.

While the Alexanders and Trevor Handley maintained a respectful silence, Charles shook his head in amazement. Although little used to giving advice, and especially to his formidable friend, he could not help observing, "It has always been your way to disappear from your friends when something troubles you. But it won't do now that you are married, Darcy. Surely you must see that."

Darcy spoke with a novel humility. "You are right beyond a doubt, Bingley. There is no value in having a discussion when one of the parties involved cannot speak to their viewpoint. It is a habit I have formed from my childhood, but I daresay that I have learned my lesson today. I regret the inconvenience and discomfort suffered by everyone on my account." He sighed deeply, for such a disclosure cost him a great deal.

It was Mr Alexander's turn to ask a question. "I am still a bit perplexed by Miss Bingley's motivation in writing the letter which precipitated the crisis."

Darcy frowned thoughtfully. "I have not spoken to her yet, but I assume that Miss Bingley mistook the affection between Lizzie and Trevor for something more than it was."

He did not wish to discomfit his friend Bingley by elaborating on that subject, but Charles grimaced, and with uncharacteristic seriousness, said, "I believe it is time for *my* frankness. I have been negligent. My criticism of your behaviour, Darcy, was an example of my natural tendency to avoid taking responsibility myself. I have been well aware that my sister has harboured ill feelings toward you and your wife for some time, and as her brother, it was incumbent upon me to speak to her, or at least to shield my friends from her anger. It is I who should apologise." Turning to Mr Alexander, he explained, "My sister has been unhappy since I first paid my attentions to Miss Bennet, for she esteemed it beneath my dignity to marry someone of what she considered inferior birth. Her misery was made complete, however, when Mr Darcy, in whom she had invested her own hopes, married Elizabeth Bennet. I blame myself in this matter for not having interceded earlier."

Fitzwilliam Darcy leaned back in his chair and folded his arms, a sanguine smile spreading across his face.

"Charles Bingley, I must say we make an amusing pair. I, who have prided myself on my strength and honesty, have allowed myself to be buffeted about like a dinghy on high seas, unable to hold a course for the squalls. You, on the other hand, portray yourself as irresolute and carefree, but you have steered your course through tempest and shoals, never moved by the forces around you. I had no idea you were even aware of the storm that has been brewing."

Charles laughed as his cheeks coloured. "I daresay we have all learned a good deal about ourselves from this bit of heavy weather."

Into this pleasant scene of reconciliation stepped Georgiana Darcy with an impish smile.

"Lizzie is going back to sleep, on condition that I promise not to leave you alone to think, Fitzwilliam." The room echoed with the united laughter of its occupants.

Fitzwilliam rose from his chair. "You may rest assured that I will not trust myself to solitary thought for a very long time, my dear. I shall henceforth form every opinion through rational dialogue with at least two people. I bid you all a pleasant night."

Trevor rose as well. "I will see you safely to your door, my friend, and then avail myself of your hospitality for a night's rest." Charles Bingley stood and declared he was ready to sleep as well, leaving Georgiana alone with the Misters Alexander. She sat down with a weary sigh.

"I shall never know how to make amends for welcoming you to Pemberley in such a fashion. You must be appalled by the state in which you find us."

Mr Alexander's answer was characteristically kind-hearted and sensible.

"It falls to us to apologise, my dear, for intruding upon you without warning. This has been, for you and Fitzwilliam, an exhausting winter, but let us hope that what has been accomplished will prove well worth the trouble."

Georgiana reached out to touch his hand. "If it were nothing more than the restoration of the friendship between the Darcy and Alexander families, I should judge it so."

"I have long hoped for that," he replied. And with a meaningful glance at his son, Mr Alexander rose to say goodnight. "You will excuse me, I hope. I think I must be off to bed as well."

When they were alone, Edward moved to sit beside Georgiana.

"You must be dreadfully exhausted, Miss Darcy."

She smiled quizzically. "When last we met, you called me Georgiana. Has your absence imposed this formality between us?"

He blushed. "Perhaps this is not the time, but in the last few weeks, I have begun to think of you in a very different light." Her surprise at his words was obvious, but she waited quietly for him to continue.

Hesitantly at first, but gaining courage from her calm attentiveness, Edward Alexander poured out his heart to Georgiana Darcy. Although, as he suspected, she was unprepared for such an ardent declaration of love, nothing in her demeanour suggested that she found it unwelcome. When, at the end of his impassioned speech, he dropped down on one knee before her to ask for her hand, she blushed prettily and answered, simply,

"Yes, Edward."

Edward laughed out loud at her straightforward response. Kissing her hand, he asked playfully, "After hours of practising arguments against imagined reservations on your part, am I to be thwarted thus with a simple 'yes'?"

Her response was earnest and kind. "Edward, I know I am young, but I believe there is not another man on earth for whom I could feel such admiration and respect. From the first day of your visit to Pemberley, I felt a pleasure and easiness in your presence that I have never experienced. I would be honoured to marry you, and I can find in my heart no reservations."

"Perhaps your brother will supply us with the arguments against it," he replied with a nervous laugh.

She pondered the question seriously. "Fitzwilliam has been almost a father to me in the years since my father's death, and I am sure he may worry that I am too young for such a commitment, but when he is assured, as I am, that no one could bring me greater happiness, I cannot doubt he will agree."

Edward raised her hands to kiss them. "Together, we will create the most magnificent symphony, my love."

Chapter Sixty One

Darcy silently took his place beside Lizzie in bed, fearful of disturbing her slumber, but she stirred and turned towards him with a sigh of contentment. He asked softly, "Are you all right, Lizzie?"

"I'm fine, really... only a little tired. I am sure in a day or two I shall be myself completely," she answered sleepily.

He kissed her forehead and said, "I should not have gone to Matlock."

"I had anticipated that it would be difficult to be apart but I had not the slightest idea how difficult. I wish I could fall asleep and wake up to find that the events of this week were only a nightmare."

"Perhaps we shall. In any case, if the sun rises tomorrow as I expect, we will be free to start over again."

"Mm-hmm," she murmured, drifting off to sleep. Darcy required a good while to still the voices in his head, but he slipped at last into a shadowy place between wakefulness and sleep where everything and nothing ebbed and flowed around him. The trembling of Lizzie's form brought him fully to himself and he tightened his arms around her.

"What is it, my love?"

"We weren't ready for the child, were we, Will? I thought…" Her voice caught on a sob.

"Shh, darling. How can I pledge my love to you when I have failed you so many times? And yet I feel so certain right now that nothing remains to haunt me, nothing will mar the peace we have built."

She sighed softly and relaxed into his embrace. A few minutes later she opened her eyes and smiled. "Look, Will. You were right. The sun is going to rise today."

After a few minutes, Lizzie ventured cautiously: "There is one more thing which is troubling me, Will. When you came into the room yesterday you were dreadfully disturbed. It was not about the baby, as I assumed." She paused to remember their conversation. "Were you convinced, then, that there was truth in Caroline's accusation?"

He could find no excuse not to tell her everything, so with as much calm and control as he could muster, he explained the manner in which he had come to believe that his mother had taken Trevor as her lover, and that Georgiana was the result of that liaison. "With Miss Bingley's accusation ringing in my ears, and the conclusion I had drawn regarding Trevor's deceitfulness, it was inevitable that I should find myself wondering if he were capable of preying on you as well. The night's ride and a few glasses of wine convinced me that I was, yet again, being a fool. I reached Pemberley at the moment when my thinking had finally cleared and I was certain that your love was what it has ever been – beyond reproach.

"When I found Jane keeping watch, and then you so miserable - your apology sent me racing back over all of the ground that had been left behind."

"It is no wonder that you looked as if you had been chased by the devil himself," she said, shaking her head. A long silence ensued while each pursued their thoughts, until Lizzie summed up the problem.

"You must promise me that if ever we disagree again, which seems unlikely, you will allow me to tie you to a chair until the matter is resolved."

This brought an appreciative guffaw from Darcy, answered by Lizzie's ringing laughter. One sobering thought still remained in Lizzie's mind: "The subject of Georgiana's birth still remains a mystery, then."

"Yes," he replied thoughtfully. "I cannot but wonder if there was another man involved, but I suppose it does not really matter." Darcy stood up slowly and took up his position of contemplation at the window. After a long while, he turned to her and said, "My mother's offences were against my father, and he suffered them in silence, taking them with him to his grave. Although I am still curious about it, I do not see how I shall ever know. Perhaps, for Georgiana's sake, I ought to let the matter rest."

Lizzie was thoughtful in turn. "Do you remember, Will, how the first time we spoke with Mr Alexander, he said he thought it best that he only answer what you ask about your parents? Perhaps he has more he could tell us."

With a broad smile, Darcy returned to sit beside her.

"Mr Alexander has one secret which I believe I have guessed, but it has nothing to do with my parents. It has to do with his son."

Lizzie looked puzzled for a moment and then her face lit up with a joyful smile.

"Has Edward come to propose to Georgiana, do you think?" His smile answered her question and she continued excitedly, "Oh, Will, of course he has! And Mr Alexander came along to make sure everything went smoothly. Only imagine what they must have thought when they arrived yesterday. It is a wonderful test of Edward's devotion to Georgiana if he does not run away before breakfast."

Fitzwilliam's smile was as broad as hers.

"Judging by the look on his face last night at supper, he will scarcely stray more than a few feet from her side, even if confronted by the furies of hell. I look forward to his proposal before the day is done."

"I am so very happy for them, Will. Could you have imagined a few months ago that Georgiana would be a woman ready for marriage by this time? She has grown so very strong and confident, and he suits her so very well."

Darcy grew suddenly still, and then leaned over to bestow a kiss as soft as down upon her forehead. He whispered, "Have I told you how much I love you, Elizabeth? I hope we shall have as many babies as you like to fill this house with merriment, and Edward and

Georgiana may make themselves an apartment around the pianoforte and play day and night if they choose. Between your laughter and their music, I shall wake each morning to feel I have been snatched from hell's portal and lifted through the gates of heaven." She leaned into his embrace with a sigh, and for a few minutes only the pleasant anticipation of the future entertained their minds.

Finally Lizzie leaned back against her pillow and asked, "What were you dreaming last night, Will? You were talking but I couldn't make it out."

His eyes narrowed thoughtfully and then he teased, "Yesterday, I recall, you disliked the truth when I told it to you, and so I hesitate to try that."

"If you mean to tell me that you dreamt that either one of us was unfaithful to the other, by all means lie. Any other truth I believe I can bear today, as I am beginning to feel quite energetic."

"Well, the truth is that I have no idea. There were faces and voices, but none of them clear enough to make out. Perhaps I was saying goodbye to all of my ghosts." He smiled confidently. "But enough about me. Why don't you tell me about your altercation with Miss Bingley? I am sorry to have missed it, if it was anything like your exchange in the carriage from Meryton."

"Oh, no, my dear," she laughed, "it was not nearly as pleasant as that. Although I must confess that I was moved to an explosion of laughter at one point." She proceeded to relate the whole of the conversation. "I do wish you had seen Jane's face, Will. She was as close as I have ever seen her to anger, but pity for poor Miss Bingley's distress quite overtook her in the end."

"From what I have heard of your condition after I fled the house, I daresay Jane has been angry at someone else recently. What a strange couple we make, Lizzie. I inspire rage in the breasts of saints and you provoke laughter in the midst of anguish."

"I must tell you how Jane roused me from my lethargy, Will."

She described her state of mind and Jane's ruse to distract her. "I should have suspected deceit when she spoke of her own discomfort, for it is so unlike her, but she took me completely by surprise. When she began to blame you, she knew it would rally my spirits, either to anger at her or at you. When I realised what she had done, I could not help but laugh. I am sure the poor doctor thought we had lost our senses completely, but he was not half so surprised as Caroline Bingley, who rushed in to find out what had happened." Suddenly serious, she said, "Have you spoken to her yet, Will?"

He explained that he had not seen her, but that Charles had described to him last night her tearful apology to the rest of the party. "I am sure she is not anxious to see me, but I suppose the kindest thing would be for me to face her as soon as possible."

"Oh, yes, Will, you must. You will not be harsh with her, will you?" she asked anxiously.

He smiled at her in admiration. "I do delight in your goodness, Lizzie. And Jane's. That anyone so maligned should have such concern for the happiness of their attacker is difficult for me to comprehend."

"She is such a miserable soul, who would not pity her, Will? She has tormented herself these past few months far more than I could ever do. And now she has embarrassed herself so heartily that she can scarcely show her face. I do hope you will treat her gently."

"For you, dear, I would make friends with the devil himself," he said, kissing her forehead. "I will go to her directly this morning and relieve her fears, for she has less to reproach herself with than I do."

"Will, if you persist in blaming yourself for what happened yesterday without recognising *my* culpability as well, I shall lose my good humour," she declared firmly.

"Anything but that! I will most graciously cede the majority of the blame to you, if you will have it."

"I will settle for the half of it, thank you." She reached out a hand

445

to shake on the bargain.

Darcy stood up. "I will go to Caroline now and tell her God knows what, and then we shall declare an embargo on blame and misery for all time."

Darcy went off to dress and sent a maid to look for Jane, knowing she would be anxious to be with her sister. Bracing himself for the unpleasant task, he walked resolutely to Caroline Bingley's door and knocked firmly. As she opened the door, he was moved immediately by the sight of her diminished spirit and, remembering Lizzie's admonition, he spoke gently.

"Miss Bingley, I believe you must be anticipating an angry speech from me concerning the events of the past few days, but I confess I have no stomach for further anguish, either on your part or on mine."

Without meeting his eyes, she invited him into the room with a weak gesture. He walked to a chair, sat down abruptly and leaned forward with arms resting on his knees, his eyes closed in concentration, and when he spoke again, his voice was so soft she scarcely heard him.

"Elizabeth Bennet is my life, and I have nearly killed her by believing her capable of betrayal." He sat up and looked into her eyes. "I reproach myself more than I do you for her distress; it was not your accusation which injured her, but my lack of faith. It was from fear that I do not deserve her love that I allowed myself to mistrust her. I will not make that mistake again. If it is in my power to prevent it, Lizzie will never be hurt again... by either one of us."

Miss Bingley nodded silently, not trusting herself to speak. She was so moved she could scarcely keep from crying out, but she held her thoughts in check as she waited for him to compose himself. At last, he continued, meeting her gaze steadily.

"She refuses to blame me and she has so eloquently pleaded your case that I dare not be angry with you." There was a most uncomfortable silence, which he broke by standing and moving about the room in obvious agitation. When he addressed her at last, she started nervously.

"Miss Bingley, I hope you will not mind if I speak frankly," he said, pausing for a sign of approval. Seeing no opposition, he continued. "I feel I must bear some responsibility for your behaviour. I was, perhaps, remiss in not considering your feelings when I asked Miss Bennet to marry me. I believe that before I met her, I allowed... perhaps even encouraged you to expect my attentions. For this I sincerely apologise. If you are angry, however, it must be with me alone, for Lizzie deserves no blame."

Caroline Bingley recognised growing within her a tender respect for this man, and she answered with a most unaccustomed serenity.

"I thought at one time that I loved you, but in the past three days I have come to understand the meaning of love as I never understood it before. I have learned to respect your wife and her sister as examples of a kind of gentility of spirit that I did not know existed. I cannot begin to express my remorse for causing them, and you, such anxiety and grief. If it were not for that, I would have to confess that this drama has so improved my own appreciation of the value of kindness as to render my suffering inconsequential."

His eyes widened in surprise at such a seemingly sincere avowal, but she was so possessed by her own thoughts that she did not notice. She continued quietly, "You have but to say 'go' and I will remove myself from Pemberley forever, but if you allow me to stay, I will try to prove to you and to all of the gentle souls gathered here that I am not the same woman I was a few days ago. I long for nothing so much as to make amends for my past behaviour and to have the opportunity to count all of you as friends, for I can think of no one whose good opinion is more important to me."

Fitzwilliam Darcy would have disbelieved such words from Caroline Bingley had they not so closely matched his own transformation of a year ago. He studied her face and found no trace of deceit or insincerity in it. Indeed, there was such an alteration in her bearing and such a softness about her eyes that he could not long mistrust her. His face broke into a wide grin of relief.

"Miss Bingley, I do not understand the power of these sisters, but if they can effect such an improvement in two such cynics as you and I, they deserve a great deal more than Charles and I can give them. I am sure that both Jane and Lizzie would want me to extend an open invitation to you to stay as long as you like. They are sitting together just now in our room, and I believe they would welcome you with open arms if you went to them."

Miss Bingley's serenity was undone by his kindness and she covered her face with her hands and cried. At last she steadied herself and took the handkerchief he offered. Her smile, when it appeared, was radiant.

"I would not be surprised by even that, Mr Darcy." He nodded knowingly and left her to compose herself while he went downstairs to breakfast.

Chapter Sixty Two

The various residents of Pemberley had all earned, one way or another, an untroubled night's rest, and the morning meal stretched nearly to mid-day before everyone was accounted for. Georgiana and Edward were the first to rise, ready to turn their attention to planning the future, and they were joined a short time later by Jane, restless and anxious for news of Lizzie. After hearing Georgiana's cheerful account of her visit last night, she was content to sit down to breakfast herself, although she scarcely touched her food, starting up each time footsteps were heard in the hall. Mr Alexander, Charles, and finally, Trevor appeared, and even as the last dish was cleared, the group lingered at the table as if they had taken root. When a maid entered to say Jane was wanted upstairs, she fairly flew from the room.

By the time Fitzwilliam Darcy entered the breakfast parlour, he was in a mood as light-hearted as any he had experienced in his life. His friends greeted him enthusiastically, eager for his news, but they needed no words to understand the happiness that radiated from his face.

"Lizzie is becoming restless already. I daresay we shall have her downstairs before another day has passed. By the way, Charles, I have made my peace with your sister, so I hope there remain no impediments to a blissful future for all of us."

Charles beamed at this news and exclaimed, "We must have a celebration this evening, Fitzwilliam. What is required here is a bit of light-hearted fun."

Trevor stood with a satisfied smile to announce that he was off to Croftwoods, but at Fitzwilliam's insistence, agreed to return in the evening. As he walked his friend to the front door, Fitzwilliam said hesitantly, "Trevor, there is one final detail that puzzles me..."

They walked out into the front garden together and Trevor turned to face Darcy with an encouraging smile, waiting for him to

449

continue.

"Your mother mentioned that she continued to receive support and correspondence from my father after your return from Pemberley. She apparently had no knowledge of your rupture with my father."

Trevor turned to survey the grounds before answering. "I learned a good many things in my brief stay at Pemberley. One of them was the unspoken code of silence." Turning to face Darcy squarely, he said, "I told my mother that I needed to move on with my life—I simply omitted the reason. I trusted that your father would be equally reluctant to dishonour his family name by sharing with her any sordid details. I was correct in assuming that."

He turned away, apparently lost in thought for a few moments and then added, "You take after your father more than you know, Willie. I imagine Mrs Darcy to be the first person to whom you have exposed your vulnerabilities. She had that effect on me, you know—I told her everything about myself when she was at Croftwoods the other day. I have wondered at times if your mother and father might have had a different relationship had he let down his guard a bit."

The two men walked in silence to the stable where Trevor waited for a mount to be prepared. Fitzwilliam finally spoke. "I believe we must follow Lizzie's example, Trevor. It will save us both a vast deal of pacing about and furrowing of the brow. We have both wasted too much time with our silence."

Trevor smiled and they embraced in silence. As he mounted his horse he looked down and asked, "Friends?"

Fitzwilliam shook his head and answered, "Brothers."

He walked slowly back to the house, pondering Trevor's words. As he entered the house, Georgiana and Edward Alexander met him in the hallway. Her face was lit with a secretive smile and she patted his arm and said, "I am going to sit with Lizzie and Jane, Fitzwilliam," and turning toward Edward, she said, "and Edward, I believe, would

450

like a word with you in private."

"Of course, Edward. Shall we go to the library?" he said, raising his brows inquiringly, giving no sign that he anticipated his request. He smiled to himself as he turned to walk ahead of the eager young man.

Edward, in spite of Georgiana's reassurance, found himself daunted by the task he had set himself. During his first weeks at Pemberley, he had formed an admiration and respect for Fitzwilliam Darcy, but he knew him by reputation to be a man capable of strong opinions and quick anger. He could not have failed to notice Mr Darcy's doting concern for Georgiana, and looking at the matter objectively, he doubted that his proposal would excite a great enthusiasm on Mr Darcy's part. However, Edward Alexander was noted for nothing if not his unabashed optimism, and as he haltingly began to express his regard for Miss Darcy, he was emboldened to see that the gentleman listened thoughtfully and with no apparent agitation to his words.

Having pronounced, at last, the formal request for her hand, Edward found that he was nearly out of breath, and, realising that he must have been rambling on dreadfully, he turned very red indeed and averted his eyes, waiting for an answer. Fitzwilliam had, but only with the utmost control, managed to maintain an air of dignity and seriousness in the face of the earnest young man's outpouring, and now he saw his opportunity to indulge himself a little. He stood up, and turning his back to Edward, stood before the window, apparently lost in thought. Before turning back to face him, he composed his smiling face into a solemn mask. "While I have the deepest respect for you and your family, Mr Alexander, there is one thing about your request that worries me." He paused dramatically while Edward squirmed in his skin and began quickly to review all of the arguments he had carefully prepared in anticipation of Mr Darcy's disapproval.

Finally, Edward could stand the silence no longer. "Sir?"

Fitzwilliam wore an air of distracted perplexity, as if he had forgotten the subject of their conversation.

"Oh," he said, shaking his head, "I was just wondering why you are asking me for permission, for other than marrying Miss Elizabeth Bennet, I have done nothing in a great many years that would indicate that my judgement is sound or my instincts unflawed. If it is a reasoned, intelligent decision you seek, I suggest you apply to Mrs Darcy, or to Georgiana herself."

He maintained his serious air so aptly that Edward was unsure how to understand him. He answered doubtfully, "I have taken the liberty of consulting Miss Darcy's feelings on the subject and she has given me reason to understand that she would not find my attentions unwelcome."

Fitzwilliam laughed out loud. "If by that you mean that you asked her and she said 'yes', I would say you have exhibited uncommon good sense. I hope you will not mind if I tell you that I took the liberty of consulting Mrs Darcy, as your demeanour last night gave me a hint of your feelings, and she is quite in agreement with me. We respect Georgiana's intelligence and good sense too much to stand in the way of her decision if she has made it, and we would both be most pleased to welcome you as a brother, for it is obvious that the two of you are perfectly suited to one another." He reached out to shake hands with Edward, whose blushing smile gave evidence of his relief and pleasure.

Fitzwilliam laughed. "Sorry to have played you along like that, Edward, but the last few days have been so overburdened with seriousness that I could not pass up the opportunity for a bit of levity. I will go and speak to the ladies, for I am sure by now they have worked out all of the pertinent details of your future. I shall send Georgiana downstairs in a few minutes."

Fitzwilliam took the stairs two at a time, feeling as frisky as a young colt. Entering his room, he heard, as he suspected, the unmistakable voices of ladies engaged in one of their favourite pastimes, the planning of a wedding. He frowned sternly at Georgiana as she rose to approach him.

"I believe it is customary for approval to be given before the festivities are arranged."

Georgiana laughed out loud, for unlike Edward, she harboured no fears as to her brother's state of mind. "I have given *my* approval, my dear brother, and as Lizzie agrees with me, I cannot seriously think you will interfere." Laughing, he picked her up and swung her around in a circle.

"I have no illusions as to who has good sense in this house. In fact, I have just told Edward that I defer to Lizzie's judgement and your own on all subjects of import, and have given him leave to do the same. You had better go down to him, my dear, for I am afraid I could not prevent myself from teasing him a bit." She gave him a quick kiss on the cheek and waving to Lizzie and Jane, started for the stairway.

Lizzie looked at him from under lowered eyebrows. "Will, I hope we have had more than enough confusion and mistaken meanings to last us a good long while."

His smile was innocence itself.

"I take you as my tutor in this, as in all things. The day that you eschew levity for the sake of serious and sincere speech is the day I do the same. In the meantime, I am just beginning to perfect my wit, and I expect from you a suitable admiration of my talents." They all enjoyed a warm laugh together as Darcy sat down in the chair Georgiana had vacated, and the three entertained themselves for some time with their thoughts on the impending marriage. Darcy stood up finally, professing a desire to speak with the senior Mr Alexander on the subject, and Lizzie attempted to arise from bed, saying she would go down with him. Both Jane and Darcy importuned her to think of no such thing, and she was at last overwhelmed by their arguments and relaxed back against the pillows, thumping the covers impatiently.

"Dr Andrews will be back this morning, Lizzie, and I promise you that if he gives you permission to leave your bed, I shall carry you down the stairs myself. In the meantime, please do not give Jane any further cause for anxiety," he said with a wink at his sister-in-law.

"All right," she said, a trifle petulantly. "But you must promise to tell our guests that I am well enough to have visitors."

He smiled indulgently and bowed. "If you like, I shall bring in builders directly to construct a theatre about the bed, and you shall have as many visitors as you please."

Fitzwilliam found Mr Alexander in the library, perusing a small and rather shabby leather book. Clamping a hand on the good man's shoulder, Fitzwilliam extended his other hand in a clasp of approval. "I hope I have given you no reason to fear the alliance of our two families, Mr Alexander."

"On the contrary, Fitzwilliam. Nothing could give me more pleasure," he answered, "although I must confess that a few months ago I would have considered it to be totally impossible. Do you have no misgivings yourself, Son?"

Fitzwilliam answered emphatically, "I am ready to sit back and relax for the next few years, and let other people fret about and meddle with the future. Georgiana and Edward are as likely a couple as any two people I have known, and if they believe themselves capable of making one another happy, I am prepared to toast them. As to Edward's fortune, both Lizzie and I would be delighted if they chose to remain at Pemberley for all of their lives and supply us with their music. In any case, they shall manage to live in a way that suits them; I have no doubt of that. And for myself, I consider it inordinate good fortune to be united forever with your house and your family."

Mr Alexander smiled broadly and shook his head. "I wonder if your father is still about. I feel the need to speak to him."

"So do I," said Fitzwilliam, turning more thoughtful. "Mr

Alexander, may I ask you a question?" The old man nodded. "Do you think my father is Georgiana's father?"

Mr Alexander took a long slow breath and looked down at the book in his hand, stroking its cover lovingly as if it helped him to think. After a long pause, he looked up at Fitzwilliam with such a serious face that it gave the young man a start. "I believe you might like to read this, Fitzwilliam. Your father kept a journal for you - he began it on the day you were born. He gave it to me before he died and asked me to read it and then put it away until you were ready for it." Fitzwilliam turned pale and did not move a hand, although Mr Alexander extended the book towards him. The old gentleman smiled compassionately and said, as he placed the book on one of the shelves, "When you feel ready, then." He moved to the doorway, stopping to say over his shoulder, "Let your heart guide you, Fitzwilliam."

When he was alone, Darcy sat down in a chair to explore the feelings raised by Mr Alexander's disclosure. At last he went to retrieve the soft red leather volume from the shelf, turning it over in his hands and finally opening its cover. Inside he found the date of his birth inscribed in his father's decorative style, with the dedication, "To my first-born son, Fitzwilliam. Your birthright is the love that brought you into being; your future, what you choose to make it." He traced the letters with his fingers and then slowly closed the cover and went upstairs to Lizzie. Jane stood as he entered the room and excused herself to look for Charles. Noticing the pensive air about him, she closed the door softly as she left. Lizzie caught his mood at once and laid her hand on his as he sat down beside her on the bed. He handed her the book without speaking, and with a quizzical look, she opened it and read Mr Darcy's inscription.

Caressing the worn leather reverently, she asked softly, "From Mr Alexander?"

He nodded and replied, "My father's journal. For so many years I have longed to understand him, and yet now that I have his own account of his life at my fingertips, I feel curiously reluctant to read it."

She smiled and leaned her head against his chest, and his arms encircled her and held her tightly to him. She murmured, "You will read it when you are ready for it, love." He smiled and, taking the book, tucked it under his pillow.

"Before my first son is born," he said serenely.

The rest of that day, and many more, were spent by the inhabitants of Pemberley Manor on the pleasant reparations and quiet celebrations of all of the forms that love may take between humans.

Finis

1109462

Made in the USA